James Lee Burke is the author of thirty previous novels. He won the Edgar Award in 1998 for *Cimarron Rose*, while *Black Cherry Blues* won the Edgar in 1990 and *Sunset Limited* was awarded the CWA Gold Dagger in 1998. He lives with his wife, Pearl, in Missoula, Montana. Visit his website at www.jamesleeburke.com.

JAMES LEE BURKE
HALF OF PARADISE

PHOENIX

A PHOENIX PAPERBACK

First published in Great Britain in 1997
by Phoenix
This paperback edition published in 1999
by Orion,
an imprint of Orion Books Ltd,
Orion House, 5 Upper St Martin's Lane,
London WC2H 9EA

An Hachette UK company

5 7 9 10 8 6 4

Reissued 2004, 2011

A CIP catalogue record for this book
is available from the British Library.

ISBN 978-0-7528-2639-4

Printed and bound in Great Britain by Clays Ltd, St Ives plc

The Orion Publishing Group's policy is to use papers that
are natural, renewable and recyclable products and
made from wood grown in sustainable forests. The logging
and manufacturing processes are expected to conform to
the environmental regulations of the country of origin.

www.orionbooks.co.uk

To Pearl

BOOK ONE

SUMMER'S DUST

AVERY BROUSSARD

After the spring rains when the first hot days of summer begin, the inland waters of the Gulf of Mexico turn smoky-green from the floating seaweed, fading to dark blue beyond the sandbars where the great white pelicans dive for fish. On an island off the Louisiana coast there is an open-air pavilion among a group of cypress trees, and in those first wisteria-scented days of May one can sit in a wicker chair, drinking chilled wine, and listen to the salt breeze rustling through the overhanging moss, or just sit and watch the whitecaps break against the beach and disappear in an iridescent spray of foam.

Avery Broussard walked up the beach with his duffle bag over his shoulder and entered the pavilion. It was midafternoon and no one was at the bar. Two fishermen sat at one of the marble-topped tables. He drank a draught beer from a thick glass mug filmed with ice on the outside, and watched the fishermen hand-wrestle. One of them was a little drunk, and he laughed loudly and used a profane expression in French when the other man forced his hand down. Avery drank down the cold beer and ordered another. He counted the money in his wallet. He had fifteen dollars, enough to buy a bottle and get him home. He had quit his job on the oil exploration crew that morning, and he wanted to catch the afternoon launch to the mainland in order to be at the house by nightfall. It was three o'clock now and the launch left at four. He sipped the beer and looked out over the beach at the few palm trees and the sun bright on the water and the sandbars white in the distance.

Avery was through with oil crews. Six months ago he had signed on as a jug-hustler on a shooting crew that did offshore exploration preliminary to putting down a well. Later he became a driller's helper. He got a pay raise, and he liked working on the drill better than pulling recording instruments out of the water ten hours a day with the sun hot on his spine and the skin on his fingers cracked and hard from being wet too long. But now he was finished. Life on the Gulf was fine, but he hadn't returned home or seen his father in the six months since he had left, and he thought that he had gotten rid of the things that had made him leave. He bought a pint of bourbon and put it in his duffle to drink on the way home.

He walked slowly down the beach towards the landing. The sky was clear and the gulls dipped their wings and circled overhead. He wondered what his father would say when he saw him again. Avery had written home only twice since he started work on the crew. Several times he had wanted to write his father and tell him why he had gone, but he could never find the proper words. His father wouldn't have understood, just as he didn't understand when Avery's older brother Henri had left. The father and the sons were apart in time. Avery hoped that now things could be different from what they had been, and that he wouldn't have to go away any more. It's in you, he thought, like it's in him. You don't belong anywhere else. He cut the seal of the whiskey bottle with his pocketknife, peeled it back and unscrewed the metal cap, and took a drink. Generations of inbreeding have put it into your blood. The land, the house, the country around it, and all that goes with it is inside you.

He waited on the dock until the launch came. He went aboard and stood on the bow and leaned against the deck rail. The deck-hands cast off the mooring lines and the boat headed for the mainland. Avery looked out towards the Gulf and saw the gray shapes of two oil tankers silhouetted against the sky; he wondered where they were going. Ahead lay the mainland, a long stretch of white beach with a heavy line of trees in the background. Off to the left he could see the salt marsh with its flat expanses of alligator grass and the blasted trunks of cypress trees half submerged in the water. A sailboat came out of the lagoon, tacking in the breeze. He took another drink from the bottle and turned his face into the wind. The air was fresh with the smell of brine. The whiskey felt hot inside him, and he was getting a good edge on. The boat churned inland and passed the sandbars and the salt marsh and neared the dock.

He put the bottle in his bag and walked down the gangplank after the boat landed. Several trawlers were tied up at the dock. The fishermen were spreading out their nets to dry. He walked up the landing, the duffle over his shoulder, past a few boarded shacks and headed down a gravel road that would take him to the highway. There was thick green foliage on both sides of the road and tall gray oaks with hanging moss, and the late afternoon sun cast dark shadows over the lane. He saw a nutria, like a huge rat, swimming in the irrigation canal beside the road. Two cranes flew up over the trees from the swamp, their wings gilded in the sunlight.

Avery came out on the highway and hitched a ride with an old man in a vegetable truck. Riding along, he thought about his family, or what was left of it. His mother had died in childbirth, and his brother had been killed at Normandy. Now it was just his father and himself, and sometimes he wondered if it wouldn't be better if they were gone, too. His family had lived for over a hundred years in Martinique parish, in the same house, on the same piece of ground which his great-grandfather had bought from the Louisiana government when he came from the West Indies in 1850. His great-grandfather had had a Negro servant who came with him as a free man into a slave country, and the two of them had built a sugarcane plantation that was later to become one of the largest in the southern portion of the state. When the War Between the States broke out, Avery's great-grandfather had enlisted in the Confederate army, although he spoke only a few words of English, and was made a captain in the infantry; he and his servant were attached to the Eighth Louisiana Volunteers under General Jackson, and at the battle of Fredericksburg he was made deaf by the explosion of a cannon ball and was captured by the Federal army and imprisoned at Johnson's Island for the remainder of the war.

When Appomattox came he and his servant took turns riding a half-starved mule through the bayou country and moccasin-infested swamps with nothing to eat except a sack of parched corn, until they returned to Martinique parish to attempt rebuilding what was left of their home after the fields had been burned, the stock killed, and the house shelled by artillery. During Reconstruction half of the land was lost to carpetbaggers, and the other half was left unplanted because there was no money to buy seed or to hire manual labor.

The great-grandfather was killed in a duel in 1870 by a Spanish aristocrat who made a profitable living as a scalawag and who had tried to buy the Broussard land at one-third of its value. Rebuffed, he had joined forces with the carpetbag government in an attempt to prove that Mr. Broussard was the leader of the night riders which terrorized the Negro voters. The Spanish aristocrat won his duel, but he was shot dead two weeks later on Rampart Street in New Orleans. A witness to the shooting said that a well-dressed Negro had approached the Spaniard, asked his name, then pulled a dueling pistol from his vest and fired from three feet. No one knew the Negro, nor did they ever see him again in New Orleans, but some believed him to be the servant of the man whom the Spaniard had killed in a duel sometime before.

Over the years the land was lost in pieces until Avery's father, Rafael Broussard, owned only twenty acres of the original two-thousand-acre tract. Now there was no one left save Avery and his father and a Negro named Batiste who was the grandson of the servant the first Broussard had brought with him from the West Indies in 1850. The twenty acres of land was mortgaged, and it no longer produced enough cane to pay their expenses.

The truck stopped and Avery climbed down and thanked the old man. He started down the lane through the wood gate towards the house. The gate swung back on its hinges over the cattle guard and clacked against the fence post. He could see his father standing on the veranda looking out over the barren fields in front of the house. Mr. Broussard wore the same black trousers and coat he always wore when he wasn't in the fields. His thin hair was steel-gray, and the red veins in his cheeks showed through his gray whiskers, and he had on a wide-brimmed planter's hat that was slanted over his eyes. Batiste was sawing logs and putting them in a cord by the side of the house. The house was built in French colonial style with red bricks covering the bottom half of the building, and a balcony ran completely around the second story.

The banisters on the veranda were broken, and the paint was cracked and peeling, the roof sagged in places, and the outbuildings had weathered gray. To one side of the house there was a pecan orchard, the trees barren and twisted like broken fingers held in the air.

"Hello, son," Mr. Broussard said.

"Hi, Papa."

"I'm glad you came home."

Avery looked about him and felt the emptiness of his home press in upon him.

"Did you quit your job?" Mr. Broussard said.

"Yes, sir."

"Batiste said you would come home. All the time you were away he said you would be back. It's been a little hard since you've been gone."

Why does he have to talk like that? Avery thought.

"Aren't you planting this year?" Avery said.

"I have to get some money from the bank."

"The oil company owes me some in back pay. They'll send it in a couple of weeks."

"That's fine, son. Maybe we'll have a good year."

Batiste came over and shook hands with Avery. His hair had begun to turn white, and his shoulders were bent; he wore suspenders and a collarless shirt, and the leather was cut away from the toe of one of his shoes.

"He's looking fine, ain't he, Mr. Broussard?" he said.

"How've you been?" Avery said.

"Been waiting for you to come home. I didn't have nobody to go hunting with."

"We'll go frogging tonight."

"I reckon you grown into a man," Batiste said. He was smiling with his hands on his sides.

"He looks older," Mr. Broussard said.

Avery felt embarrassed.

"Yes sir, you grown into a man," Batiste said. "It's sure good to have you back. I ain't had no fun hunting by myself."

"We'll get plenty of honkers this year," Avery said.

"Going to fix the blind up so we'll be ready for them in the fall."

Avery remembered when he and his father used to go hunting together. They would get up early in the morning and put on their waders and quilted hunting jackets. They used the outboard to cross the mouth of the river, and Avery would sit on the bow, letting the cold spray sting his face, and listen to the gulls that cry over the water before dawn. They would stand waist-deep in the freezing water, waiting for the ducks as they flew over the willow trees to feed in the rice field, then fire when the lead ducks dropped through the mist to land, he with the pump and his father with the double-barrel The ducks would fold and fall heavily through the air, making a loud crack and splash when they broke through the thin sheet of ice. Avery would keep firing until his gun clicked empty, pumping the smoking shells into the water. The dogs would bark and jump off the levee into the reeds and swim towards the fallen birds. Then his father would break the double-barrel and wink at him as the empty shells plopped into the water. Keep shooting like that and we won't have any birds for next season, he would say. They would wade to the levee and sit on the bank, drinking black coffee from thermos jugs, and listen to the geese honking in the marsh.

But that was then and not now. Mr. Broussard didn't hunt anymore, and the double-barrel stayed over the fireplace. After his father quit hunting Avery went with Batiste, but it wasn't the same.

"We'd better go in and have supper," Mr. Broussard said.

"I'll carry your duffle for you," Batiste said.

Inside, Mr. Broussard and Avery ate at the kitchen table, which was covered with a red-and-white checkered oilcloth.

"How much do we owe the bank?" Avery said.

"There's no need for you to worry about it, son."

Why does he have to speak to me like that?

"How much is it?"

"Three hundred dollars," he said.

"We can take another mortgage," Avery said.

"Yes, we might be able to."

"What do you say it like that for?"

"I'll go see them about the mortgage tomorrow."

"There's something else, isn't there?"

"I couldn't meet the land taxes this year. The farm will go up at the sheriff's tax sale unless I pay them soon."

"My check from the company will pay the taxes."

"It's good of you to offer the money, but you know I didn't approve of you taking that job."

"Yes, sir."

"There are all manner of men on those oil crews. You should always seek your own level in associating with people."

"Yes, sir."

"Those men are from a different background than you."

"What difference does it make?" Avery said, and then wished he hadn't.

"When you associate with people of a lower social class as an equal, they bring you down to their level. You don't bring them up to yours."

"All right, Papa."

"I let you take the job because you were old enough to make decisions for yourself, but I never approved of it."

"I'm not on the job any longer."

"I know that, but you must always seek out your equals."

"All right. I'm not going to work on any more crews."

"I wanted to go to sea when I was a young boy, and my father wouldn't allow me to. At the time I thought he was wrong, but as I got older I realized that he had done the right thing."

"Let's finish dinner, Papa."

"Why did you take that job to begin with?"

"I thought I might like working on the water."

"Try to understand, son. I'm not attempting to keep you at home. You can get a job in town or go to the college if you like. But you should do something suited to your background."

"I'll help with the farm this summer."

"Would you like to go to the college? I had hoped you would."

"Maybe next year."

"There's something else I'd like to talk with you about. When you unpacked your clothes I thought I saw a bottle. Are you still drinking?"

"Not too much. Just once in a while."

"You're older now and you make your own decisions, but I don't like to see you drinking," Mr. Broussard said. "It killed your grandfather."

"I'm all right."

"Maybe it's in your blood. They say the odd generation gets it. Henri started drinking early, too."

"A friend of mine left the bottle with me."

"I hope I haven't raised you wrong. I brought you up the same way I was brought up. That's the only way I knew."

Avery began to wish he hadn't come home.

"I leave it alone now. I haven't been tight since I went to work."

"I want to believe that's true."

Avery felt guilty for lying, but he had learned long ago that it was better to tell his father certain things, whether they were true or not.

"You know how disappointed I was in you the night the sheriff had to bring you home from that bar," Mr. Broussard said.

"That was a long time ago, Papa. Let's don't talk about it."

"He had to carry you up the front steps."

"Yes, sir, I know. I told you I was sorry for it."

"Well, it isn't worth talking about now. I just don't want to see you let liquor ruin your life."

Avery got up. "Batiste and I are going frogging."

"Will you get rid of that bottle?"

"All right."

"Good night, then."

"Good night."

Avery put his dishes on the sideboard and went upstairs to get his flashlight and frog gig.

The next week Mr. Broussard paid the land taxes with Avery's oil check and took out a second mortgage on the twenty acres. They bought seed, rented a tractor, plowed and planted. They worked hard, six days a week from dawn to nightfall, and Avery became aware of how badly his father had aged. Mr. Broussard was losing weight and his face became more drawn. He would not listen to either Avery or Batiste when they asked him to take things easier. He worked in his long-sleeve undershirt without a hat, and his face and neck became coarsened by the sun, and in the evening he went to bed right after dinner, sometimes with his clothes on. Once he stayed outside and continued working during a rainstorm. He caught a bad cold which almost developed into pneumonia. Three weeks later he was back in the fields. He did more work than Avery thought him capable of. Sometimes he spoke of the good year they were going to have, and how he would repay the bank and possibly improve the farm. Then during the next years they could repair the house (he never once considered living in another house), buy new farm machinery, and rent pasture land for the stock. The summer was hot and the rains were like steam, and the cane grew tall and purple and gold.

In September they began cutting the cane. They were working in the fields behind the house when it happened. Mr. Broussard stepped up on the running board of the truck to get into the cab, then suddenly his face whitened as he tried to hold on to the doorjamb, and fell backwards into the stubble and the broken stalks of sugarcane. He held his hands to his heart and gasped for breath while Avery tried to loosen his collar. Batiste and Avery put him in the cab, and the Negro folded his coat into a pillow. On the way to the house Mr. Broussard's eyes remained glazed and staring.

That afternoon the doctor and the priest came. Avery stood on the veranda while they were inside. He looked off into the distance at the oil wells. The gas flares were red against the rain-clouded sky. Across the meadow a wrecking crew was tearing down the remains of the old Segura home. The roof was gone and the board planking was being stripped away with crowbars to be stacked in a large pile for burning. Two men were attaching chains to the brick chimney to pull it down with a bulldozer. A new highway was coming through, and a filling station was to be built on the site of the Segura house.

The doctor came out and walked past Avery to his car. Avery went inside and met the priest in the hallway. "Your father died in a state of grace," the priest said. "He is in heaven now." Avery went into his father's bedroom without answering. The room was dark and smelled of dust. His father lay in the big mahogany tester bed with the ruffled and pleated canopy on top. Avery looked at the outline of his body under the sheet. He walked to the bed and pulled back the sheet. Mr. Broussard's face was gray, and the flesh sagged back from the skull. The skin was tight around the eye sockets. He seemed much smaller in death than in life. Avery turned his head away and pulled the sheet over his father. He sat down in the chair and cried.

It rained the day of the funeral. It rained all that week. The freshly dug earth was piled beside the open grave among the oak trees. Water collected in pools and washed over the side of the grave. Batiste stood bareheaded in his only black suit with the rain streaming down his face. Avery watched the men lower the cloth and pine board casket with the pulleys. The priest read aloud from the book opened in his hands. Both of the gravediggers kept their hats on. The men from the funeral home coughed and sneezed and wanted to get out of the rain. A few people stood on the other side of the grave under umbrellas. Most of them were Negroes who had worked on the Broussard land in the past. The dye in the cloth on the outside of the casket ran in the rainwater.

J. P. WINFIELD

He was twenty-seven years old and he had a seventh-grade educa-
tion, and he had never been more than sixty miles from his home.
J.P. sat in the corridor outside the audition room and smoked
cigarettes. The fans were off and he was sweating through his
clothes. The Sears, Roebuck suit he wore was light brown, almost
the color of canvas, and the sleeves and trousers were thread-worn
and too short for him. Some people went by and he put his shoes
under the chair so they wouldn't be noticed. They were unshined
and the stitches were broken at the seams. His polka dot clip-on
bow tie was at an angle to his shirt collar. He took his guitar out
of its case and tuned it again to pass the time. It was the only
thing he owned of value. He had paid forty dollars for it in a
pawnshop. It had twelve strings, and he kept the dark wood shined
with wax. His fingertips were callused from practice.

He looked at the secretary behind the desk. She had on high
heels and hose and a white blouse. She held her back very straight
and her breasts stood out against the blouse. He thought how he
would like to sleep with her. She went inside the audition room
and came back out again.

"Mr. Hunnicut will see you now," she said.

J.P. put out his hand-rolled cigarette under his shoe and placed
the guitar back in its case. From the corner of his eye he watched
the secretary sit down in her chair. Her skirt creased across the

top of her thighs. He went into the audition room and saw a fat sweating man dressed in a white linen suit and candy-striped necktie sitting in a folding chair with a pitcher of ice water by his side. There were some other men standing around whom J.P. didn't look at. The man in the linen suit filled his glass from the pitcher and swallowed two salt tablets.

"What do you do?" the man said.

"Play twelve-string guitar and sing," J.P. answered. "I seen your ad in the paper about the talent show."

"You know there's an entrance fee of five dollars."

"I give it to the secretary."

"All right, go ahead. Sing."

J.P. felt nervous. The other men were watching him. He thought they were smiling. He put the leather strap around his neck and began. He hit the wrong chords and his voice cracked. One of the men laughed.

"Shut up, Troy," said Hunnicut, the sweating man in the white linen suit.

"I reckon I'm nervous," J.P. said.

"Try it again," Hunnicut said, bored.

> *Good morning, blues*
> *Blues, how do you do?*
> *I'm doing all right*
> *Good morning, how are you?*
>
> *When I got up this morning*
> *Blues was walking round my bed*
> *Yes, the blues walking round my bed*
> *I went to eat my breakfast*
> *The blues was all in my bread*
>
> *I sent for you yesterday see me baby*
> *Here you come a walking today*
> *Yes, here you come a walking today*
> *Got your mouth wide open*
> *You don't know what to say.*

Hunnicut leaned his weight back in the wood chair and looked at him. He spit on the floor and took a drink of water.

Good morning, blues
Blues, how do you do?
I'm doing all right.
Good morning, how are you?

J.P. finished and put his guitar back in its case.

"Do you write your own music?" Hunnicut said.

"That's one of Leadbelly's songs. I heard him once when he first got out of the pen."

"Who's Leadbelly?"

"He was in Angola. He's the man that made a twelve-string guitar."

"Here's a card. It will get you in the door tonight," Hunnicut said.

"Do I get my five dollars back?"

"No, you don't get it back. Do you want to use one of the electric guitars tonight?"

"I don't play on no electric guitar," J.P. said. "It ruins the tone."

"You got another suit besides that one?"

"What's wrong with it?"

"Nothing. It looks fine."

"Let him wear a pair of overalls," one of the other men said.

"Don't mind Troy," Hunnicut said. "He's got a mouth disease. It don't know when to stay shut."

Troy was a member of Hunnicut's show. He was from back-of-town Memphis, and he had black marcelled hair, sideburns, a high oil-slick forehead, and gold plating around the edges of his teeth. His lean jaws worked slowly as he chewed a piece of gum. The man with him was named Seth. He was tall and he had coarse brown hair like straw, and his face was scarred from smallpox. The skin was deeply pockmarked and reddened, and there was a scent of whiskey on his breath.

"I got something for you to sign," Hunnicut said. "This is just a talent show and you don't get paid. If you win you appear on the Louisiana Jubilee, and then we'll talk about a salary. Seth and Troy will be on the show tonight, but they're not in the contest."

He gave J.P. a release to sign. J.P. put his signature at the bottom in pencil in large awkward letters.

"What's your full name?" Hunnicut said.

"That's it."

"Your initials stand for something, don't they?"

"J.P. is my name, mister. I ain't got no other."

"Where are you from?" Troy, the man with the black marcelled hair, said.

"Up north of here by the Arkansas line."

"All right, boy. You're all set to go. We'll see you this evening," Hunnicut said.

J.P. picked up his guitar case and left the audition room.

"You figure he come to town on a mule?" Troy said.

"He's going to do all right," Hunnicut said.

"You ain't going to let him win?"

"He's the man."

"He's a hillbilly."

"You want to know something? I'll tell you why you'll never be anything but a dime and nickel picker in somebody's troupe. Because you got no idea of what it takes to get on top of the pile. You either got to know how to act like a hick and make the real hicks think you're as stupid as they are, or if you're a real hick you got to have somebody with brains enough behind you to make the other hicks think like you want them to. The way to make money from hicks is to sell them a hick. And that boy is just what they want."

"He's still got fertilizer on his shoes," Troy said.

J.P. crossed the street and walked towards the hotel. He had rented a room without a bath in the older part of the business district. The hotel was an ugly three-story building with rusted fire escapes and one wall had been blackened by a fire. He took his key from the desk clerk and went upstairs.

The room had a musty odor to it. He turned on the ceiling fan and opened the window. He leaned on the sill and looked down into the street. He saw the cotton exchange and the sample bales wrapped in brown paper and partially torn open and stacked by the side entrance; there were drygoods stores, a Negro peddler selling fruit from a wagon, groups of men in overalls and seersucker suits who talked and chewed tobacco and spit over the curbing, women in cotton-print dresses looking through the store windows at the cheap machine-made merchandise, and the late afternoon sun beat down on the asphalt and filled the air with a hot, humid odor. A man who had his legs amputated at the knees sat propped against one of the buildings with a hat in his hand. There were several pencils in the hat. People passed him by without notice, some looked at him in curiosity, one woman dropped a coin into his hat. He sat on a board platform with small metal wheels underneath. He rolled himself along the sidewalk by pushing with his hands against the pavement. J.P. watched him disappear around the corner. He turned away from the window and lay down on the bed.

He took out his guitar and drew his thumb slowly across the strings. Sometimes he used a beer cap for a pick as the cotton field workers did who used to play guitar in the juke joints on the edge of town. He had first liked music as a small boy when he used to sit on the levee in the late evening down by the nigger graveyard and listen to the funeral marches and see the sweating faces in the glow of pine fagots and hear the music that seemed to tell the sorrow of an entire race.

He wanted to write a song. It would contain all the things he felt inside him. It would have the sadness he saw in the country around him, the feeling of the niggers singing in the fields, it would be like the songs they sang on the work gangs and in the Salvation Army camps, or like sitting on the back porch alone, watching the rain fall on the young cotton.

He went down the hall to bathe and dress. At six o'clock he left the hotel and walked to the city auditorium where the contest was being held. The stores had closed and there were few people on the street. He passed the movie house and saw the man with the amputated legs on his wood platform off to one side of the entrance holding his hat and pencils in his hand. The beggar smelled of wine and dried sweat. The buttons of his shirt were gone and his bony chest showed. The theater manager asked him to move farther down the street; he was in the way of the people who wanted to go to the show.

J.P. went to the back door of the auditorium and gave the doorman his card. It was crowded backstage. He saw Hunnicut and Troy talking in the wings.

"Evening," he said.

"Hi boy, how's it going?" Hunnicut said, then shouted at one of the prop men, "You got the lights out of place—over there, no, I said over there." He turned back to J.P. and Troy. "I got to do everybody's job for them. Go show him where to put the lights, Troy. I should fire the whole goddamn crew of them."

"Where am I supposed to go?" J.P. said.

"Let's get you another suit of clothes first."

"My suit don't have nothing to do with playing guitar."

"Hey, Seth, get over here."

Seth was talking with a short, well-formed brunette.

"Take him into Troy's dressing room and find him some clothes," Hunnicut said.

"You sure Troy don't mind?"

"To hell with Troy. Get Winfield a suit that don't look like a piece of canvas."

They walked behind the sets to the dressing room. Seth took a gray sports suit from the closet and laid it over the chair. The pockmarks in his face showed more deeply in the artificial light of the room. He took a pint bottle out of his coat pocket and unscrewed the cap. He drank out of the bottle while J.P. dressed.

"You want a shot?" he said.

"Thanks. You reckon I got a chance tonight?"

"You'll be all right."

"I spent my last few dollars to come to town."

"Virdo will give you a job. You're real good on a twelve-string."

"Who's Virdo?" J.P. said.

"It's Hunnicut's first name, but he don't like nobody to call him by it."

"Is that girl you were with in the show?"

"Yeah. She sings some. Mostly she's out there to give the farmers something to look at. I never could get no place with her. She gives it to Troy pretty steady. He can have it, though. She's on the powder. Mainline stuff."

"You know some girls around town?"

"Just whores."

"I'm busted."

"Get Hunnicut to give you an advance after the show and I'll take you to a place."

"I ain't got the job yet."

"You ain't seen the other people that's going to be out there.

There's one fellow that beats on a washboard while he plays the harmonica. You ain't got to worry about the job."

They left the dressing room and went back to stand in the wings. Troy was onstage with the band, waiting for the curtain to open. Seth smoked a cigarette, then went onstage and picked up his banjo and adjusted the microphone. He smiled out at the crowd as the curtain opened.

"A great big howdy, friends and neighbors," he said. "This is Seth Milton. Tonight we're going to have some of your favorite artists from the field of country and western music, along with some of the best in local talent. The contest is going to start directly, but first me and the boys is going to pick and sing some of your favorite tunes. This show is being put on by Mr. V. L. Hunnicut of the Louisiana Jubilee, who has encouraged so much young talent and brought some of the major stars of country music into the national spotlight. Also I want to tell you about the big one hundred page color picture book that we have on sale at the entrance. It contains one hundred actual color photographs of your favorite country singers, ready to cut out and put on the wall at home. This big color picture book is selling for the low figure of two dollars and fifty cents, and if you ain't got the money on you, you can put in your order and it will be sent to you collect. The pages is in bright glossy color, and when you're listening over the radio to your favorite country entertainer you can look up his picture in the big-print table of contents and it's just like he's in the room with you.

"Now, I want you to meet somebody that many of you already know. He's one of the best guitar pickers in the field, and he's just put out two new records. Come on up here, brother Troy."

J.P. stood in the wings and listened to Troy sing and the applause afterwards. Then the brunette came on and sang "I Want to Be in My Savior's Arms," and he looked at her short-cut hair and Irish peasant face and her abnormally large breasts. She had a slender waist, flat stomach, and wide hips. He thought about laying her, and then he thought about going to a whorehouse later in the evening with Seth. He hoped he could get the job and the advance on his salary. It had taken all his money to come to town and enter the show, and it had been three weeks since he had slept with a woman; if he lost the contest he would have to hitchhike back home, and it would be another month before he could afford Miss Sara's house out in the country.

The band left the stage, and the contest started. The man with the harmonica and washboard went on first. He held the harmonica in his mouth with his lips and played while he beat out the rhythm on the metal ripples in the washboard with his knuckles. Three others went on, and it was J.P.'s turn. He walked out on the stage from the wings with his guitar. The lights were hot in his face. The audience was a dark, indistinct mass behind the lights. He sang "Good-Night, Irene," which had been Leadbelly's theme song.

> *I asked your mother for you,*
> *She told me that you was too young.*
> *I wish the Lord I never seen your face,*
> *I'm sorry you ever was born.*
>
> *Stop rambling and stop gambling,*
> *Quit staying out late at night.*
> *Go home to your wife and your family,*
> *Sit down by the fireside bright.*
>
> *I love Irene, God knows I do*
> *I love her till the sea runs dry,*
> *If Irene turns her back on me*
> *I'm going to take morphine and die.*

The crowd liked him and they applauded until he sang it again. They were still applauding when he left the stage.

J.P. propped the guitar against one of the sets and wiped the perspiration off his forehead on his coat sleeve.

"You got on my suit," Troy said.

"You can have it back. It don't fit me, nohow."

"I told him to take the suit," Hunnicut said.

"I had it cleaned yesterday. He got sweat on the sleeve."

"Take the goddamn thing back, mister. I didn't want it in the first place."

"Take it easy, Winfield. You did fine tonight."

"Do I get a job with you?"

"You haven't won the contest yet."

"Seth said I already had the job."

"All right, you're working for me."

J.P. took a crumpled one-dollar bill out of his pocket and gave it to Troy.

"This will pay for the goddamn cleaning," he said.

"Where are you going?" Hunnicut said.

"To get my clothes."

He went to Troy's dressing room and changed into his Sears, Roebuck suit. After all the contestants had gone on, Hunnicut announced that the winner was J.P. Winfield, who would soon be appearing on the Louisiana Jubilee with the rest of the band. J.P. combed his hair in the mirror and clipped the comb inside his shirt pocket. He left Troy's sports suit unfolded on top of the chair. He rolled a cigarette and walked back to the wings where Hunnicut, Troy, Seth, and the brunette were talking. The auditorium had cleared.

"You ain't met April yet," Seth said.

J.P. looked at her.

"This is April Brien," Seth said.

"Glad to meet you," she said. Her eyes moved up and down him. Her peasant Irish face had a dull expression to it.

"Evening," he said.

"April does all the spirituals in the show," Seth said. He put his hand on the small of her back and let his fingers touch her rump.

"Cut it out," she said.

He gave her a pat.

"Lay off it," Troy said.

Seth winked at J.P.

"Come in the office," Hunnicut said. "I got a contract for you to sign."

They went into Hunnicut's office, which he had rented with the auditorium. His white linen suit was soiled and dampened. The candy-striped necktie was pulled loose from his collar, and the great weight of his stomach hung over his trousers.

"I start you on a straight salary at three hundred and fifty a month," he said, "plus any commissions we make off records and special appearances. This contract says that I'm your manager and agent, and I take twelve percent of your earnings. We'll see how you do, and later on maybe we can work out a pay increase."

"You take a commission off the same salary you give me?"

"That's right. But I'm the man that schedules all your appearances, and if you've got the right stuff I can push you right up to the top. I put a lot of people on the Nashville Barn Dance."

"How about an advance? That was my last dollar I give to that fellow for his suit."

Hunnicut took a black square billfold out of the inside pocket of his coat. He flipped it open flat on the desk and counted out several bills.

"Here's fifty dollars. Will that do?"

"That'll do just fine."

That night he and Seth went to a juke joint and got drunk and picked up two prostitutes. They spent the night in an apartment next door to the bar, and J.P. awoke in the morning with a hangover and looked at the woman beside him in the light and wished he had stayed sober the night before. He put on his clothes and counted the money in his wallet. He couldn't find his clip-on bow tie, then he saw the prostitute sleeping on it, and he pulled it out from under her leg and left the room and caught a taxi to his hotel.

He bought a new suit and a new pair of shoes and gave his old clothes to the porter. He checked out of the hotel and walked down the street, holding the guitar case by its leather handle. He thought about the long bus ride ahead with the band through the sun-baked, red clay country of north Louisiana. He thought about the money he would make singing, three times the amount he made as a sharecropper back home. And Hunnicut had said that he might go up to the Nashville Barn Dance. The sun was very hot, and he had to squint his eyes in the white glare off the pavement. It would be a long trip in the summer heat.

TOUSSAINT BOUDREAUX

A South American freighter had come into port the day before to unload a shipment of coffee and to pick up another load of machine parts. Down in the hold a gang of stevedores waited for the gantry to lower the cargo net through the hatch. The temperature was over a hundred degrees in the hold. The iron plates on the bulkhead would scald your hands if you touched them. Toussaint looked up through the hatch at the bright square of sky. The Negro watched the gantry boom swing around from the dock and drop the cargo net into the hold, loaded with crates of machinery. The gang loosened the net and pulled the crates free with their hooks and dragged them across the floor. Toussaint and another man whipped their cargo hooks into the wood and slid a crate into position against the bulkhead. It was almost quitting time. He watched the empty net go back up through the hatch. The work whistle blew and the men picked up their lunch kits and walked up the metal steps to the deck and down the gangplank to the dock.

Toussaint was fighting a four-round heavyweight bout at the arena that evening against an Italian from Chicago. He had wanted to get off work early, since his manager had promised him a main bout with a contender if he won tonight; but his gang boss wouldn't let him off, and he had only a short time to rest before the fight. He ate a light supper and went to the pool hall to pass the time. He found a table in back and shot a game of nine ball. He liked the smooth felt green of the tables and the click of the balls. There was a horse board along one wall and a ticker tape machine that gave the race results. A couple of hustlers tried to get him into a game. He ignored them, chalked his cue, sank the nine ball, and had the boy rack the balls for another game. The hustlers played the slot machine and waited for someone else to come in. Toussaint looked at their clothes: the high-yellow pointed shoes, the knife-cut trousers, open-collar shirts without a coat, and short-brimmed hats with a wide hatband and a feather. He threw a dime on the table for the game and left.

He caught a bus to the arena. The preliminaries began at eight and he had the third bout. He carried his canvas athletic bag into the locker room and changed into his trunks and robe. The job he had on the docks was the best job he could find in New Orleans when he came to the city from his home in Barataria five years ago. But it was tough in the union and on the docks, and each man did his work and looked out for himself. It was very different from what Toussaint had known in Barataria. Most of the men on the gang, save a few, had accepted him by now; but when he first went to work he was treated with either indifference or resentment, and two men complained to the union about working in the same hold with a Negro.

He did some calisthenics to loosen up and sat on the rubbing table. There was no fat on his body, and the elastic band on his scarlet trunks was flat and tight across his stomach. He had fought once a month in the preliminaries for the last year. He had lost one bout, and it was after a split decision and the referee had decided against him because of a foul. Some of the people around the arena thought he could move up to the big circuits if he was handled properly, except he was thirty years old and his best years were behind him. He could punch hard, move around fast, and stand up under a beating. He had gotten his start when a fight manager had seen him in a fistfight down on the docks. Toussaint had fought another stevedore who had said that he didn't like working with a Negro. The manager called him aside after the fight and told him he could earn fifty dollars for coming down to the arena and putting on the gloves. Since then Toussaint had become a promising club fighter with a good classic style.

Archie, his trainer, came into the locker room. He was an ex-navy man who ran a men's health club downtown and picked up extra money as a part-time trainer. He wore white duck trousers, a T-shirt, and white low-topped tennis shoes. He had a thick chest and shoulders and bicepses, and his face was tanned and part of his brown hair had been bleached out by the sun.

"You're early tonight," he said.

"I'm stiff. I need a rubdown."

"I saw the dago in the hall. He says he's going to crack you open."

"What do you think?"

"I've never seen him fight before."

"They say he's good," Toussaint said.

"He's a ham and egg boy."

"I want to get him fast. I don't want no decision tonight."

"He's going to have the reach on you. You'll have to get under him."

"Where's Ruth?" Ruth was Toussaint's manager.

"Down at ringside with the money boys. They'll be watching you."

"What are the gamblers giving?"

"Two to one on you."

"I wish I seen this boy fight before," Toussaint said.

"How do you feel?"

"Tight."

"Lay down. I'll work on your back."

Archie massaged his shoulders and taped his hands. Some of the other preliminary fighters came into the locker room and began dressing. The buzzer sounded for the first bout. One of the fighters left with his trainer. Fifteen minutes later they were back. The fighter was bleeding from the nose and mouth. He slammed the door and threw his robe into a locker. His chest and stomach were covered with red welts. He lay back on the rubbing table.

"I tell you he had oil on his gloves. I couldn't see what I was doing," he said.

His trainer pinched the bridge of his nose to coagulate the blood.

"Every time I got in close he slapped me across the eyes. It ain't right."

"You were lucky to last three rounds. He had it all over you," his trainer said.

"I could have chewed him up and spit him out if he fought fair," he said, still bleeding from the nose.

"Did Ruth say anything about talking with the promoters?" Toussaint said.

"They'll give you a ten-round bout next month if you knock over the dago," Archie said.

"I got to get out of the prelims before long. I ain't got many years left fighting."

"How does your back feel now?"

"I'm okay." He rolled his arms and shoulders.

"You don't pick up any fat on the docks."

"Loading machinery don't do nothing for me before a fight neither."

"The second bout is almost over. Move around a little bit."

Toussaint stood up and threw some shadow punches. Archie laced his gloves and snipped the plastic tips off with a pair of scissors. He put a mouthpiece, a water bottle, and some towels into a canvas bag.

"There's the buzzer. Let's go," he said. He picked up the canvas bag and the first-aid kit, and they went out into the corridor and up the concrete ramp that led to the arena.

The arena was overcrowded and the air was heavy with a drifting haze of cigarette smoke. The house lamps dimmed for the third bout as they walked down the aisle. The lights above the ring were bright through the smoke. There was a steady noise of talking and scraping of chairs. Some of the people shouted to Toussaint as he passed them. He looked at his opponent, who was already in the ring. The Italian had a scarred face and was a few pounds heavier than Toussaint. He was rubbing his feet in the rosin and pressing one glove into the palm of the other. Toussaint climbed into the ring and did some footwork while the announcer tried to get the crowd's attention.

"Ladies and gentlemen," the announcer said. He was dressed in a tuxedo. "Tonight we have two good boys with us for the third bout. Wearing scarlet trunks at a hundred and ninety-five pounds is Toussaint Boudreaux, a local boy with eleven wins and one loss. His opponent in the opposite corner, wearing black trunks, at two hundred pounds is Anthony Pepponi from Chicago, Illinois, with seventeen wins and two losses—"

Toussaint and Archie went to the center of the ring to get the referee's instructions. They came back to the corner and Archie climbed down through the ropes. Toussaint handed him his scarlet robe.

He moved out fast with the bell and started punching. Pepponi had the reach on him, but Toussaint stayed in close and kept his head low to catch most of the heavy blows on his forearms and to work in for a body attack. Pepponi opened his guard when he hooked, and Toussaint unloaded on him. His head jerked back and the Negro hit him twice in the rib cage with his left and slammed another right on his jaw before he could recover. Pepponi backpedaled, fighting defensively, then caught Toussaint on the chin with a long one. Toussaint moved in and worked on his midsection. He crouched low to keep under Pepponi's arms. Pepponi fought his way out of the corner, jabbing with his left to keep Toussaint away, and sent a right to his brow. Toussaint took a punch on the forehead for every two punches to Pepponi's body. The Italian was breathing hard. They tied up in the center of the ring and worked on each other's kidneys until the referee separated them. The crowd applauded at the bell.

Archie climbed up on the apron with the wood stool. Toussaint had a thin split over his eye. Archie took out his mouthpiece and Toussaint rinsed his mouth from the water bottle and spit into the funnel.

"Stay in close and wait till he opens up," Archie said, rubbing the Negro's chest with a towel. "You hurt him with that first right. Keep working on his body. He's winded, and he'll have to try to put you away. If it keeps up like this you'll have him on a decision."

"He knows how to hit," Toussaint said. He could feel the flesh draw tight around his eye.

"Ten seconds," Archie said. "Remember, don't try to cool him till he comes after you."

Toussaint kept his guard high to protect the cut over his eye. Pepponi concentrated his punches on the Negro's forehead. The leather slapped as Toussaint brushed away the jabs, and then there was a raw crack when Pepponi connected with that long right. The blood came down in Toussaint's eye, hot and sticky. He straightened up and gave Pepponi a target, and then ducked a right and caught him in the solar plexus. The Italian wheezed and pulled his elbows in to cover his stomach. Toussaint tried to move in on him, but Pepponi clinched him. The Negro took two more punches on the eye. Pepponi was throwing everything he had to keep Toussaint away. Toussaint worked on his body to open him up. Pepponi fought more carefully. He knew that Toussaint was waiting to unload on him, and he was going to try to take the fight on a technical knockout.

Toussaint was badly hurt in the third round. Pepponi butted him in a clinch and lengthened the split over his eye. He could no longer see out of his left eye, and Pepponi's right hand was outside his vision. His nose was swollen and the inside of his mouth was cut. He knew that he had lost the round.

In the corner, Archie wiped his face with a wet towel and worked on the left eye with a cotton swab. The taste of blood in Toussaint's mouth made him faintly nauseated. He drank from the water bottle and spit it out. The fourth round was the last one. He would have to get Pepponi then, or it would probably be a split decision. Toussaint had the first two rounds on points, but Pepponi had the third and he would probably get the fourth.

Toussaint was unsteady on his feet as he came out of his corner. Pepponi hit him on the bridge of the nose. Toussaint feinted with his left and drove a right hook into his side, just below the heart. Pepponi dropped his glove and Toussaint hit him hard across the side of the head. It knocked Pepponi against the ropes. Toussaint pinned him in the corner and went to work on him. He hooked a right into the Italian's jaw, and then he felt a bone snap in the back of his hand. The pain rushed up his arm through his body, and made his eyes water. It had cracked like a dry stick. Pepponi got out of the corner and came towards him punching. Toussaint held his right glove in front of his face and tried to keep him away with his left. Toussaint feinted with his good hand to make him drop his guard, and shifted all his weight onto his left foot and drove an uppercut straight into the Italian's throat. The pain almost made Toussaint pass out. Pepponi spit out his mouthpiece and stiffened as he bounced off the turnbuckle and sank to the floor with his head and arms hanging through the ropes.

He couldn't get up before the final count. The referee came over and raised Toussaint's arm to the crowd. Archie climbed up on the apron with the robe, and sponged his face and chest. The Negro's eye was completely closed. Archie draped the robe on Toussaint's shoulders, and they left the ring and made their way down the aisle to the locker rooms.

Toussaint lay down on the rubbing table while Archie tried to remove his glove.

"Your hand is swollen up like a rock," he said. He cut away the glove with a razor blade. The leather peeled back from the edge of the razor. "That punch may've ruined your hand for good."

Toussaint put his left arm across his face.

"The ring doctor will be here in a minute. Is it hurting bad?" Archie said.

"It's numb now."

"I don't see how you did it."

"I didn't think about it. I saw him coming and it was over."

"You got a rough shake. Maybe I didn't have your hand taped tight enough."

"The tape was all right. When I hit him he pulled his head in and I caught him with the back of my fist."

Toussaint's manager came into the locker room. He wore his hair in a crew cut and dressed in a dark business suit and silk tie with a jeweled tie clasp, and there was a Mason's ring on his finger. His face was ruddy and there was hair on the back of his hands.

"What happened?" he said.

"He busted his hand."

"Let's see it."

Toussaint held it up.

"Where's the ring doctor?" Ruth said.

"He's coming," Archie said.

"We'll get an X ray at the hospital and see how bad it is," Ruth said.

"It's a compound fracture," Archie said. "He's bleeding under the skin."

"I'm sorry, Toussaint. I had it arranged with the promoters for you next month."

"He'll get another chance. The money boys are watching him."

"They thought you'd make a good drawing card to fight an out-of-town boy."

"How's Pepponi?" Toussaint said.

"He was all right after he got up. You just took the wind out of him," Ruth answered.

Archie cleaned the blood out of Toussaint's eye with a piece of cotton.

"Here's what I owe you for the fight," Ruth said. "There's a little bit extra to hold you over. Tell the doctor to send his bill to me."

"I ain't asking for no handout, Mr. Ruth."

"I know you're not. I always give a boy something extra when he gets hurt and has to lay off a while."

Ruth tucked the money in Toussaint's robe pocket.

"When your hand is all right come down to the arena and we'll see what we can do," he said.

Ruth left the room. The ring doctor came in and put Toussaint's hand in a temporary sling. He cleaned the cut over his eye and closed it with twelve stitches. Toussaint dressed without showering, and he and Archie drove to the hospital for an X ray. The intern said that he had broken several bones in the back of his hand and it would take a long time to mend. The intern set the hand in an aluminum brace that was shaped to the curve of the palm and fingers and didn't allow any movement of the fractured bones. Archie drove Toussaint to his flat.

"Ruth meant it about you coming back to the arena when your hand is well," he said.

"The doctor told me I got to wait six months before I fight again."

"What about your job on the docks?"

"They ain't hiring one-arm men to handle freight."

Toussaint lived in a tenement building a few blocks from the warehouse district. He went up the narrow stairway through the darkened corridor to his room. The room was poorly furnished, and dingy like the rest of the building, with a tattered yellow shade on the window, a single bed with a brass bedstead, a wall mirror and a scarred chest of drawers by an old sofa that was faded colorless; the wallpaper was streaked brown by the water that seeped through the cracks every time it rained. He turned on the single bulb light that hung by a cord from the ceiling. He took off his sling to undress, and rinsed his face in the washbasin. He looked in the mirror at the row of black stiches across his eye;

one side of his face was swollen into a hard knot. He showered, turned out the light, and went to bed.

Outside in the alley he heard drunken voices and the rattling of garbage cans. He looked up through the darkness and thought of his home in Barataria, south of New Orleans. He wondered if he would ever go back. A woman yelled for the drunks to be quiet. Toussaint rolled over in his bed and closed his eyes. He thought of himself on the deck of a trawler with the nets piled on the stern and the steady roll of the Gulf beneath his feet, the horizon before him where the dying sun went down in the water in a last blaze of red, the smell of the salt and the seaweed and the sound of the anchor chain sliding off the bow. He turned in his bed and couldn't sleep. He remembered the tavern where they used to go after coming into port. It was a good place with a long polished bar and small round tables covered with checkerboard cloths. They served boiled crabs and crawfish, and you could get a plate of barbecue and a pitcher of draught beer for a dollar. It was always filled with fishermen, and Toussaint would stand at the bar and talk and drink neat whiskey from the shot glasses with water as a chaser.

The next morning he looked for a job. He tried the state employment agency first. The only jobs to be had were those of bellboy, bus hop, and janitor. He went to warehouses, trucking firms, auto garages, and was told that there was either no job to be had, or to come back when his hand had healed. The third day he went to a clothing store on Canal that had advertised for help in the stockroom. Toussaint applied and got the job. When he reported for work he was shown where the brooms, mops, dustpans, and cleaning rags were kept, and was told to mop the floor of the men's and women's restrooms. He left the store and looked for another job. A week passed and he found nothing. The landlord of his building asked for the rent, which took Toussaint's last twenty dollars. He rode the streetcars and buses and walked over most of the city to find work. He went to a private employment agency. They said he might try cutting lawns; there wasn't much else for a man in his condition.

Two weeks later he was sitting in the pool hall, reading the want ads in the newspaper. All the tables were being used. A man with a cigarette between his teeth sat down on the bench beside him. It was one of the hustlers who had tried to get him into a game the afternoon of his last fight.

"Out of work?" he said.

"That's right."

"See anything in the paper?"

Toussaint looked towards the pool tables.

"I see you got a bad hand. Work must be hard to get."

Toussaint folded his paper and put it on the bench.

"If you're looking for a job maybe I can fix it up," the hustler said.

"You run an employment agency?"

"I got a friend that needs a guy to drive a truck."

"You drive it for him."

"I make my bread in other ways."

"Who's your friend?"

"That's him by the horse board."

"I don't know him," Toussaint said.

"He don't know you either."

"Say what you got on your mind or go back to your friend."

"He needs a driver and he figured you might want the job."

"That ain't telling me nothing. What's he want to hire me for?"

"This is a special kind of trucking service. He don't take on union drivers."

"What's he hauling?"

"That's what the union asks," the hustler said.

"And his drivers don't ask nothing."

"You got it."

"I want to ask him some questions."

"He ain't used to it."

"Get off it, boy. He wouldn't have sent you over here to hire a one-arm man unless he needed a driver pretty bad."

"You're cool, daddy."

They went over to the man by the horse board. He was a well-dressed, light tan Negro with thick, rimless glasses. He looked like a Negro preacher, except for the glass ring on his little finger.

"This guy might want to be a truck driver," the hustler said.

"Did Erwin explain it to you?"

"What are you hauling?" Toussaint said.

"You make an out-of-state delivery. I take care of the rest."

"What's the pay?"

"A hundred dollars."

"I want two hundred if I'm carrying a blind load."

"I don't pay a driver more than a hundred."

"Get somebody else, then."

"A hundred now, and a hundred when you get there."

"Where am I going?"

"You'll learn that tonight. Erwin will give you the address of the warehouse."

"Is this a one-man job?"

"Another truck will go with you."

"What is it? Whiskey?"

"Give him the address, Erwin."

The hustler tore open an empty cigarette pack and flattened it against the wall and wrote something on it in pencil. He gave it to Toussaint.

"Here's your bread ticket, daddy," he said.

"Bonham Shipping Company," Toussaint read. "Are you Bonham?"

"Yes. I am. Pick up the truck at nine."

"You ain't give me the money yet."

"He's real sharp, ain't he, Mr. Bonham?" the hustler said.

AVERY BROUSSARD

It was night and the moon was high, and Avery sat on a log in the clearing while Tereau took the coffeepot off the fire. Tereau was three parts Negro, one part Chitimacha Indian, and he made the best moonshine in southern Louisiana. No one knew how old he was, not even Tereau, but a Negro must live very long before his hair turns white. He had fought sheriffs and federal tax agents to keep his still, and some people said that he carried a double-edged knife made from a file in his boot.

Tereau poured coffee in their cups and added a shot of whiskey from the pint bottle he carried in his coat pocket. They were waiting for the bootleggers who were to slip through the marsh in an outboard and meet them. The mules and the wagon were off to the side of the clearing by the trees, with the heavy kegs of whiskey loaded on the bed. Avery took another shot in his cup.

"Tonight ain't a good time to be drinking too much corn," Tereau said.

"What happened to the bootleggers?"

"They'll be along. There's a lot of moonlight. They got to be careful."

"Do the state police ever catch any of them?"

"Sometimes, but they usually get rid of the whiskey before they're caught. It don't take long to dump them barrels overboard."

Tereau rolled a cigarette and handed the package of rough-cut string tobacco to Avery.

"Them bootleggers don't take much chance," Tereau said. "They're always moving and they got nobody except the state police to look out for. I got to worry about federal tax agents. They never give up looking for my still. Every month there's a couple of them wandering around in the marsh trying to find it."

Avery laughed.

"They almost got me once," Tereau said. "When I leave the still I run a ball of string around it in a big circle, about a inch off the ground. One day I come back and the string was slack on the ground. I snuck around to the other side and seen one of them tax people hid behind my boiler. I went and got my brother and two cousins and we brung the wagon up close to the still, then I sent my brother down to the tax fellow's car. It was parked about a mile away on a side road. My brother stuck a match in the horn button to keep the horn blowing, and the tax fellow took off to see what the matter was, and while he was stumbling through the briars we took the still to pieces and loaded it on the wagon and moved the whole outfit to the other side of the marsh."

"You crazy old man," Avery said.

"I don't see no old men around here." Tereau puffed on the cigarette and flicked it into the fire.

"Why'd you want to come with me, Avery? You ain't never been one to break the law," he said.

"Since they took the farm I got nothing else to do. Breaking the law seems like a good enough way to pass the time."

"If you don't end up busting rocks on a work gang."

"They never caught you."

"That's because I been at it a long time. My granddaddy taught me all the tricks when I was a little boy. When he was a young man he sold moon to both the Confederate and Federal army, except he might have added some lye or fertilizer when he sold it to the Yankees. I hope you ain't planning on making this your life's work."

"You'd put me out of business."

There was a rustle in the bushes, and two men came into the clearing. They were bootleggers who picked up Tereau's whiskey to run it through the marsh downriver to Morgan City, and eventually to New Orleans and the dry counties in Mississippi. The whiskey was sold for four dollars a gallon at the still and twelve dollars a gallon at the retailers. It was clear and tasted like Scotch, and sometimes coloring was added and the whiskey was sold with a bonded Kentucky label, although its maker had never been out of Louisiana. The bootleggers were sunburned, rawboned men; their hands and faces were smeared with mud and handkerchiefs were tied around their necks to protect them from the mosquitoes; they were dressed in heavy work trousers and denim shirts with battered sweat-soaked straw hats. They were from the Atchafalaya basin, where there is nothing but lowlands, swamps, mud-choked bayous, scrubby timber so thick it is almost impassable in places, and swarming clouds of mosquitoes that can put a man to bed with a fever.

The bootleggers came into the light of the fire. Their names were LeBlanc and Gerard. LeBlanc was the taller of the two, with an old army .45-caliber revolver stuck down in his belt. He was dark and slender, and his eyes were bright in the light. Gerard was thick-necked, unshaved, with heavy shoulders that were slightly stooped; he had long muscular arms and a crablike walk. He cut a slice off his tobacco plug and dropped it into his mouth.

"You all are late tonight," Tereau said.

"We had to take the long way," LeBlanc said. "State police is on the river."

"We're going to have to change our pickup night. They got it figured when we move our stuff," Gerard said.

LeBlanc looked at Avery.

"Who's the boy?" he said.

"He's all right," Tereau said.

"What's your name?"

"Avery Broussard."

"I reckon Tereau told you it ain't good to talk about what you see in the marsh at night," he said.

"He told me."

"Tereau says he's all right," Gerard said.

"Sure he's all right," LeBlanc said. "I'm just making sure he understands how we do things down here."

"He knows," Tereau said. "Where's the boat?"

"Down in the willows. We got it covered up good," Gerard said.

Avery looked at the wild stare in LeBlanc's eyes.

"There's too much moonlight. You can see us for a half mile on the river. We had to come down the bayou," LeBlanc said.

Tereau went to the wagon to get tin cups for their coffee. "I got some rabbit. You want to eat?" he said.

"We ain't got time. It's about four hours till dawn. We got to reach Morgan City before daylight," LeBlanc said.

They sat down on the log while Tereau filled their cups. LeBlanc stretched out his legs and removed the pistol from his belt and placed it on the log.

"Do you use that thing?" Avery said.

"They ain't nobody around to say I have," he said. He picked it up and rolled the cylinder across his palm. "I got it in the army." He snapped the cylinder open into a loading position and snapped it back again. His eyes were hard and distant as he looked into the fire. "They teach you how to shoot real good in the army. I was a B.A.R. man. I could knock down nips at a thousand yards with a Browning."

Gerard stood up and threw the rest of his coffee into the fire. "We better get moving," he said. LeBlanc continued to stare ahead with the pistol in his hand. Gerard nudged him with his foot. "Come on, we better move. We still got to load the boat."

LeBlanc rubbed the oil off the pistol barrel on his trouser leg. He put the gun on half cock and slid it back in his belt. He still had that same hard, distant look in his eyes. He finished his coffee in one swallow and got up and went over to the wagon to count the kegs of whiskey with Tereau.

"Don't get him talking about the army no more," Gerard said to Avery. "He ain't been right since he come back from the war."

"Did he ever use that gun on anybody?"

"I don't ask him no questions. He knows his job, and what else he does ain't my business. The only time I got to watch him is when we have a scrape with the law. Soon as he thinks they're around he takes out his pistol and puts it on full cock. His eyes get like two pieces of fire when he sees a uniform."

Avery looked over to the wagon. Tereau was fastening the tailgate after LeBlanc had climbed down from the bed. The mules shuffled in their harness.

"What happened to him in the army?" Avery said.

"He was in the South Pacific about a year. He even got decorated once. Then one day he tried to shoot his commanding officer and deserted. They found him about a month later and put him in the stockade. He went kind of crazy in there. They sent him to a hospital for a while, but it didn't do no good. They finally give him a medical discharge because there wasn't nothing else they could do with him."

Gerard took the coffeepot off the iron stake and poured the coffee over the fire. The coals hissed and spit as the fire died and the clearing darkened except for the light of the moon. He pulled the iron stake out of the ground and kicked dirt over the faintly glowing embers.

"Don't let LeBlanc worry you," he said, and went over to the wagon in his slow, crablike walk, his shoulders slightly rounded, with the iron stake and coffeepot in each hand. Avery followed.

"Twenty-five kegs," LeBlanc said.

"I reckon you want some money," Gerard said to Tereau.

"I reckon you're correct, Mister whiskey runner," Tereau said.

Gerard loosened his shirt and unstrapped a money belt from his waist. He propped one foot on the hub of the wagon wheel and counted out the money on his thigh. He put the bills in a stack and handed them to Tereau and strapped the belt around his waist again.

"When you going to start putting my name on the labels?" Tereau said.

"Soon as you start paying federal taxes and we both go out of business," Gerard said.

"I hear something out there," LeBlanc said.

They listened for a moment.

"I don't hear nothing," Gerard said.

"It's out on the river somewheres," LeBlanc said.

"There ain't nothing out there. We got rid of the police three miles back."

LeBlanc moved his hand to the pistol and looked off into the darkness. "There's something wrong," he said. "Everything is going wrong tonight. I can feel it. There's too much moonlight, and there's somebody out on the river."

"There ain't nobody out there."

"I heard it I tell you."

Gerard looked at Tereau.

"Maybe he did hear something. Let's go to the boat and don't take no chances," Tereau said.

Gerard threw the coffeepot and iron stake into the back of the wagon. Tereau got up on the seat and wrapped the reins around his fist. He drove the wagon around the edge of the clearing through a narrow break in the trees that opened onto a wheel-rutted road leading between the levee and a deep gully. They could hear the nutrias calling to each other in the swamp, a high-pitched cry like the scream of a hysterical woman. The oak trees stood at uneven intervals along the rim of the gully, and the moonlight fell through the branches, spotting the ground with pale areas of light against the dark green of the jungle. Tereau sat forward with the reins through his fingers. He looked back at Avery and Gerard, who were following, as the wagon banged over the ruts. LeBlanc walked ahead of the mules, straining his eyes against the darkness. He stopped and without turning put one hand in the air.

"What's the matter?" Gerard said.

"There it is again. It's a boat laying out on the river. I can hear the water breaking against its sides," LeBlanc said.

"How in the hell can you tell it's a boat?" Gerard said.

"I know it's a boat."

"I can't hear nothing," Tereau said.

"I'm going ahead to take a look," LeBlanc said.

"You stay here. Me and the boy will go," Gerard said.

"I reckon I don't need nobody to tell me what to do."

"We need the gun here," Gerard said.

"Tereau's got a rifle in the wagon."

"I ain't carrying it this time," Tereau said.

Gerard touched Avery on the arm and they moved up the road past LeBlanc.

"I don't like nobody telling me what to do," LeBlanc said.

"I ain't telling you nothing," Gerard said. "I'm just asking you to watch the wagon."

They walked on out of sight. The road continued in a straight line between the gully and the levee. Directly ahead was the cove where their boat was moored in the willows. The cove was about fifty yards wide, but the entrance was a bottleneck formed by sandbars, deep enough for small craft to enter and too shallow for anything larger. The river was swollen from the rains, flowing swiftly down to the Gulf. Avery and Gerard left the road before they got to the landing, and worked their way around the edge of the cove to where it met the river. From there they could see the willow trees, the cove, and the river without being seen. They went through the brush until they reached the river's edge where the backwater rippled over the sandbar that formed one side of the bottleneck of the cove. They squatted in the sand and looked out through the reeds.

"There ain't nothing here," Gerard said.

"Look over yonder."

"Where?"

"Just out from the sandbar. It's an oil slick," Avery said.

"It could have come from upriver."

"It's not spread out enough. A boat has been here in the last hour."

Gerard spit a stream of tobacco juice into the sand. "Let's get further downriver. Maybe we can see something."

They worked back along the shore away from the cove. They kept in the shelter of the trees and didn't speak. The frogs and crickets were loud in the marsh. Gerard walked ahead, not making any sound. They arrived at a small inlet that washed back through the trees. They waded into the water until it was around their thighs. Gerard stood with his hand on a tree trunk, looking out over the river.

"I can't see a goddamn thing," he said.

"Maybe they went on past us," Avery said.

"Let's go back to the other side of the cove. If there ain't nothing there, we'll load the boat and get out of here."

"There's another slick."

Gerard looked at the metallic blue oil deposit floating on the water. He raised his eyes and studied the opposite bank.

"Sonsofbitches," he said. "They're hid back in the shadow against the bank. They must have cut their engine and floated downstream to wait for us."

"What do you want to do?" Avery said.

"There ain't no way to get my boat out as long as they're sitting there."

"Sink your boat and go back on foot."

"They'd find it sooner or later and get my registration number."
Gerard spit into the water and waded to the bank. "We got to get
rid of them. Let's go get the others."

They started towards the cove.

"What's the sentence for running whiskey?" Avery said.

"One to three years."

"Do you have a drink on you?"

"I never touch it."

They went through the underbrush to the cove where the sandbar
jutted away from the shore. They could just see the hard-packed
crest beneath the surface in the moonlight. Gerard stopped for a
moment in silence and looked out over the water at the sandbar, and
then followed Avery back through the trees towards the road. They
passed the clump of willows and turned along the gully. They could
see the outline of the wagon and the kegs on its bed in the shadows.
LeBlanc was sitting up on the seat with Tereau.

"What did you see?" Tereau said.

"They're there," Gerard said.

"Bastards," LeBlanc said.

"I think I got a way for us to get out," Gerard said. "We'll have
to load the whiskey first."

"You can't outrun them with a boatload of them kegs," Tereau
said.

"They ain't going to chase us. They're going to be piled up on
the sandbar. Take the wagon up to the boat and we'll get loaded."

Tereau slapped the reins against the mules' backs. The kegs
lumbered from side to side as the wagon creaked forward. LeBlanc
sat beside the Negro with his hand on the butt of his revolver.

"You ain't going to need the gun," Tereau said.

"I'm the judge of that."

"We never had no shooting. We don't shoot and they don't
shoot."

LeBlanc looked grimly ahead. Gerard and Avery took the mules
by their harness and turned them around so the tailgate would
face the boat. Tereau tied the reins to the brake, and climbed down
and went to the rear of the wagon. He pulled the metal pins from
their fastenings and eased the gate down.

"It ain't too late," he said. "I'll give you your money back and
take the whiskey to the still."

"We'll make it," Gerard said.

"It's your three years," Tereau said, and took the first keg off the bed onto his shoulder.

Avery got up on the bed and handed the kegs down. In a quarter hour the boat was loaded.

"Now what?" Tereau said.

"You better get ready to move," Gerard said.

"It ain't smart what you're doing."

"I never had to ditch a load yet."

LeBlanc got into the long flat outboard and climbed over the kegs to the bow. Gerard got in and sat on the board plank in front of the motor. He took a flashlight from under the seat and placed it beside him. He wrapped the rope around the starter, put the motor in neutral and opened the throttle; he yanked hard on the rope. It caught the first time, and he increased the gas feed and raced the motor wide open in neutral. They heard the two Evinrude seventy-five horsepower engines of the police boat kick over across the river.

Gerard took up the flashlight and shone it through the willows so it would be visible from the river. The throbbing of the police boat's engines became nearer, then they saw it come around the river bend full speed towards the mouth of the cove, the water breaking white in front of the bow, the flat churning wake behind and the spray flying back over the uptilted cabin. Someone on board must have seen the sandbar, because the boat swerved to port just before it struck the crest. The bow lurched in the air, and the engines, still driving, spun the boat around on its keel until it came to rest with part of the stern out of the water and the starboard propeller churning in the sand.

LeBlanc stood up in the outboard and shouted at the police boat.

"Sit down!" Gerard said. "I got to get us out of here." He threw the motor into gear and shot forward through the willows. The police boat's searchlight went on, and the trees were flooded with a hard electric brilliance. "Bastards," LeBlanc shouted. He stood up again and took aim with the pistol. The glass broke with the first shot, but the lamp still burned. He fired twice more, and the searchlight went out.

Avery and Tereau ran for the wagon. They climbed into the

seat, and Tereau slashed the reins down on the mules. The mules jumped against their harness, and the wagon banged over the ruts, pitching back and forth, so that Avery had to hold on to the brake to keep from being thrown from the seat. He looked behind him and saw LeBlanc's pistol flash three times in the dark. Tereau whipped the mules to a faster pace until the boat was out of sight. They could still hear LeBlanc cursing.

"He's done it," Tereau said. "We never had no shooting, but we're going to have it now."

"Where we going?"

"To the still. I'm going to move out everything I can. The swamp will be full of police before morning."

The wagon swayed against a tree and careened back on the road.

"My God," Avery said.

"Got no time to waste." Tereau whipped the mules harder.

"You think he hit anybody?" Avery said.

"It ain't our doing."

"We were with them."

"When they got in the boat they were on their own," Tereau said.

"Look out!"

The left front wheel of the wagon struck a large oak root that grew across the road. The rim of the wheel cracked in two, and the spokes shattered like matchsticks as the wagon went down on its axle, skidding across the road to the edge of the gully; it turned on its side and balanced for a second, then toppled over the brink, pulling the mules down with it. Avery was thrown free and landed on his stomach in the middle of the road. The breath went out of him in one lung-aching, air-sucking rush, and the earth shifted sideways and rolled beneath him, and a pattern of color drifted before his eyes; then he could see pieces of dirt and blades of grass close to his face, and his chest and stomach stopped contracting, and slowly he felt the pressure go out of his lungs as he pulled the air down inside him. He turned over on his back and sat up. He looked for the wagon. There was a scar of plowed dirt where the axle had skidded across the road. He stood up and walked to the brink of the gully.

"Get down here and pull it off me," Tereau said.

Avery could see the top portion of the Negro's body lying among the splintered boards. The wagon had come to rest upside down, pinning Tereau's legs under it. The mules lay at the front, twitching and jerking in the fouled harness. The kegs had broken open and there was a strong smell of whiskey in the air. The broken slats (their insides burned to charcoal for aging the whiskey) and copper hoops were scattered on the ground. Avery slid down the bank and tried to lift the wagon with his hands. It came a couple of inches off the ground and he had to release it. He moved to the front of the wagon and tried to raise it by the axle. It wouldn't move. He stooped and got his shoulder under the axle and tried again. He pushed upwards with all his strength until he went weak with strain.

"Find something for a wedge," Tereau said.

Avery hunted along the gully for a stout fallen limb. He found several thick branches, but they were rotted from the weather. He searched in the grass and saw a railroad tie that had been discarded by one of the pipeline companies that worked in the marsh. The tie was embedded in the dirt. Avery pried it up with his fingers and saw the worms and slugs in the soft mold beneath. He carried it back to the wagon.

"I'll slip it under close to your legs," he said. "When I lift up you pull out."

"I'm waiting on you," Tereau said.

Avery fitted the wedge under the side wall of the wagon and lifted.

"Hurry up and get out. I can't hold it up long."

"I don't feel nothing in my legs. The blood's cut off."

"I got to drop it."

Tereau reached under the wagon and grabbed his legs under the knees and pulled.

"I'm out. Let it go," he said.

Avery released the tie and let the wagon drop.

"Is anything broken?" he said.

"I don't know. Hep me up."

He put Tereau's arm over his shoulder and lifted him to his feet.

"They ain't broke, but I can't go nowheres."

"You can't stay here."

"We ain't getting out of the marsh this way."

"I'll help you. Can you walk if I help you?"

"I ain't going far."

"Let's get away from the wagon. They can probably smell the whiskey out on the river."

"There's something you got to do first."

"What?"

"Them mules is suffering," Tereau said. He took the long double-edged knife from his boot. The blade shone like blue ice in the moonlight. "Put it under the neck. They won't feel no pain that way." He handed the knife to Avery.

Tereau leaned against a tree while Avery went over to the mules. The knife cut deeply and quick. He cleaned the blade on the grass and came back.

"Let's get out of here," he said.

Farther down the gully there was a rainwash that had eroded a depression in the bank. It was dry now and overgrown with vines and small bushes. Avery was able to get Tereau up the wash to the road. They crossed to the other side and entered the thicket and headed towards the opposite end of the marsh where the still was. Tereau could take only a few steps at a time. For the next hour they worked their way through the undergrowth. Tereau was breathing hard and had to rest often. The vines scratched their faces and necks. In some areas the mosquitoes were very bad and swarmed around them and got inside their clothes. It took all Avery's strength to keep the Negro on his feet. Tereau took his arm from Avery's shoulder and sat on the ground.

"Go on and let me be," he said.

"You know I can't do that."

"Go on. You don't belong down here nohow."

"You're not helping anything. You're making things harder," Avery said.

"My legs are gone. You'd have to carry me."

"All right. I'll try it."

"You ain't talking good sense."

"I'll get somebody to help. Will you be all right if I hide you here?"

"I'll get along."

Avery put him in the bushes and cut some branches from the trees to cover him.

"Leave me the knife," Tereau said.

"What for?"

"I need it."

"No."

"Give me my knife and get away from here."

"I'm not going to give it to you. Stay put till I get back." He put the knife in his belt.

"I'm too old a man to go to prison."

"Stop talking like that."

"Ain't you got any sense at all? You won't be back in time, and I ain't going to no jailhouse."

"Don't talk so loud."

"I don't know why I ever took a young boy with me in the first place."

"I'm going to Jean Landry's houseboat. We'll come back in his pirogue."

Avery left him in the thicket and splashed into the knee-deep water of the swamp. It would take him a half hour to get to Landry's, and about half that time to come back in the pirogue. The bottom of the swamp was mud and sand. His feet sank in to his ankles. He thought he heard the police in the distance. The branches of the trees overhead grew into one another, and there was almost no light in the swamp. He had trouble finding the direction to the houseboat. He believed that old man Landry would help them, since he disliked any type of authority and had moved out in the swamp years ago to avoid paying taxes and obeying the law. Unconsciously Avery felt at his side for the knife. It was gone. He thought he would have heard it splash if it had fallen in the water. It must have slipped out of his belt before he left Tereau. He headed back towards the shore, breaking through the overhanging vines with his forearms. A water moccasin slithered across the water in front of him. Avery's foot caught on a tree root and he went under. He struggled to free himself and plunged through the reeds onto the bank.

The cut branches were still in place over the bushes where Tereau was hidden. Avery ripped the branches away. The Negro was sitting upright, just as he had left him, with the knife on the ground by his side.

"You ain't forgot nothing, have you?" Tereau said.

"You and that goddamn knife."

"Take off. You ain't got much time. I heard the police on the road a few minutes ago."

"Let's get moving, then."

"It ain't no use. There's a big tree out in the water I can hide in. Leave me there and Landry'll find me in the morning when he picks up his nets. You can go through the grass flats to the other levee and get back to town. There ain't nobody going to follow you through there."

"I have to take the knife with me."

"You'll probably cut yourself with it."

Avery picked up the knife and threw it through the air into the water. They heard it splash in the dark.

"Ain't that a foolish thing to do."

"Let's go," Avery said. He helped Tereau to his feet and picked him up over his shoulder in a cross-carry. He moved out of the thicket and waded into the water. Away from the bank there was a great cypress tree with one side split open and blackened and hollowed out where it had been struck by lightning. He slid the Negro off his back into the hollow. Tereau adjusted his position with his hands so that he could sit upright fairly comfortably, and pulled his feet out of the water inside the tree. He took off his boots and wrung out his socks.

"I reckon you'll let me alone now," he said.

"I reckon."

Tereau took the pint bottle of whiskey from his pocket and pulled the cork out.

"Would the young gentleman care for a drink?" he said.

"You crazy old man."

Avery and Tereau each took a swallow from the bottle. Avery waded back to shore and made his way through the thicket, walked down the gully and across the road and over the side of the levee, and began circling behind the police. He hoped the police would be searching the road so he could get to the big expanse of alligator grass without being seen and cross to the opposite end of the marsh. He could hear voices ahead. He crawled up the side of the embankment and looked down the road. Several flashlights shone through the trees opposite the gully. Two officers with Springfield rifles stood with a third man between them. The man's hands were handcuffed behind him. He turned his face in the beam of one of the flashlights. His clothes were wet, he had lost his hat, and his black hair fell over his ears. His skin looked white in the flashlight beam. A captain and another state policeman climbed out of the gully onto the road.

"Why don't you tell us where they headed for, and we can all go home," the captain said.

LeBlanc glared at him in silence.

"We're going to get the others whether you help us or not," the captain said. "Your friend probably drowned trying to swim the river, and the ones in the wagon aren't going far after the crackup they had. It'll make it easier if you cooperate."

"You go to hell," LeBlanc said.

The captain motioned for the other men to continue down the road. Avery crawled back down the levee into the brush and started towards the grass flats. The glow of the flashlights shone above the levee. He entered the wide field of alligator grass where there were bogs of silt and quicksand. The quicksand wasn't deep enough to be dangerous, but usually a man was helpless in it if he didn't have somebody to pull him out. The bogs looked like solid ground because they were covered with dead leaves and grass. He traveled slowly as he went deeper into the field, his head held down, watching the ground carefully. The sharp-edged grass cut his face. He saw a bog ahead and went around the side of it. The sand was wet and cold and came over his shoes. There was a dead nutria, half submerged, out in the middle of the bog. The buzzards would have gotten it if it had died anyplace else, but they couldn't stand on the sand to feed. Avery looked up at the hard ivory brightness of the waning moon. It would be morning in a few hours, and old man Landry would get Tereau out of the tree. Avery went on for another mile and came out on the far end of the marsh. He walked through the sand and water and reeds onto the bank. He sat down exhausted. Someone on top of the levee shone a flashlight down at him. Avery whirled and started to his feet. It was a state policeman. He could see the campaign hat and the leather holster and the dust-brown uniform. The policeman had a revolver in his hand, the moonlight blue on the barrel.

"Stay still. You got nowhere to go," he said.

J. P. WINFIELD

He appeared on the Louisiana Jubilee every Saturday night for the next five months. The show was broadcast throughout four states, and J.P.'s name became well known to those people who sit by their large wooden radios with the peeling finish and tiny yellow dial on Saturday night to listen to their requests and hope that their letters will be read between the advertisements of cure-all drugs and health tonics. J.P. came to be one of their favorite entertainers. They bought his records and wrote him letters, and he replied by sending them an autographed picture of himself and the band. He also received an increase in salary and replaced Seth as the main figure of the show. When the band appeared onstage J.P. acted as the spokesman and did most of the solos. He never used any accompaniment except his own guitar when he sang, his third record sold two hundred thousand copies, and Hunnicut had his name featured on the placards that were nailed to the fronts of the dance halls and roadhouses where they played.

During the week the show toured the small towns and played one-night performances in any dance hall that was willing to pay three hundred dollars to have a band from the Louisiana Jubilee. Each weekday night J.P. sang his songs in the juke joints and highway clubs, and the days were spent traveling across the country in a state of complete fatigue. The band didn't quit until early in the morning, and there was little time for sleep except while riding in the bus. When they returned at the end of the week for the Saturday night performance on the Jubilee, J.P. was physically spent. It was at this time that April introduced him to a doctor who pushed narcotics. She had begun to pay attention to J.P. since he had moved to the front of the band, and on Sunday afternoon she called him into her hotel room to meet a man whom he would not forget for a long time.

"This is Doc Elgin," she said. "He can give you something to make you feel better."

Elgin was a thin sallow man who reminded J.P. of a rodent. His body was wasted and bent, and his hands were like bone. He had an ingratiating smile that made you want to look away, and his body structure seemed so fragile that J.P. thought a sudden blow would cause it to break to pieces like brittle candy.

"April says you need something to lift you up," he said.

"I feel wore out all the time," J.P. said.

"It happens to all of us, honey," April said. "Doc will make you right."

"I have something that will help you," he said. His black bag rested on a chair. He opened it and took out a small cardboard box. He handed it to J.P. "Take one of these whenever you need a push."

"This ain't joy stuff, is it?"

"It's Benzedrine."

"What's that?"

"It won't harm you."

"I don't want no happy stuff, hear."

"This is just a stimulant."

J.P. slid the box open and looked at the row of pills on the cotton pad.

"What do I owe you?" he said.

"There's no charge. That's a sample a drug company sent me."

"Ain't you supposed to have a prescription for this?"

"No. These are mild. They won't hurt you." Elgin turned to April. "I'm going now. Give me a call when you need me."

"All right, Doc."

"It's enjoyable meeting you, Mr. Winfield."

"Yeah. You bet."

Elgin went out. J.P. took one of the pills from the box and filled a glass of water from the pitcher on the dresser. He put the pill in the back of his mouth and drank the water.

"I reckon I'll go lay down," he said.

"You don't have to leave."

J.P. looked at her. She was standing close to him. She held her face up. He could see she wanted to be kissed. He wondered if he could lay her. He didn't want to lead up to it and get hot for her and then be rejected. He looked at her black hair and the blunt features of her face.

"Troy figures you're his girl," he said.

"Troy is an ass. Don't you like girls?"

"I ain't interested in trading valentines."

"You're a big boy."

He leaned down and kissed her. She moved her body against him and put her arms around his neck and breathed in his ear. He wanted her badly now. She widened her thighs and pressed her stomach tight against him. He worked his hand up her side and felt her breast.

"Let's go over to the bed and I'll teach you a nice game," she said.

She pulled away from him and drew the blinds. The room fell in a yellow twilight. She undressed and sat on the bed and pulled off her stockings. He looked at her large breasts and flat stomach and white thighs. There was a weak feeling in his throat. She lay down on the sheets and waited for him.

"It isn't nice to keep a girl waiting," she said.

He got in beside her.

"That's a good boy. Don't you like this better than giving your money to those girls?"

"What girls?"

"I know you and Seth go to one of those places back of town. Tell me how they act when you're in the room with them."

"Ask Seth."

"I bet he's lovely when he finds somebody who will give it to him."

"I couldn't tell you."

"Here, how's this?" she said. "That's a good boy. Let April do the work."

* * *

That evening he returned to his room. He had a headache and felt depleted. He sank down in the armchair before the window and let the perspiration roll down his neck into his shirt collar. He wished he had let April alone and had slept during the afternoon. After they had been together for a while he had wanted to rest, but she wouldn't let him go. Whenever he tried to stop she got him worked up again and forced him to continue, and now he felt sick. The Benzedrine had built him up, and then it abruptly dropped him. He put his feet on the bed and let his arms hang over the sides of the chair to the floor. He looked out the window at the late red sun slanting across the rooftops and the now russet-colored buildings. The swallows spun in black circles over the chimneys.

It was seven-thirty. He had to meet Virdo Hunnicut in his room at nine. Why couldn't he have stayed away from April and rested during the afternoon? He felt like going to sleep and not getting up until the next night, but Hunnicut had said that there was something important for them to discuss. J.P. called the desk clerk and asked to be awakened at eight-thirty. He lay down on the top covers of the bed and went to sleep.

He dreamed he was sitting on the back porch of his home, looking out over the cotton field and its red earth and long green rows. The sky was dark with clouds, and the heat lightning flashed in the east. He breathed the wet smell of the rain as the first drops fell on the field. He was very alone on the porch of the tenant cabin, and he watched the lightning illuminate the edges of the clouds, and the showers burst from the sky. He leaned back in the wooden chair and put his feet on the railing and thought how he wanted to put it all into one song.

J.P. sat upright in bed just before the desk clerk rang the telephone to wake him. He sat on the edge of the bed and rubbed his face. He was sweating all over, and his headache had increased. He stripped to the waist and went to the bath and turned the shower on his head. He let the cold water run over him until his mind had cleared. He dried himself with a towel and looked in the mirror. His face was dull with sleep and fatigue. He combed his hair and went back into the bedroom and took a clean shirt from the dresser. His head kept throbbing.

He started to leave the room and stopped. He took the cardboard box of pills from his pocket and slid it open. He hesitated for a moment, then went back into the bath and filled the water glass. He would need something to get him through the evening. A few minutes later he knocked on Virdo Hunnicut's door.

"It's open."

J.P. went in. Hunnicut sat in the stuffed chair by the desk with an electric fan blowing on him. He wore a flowered silk sports shirt that was stained with perspiration. There was a bowl of ice cubes in front of the fan. His face was flushed pink from the heat.

"Have you ever seen it so goddamn hot for September?" he said. "I got one window in the room and it opens on the air shaft. It feels like they got the heaters on."

J.P. sat in the straight-backed chair opposite Hunnicut. He watched the big man sweat and wipe his face.

"What did you want to talk about?" he said.

"I'll tell you if you give me the chance."

"I ain't feeling too good. I want to get some sleep tonight."

Hunnicut leaned his weight forward, opened the desk drawer, and handed him an envelope.

"What is it?"

"Look for yourself."

He opened the envelope by tearing off the end and looked inside.

"Train tickets," he said.

"You're going to Nashville."

"The Barn Dance?"

"Your train leaves at midnight."

"When did I get on the Barn Dance?"

"About three hours ago, after I finished talking with Jimmy Lathrop."

"Who in the hell is Jimmy Lathrop?" J.P. said.

"He's the man that makes Live-Again, one of the biggest selling vitamin tonics on the market. From now on you make people drink Live-Again."

"Why don't you tell me first before you hire me out to somebody I never heard of?"

"You wanted to go to Nashville, didn't you?"

"Yeah. But I like to be told before I'm hired out."

"I got a contract in my office, signed by you, that says I manage your engagements and you got nothing to say about it."

"I don't feel like making no train trip tonight."

"There's something else in the envelope. Maybe it will make you feel better."

J.P. took out the check and held it in the light from the desk lamp. It was for four hundred dollars, payable to him.

"Lathrop told me to advance it to you," Hunnicut said.

"I still ain't up to making a five-hundred-mile train trip tonight."

"You're giving me a burn in the ass, J.P."

"You want me to take off in the middle of the night on two hours' notice without telling me nothing except I'm going to sell vitamin tonic for somebody I ain't even seen. That money won't do me no good in a hospital or a cuckoo ward."

"I want you to listen to what I got to say, J.P. Lathrop is one of the biggest men in the state. There's a dozen of these fine politicians in the capitol who get their bread buttered by Jim. He could have bought a boxcar load of hillbilly singers to push his product, but he picked you because me and him has done business before. If you think you've gotten big and you can tell me what to do, or slough off Lathrop's offer, tear up that check and there will be someone else riding the train tonight."

"I ain't sloughing off his offer. I said I'm wore out and I want to be told about something once in a while."

"I'm fed up talking with you. Either do what I tell you, or you can start back for the tenant farm and chop cotton like a nigger for three dollars a day."

"You can't break my contract."

"I can do any goddamn thing I please."

"Why does it have to be tonight?"

"Because I say so," Virdo Hunnicut said, and slammed the flat of his hand on the desk. He wiped his sweating face. "Pack your things and get down to the station. When you get into Nashville go to the Grand Hotel. A man from the radio station will meet you there."

J.P. sat for a minute and looked at Hunnicut. The room was quiet except for the creak of the straight-back chair and Hunnicut's wheezing. He folded the check and put it in his shirt pocket with the tickets and walked from the room.

He packed the clothes he would need into a single suitcase, picked up his guitar, and took a cab to the depot. He rested his head on the back of the seat and looked blankly out the window while the cab rode downtown. The neon signs were a long blur of colored light without shape or form. The smell of the street, the tar and asphalt, and the dryness of the September night came to him through the open window. It was the end of day in the city; there was the burnt, electric odor of the streetcars and the dry scratch and flash of red as they crossed the electric connections; the pages of newspaper scudding along the sidewalks; the faint smell of rubber and gasoline from the automobiles; the Salvation Army band on the corner, with their high-collar blue uniforms and homely faces and loud brass instruments and tambourines and shrill voices, singing "On Jordan's Stormy Banks We Stand"; and the missions where the bums could get a meal and a cot if they would sit through a sermon on salvation and Jesus Christ.

J.P. closed his eyes and let his head sag to one side. He didn't know the cab had stopped at the station until the driver woke him. The redcap carried his bag into the waiting room; he sat down on one of the pewlike benches, put his guitar case beside him, and read the train schedule on the opposite wall. There were a few people in the waiting room. A porter slept in a chair by the platform door. J.P. took out his tickets and looked at them. Hunnicut had put him in a chaircar. He went to the ticket window and talked with the stationmaster and tried to get reservations on a Pullman. The stationmaster told him that there were no more reservations to be had, and he would have to ride in the chaircar.

His train was announced over the loudspeaker, and he carried his bag and guitar case out on the platform. The ice and baggage wagons rumbled over the wood planks. The trainmen opened the vestibule doors of the coaches and put down the stepstool for the passengers. Men in overalls moved along the cinder bed by the side of the train with copper oil cans. J.P. walked down the platform and found his car. The conductor looked at his ticket and helped him up into the vestibule.

The car was crowded and the air was thick with smoke. He

made his way down the aisle, bumping people with his guitar case, and took a seat at the end of the car. A soldier snored loudly next to him. J.P. pushed back the seat and tried to relax. His legs were cramped and he couldn't stretch out. A child close by began to cry. The train hissed and jolted and moved slowly out of the station. The lights in the car went down, and J.P. felt the darkness go over him.

The telegraph wires are weaving through the air outside the window and I'm going to Nashville Tennessee for Big Jim Lathrop Big Jim sends bread and butter checks to the state capitol the train is rocking back and forth rocking and I lean back and sleep in the dusty smell of old cushions and the train rocks me down past the dust of the cushions to where it is cool like sheets against my back and then the hot wetness of her on top of me I felt the bone in Doc Elgin's hand and I had to look away when he stared at me and he give April something in a package because I seen it in her drawer and she covered it over with a slip when she seen me looking at it she has small blue marks on her arms

Hunnicutt said You can start back to the tenant farm and chop cotton like a nigger for three dollars a day but he don't know nothing about chopping cotton the hoe goes up in the air and thuds down in the dirt and I see the shadow of my straw hat on the ground I never been in Tennessee Troy is from Memphis he ain't picked cotton for two cents a pound none of them knows how to drag the half-full burlap sack through the rows with one hand and pick the white puff with the other and put it in the sack

they were singing On Jordan's Banks and the bums stood in line to get inside because it was night and they had to find a place to sleep I heard them singing in the camp back home and they slept on army cots and mixed lighter fluid with orange juice and I seen one trade his overcoat for a quart jar of moon they put up the cots around a big iron stove and their faces looked like corpses sticking out from under the blanket sometimes I watched the evening train run across the sun and stop by the water tower and they would crawl out of the rods and that night I heard them singing hymns in the camp like the nigger funeral marches they're not niggers their faces are white like ash under the blanket and they take off their coats and wrap them around their feet to keep warm.

Doc Elgin said to take one when I need a push it ain't happy stuff I seen niggers taking cocaine and it comes in a powder and it gets them high and you can tell when they're on it by their eyes her eyes were shrunk up like pinpoints and I started to ask her if Elgin done that too but I didn't because she said not to talk about him no more the skin on her breasts looked thin and milky like a candle flame was behind it and you could see through it I could feel it coming on inside me and I held the back of her legs and felt it swell and burst and then she started it over again

whistle blowing down the line and I watch the sun plunge out of the sun across the fields and the crimson evening fade behind the trees

TOUSSAINT BOUDREAUX

There were two trucks backed up to the loading ramp on the side of the warehouse. The side street was dark except for the glow of light that shone through the open freight doors of the building. A sign above the door said Bonham Shipping Company. A white man and a Negro were bringing out crates and loading them in the trucks. Bonham, the light tan Negro who looked like a Baptist deacon, stood on the ramp. Toussaint waited beside his truck and watched the loading. His arm was in a black sling. The driver of the other truck, a white man, sat in his cab behind the steering wheel. He wore yellow leather gloves and an army fatigue cap and smoked a cigarette without taking it out of his mouth. There were ashes on the front of his shirt.

"You been working here long?" Toussaint said.

"A while," he answered, without looking at him, his gloved hands resting on the steering wheel.

"You got any notion where we're going?"

"Bonham will tell you," he said, still looking straight ahead.

"I asked you."

"I don't know."

Toussaint turned away and looked up at Bonham on the ramp. He was dressed in a brown suit, with a good shoeshine, and his glass ring and rimless glasses glinted in the light from within the building. The last of the crates was loaded. One of the men closed the truck doors and locked each one with a heavy padlock. Bonham came down the ramp.

"Take highway ninety straight to Mobile," he said. "There's a street map of the city in your glove compartment. The place where you're supposed to go is marked in red pencil."

"Who's going to pay me the other hundred dollars?" Toussaint said.

"My partner in Mobile will give it to you as soon as you get to his warehouse."

"I'll follow you," Toussaint said to the other driver.

"Go on ahead," Bonham said. "I have to talk with him about something."

"He knows the road better than me."

"It's a good road all the way. You won't have no trouble," the other driver said.

"What about the weigh stations?"

"You're under the load limit. The police won't bother you," Bonham said.

"I ain't got any shipping papers."

"They don't ask for them unless you're over the limit," Bonham said.

"Go ahead. I'll be right behind you," the other driver said.

Toussaint climbed up in the cab and took the black sling off his arm so he could shift gears. He started the engine and put the truck in low and drove down the side street away from the warehouse. He turned at the intersection and headed towards the highway. He watched for the other truck in the rear-view mirror. Toussaint didn't like the way Bonham and the other driver had sent him ahead. There was something wrong about it. Why would they send me on alone with a load of stuff that must be worth plenty, he thought. I could hide the load and drive the truck into the river and they'd never see me again.

Bonham was careful enough at first. He wouldn't tell me where I was going until the last minute, but now he sends me on by myself. And why did he need two drivers? He could put all them crates in one truck. He didn't need me. He hires a one-arm man out of a poolroom for no reason. It don't fit.

Toussaint looked in the rear-view mirror again. There were two automobiles behind him. He slowed and let them pass. He turned into the main road that led to the highway. The river levee was on his left, and ahead he could see the looming black structure of the Huey Long Bridge. He accelerated to keep up with the traffic. Why don't he come on, he thought. He's had plenty of time. I can't drive no slower without tying up traffic.

He entered the circle before the bridge and turned out on the highway. He drove on a mile to where the cars had thinned out, and pulled off on the gravel shoulder of the road. He opened the glove compartment, and under a street map of Mobile he found the red reflectors. He walked back down the highway and set them on the shoulder at intervals to warn the oncoming automobiles. He went back and stood by the running board and waited for the other truck.

A half hour later it came. Toussaint waved the driver down. The truck slowed and pulled off on the shoulder in front of the Negro. The driver opened the door and swung out of the cab as Toussaint walked up.

"Why did you pull me over?" he said. "You ain't supposed to stop till you hit Mobile. You should be almost out of the state by now."

"I got my markers out. Nobody is going to bother us."

"You ain't supposed to stop."

"What have you and Bonham got on?"

"Mind your business," the driver said.

"Why did you wait thirty minutes to follow me?"

"You ain't paid to know anything."

"You could have carried the whole load. He don't need another driver."

"He splits a shipment so he don't take a chance on losing it all. The police ain't going to get us both."

"He ain't the type man to trust a hot load with somebody he don't know."

"Ask him about it."

"You're the man I'm talking to."

"Quit if you don't like it."

"I got another hundred dollars coming."

"Earn it, then. I ain't going to stand out here no longer."

"What's Bonham got planned?"

"Nothing."

"You're shitting me."

"I ain't got to take that from you."

"You work for a nigger," Toussaint said.

The man tried to hit him, but Toussaint caught his arm in midair with his good hand and held it helpless before him.

"I'll break your arm like a stick, white man."

"God damn you."

Toussaint pushed him away.

"Get in your truck," he said. "I'm following you this time. I'm going to be on your bumper all the way to Mobile."

The man climbed up in the cab and slammed the door. Toussaint picked up the reflectors from the roadside and got in his truck. He dropped the reflectors on the seat and followed the other truck off the shoulder onto the highway. He kept close behind so no cars could get between them.

As the road straightened out, the other truck began to widen the distance. Toussaint pressed on the accelerator to keep up. The speedometer neared fifty and the truck in front continued to gain. Toussaint pressed the gas pedal to the floor, but his speed didn't increase. It's got a governor on it, he thought. The gas feed is fixed so it can't do more than fifty. He knows it too. He might have even put it on. They want to make sure I don't stay with the other truck. He must be making seventy. He's got a clear stretch ahead of him. I can't catch him unless he runs into traffic.

Toussaint watched the taillights grow dimmer. The lead truck went over a rise and disappeared. The glow of the headlights reflected against the night on the other side and then disappeared too. Toussaint approached the rise and shot the truck into second gear to pull the grade. The highway before him was empty when he reached the top. He looked off to the side of the highway. There was a dirt farm road that led between two fields into a wood. He must have turned out his lights and took the side road, Toussaint thought. He couldn't have got that far ahead of me.

Toussaint pulled into the road and hit his brights, illuminating the grove of trees. A yellow haze of dust still lingered in the air over the road. There were two lines of heavy tire marks crushed into the dry ruts. He stopped the truck and turned off the engine and cut the lights. He could faintly hear the engine of the other truck toiling along the back road through the woods. In a few minutes the truck would take another road and cross the border into Mississippi.

Toussaint felt among the tools beneath the seat until he found a heavy tire iron. He went around to the back of the truck and inserted the flat end of the iron behind the padlocked hinge on the two doors. He pried the screws loose and twisted the tire iron sideways until the hinge snapped. He pulled the doors open and climbed in. The crates were stacked against one wall. He fitted the iron under one of the crate tops and wedged it ajar, and then pulled it loose with his hand. He took out the packing and looked at the fur pelts inside. He turned the crate over on the floor and struck a match. They were nutria and rabbit pelts. He splintered another crate open with the iron. It was the same thing. He smashed in the sides of three more and scattered the furs over the floor. They were all rabbit and nutria pelts. The whole thing is almost worthless, he thought. They hired me to carry a load that ain't worth two hundred dollars. The other truck is carrying the good stuff, and they was going to let me be picked up. They robbed a fur company, and the stuff is so hot they can't get it out of the state. Bonham loaded me with cheap pelts and was going to feed me to the police while his other boy slipped out on the back roads. The police don't know the difference between nutria and beaver. They'd think they had the real stuff. By the time they found out, the other truck would be gone. Bonham set me up for a stretch in the penitentiary, and I stepped right into it.

He climbed down from the back and shut the doors. He was going to leave the truck and hitchhike to the city. It would be better to leave it here than in town. An automobile came down the highway and slowed as it passed the farm road. It pulled off on the shoulder to make a U-turn and came back towards Toussaint. He threw the tire iron under the truck as the car turned into the road and caught him in its headlights. He walked to the cab and opened the door to get in. The car drew abreast of him and stopped. On the door was the white emblem of the state police. Two officers sat in the front seat. The driver turned a flashlight on Toussaint.

"What are you doing back here?" he said.

"Pulled off the road to get some sleep."

"Most companies tell their drivers to stay on the highway."

"Mine's different."

"Who do you work for?"

"Bonham Shipping Company in New Orleans."

"Let me see your papers."

"I ain't got any. Take the light out of my eyes."

"See what he's carrying," he said to the other officer. The far door opened and the second officer got out and went to the back of the truck.

Toussaint looked around him. It was too far to the woods, and the fields afforded no cover. There was nothing to do except stand there and listen to the whirr of the cars on the highway and look into the hot circle of light held in his face.

"The lock's broken," the second officer said from behind the truck, and then, "This is the one. There're furs all over the place. He's been breaking open the crates."

The driver got out of the car and took the handcuffs from the leather case on his belt. He snipped them open.

"You don't need them," Toussaint said.

"Put out your wrists."

Toussaint held them out.

"What's wrong with your hand?"

"I broke it."

"All right. Get in the back."

The second officer returned and got in beside the Negro. He handed a small notebook to the man in the front seat.

"Here's the license number," he said. "It's the truck that was stolen out in Gretna yesterday."

Toussaint looked out the window at the fields and listened to the whirr of the cars on the highway.

"They add on three years for auto theft," the driver said.

"I didn't steal it," Toussaint said.

"Where did you get the furs?"

"Bonham paid me to drive them out of the state."

"How did you think you were going to get past us?" the second officer said.

"I didn't have nothing to do with no robbery. The stuff you want is already in Mississippi. Them pelts is worthless."

They didn't understand Toussaint and ignored him. He looked at the fields and said nothing while the officer in front used the radio to put in a call for another car to come pick up the stolen truck. Both of the policemen felt they had done a good job in capturing Toussaint and the load of furs. While they waited for the other car to arrive, the driver asked Toussaint how he had hurt his hand. When the Negro told him the driver said he should have stuck to prizefighting.

BOOK TWO

BIG MIDNIGHT SPECIAL

for Robert Lee Sauls
executed in the Calcasieu parish jail
Lake Charles, 1955

AVERY BROUSSARD

The main room (called the drunk tank) of the parish jail was on the second story of the building. The walls and floor and ceiling were made from concrete. There were two barred and wire-grated windows to each wall. In the summer the room was damp and foul smelling from sweat and lack of ventilation. Once a month the trusties cleaned the room with disinfectant, but it did no good. The stench was always there. There was no way to get rid of it. They scrubbed the concrete with sand and brushes and whitewashed the walls and ceiling, and even sprayed the room with insecticide, but it was useless. The stench was on the men's bodies, in their clothes, in the tick mattresses; everything in the room had that same thick, sour odor to it.

In the center was a low boxlike structure made entirely of iron that was called the tank. It sat squat and ugly in the middle of the floor, like a room within a room. The walls were painted gray and perforated with small square holes. The tank was divided into cells, each containing four iron bunks welded to the walls. There was a narrow corridor that ran the length of the structure, separating the cells into two opposite rows. It was here in the tank where the stench was worst. There was little air and no lighting and the walls were covered with moisture. Every afternoon at five o'clock the inmates were locked in the tank for the night. It was usually overcrowded, and some of the men slept on the floor in the corridor.

At seven in the morning the jailer opened the door to the main room and the trusties wheeled in the food carts and unlocked the tank. The area outside the tank was called the bulipen, where the men were allowed to move about during the day. The jailer always stood in the doorway and watched the men line up with their tin plates and spoons for breakfast and lunch (there was no supper). There was a white line painted on the floor, forming a six-foot square around the doorway where he stood. This was the deadline, and none of the inmates was allowed across it when the door was open. If they did come past the line, they would be knocked to the floor by either the jailer or one of the trusties. The jailer, large and heavyset, was a careful man and took no chances.

During the day the men could do as they pleased in the bullpen. The room had to be kept clean, and it was forbidden to throw anything out the windows, whether a cigarette end or a scrap of paper, or call down to the people in the street. If a rule was broken, one of two things could happen. Everyone could be thrown in the tank and left there for several days, or the person who broke the rule would be dragged off to the hole, which was in another part of the building. The hole was a cast-iron cage, like the tank, except much smaller in size with enough room for only two men. It was ordinarily used to hold men who were condemned to death and awaiting execution, but since these men were there for only a short time it was usually left free to be used as a place of solitary confinement. On one wall of the hole there was a list of names written in pencil with a date beside each one. These were the men who had been put to death upstairs.

Avery's trial had been over for a week. He had pleaded guilty and received a sentence of one to three years to be served in a penal work camp. LeBlanc had drawn the same sentence as Avery for running moonshine, plus seven years for armed assault. Both of them were being held in the parish jail until they would be transferred to the work camp. When they came into the jail their personal belongings were taken from them and put into two brown envelopes, and they were each issued a tick mattress, a tin plate, a tin cup, and a spoon. The tank was full, and they were among the men who slept on the floor.

Avery and LeBlanc had their mattresses pulled against the wall to leave room for a walkway. There was a card game going on in the corridor. Five of the inmates sat or lay in a circle. A candle stub was melted to the floor in the center, and the thin flame flickered on their faces. Every night they played cards with the same faded incomplete deck. They used matchsticks for stakes, and the two winners were exempt from the cleaning detail in the morning.

Avery watched the game in silence. LeBlanc was playing, although none of the men wanted him. He had caused trouble since the first day he was brought into the jail. He had cursed the jailer and tried to hit a guard, for which he got a week in the hole. He refused to eat for three days when he came out. One of the inmates gave him a plate of food and told him to eat something, and LeBlanc threw it against the wall beside the doorway where the jailer stood. He was given two more days in the hole. He told everyone he would kill the jailer or a guard if given the chance. When he got out of the hole the second time he set fire to his mattress and filled the room with smoke. The men lied to the jailer and said that someone had dropped a cigarette on the mattress and the fire was an accident. They didn't lie because they liked LeBlanc; whenever someone did something wrong, Ben Leander the jailer punished all the inmates. He didn't look upon the men as individuals. They were a group, and when one of the group went against him the entire lot was to blame.

It was LeBlanc's deal. He shuffled the cards and set them down to be cut.

"Five-card stud," he said.

"We been playing draw," one man said.

"I'm dealing stud. You ain't got to play."

The other men told him to deal draw poker.

"I ain't playing draw," he said. "It's dealer's choice, and I call stud. One card down and four up. If nobody don't want to play I take the ante."

"Play like we been doing."

"We always play the same game," another said.

"The game is stud," LeBlanc said, dealing the cards.

Avery sat and watched. Sherry, the man next to him, rolled a cigarette from loose tobacco in a shred of newspaper. The men had given him his name because he had been able to conceal a bottle of wine in his overalls when he was brought in. He was being held for the robbery of a liquor store.

"Your podner acts like he ain't right in the head," he said.

"It's because he's locked up," Avery answered.

"We all locked up. That don't give him no excuse."

"He was in the war."

"He's got a crazy look in his face," Sherry said. "Setting fire to his mattress like that. We like to coughed our lungs out from the smoke. He's lucky they give him another mattress to sleep on."

"The jail is rough on him."

"Wait till he gets to the pen."

"They're sending us to a work camp."

"That's worse. They treat you better at the pen."

"You been up before?"

"Three times around," Sherry said. "It ain't too bad for me. I'm used to it. Only thing I miss is drinking. With some of the cons it's women. That's all they talk about in the pen. With me it's liquor. I can go without pussy, but I miss my drinking."

Avery looked at Sherry. His face was an alcoholic's. The lips were a bluish color in the darkness, and his jaws were flecked with small blue and red lines. His eyeballs twitched nervously.

"I go on a drunk once a month," he said. "I stay drunk about a week and then I'm okay. But I got to have that week."

"What are you in for?" he asked.

"Running moonshine."

"Was you and LeBlanc working together?"

"There were two others. One got away and one drowned."

Sherry looked from side to side and lowered his voice.

"It ain't my business, but maybe it'd be better if you found yourself another podner."

Avery didn't answer and Sherry continued.

"He's trouble, and you don't want no trouble in the pen. You got to do like they tell you. He'll crack up in the work camp. They'll have to put him in a crazy house," he said. "I'm just telling you what I think. You can podner with him if you want. But he's going to get it at the camp."

Avery turned back to the game. LeBlanc had finished his deal, and the man next to him was shuffling the cards. Every time LeBlanc drew a bad hand he threw down his cards and cursed the man who had dealt. When it was his turn to deal again he said he was going to change the game and called stud poker. The other men complained.

"Then nobody plays at all!" he shouted, and began to tear the cards in pieces and throw them in the air.

There was a brief fight. Two men held his shoulders to the floor while another wrenched the remaining cards from his hands. LeBlanc thrashed his feet and struck a man in the groin. The man reeled against the wall with a stupid expression of pain on his face. LeBlanc fought to get up, shouting at the top of his voice. The other men were coming out of their cells into the corridor to watch. He got one hand free and hit blindly at the figures around him.

"Somebody shut him up!"

"Leander is going to keep us in the tank for a week!"

"Belt him and get it over!"

"Bust him with a shoe. That'll keep him quiet."

A fist struck out and snapped LeBlanc's head back against the iron floor. His eyes rolled, and he was unconscious. The men who had been holding him stood up.

"The sonofabitch can fight."

"Leander ought to keep him in the hole till he starts beating his head on the walls."

"Look what he done to Shortboy."

"Does it hurt bad, Shortboy?"

Shortboy stood against the wall with a dazed look on his face. He couldn't answer.

"See what he done?" Sherry said to Avery as the men moved away from LeBlanc, leaving him stretched out on the floor. One man picked up the candle stub and the scattered cards.

"Help me get him on his mattress," Avery said to Sherry.

"Let him be. He ain't our lookout."

"Are you going to help me or not?"

"It ain't good to podner with a guy like that."

Avery went over to LeBlanc and dragged him by his arms to his mattress. The men stopped talking and watched him. Sherry moved to the other end of the corridor. There was a small patch of red in the back of LeBlanc's hair. Avery rolled him over on his stomach.

The men looked at Avery and began to talk among themselves. It was accepted by the inmates that no one was to help the victim when they dealt out punishment to one of their own members. Avery had broken the rule. Sherry came back and took his mattress to the end of the corridor. None of the men spoke to Avery for the remainder of the night.

In the morning the main door clanged open and the trusties entered with the food carts. The tank was unlocked, and the men picked up their cups and spoons and tin plates and shuffled out in the bullpen for breakfast. Avery shook LeBlanc by the shoulder to wake him. He lay in the same position as last night. There was a yellow and purple bruise along his jawbone, and a matted area of red in his hair. His face was the color of ash; Avery was afraid he might have had a concussion. He shook him again.

"Let's go. It's time for breakfast," he said.

LeBlanc opened his eyes and sat up on his hands.

"My head hurts," he said.

"Let's go eat."

LeBlanc felt the back of his head.

"It's blood. Somebody hit me in the head."

"Forget about it. We don't want any more fights."

"What fights? I don't remember nothing."

"You were playing cards and you got into a fight."

"I remember the cards, but I didn't get in no fight. Somebody slipped up and cracked me in the back of the head."

"Don't worry about it now. Let's get in the line."

"Which one of them done it?"

"There were a lot of them. You can't get them all."

"I can get the one that give it to me," LeBlanc said.

"Here's your plate. I'm going to eat."

He went out into the bullpen, and a minute later LeBlanc followed him. The men were in line before the food cart. The trusties were serving grits and sausage and coffee from the aluminum containers. The men sat down on the floor with their backs against the wall and ate. When Avery and LeBlanc came out of the tank and got in line the talking stopped, and there was no sound but the scraping of the spoons in the plates. Leander the jailer looked at LeBlanc from the doorway. He had been a jailer long enough to know what had taken place the night before. He didn't mind if LeBlanc had been ganged by the other men; maybe that was better than throwing him in the hole, and he wouldn't be bothered with him anymore. But once a man had been beaten to death in the tank, and that had brought about an investigation, which cost the old jailer his job and caused the city officials a good deal of work.

"Who worked you over?" he said.

LeBlanc looked at him in hatred.

"Answer me."

LeBlanc spit on the floor.

'Get out of the chowline," Leander said. "You don't eat breakfast this morning." He turned to the other men and pointed his finger. "I'm not going to stand for this sort of crap in my jail. I'm a fair man until somebody crosses me, then I step on his neck. I don't know which ones worked on LeBlanc, but that don't matter because I'll make every one of you pay for it. Any more fighting and I'll lock you up in the tank until the stink gets so bad you won't be able to breathe. Some of you ain't been locked up for a week, but you can ask Shortboy what it's like."

Ben Leander told the trusties to take the food cart out. The men were usually given a second serving, but this morning they were being punished. Leander looked around the room once more and went out, clanging the iron door shut behind him.

"You fixed us good," one man said to LeBlanc.

"He'll cut us short on lunch, too," another said.

"We was all right before you and your buddy come in."

"Was you ever locked in the tank, Shortboy?" a third inmate said.

"He can't keep nobody in there a week."

"Shit he can't."

'Tell them about it, Shortboy."

"It's just like he says," Shortboy said. He was a short, thick-bodied man, with a square build and a big nose and close-set eyes. 'The stink seeps into your guts and they don't send the trusties in to clean the crappers and them goddamn flies is all over the place and you think you'll puke when they hand you the food through the slot in the door. About six months ago there was an old man in here. He used to walk around in his drawers all the time, and there was something wrong with one of his legs. It was red and swole up like rubber. One time the door was open and the old guy forgot and stepped across the deadline. Leander pushed him down on the concrete, and he got all skinned up. We wrote what happened on a piece of paper and everybody signed it. One of the guys took it to a newspaper when he got out. Soon as the paper come out Leander threw us in the tank for nine days. Nine fucking days, crowded up together like a bunch of pigs. We even set fire to them Bibles to get rid of the stink. There wasn't none of us fit to piss on when we come out of there."

"It ain't right to lock everybody up for what one guy does," a man said. "He ought to put LeBlanc in the hole and let us be."

"You got no rights in here," another said.

Avery and LeBlanc were over by the window. Avery had his plate and cup on the sill. He was standing. LeBlanc sat on the floor against the wall with his knees pulled up before him. His black hair hung in his face.

"We don't have a lot of friends here," Avery said.

"I don't give a damn for that. Bunch of white trash."

"Listen. If Leander locks us all in the tank, you and me aren't going to be worth twenty-five cents."

"I got some people to pay back. It's them that's got to be on the lookout."

"There're thirty of them. They'll get started, and there won't be any way to stop them."

"I ain't afraid of no white trash."

"That isn't it," Avery said. "You've got to learn how to live in here if you're going to make it."

"I ain't got to learn nothing."

"Eat some breakfast."

"I don't want none."

"Suit yourself."

"You're good people, kid, but you ain't got to watch out for me. I seen more stuff than you could think about."

"I was trying to keep you from getting your throat cut."

"I didn't know about you back in the marsh, but you're good people. There ain't many people worth anything."

"Don't start any more fights in here, and we'll be all right."

"I got to even everything up."

"You'll go back to the hole."

"Screw it."

"Don't get us into more trouble."

LeBlanc stood up and jerked his shirt out of his trousers.

"You see this scar on my belly?" he said. "A Jap bayonet done that. Look at my back. That's what a army M.P. done. I got a lot of paying back to do."

Avery poured some of his coffee into LeBlanc's cup.

"Drink the coffee," he said.

LeBlanc tucked his shirt in and drank from the cup.

"You ain't been in a war. Don't ever go to one, even if they stand you up against a wall," he said. "I went over in '43. They sent us in at the Marianas. The Japs pasted us on the beach, but we done our share of killing too. That's where I shot my first man. I forgot what the rest of them looked like, but Christ I remember that first one. He was buck naked except for a strip of rag around his loins, up in the top of a palm tree. I cut him down with my B.A.R. and he fell out and there was a rope tied around his middle and he was swinging in the air and I kept on shooting and the bullets turned him around like a stick spinning in the water."

"I'm going to sleep for a while," Avery said.

"You ain't finished eating."

"I was awake most of last night."

He went through the open door of the tank and lay down on his mattress. He put his arm behind his head and looked up at the top of the tank. He thought of his brother Henri who had been killed at Normandy. Avery could remember the day he enlisted. Henri was seventeen at the time and would not have had to go into the service for another year, but he volunteered with the local National Guard outfit that had just been activated for training. It was his way of leaving, Avery thought. He was getting away from the house and Papa and all the rest of it.

Henri finished training and was shipped to England in February of 1944. They received one letter from him in the next three months. In late June a telegram arrived at the Broussard home. Mr. Broussard didn't open it. He held the envelope in his hand a moment and dropped it on the table and went to the back part of the house. Henri had been attached to a rifle company as a medic. He was among the first American troops to invade the French coast. Many of the men in his company didn't make the beach. He dragged a wounded man out of the surf and was giving him a shot of morphine when a mortar shell made a direct hit on his position. The burial detail put him in a pillowcase.

And that's it, Avery thought. Somebody in Washington sends you a yellow square of paper with pasted words and your brother is dead. Just like that, dead. No more Martinique parish, no more Papa, no more fallen down house that somebody built a hundred years ago for a way of life that is as dead as Papa and Henri. And the last of the noble line of French and Spanish aristocracy is now lying on his back in the parish drunk tank on a mattress that smells of vomit, waiting to go to work camp where he will have prison letters stenciled on his back and they'll give him a pick and shovel to work with at hard labor from one to three years, and he may be one of the few aristocrat convicts in the camp.

Avery remembered the things his father used to say to him when they sat on the veranda together during the long summer afternoons. Mr. Broussard spoke of the early American democracy and the agrarian dream of Thomas Jefferson, and how they had died and there was nothing left of them save a shell. The agrarian dream had been destroyed by an industrial revolution that pierced America to its heart. The republic was gone and had been replaced by another society which bore little semblance to its predecessor. Mr. Broussard had been raised to live in a society and age that no longer existed. By blood and by heritage he was bound to the past, which was as irreclaimable as those vanished summer days of heavy cane in the fields and the Negroes going to work with the hoes over their shoulders and the full cotton wagons on the way to the gin. Only an inborn memory remained, a nostalgia for something that had flowered and faded and died before he lived. Possibly in the mellow twilight of evening he could look out from the veranda and see the column of men in their worn butternut-brown uniforms, retreating from the Union army, and hear the jingle of the saber and the labor of the horses, the creak of the artillery carriages, as the column moved up the river road to make one last fight against General Banks' advancing troops.

He should have lived back then, Avery thought. He should have died when it died, and never had sons that end up torn to bits in France or serving time on a work gang.

Avery heard a metal object strike the side of the tank and rattle across the floor. There was angry swearing from the bullpen. He got up and walked to the door. The men were looking at LeBlanc, who sat on the floor. A tin cup lay by the wall of the tank. The men moved towards LeBlanc and circled about him. He stood up to face them with his fists clenched by his sides.

A stout, bull-chested man led the group. He walked with the clumsy motions of a wrestler, flat-footed, his thick legs slightly spread, his big hands awkward. He wore a crushed felt hat, which always remained on his head except when he slept. The men called him Johnny Big, because he was thought to be the toughest man in the tank, and the others did what he told them. He also acted as spokesman for the group. When the men needed something, they talked to Johnny Big, and he talked to Leander, and sometimes they got what they wanted. Each inmate contributed two cigarettes a day to Johnny Big. He was head man and no one questioned his authority.

Avery caught a man by the arm and pulled him aside.

"What happened?" he said.

"Let go."

"Tell me."

"LeBlanc slammed his cup against the tank and almost bust Sherry in the head."

Avery released him. The man crowded into the group with the rest.

"How come you to try and hit Sherry?" Johnny Big asked.

"If I wanted to hit him he wouldn't be walking around," LeBlanc said. "I wouldn't use no cup to do it with, neither."

"You're screwing things up for us. We got to teach you."

"I'll get toe-to-toe with anybody in here."

"There ain't going to be a fight," Johnny Big said. "Leander said he don't want no more. This is something else."

"Take it easy," an older inmate said. "Leander will put us in the tank."

"He ain't going to know. There ain't anybody going to tell him." He looked into each face. "There's a way to do it that don't leave any marks."

He took a newspaper out of his back pocket and rolled it into a tight cylinder. He patted it in his open palm.

"You should know about this, LeBlanc," he said. "It just leaves a few red marks on the ribs. It does all the work on the inside. Nobody can tell you been worked on except yourself."

"Let him be, Johnny," the older inmate said.

"Keep shut."

Most of the inmates pressed forward. A few shrank back from what was about to happen.

"Grab hold of him and pull his shirt off," Johnny Big said.

LeBlanc lunged at him, but the men caught him and pinned his arms behind him. He struggled to get free, cursing, his eyes wild. Johnny Big whipped the newspaper across his ribs. He hit him on the other side with a backhand stroke and started again. He swung harder with each blow. He was a heavy man, and he threw all his weight into his arm and shoulder. LeBlanc's body twisted with each stab in his side. The newspaper swished through the air and whapped across his ribs. The beating became faster. The newspaper was in shreds, and suddenly all the men were upon LeBlanc, striking him with whatever they could.

Avery had plunged into the men and was tearing at bodies and clothing to get to LeBlanc. He was shoved to the floor, and someone stepped on his hand. He came back and hit the man in front of him with his fist in the back of the neck. The man he had struck didn't seem to feel the blow. He hit again and again and could hurt no one. They were intent upon hurting LeBlanc and he could do nothing to turn their attention. An inmate pushed him in the face. He felt the sweat and grit of the man's palm in his mouth. He drove through the men, and then he was free, stumbling forward off balance. The beating was over and they had drawn back. He looked down at LeBlanc; his lips were split and his face was covered with red swellings that were already beginning to turn blue and his forehead was knotted with bumps. He lay contorted on the floor with his bloodied and ripped shirt hanging loosely from his trousers.

"You dirty bastards. Oh, you dirty bastards," Avery said.

"Let's get him, too," someone said.

"He ain't any better than LeBlanc."

"He hit me in the back of the neck."

"Yeah, Johnny. Teach them both."

Johnny Big had the stub of the frayed newspaper in his hand. He let it drop to the floor by LeBlanc's feet.

"This one don't look tough enough for all of us," he said.

The men knew what Johnny Big was going to do. They had already forgotten that the jailer would lock them in the tank for what they had done to LeBlanc. They had watched or helped beat one man senseless, and they didn't want to stop. They formed a circle around Avery and Johnny Big.

"What do you say, boy? You want to find out how good you are?" Johnny said.

Avery set himself and caught him on the chin with the first punch. Johnny Big's head jerked back and his felt hat flew in the air. Avery hit him twice more in the stomach, and then Johnny was on him, clubbing with both fists. Avery recoiled backwards under the blows. The men were shouting and enjoying it. He felt that everything in his head was shaken loose. Each blow struck him like a hammer and sent a wave of nausea and weakness through his body. He ducked and weaved and tried to get out from under him and took one full in the face. The room tilted upwards and he spun into the wall of the tank and fell to the floor. Johnny came on. Avery tried to get up, and Johnny Big knocked him back against the tank with his knee. He lay stunned, tasting the blood in his mouth and smelling the damp concrete. A pair of thick legs stood before him. He could hear voices from afar, as though someone were shouting down a well. His eyes fixed on the rough leather work boots and the pair of legs.

Someone laughed and the pair of legs moved away. Avery dove forward and tackled him below the knees. He caught him from behind and locked his wrists and jerked upward. He felt the man struggle for his balance and leap out at the air as he went down. Johnny Big hit the concrete with his full weight. Avery freed himself and got up. He didn't know if he could stand. His limbs felt disjointed from his body. Johnny Big pushed himself up from the floor. There was a cut right at his hairline. Avery clenched both his hands together and swung his arms downward in one motion like an axe and hit him across the bridge of the nose. Johnny Big fell back to the floor with his hands to his face. He was sitting on his rump, and he took his hands away and looked at them dumbly and put them back. His nose was broken. He got to his feet and swayed across the room to where his felt hat lay. Avery watched him, believing he had quit. Johnny Big put his fingers in the hatband and pulled out a thin, single-edged razor blade. He came forward, holding the razor between his thumb and fingers, low and out to the side like a knife fighter.

Avery backed away. The men scattered about the room. He looked around for a weapon. There was nothing he could use except a broom propped against the opposite wall, and Johnny Big was between him and it. He moved along the side of the tank, watching the razor blade all the while.

"Let him go, Johnny. We don't want a cutting," Shortboy said.

Johnny Big backed Avery towards the wall.

"He fought you square. You got no right to cut him," the older inmate said.

Some of the men agreed and told Johnny Big that he should let Avery go. Johnny had been beaten in a fair fight, he had had his nose broken, and he was no longer head man of the tank. He had betrayed the others by losing the fight.

"You ain't got call to cut on him."

"You done beat one man almost to death," the older inmate said.

"Yeah," Shortboy said.

"I'll cut any man that comes near us," Johnny said.

Shortboy stepped back, although he was already twenty feet away.

The main door swung open and Ben Leander and two of the guards came into the room.

"I told you what would happen if I caught you at it again," the jailer said. "There isn't one of you going to get out of it this time." He saw LeBlanc lying on the other side of the room. Johnny Big pushed his razor blade down into the back pocket of his denims. Avery was standing against the wall, and his face and neck were beaded with drops of perspiration.

"You guys don't know when you got it good," Leander said. "The only time you're going to get out of the tank is to sandpaper the concrete. I told you I don't take crap in my jail. It hasn't been two hours since I warned you. Now it's your ass." He turned to the guards. "Go see if the sonofabitch is dead."

The guards went over and looked at LeBlanc. One of them lifted his head and put it down again.

"He's bleeding inside."

"Did you start this, Johnny?" Ben Leander said.

"No sir."

"Who did?"

"I don't know."

Leander walked over and picked up the stub of frayed newspaper from the floor. He held it towards Johnny Big.

"Is this yours?"

He shook his head.

"This is one of your tricks."

"I didn't start the fight. It was LeBlanc and his buddy. LeBlanc started throwing things around after you left and we tried to stop him and the kid jumped in."

"You don't look too good, boy," Leander said to Avery.

"Johnny Big don't look too good, neither," the older inmate said.

"That's enough from you," Leander said.

"Everybody beat up on LeBlanc and the boy tried to help him," the older inmate said. "Johnny thought he could have some fun knocking him around and he got his nose broke."

"Is that straight, Shortboy?" the jailer asked.

"I didn't see it too good," Shortboy said.

"It don't make any difference who started it," Leander said, "because all of you are going into the tank until I see fit to let you out." He spoke to the guards. "Get LeBlanc out of my sight. Put him downstairs and keep him there till I call an ambulance. I don't want to see him again. Take Johnny with you and get his nose fixed."

The guards put LeBlanc's arms over their shoulders and lifted him. His head hung down and his feet dragged across the floor. Johnny Big followed them.

"Wait a minute," Leander said.

Johnny Big stopped.

"You put something in your back pocket when I came in."

"I ain't got nothing."

"Take it out."

"Yes sir."

"Now throw it on the floor and get out of here."

"Yes sir."

Leander picked up the razor blade and dropped it in his shirt pocket.

"Come with me," he said to Avery.

Avery went out of the room and Leander pulled the door shut behind him. He shot the steel bolt in place and clamped down the handle of the safety lock. They went down a corridor and up a spiral metal stairwell to the third floor of the building. Leander opened the door to a bare white room with a single window and an iron cage in the center. Avery stood by the window and looked down into the street while Leander unlocked the hole. The courthouse was across the square, with its white pillars and classic façade, and the well-kept lawn in front, green and wet from the water sprinklers in the sunlight, and the Confederate monument in the shade of the trees.

"Get inside," Ben Leander said.

Avery walked to the open door.

"What do you get out of it?" he said. "Is it the money?"

Leander pushed him inside and swung the door shut. He twisted the key in the iron lock.

"They're taking you to the work camp next week. You're goddamn lucky," he said.

That afternoon Avery had a visitor. Batiste had ridden the bus from Martinique parish to see him. He sat in the waiting room with his hat in his hand, wondering who to ask about Avery. There was a package wrapped in brown paper and tied with cord by his side. Ben Leander came out of his office and asked him what he wanted. Batiste said he wanted to see Avery Broussard, he had some tobacco and breadcake for him. Leander said that he was not allowed to have visitors, no one could see him on that day or any day as long as he remained in the parish jail. Batiste wanted to leave the package.

"He's in the hole. He can't get anything from outside when he's in the hole," Leander said, to make him understand how things were run in the parish jail.

J. P. WINFIELD

He was in the recording studio of a Nashville radio station. Three mornings a week he did a half-hour show which was put on tape and broadcast in the afternoon. The show was almost over. He stood at the microphone and sang the last number. The announcer sat at the table before another microphone, reading over the type-written pages in his hand. A very plain woman in a cotton-print dress sat on the other side of the table, nervously twisting a handker-chief around her fingers. There were two men standing beside J.P., one with a guitar and the other with a banjo. They were waiting to do the advertisement. One of the sound engineers in the control room behind the sheet of glass signaled to them when J.P. finished. They strummed and sang the Live-Again slogan:

> *Live-Again, Live-Again, the sick man's friend,*
> *It helps you every time,*
> *There ain't anything like it*
> *That makes you feel so fine.*
> *Drink Live-Again today,*
> *Chase them miseries away,*
> *Get out of bed and holler,*
> *Live-Again for a dollar.*

"Yes sir, neighbor, there ain't anything like it," the announcer read. "Live-Again has got everything you need to make you get up and stomp around like your old self again. It's got vitamin potency that drives through your body and makes you shout and holler like you was never sick a day in your life. It ain't right to waste your life in a sickbed. There's people all over the country setting around doing nothing because they don't have the energy to get out and have a good time. Well, you don't have to be a shut-in anymore. Go down to the drugstore or the grocery and ask for Live-Again vitamin tonic in the black and yellow box with the big bottle inside. There's a lady with me now who used to be a shut-in. She couldn't do her chores and her family was falling apart because of her poor health. She heard about Live-Again and she tried it, and now she's healthy and strong and her family is back together again. Tell the people about it, Mrs. Ricker."

Mrs. Ricker read in a steady, flat monotone: "I don't know how to thank the good people who make Live-Again. They made my life worth living. Before I tried Live-Again I didn't think I could go on anymore. I had to stay in bed all the time and I couldn't take care of my children and my husband had to spend all our money on doctor bills. The deacon of our church told us about Live-Again, and in a few weeks' time I was a new woman. This wonderful medicine has saved me and my family and we are happy once more."

"And believe me, neighbor, it helps everybody," the announcer said. "Well, that does it for today. You've been listening to the J. P. Winfield show. Remember to send us your cards and letters and to buy Live-Again. There ain't anything like it. So long, neighbors, and may the good Lord watch after you."

> Drink Live-Again today,
> Chase them miseries away,
> Get out of bed and holler,
> Live-Again for a dollar.

The red light over the door went off. The two singers put away their banjo and guitar. Mrs. Ricker twisted her handkerchief around her fingers and looked at the announcer.

"Did I sound all right?" she said.

"What do you think, J.P.?" the announcer said. "Have you ever heard anything like this good woman?" He was a business college graduate who was employed by the station to sell vitamin tonic, glow-in-the-dark Bibles, tablecloths painted with the Last Supper, and pamphlets on faith healing.

The singers laughed and went out. J.P. put his guitar in its case.

"I was never on the radio before," Mrs. Ricker said. "Will I be on the air this afternoon?"

"Yes ma'am. They'll hear you all over the South. Mrs. A. J. Ricker, voice of the Southland."

"I declare," she said. "Do you think they'll want me to make any more recordings?"

"I don't think so. You'd better run along home now. You don't want to miss the afternoon show."

"I'll leave my phone number in case they want me again."

"That's fine. Goodbye."

The door clicked shut after her.

The sound engineer stuck his head out of the control room.

"You want to hear the playback?" he said.

"Why not?" the announcer said. "Let's hear Mrs. Ricker tell us of the wonderful medicine that saved her husband and brats from ruin."

"I'm going back to the hotel," J.P. said. "I don't want to hear no more about vitamin tonic."

He picked up his guitar case and left the studio. He walked out on the street and turned up his coat collar. It was November and the air was sharp with cold. The wind beat against him and almost whipped the guitar case from his hand. There were snow clouds building in the east, and the sky was lavender and pink from the hidden sun. He turned around the corner of a building to protect himself from the wind. There were no taxis on the street. An old woman sat in the doorway of the building with an army coat around her shoulders. She had a wagon made from apple crates, filled with old rags, newspaper bundles, and things she had taken from garbage cans. Her hands were raw and chafed. She dipped snuff from a can and spit on the sidewalk. J.P. started up the street and walked the six blocks to the hotel.

He went through the lobby into the coffee shop. The waiter

brought him coffee and a plate of sandwiches. Nothing but a poor-white tenant farmer with one pair of shiny britches and a polka-dot bow tie, he thought. I paid my last five dollars to enter a crooked talent show and now I'm on the Nashville Barn Dance. Everybody from Raleigh to Little Rock can listen to me on Saturday night. Seven weeks on the Barn Dance and an afternoon show besides. Ain't that too goddamn nice?

He thought about the few days he had taken off from the show to go up to the mountains. He had worked almost constantly since coming to Nashville. The director of the radio show had given him three days' leave. J.P. went up by the Kentucky line and stayed in a hunting lodge. The mornings were cold and misty, and there was always a smell of pine smoke in the air. When he walked out on the front porch after breakfast he could see the log cabins spread across the valley, their stone chimneys stained white by the frost. The first snowflakes were just beginning to fall, and the mountains were green with fir and pine trees. There was a trout stream just below the timber line that wound across a meadow and rushed into a great rock chasm behind the lodge. It was good country, some of the best he had seen. He wanted to stay, but he went back to Nashville to sell Live-Again.

He took out an aspirin bottle and shook a Benzedrine and a Seconal into his hand. A month ago he had used up the supply Doc Elgin had given him. Several days later he bought ten rolls of yellow jackets, bennies, and redwings from a junkie on the other side of town. He had learned to mix the three in a combination that gave him a high alcohol never had. Soon he would have to buy more. He had only a half roll left in his room.

A porter came into the coffee shop and gave him a telegram. J.P. tipped him and tore the end off the envelope. GET READY TO LEAVE WILL PHONE THIS AFTERNOON HUNNICUT.

He paid his check and went out to the lobby. He told the desk clerk to page him in the bar if he received a long distance phone call. He left the guitar case with the porter to be taken up to his room. The bar was done in deeply stained mahogany with deer antlers and antique rifles along the walls. There was a stone fireplace at one end of the room, and the logs spit and cracked in the flames. A thick wine-colored carpet covered the floor. Brass lamps with candles and glass chimneys were placed along the bar. He drank a whiskey and water and wondered what Hunnicut had planned for him now.

Later the porter paged him. He went into the lobby and took the call at the desk.

"Is that you, J.P.?" Hunnicut said over the wire.

"I got your telegram."

"How's Nashville treating you?"

"All right."

"A lot of things have been happening since you left."

"Why am I going back?"

"We got some big things planned. Jim Lathrop is with me now. I want you to get back as soon as you can."

"What for?"

"Jim is going into politics. He's running for senator, and we're campaigning for him. We're going to organize a show and tour the state."

"I don't know nothing about politics."

"You're a star on the Barn Dance. People will listen to you."

"Who else is going on the show?"

"Everybody in the band except Troy."

"What happened to him?"

"He's in a hospital. He was taking heroin. I never knew anything about it until he came out on the stage so jazzed up he couldn't remember his lines."

"I didn't know he was on it."

"When can you come back?"

"I'll take the afternoon train."

"I can wire you some money."

"I don't need none."

"Are you still hot about that run-in we had before you left?"

"No."

"Because we have some big things ahead of us, and we don't want anybody to mess it up."

"I'll see you tomorrow morning," J.P. said.

"Is something wrong? You don't sound very interested."

"I'm interested. See you in the morning."

He put down the receiver and went to his room. He called the railroad depot and made reservations on the three o'clock train. He opened his suitcase on the bed and packed. The porter came up for his bag. J.P. had an hour and a half before train time. He took out his guitar and thumbed the strings to pass the time. *Oh the train left Memphis at half past nine. Well it made it back to Little Rock at eight forty-nine.* It was a blues song he used to hear the Negroes sing around home. *Jesus died to save me and all of my sins. Well glory to God we're going to see him again.*

He took a private compartment in a Pullman car. He had the porter make up his bed, and he slept through the afternoon. The train moved down from Nashville into southern Tennessee, rolling through the sloping fields of winter grass partly covered with snow. The land became flat as the train neared Memphis and entered the Mississippi basin. The river was high and yellow under the winter sky. The train rushed southward into Arkansas, and the land was sere and coarse. For miles he saw the board shacks of tenant farmers, all identical, with their dirt floors and mud-brick chimneys and weathered outbuildings, which were owned by the farming companies, along with the bleak fallow land and the rice mills and cotton gins and company stores.

He changed trains at Little Rock and arrived in Louisiana the next morning. He checked into the hotel, shaved, and went to Hunnicut's room. He met Seth in the hall.

"The Live-Again man is inside with Virdo now. They're waiting for you," Leroy said.

"I come straight from the depot. I couldn't get here no faster."

"Do you know about the show?"

"Virdo told me over the phone."

"We're going all over the state, and Lathrop is picking up the bills. He give me a two hundred dollar advance for pussy money."

"What's this about Troy?" J.P. said.

"He's in the junkie ward. They had to strap his arms down when they took him in. The doctor said he's a mainliner. Shooting it in the arm twice a day. The last time he was on the show he come out on the stage and started cussing in the microphone. They had to cut us off the air. I think April got him started on it. Her and that quack that comes in to lay her every Sunday."

"What do you know about it?" J.P. looked at the pockmarks on his face and the reddened skin and the coarse brown hair that was like straw.

"That's how she pays her bills, spreading her legs for Doc Elgin. He comes up here every Sunday morning to collect."

"The hell he does."

"I seen him go in her room with a bulge in his fly and his tongue hanging out. He always walks down the hall with his hand in his pocket. Stay away from her, J.P. I found a new place if you want some good girls."

"I ain't got time to talk anymore."

He knocked on Virdo Hunnicut's door and went in. Hunnicut sat in a leather chair with his feet across a footstool. He wore a purple robe and house slippers. Big Jim Lathrop sat at the desk, eating breakfast from a tray that had been brought up from downstairs. He was in his early fifties, dressed in a tailored blue suit with an expensive silk necktie. His fine gray hair was combed straight back. A gold watch chain was strung across his vest. He cut the pork chop on his plate and raised the fork to his mouth with his left hand. His hard gray eyes looked at J.P. as he chewed.

"Come on in," Hunnicut said. "Meet Mr. Lathrop."

Lathrop turned in his chair, still chewing.

"How do, boy. Sit down," he said.

"Are you ready to go into politicking?" Hunnicut said.

"I reckon."

"Jim and me have been making arrangements for the show. We're going to Alexandria tomorrow night. We'll have everybody down at the auditorium. No admission. All you got to have is a Live-Again box label."

"Who you running against?" J.P. said.

"Jacob Arceneaux from New Orleans," Lathrop said. "He's French and he's Catholic, and he'll take most of the parishes in the southern part of the state unless we swing them over."

"How are you going to do that?"

"Nigger politics," Virdo Hunnicut said. "Arceneaux has a reputation as a nigger lover. He hasn't tried to stop the nigger kids from getting in the white schools, and it's going to hurt him."

"We're running on the segregation ticket," Lathrop said. "We're going to show the people in south Louisiana what will happen when Arceneaux gets in office. Their children will be mixing with the colored children, and pretty soon they won't be able to tell one from another. The future generations will be one race of high-yellow trash."

"We're going to get the nigger vote, too," Hunnicut said. "We'll put on special shows across the tracks in the shanty towns."

"My singing ain't going to put nobody in office."

"People know you and they'll listen to you," Virdo Hunnicut said. "They know you're one of them as soon as you open your mouth. One good country boy talking to the hicks is worth all the nickel and dime politicians in Louisiana. If a man can get the rednecks and the niggers and the white trash behind him he can do anything he's a mind to."

"I think J.P. understands," Lathrop said. "He knows where the money is, whether in politics or selling Live-Again."

"It's in the hicks with eight bits in their pocket for a bottle of vitamin tonic that don't do them no good."

"All right, J.P.," Hunnicut said.

"The boy is being honest," Lathrop said. "The people want something and we give it to them. This time it's a pro-segregation administration." He chewed on the pork chop bone and dropped it into his plate.

"We already got the north part of the state," Hunnicut said.

"Jacob Arceneaux is the man we have to break," Lathrop said. He wiped his fingers with a napkin. "I want you to write a song about him."

"Have something in it about him being partial to niggers," Hunnicut said.

"I ain't a songwriter."

"It don't have to be much," he said.

"Get Seth to do it."

"I don't think Seth can read."

"I can't write no song for you."

"You gotten high-minded since you went up to the Barn Dance," Hunnicut said. "Remember it was Jim sent you there."

"I ain't high-minded about nothing."

"Let the boy alone," Lathrop said. "He's just gotten off a long train ride and he's full of piss and vinegar. He'll be all right when he has some sleep."

"I ain't writing no song, Mr. Lathrop."

"We'll talk about it later."

"It don't matter. I ain't going to do it."

"What's wrong with you?" Hunnicut said.

"I got rights about what I'm going to do and what I ain't."

"We've been through this before. I told you over the phone I didn't want any more of it."

"Let's drop it, Virdo," Lathrop said. "He can eat breakfast and come back later. We'll talk over the money situation then. I think he'll find he can do real well with me."

"I ain't bitching about my salary."

"I'm not a hard man to deal with. You don't have to do anything you don't want to," Lathrop said.

"He can walk out that door anytime he takes a mind to," Hunnicut said.

"You ain't in no rush to get me out. You made a lot of green off me."

"I pushed you up to the top. You didn't know how to button your pants till I taught you."

"Let's stop this," Lathrop said. "Go eat breakfast, J.P. Have one of those pork chops."

Lathrop walked to the door with him and opened it.

"We can straighten out whatever differences we have," he said. "We talk the same language. I'm a country boy myself."

"You talk pretty smooth to be from the country."

"I've been with these city folks too long."

Lathrop closed the door after J.P. and went back to finish his coffee.

"When did you start soft-gloving people?" Hunnicut said.

"I'm an old fellow now."

"The best way to handle J.P. is to walk all over him," he said, his face big and sweating.

"He'll do as I tell him, just as you do, Virdo, and I don't think any more needs to be said about it."

Hunnicut's eyes flicked away from Lathrop's face. He wanted to say something to regain his pride, but the words wouldn't come and he sat silent in his chair.

J.P. had breakfast in the dining room, and then asked at the desk for April's room number. He had to get her to contact Doc

Elgin. He took the elevator to the fourth floor and walked down the hallway to her room. She was in bed. She pulled the sheet up to her chin and told him to kiss her. Her mouth tasted bad.

"It's a long time for a girl to be alone," she said.

"I heard about Troy."

"For God's sake, don't bring up Troy. That's all anybody talks about. Everyone feels so sorry for Troy. I wish you'd seen him the last night he was here. He broke in my room and tried to climb all over me. The hotel dick had to drag him out of the room."

"How long was he taking it?"

"What do you want to talk about him for? You haven't seen me for seven weeks and all you've got on your mind is Troy."

"I take a personal interest."

"Troy was an ass."

"I'm on it, too. I found out in Nashville."

"Rot."

"I had to hunt all over town to find a pusher."

"Benzedrine is baby food."

"My nerves was like piano wire. I thought I was going to come apart."

April chewed on a hangnail and looked out the window.

"Listen to me," he said.

"I'm listening."

"I got a habit."

"Fly away with the snowbirds."

"I ain't on cocaine."

"The snowbirds stay high in the sky. They don't worry about the habit." She bit off the hangnail and took it off her tongue with her fingers.

"Call Elgin. I need some pills."

"He comes around on Sunday."

"I need him now. I took my last pills on the train."

"You can have some of my stuff."

"I don't want no cocaine."

"You don't have to take it in the arm. Put a little powder under your tongue."

"Call Elgin."

She picked up the telephone from the bedtable and dialed a

number. She chewed on another fingernail while she talked to Doc Elgin.

"He'll be over in a little while," she said. "He has some other people to see."

"He wouldn't hurry if I was going to jump through a window."

"Doc is better than a regular pusher. He don't cut his stuff."

"Seth told me something about you and him."

"I know what you're thinking, and you can shut up right now. I pay him cash like everybody else," she said. "He don't come near me."

She sat up in bed and fixed the pillow behind her. She held the sheet up to her shoulders with one hand.

"How much does your habit cost a week?" J.P. said.

"I pay for it."

"That ain't what I asked."

"He gives me a special rate. I bring him customers sometime."

"Like me and Troy?"

"I didn't twist your arm."

"How did Troy start on it?"

"He was burning maryjane before I met him."

"I almost feel sorry for the poor bastard."

"Feel sorry for yourself. You've got a one-way ticket to the same place he's in."

"There's cures. I've heard about them. There's a place in Kentucky."

"Don't believe it. There isn't any cure."

"I heard about this place. They say you can go there for a while and come out clean."

"I took a cure once. I got out of the hospital and two weeks later I was popping it again."

"Some people have kicked it."

"Learn it now, J.P. You bought a one-way ticket. First you break down all the veins in one arm and you start on the other one. Then the veins in both arms are flat, and you take it in the legs. When your legs are gone you take it in the stomach, and by that time you're finished."

He ran his hand through his hair. "I ain't on snow. I ain't past them pills yet."

"The habit grows. Soon you'll have to use something stronger. You can't kick it."

She smoothed the sheet against her.

"Put your mind on something else. It's no good to think about it," she said. "Come sit here."

He sat on the side of the bed.

"That's better," she said.

"Nothing is better."

"Wouldn't you like to do nice things?"

"I don't feel like it this morning."

"I don't believe you."

"I don't give a damn for doing anything right now," he said.

"Did you do any running around in Nashville?"

"No."

"You like girls too much for that."

"All right. I whored the whole time."

"Don't be like that."

"I got too much on my mind."

"It don't help to think about it."

"I feel like hell."

"Pull down the shade and get in bed." She dropped the sheet from her shoulders and uncovered herself.

"People can see you through the window."

"Pull down the shade if you don't want them to."

He went to the window and dropped the shade.

"Do you always sleep like that?" he said.

"Doc Elgin says bedclothes cuts off your circulation."

"Put the sheet over you."

"Don't you like me?"

"You ain't got to act like a two-dollar whore."

"You need a benny bad," she said. "Do nice things to April. It will keep your mind off it till Doc comes."

J.P. wiped his face with his hand. He was beginning to perspire. He wished Elgin would get here. They made love in the half-light of the room. He could feel his heart click inside him from the strain. He was sweating heavily now, and his muscles began to stiffen.

"When is Elgin going to get here?" he said.

"He'll be along."

"Phone him again."

She called Elgin; there was no answer.

"Is there any place else you can call him?" he said.

"He makes deliveries all over town."

"Phone him one more time."

"He's not there."

"Why don't the sonofabitch hurry?"

"Let's do it again," she said.

"I ain't up to it."

"Come on."

"Goddamn it, no."

"Here."

"Don't do that."

"You're a little boy."

"Where is Elgin?"

"I don't know. Stop asking me," she said.

"I feel raw inside."

"I can't do anything for you unless you want snow."

"Give it to me."

"You said you didn't want it."

"Let me have it."

She walked naked to the dresser. She took a white packet from the bottom of a drawer and came back to the bed. She untwisted the paper at one end.

"Hold out your hand," she said.

She shook a small amount of white powder into his palm.

"Put it under your tongue and let it soak into your mouth. Try not to swallow any of it. It won't do as much good and it might make you sick."

"I don't have to stay on it. I can go back to Benzedrine."

"You have to take stronger stuff."

"You don't get hooked by just using it once."

"The habit grows. Big boys use big stuff."

"There's cures."

"Not for us."

"They have treatments to let you down easy."

"It's getting to you already. I can see it in your eyes."

"There's a place in Kentucky."

"That's a dream. There's not any place for me and you."

"I feel flat. Everything is lazy and flat."

"Close your eyes and let it slip over you. It makes you have nice dreams."

"Why is everything flat? You and the room are flat," he said.

"You're sleepy and far away, and nobody bothers you. It's like laying out in the snow, except it's warm and nice."

"A hospital in Lexington. I was up by the Kentucky line. It started to snow."

"You're far away."

"Yes," he said. "It was snowing."

The Live-Again show began its three-week tour the next day. People from all over the parish came to hear J.P. and Big Jim Lathrop. Big Jim was the common man's friend. He promised to fight federal intervention and the integrationists. The other outfit would have the niggers with the white children. Jim was going to fight it. He didn't know much about politics, but he knew when he was right about something. He was a country boy himself, and a man should be from the country if he was going to represent country people. City people didn't have any business in the state government. The common man should vote for his own kind. J.P. was from the country. He sang country music. He knew that Lathrop was the only man for the job. It was time that the people of Louisiana stood up for their way of life and not let any city politician destroy it. Everybody knew that J.P. was a good man and they agreed with what he had to say. They had heard him on the radio. He used to chop cotton and tenant farm like everybody else. He was supporting Jim Lathrop, and so would every man who didn't want to see the government in the hands of people not his own. J.P. and the common man were behind Lathrop. They were not going to be run over by city politicians and Northern integrationists. The common man had been kept down, and now his time had come as surely as there was a day of reckoning for all created things.

TOUSSAINT BOUDREAUX

The Barracks in the work camp were oblong wooden buildings set in a clearing among the pines. The buildings were originally constructed by the W.P.A. for the army, but had later been sold to the state for use as a penal camp. There were seven barracks, each painted white, with barred windows and barred doors. A tall wire fence enclosed the clearing. At the top were three additional strands of barbed wire. No grass grew within the boundary of the fence. The clearing was dirt smooth from the ceaseless tread of feet. Pine needles often blew across the fence from the trees, but they too were soon pressed down and covered in the dust. The sweet smell of the pines came through the fence on the wind, and the cones dropped on the bare earth, but the pine seeds, like the grass, would not grow inside the clearing.

It was early morning. The night guards walked out in the sun to warm themselves while they waited for their relief. A whistle blew and there was the sound of keys twisting in iron locks and of men stirring from sleep. The sun rose above the dark green of the trees and burned down into the clearing. The moon was a thin pale shape in the western sky. The men filed out of six of the barracks and formed a line before the dining hall. The day guards came on duty and stood by the line while it moved slowly inside. All the men were dressed in the same blue denim uniforms with LA. PENAL SYSTEM stenciled across the backs of their shirts. Some were bareheaded, others wore straw hats. The inmates were deeply tanned, and their hands were callused and roughened. They shuffled through the dust, some talking, some half asleep, into the dining hall to file past the serving counter and sit at the board tables and eat breakfast before the whistle blew again for roll call.

Outside they broke up into squads of seven and waited for the work captain to come by and call their names from his list. There were seven men to a gang, and one guard to every seven men. No one had ever escaped from the work camp because it was too well organized and the guards could account for each inmate every minute of the day. The gangs formed and waited. The work captain came down the line with his clipboard in his hand. He wore the same brown khaki as the other guards, except he had on a campaign hat like that of the state police instead of the conventional cork sun helmet, and his trousers were tucked inside his high leather boots.

"Adams!"

"Yo!"

"Ardoin!"

"Yo!"

"Benoit!"

"Yo!"

"Boudreaux!"

"Yo!"

The captain looked up from his board. He had been prepared to put a mark by Toussaint's name.

"I thought you were supposed to go back into detention today," he said.

"Nobody come for me this morning."

"Evans might put you in there for the rest of your stretch if you start more trouble."

A guard standing by the fence in the shade turned around when he heard his name mentioned. He was John Wesley Evans, the guard for gang five. His face was burned pink by the sun. He was never able to get a tan. His face would burn and peel white and then burn again. He wore a cork sun helmet that was stained brown by sweat, and there was a pair of green sunglasses in his shirt pocket. He was fat about the waist and he wore a holster and sidearm to take notice away from his stomach. He put on his sunglasses and walked out into the sunlight and stood beside the work captain.

"You want me, sir?" he said.

"I thought Boudreaux was supposed to go back in detention for another day."

"A guy in gang three started a fight. We had to turn Boudreaux out to make room."

"Then you're one day to the good," the captain said to Toussaint.

"He can go back and finish it later," Evans said, looking at the Negro.

"Broussard!" the captain continued from his roll.

No reply.

"Broussard! Answer when your name is called."

"Here."

"Louder."

"Right here!"

"This is your first day on the gang. Obey the rules and you'll get along. Don't talk during roll call and don't quit work till you hear the whistle blow. When you're inside the clearing never get closer than five feet to the fence. When you're working outside don't get out of the guard's sight. Got it?"

"Yes."

"You mean yes sir."

"I said I got it."

The captain turned to Evans. "It looks like you have another one."

"He'll come around," Evans said.

The guard faced Avery.

"Let's hear it again," he said.

"I understood the rules."

"I want to hear you say yes sir."

"I understood what the man said."

"That's not enough. Let's hear it."

Avery stood still with the sun in his eyes. Evans looked at him from behind his dark sunglasses.

"You'll come around," he said. "This is only your first day. We'll have lots of days together."

The whistle blew and the main gate opened to let the trucks in. The trusties went to the tool shed to check out the picks and shovels. The men climbed into the trucks and the back doors were locked from the outside. The trusties threw the tools into the bed of a pickup. Gang five and gang three rode out to work together. The men sat in the darkness on two wood benches that were placed along the walls. The guards rode up front in the cab with the driver.

Toussaint took a package of Virginia Extra from his shirt and rolled a cigarette. He licked the paper, rolled it down, and pinched the ends together with his thumbnail.

"How about a smoke?" the man next to him said. "I left my tobacco in the barracks."

Toussaint gave him the package and the cigarette papers. The man was named Jeffry. He was lean and thin-featured, and his eyes were as pale as his hair. His hands were slender and white, almost like a woman's, and they blistered easily. He suffered from repeated attacks of dysentery, and he would trade his tobacco for an orange from the kitchen so he could suck the juice and not have to drink the camp water.

Next to him sat Billy Jo. He had sandy red hair and a fine red scar that came down from one eye to his lip. He said that he had gotten the scar in a prison riot, but two inmates who had known him before said that he had been cut in a fight over a Negro woman. Billy Jo bragged that he had been in six penitentiaries.

Brother Samuel sat between Billy Jo and Avery. He was a red-bone from around Lake Charles, a mixture of white, Negro, and Indian. His clothes didn't fit him and his straw hat came down to his ears. He had once been a preacher, but he also practiced black magic and conjuring. A disk of wood with unreadable letters on it hung from a leather cord around his neck. He said that the disk had been given to him by the Black Man, who roamed the marsh at night when the moon was down. He carried bits of string with knots tied in them, a fang of a water moccasin, a shriveled turtle's foot, and a ball of hair taken from a cow's stomach. The men liked him. He took care of them when they had dysentery, and he would share his tobacco with others if asked to. He was serving a life sentence for murdering a white man.

Daddy Claxton sat on the other side of Avery. He was the oldest man in the work camp. His skin was dry and loose with age, and there were faded tattoos of nude women on his arms. He had been a professional soldier once, and he claimed to have known John Dillinger while he was stationed in Hawaii. He had been dishonorably discharged from the army for operating in the black market, and after his third conviction in Louisiana he had been sent to prison for life as a habitual criminal.

"How come they call you 'Daddy'?" Billy Jo said.

"I don't know. That's what they always called me," Daddy Claxton said.

"Did you really know John Dillinger?" Billy Jo asked.

"Sure I knowed him. John was a mean one, all right."

"You ain't just telling us that?"

"I knowed him. You can ask anybody. They'll tell you."

"I don't believe you was ever in the army, Daddy."

"I was a soldier. They give me some papers when I got out. I could show them to you if I had them."

"What kind of guy was Dillinger?" Billy Jo said.

"He was a mean one."

"He'd break out of this place," one of the men from gang three said.

"No, he wouldn't. He's dead," Billy Jo said.

"Your ass, Billy Jo."

"He was killed in front of a movie somewhere," he said.

"Your bloody ass."

"I knowed John when they put him in the stockade," Daddy Claxton said.

"Was he really tough like they say?" Billy Jo said.

"He was plenty mean," Daddy said.

The truck bounced over some railroad tracks and drove down a gravel road. Rocks spun up from the tires and banged under the fenders.

"What's today?" Jeffry said.

"Friday," Toussaint said.

Jeffry frowned and counted on his fingers.

"When are you breaking out?" a man across from him said.

Jeffry counted and moved his thin lips silently.

"When are you guys going to leave us?" the same man said.

"Shut up," Billy Jo said.

"Everybody in camp knows about it, you dumb bastard."

"Keep shut."

"You guys talked it all over the place."

"There ain't anybody going to tell," Billy Jo said.

"What about him?" The man pointed to Avery.

"What are we talking about?" Billy Jo said to Avery.

"I wasn't listening."

"Then you're deaf."

"I don't care what you do, podner."

"The hell you don't. You was listening," Billy Jo said.

"He wasn't paying you no mind," Brother Samuel said.

"Glory to the Lord, Brother," someone said in the darkness.

"Glory be," Brother Samuel said.

"Amen, Brother."

"I don't like nobody listening to what I'm saying," Billy Jo said.

"I bet the hacks already know about it," the man across from them said. "They'll bring you all back on a leash."

"I'll be down on Gayoso Street in Memphis greasing in some whore while you're breaking your back on the line."

"Jam it."

"Why don't you guys quit bitching at each other?"

"We only got twenty-nine days left," Jeffry said.

"Twenty-nine days and they're on their way to glory. Right, Brother Samuel?"

"How about a sermon, Brother?"

The truck was almost out to the line, and they wanted to forget the long day that was before them.

"I ain't got the power to save no more," Brother Samuel said.

"That don't matter. Save us, anyway."

"My powers ain't the same no more. I tried to heal Jeffry and it didn't do no good."

"Why didn't you let Brother Samuel heal you, Jeffry?"

"That ain't funny. You guys don't have a belly full of dysentery," Jeffry said.

"Kneel down and pray, Jeffry. Let Brother Samuel clamp his hand on your forehead and clean out your belly."

"It ain't funny."

"Let's wade on the banks of the Jordan, but don't drink none of the water or you'll get the runs."

"You guys don't have your bellies tied up in knots," Jeffry said.

"Repent sinners before you catch the runs for all eternity."

"It ain't right to make fun of the Word," Brother Samuel said.

The truck made a sharp turn, stopped, and the back doors were unlocked and opened. The men blinked their eyes in the light. Evans and another guard stood at the tailgate. Evans looked at them from the shade of his sun glasses and cork sun helmet.

"Gang five follow me," he said.

The men dropped out of the back one by one and walked in single file behind him. The truck was parked by an irrigation canal that was being dug into a flood basin. The canal ended abruptly where yesterday's work had stopped. Two long banks of dusty red clay were piled on each side of the ditch. The pine trees were green and sweet smelling in the morning air. The trees stretched away over the loam down to the river. The breeze from the river blew through the woods and scattered the pine needles over the ground.

The men in gang five followed Evans to the line shack where the tools were handed out. Two trusties stood at the door of the shack to check out the tools. Each man could ask for either a shovel or a pick. Those who got there first took all the shovels. It was harder work with a pick.

Billy Jo stepped forward in the line.

"Shovel."

"Ain't no more. Claxton got the last," the trusty said.

"My goddamn luck."

"Move along," Evans said.

It was Jeffry's turn.

"Hey Evans, can't I get a shovel? I was sick again last night."

"You should have got at the head of the line."

"I'll pull my guts loose with a pick."

"You're slowing up the line."

Jeffry lifted the pick on his shoulder with both hands and walked over to the irrigation canal.

"What's your name?" the trusty said to Avery.

"Broussard."

"There's supposed to be another guy here—LeBlanc."

"Scratch him off. He's in the hospital at Angola," Evans said.

"I ain't supposed to scratch nobody off till I get an order."

"I'm giving you the order. He won't be here for three weeks."

"Why don't somebody at the office get things straight and stop screwing up my list?" the trusty said. "What are you doing here, Boudreaux? I got you marked down in detention."

"I'm out."

"I can see that."

"Give me a pick and I won't take up any more of your valuable time."

"How am I supposed to keep my list straight when half the guys in your gang is someplace they shouldn't be?" the trusty said to Evans.

"You can bitch to the warden and maybe he'll give you another job. We need more people on the line," Evans said.

The trusty wrote in his book. "Boudreaux—one pick," he said.

Evans turned to Toussaint.

"What are you staring at?"

"Nothing." He shouldered his pick with one hand, the point sharp and shiny in the sun. His hand was tight on the smooth wood handle. Evans looked at him, his face pink and peeling from sunburn. Toussaint stared back.

"Don't ever think you could get away with it," Evans said. "You wouldn't no more get the pick over your head and I would have my pistol out."

"A man that's been on the gang can swing pretty fast. Even with one hand and from the shoulder."

Evans started to step back and checked himself.

"Talk like that can send you to detention," he said.

"I been there before."

"One of these days you ain't coming back. You'll go crazy in there and start mumbling and pissing on yourself like the loonies."

Toussaint let the pick drop to his side and swing loosely by one arm. Evans' hand jerked to his holster involuntarily and then relaxed. The Negro walked past him to the ditch.

"What was Evans on your ass about this time?" Jeffry said.

"He said I might make trusty this year."

The men were working at the end of the canal with the picks. They thudded them into the wall of dirt and pulled the broken tree roots loose with their fingers. The sweat rolled down their bare backs, and their faces were already filmed with dust. Jeffry rested his pick and looked over at Evans.

"Somebody should kill that sonofabitch," he said.

"He's a mean one," Daddy Claxton said.

"I'd like to pop his head open like you break a matchbox," Billy Jo said.

"He's going to make me pull my guts out," Jeffry said.

"You ain't the only guy in camp with the runs," Billy Jo said.

"I got to go thirsty all the time," Jeffry said. "I can't never drink a sip of water without puking it right up again. When I get out I'm going down home and stick my head in a well we got and drink till there ain't any fever left in my insides."

"I ain't seen a woman in four years," Billy Jo said. "I'm going to hire the two best-looking whores in Memphis and jazz them till they're bleeding. I ain't done any belly-rubbing in so long I forgot what it is."

"It ain't but a month now," Jeffry said.

"Why don't you guys write it on a piece of paper and tack it on the warden's bulletin board," a man working next to Billy Jo said. *"Jeffry and Billy Jo is breaking out in one month."*

"I remember in Folsom a guy stooled on a break," Billy Jo said. "Somebody used a razor on him like you slice up a ham."

"That didn't do no good to the guys that got their butts shot off," the man said.

Billy Jo swung his pick down hard into the wall of dirt.

"I don't reckon you're aiming to make trusty by turning us in?" he said.

"I got no truck with fellows like that."

"You're a good boy." Billy Jo swung his pick down again.

"What are you going to do when you get out, Toussaint?" Jeffry said.

"I don't think that far ahead."

"That's the best way to do it. You go nuts when you start counting time."

Two men moved the wheelbarrows up to the front of the ditch and shoveled in the loose dirt.

"It don't do you no good to count time," Jeffry said. "It makes you feel like shitting in your britches when you think of what's out there and you can't get to none of it."

"There's pussy out there," Billy Jo said. "Christ, I'm going to bathe in it when I get out."

"This is the worst goddamn camp they got in the state," Jeffry said. "Them goddamn Carolina chain gangs ain't any worse off than we got it."

"This place ain't tough," Billy Jo said. "I was in five pens before they sent me here."

"You had a real successful career," a man said. It was the same man who had baited him in the truck.

"Someday I'll sent you a postcard and you can play with yourself while you think about me climbing between some girl's legs."

"How did you get that scar on your face?"

"In the Tennessee pen," Billy Jo said.

"I heard you was cut for rutting over a nigger girl."

"You sonofabitch."

"Your scar is turning red, Billy."

"I'll drive this pick through your goddamn chest."

"Your bleeding ass."

"I done warned you."

"Hack watching," Brother Samuel said.

They looked up. Evans stood in the shade by the trees.

"He ain't watching us. He's thinking about what he's going to do to his old lady when he gets home," Billy Jo said. "Why'd you say he was watching us?"

"I don't reckon I see too good," Brother Samuel said.

"Don't go getting in no fights," Jeffry said. "They'll put you in detention and we'll be out in another month."

"You boys better keep quiet about it," Brother Samuel said.

"We'll make it out," Jeffry said.

"I ain't saying you won't. It's just that it don't hurt none to keep it to yourself."

"You ever been in a break, Daddy?" Billy Jo said. The man whom he had almost fought had moved to the other side of the ditch and was working by himself.

"No. I seen one, though. I was in Angola when they lined the guards up along the block and was going to set fire to them with torches."

"Too bad Evans wasn't there," Billy Jo said. "I'd give up the best piece of ass I ever had to see him get caught in a riot. And that pop-off bastard over there. I'd like to see him get his tail burned, too." He looked towards the man working on the other side of the canal.

"Why don't you quit talking about women?" Jeffry said.

"Because I love pussy, fruit man. That's the only thing I can't go without. The best lay I ever had was from a gal in Birmingham. I picked her up in a beer joint. She had a belly as smooth as water, and she was like wet silk inside. I give her everything I had and she still wanted more."

"I run after women when I was a young man," Daddy Claxton said.

"How long has it been, Daddy?" Billy Jo said.

"I got too old to think about it anymore."

"You ain't too old to play with them."

"I done eight years and I still got life to go. I don't think about them no more."

Evans walked closer to the ditch and looked down at the men. They stopped talking and swung their picks into the dirt. He went back to the shade of the trees.

Toussaint watched Avery work with his pick. He raised it over his head and swung down with his arms.

"You're doing it wrong," the Negro said.

"What?"

"You won't last the day like that."

"I know how to use a pick."

"You ain't worked eight hours a day with one before."

"How do you do it, then?"

"Swing with your shoulders. Let the pick do the work," Toussaint said. "Don't tire yourself out. You ain't working for nothing except that ten-dollar bill they give you when you get out of here."

"You talk like you're from the Delta."

"Barataria."

"I'm from Martinique parish."

"What are you serving?"

"One to three for running moon."

"You don't look like a whiskey runner."

"I wasn't in business long enough to be a professional."

"You can be out in a year on good behavior."

"I already had trouble with the captain."

"How'd you get on this gang? Gang five is supposed to be for lifers and troublemakers."

"There was a fight when I was in the parish jail."

"Who was doing the fighting?"

"I was part of the time. The man I was brought in with had to be sent to the prison hospital at Angola."

"Stay out of fights in the camp. It will get you time in detention, and they won't let you try for parole when your first year is up."

"What's detention like?"

"It's a tin box no bigger than a baggage trunk setting out in the sun."

"How many days do they put you in there?" Avery said.

"As long as they want, but they got to take you out each night. The camp doctor makes them."

"They kept me in the hole eight days at the parish jail. After the third day I couldn't go to sleep. It was too hot to sleep during the daytime and at night I'd start imagining things."

"If they put you in detention try counting the rivets on the inside of the door. When you get tired of that you can count the heat waves bouncing off the sides."

"What are you in for?"

"Ten years."

"Jesus Christ. What did you do?"

"They said I robbed a fur company."

"You didn't do it?"

"They give me ten years. They're outside and I'm inside. That makes them right."

"How does anybody beat a place like this?"

"They say nobody beats it. Nobody escapes and nobody comes out the same."

"Those two men in the truck think they're getting out."

"Jeffry and Billy Jo?" Toussaint said.

"The one with the red scar and his podner."

"If they bust free they'll be the first. Two years ago somebody in gang three tried it. He was climbing over the wire fence when they caught him with the shotguns. They make everybody in camp come outside and look at him hanging in the wire."

The sun was high above the trees now, and it shone directly down in the ditch. Brother Samuel and Daddy Claxton tied their handkerchiefs around their foreheads to keep the sweat out of their eyes. Jeffry complained of the heat and his stomach, and he held both hands close to the iron head of the pick and scratched at the dirt and roots. Billy Jo continued to talk of the women he had slept with, although no one listened to him now. The wheelbarrow was brought up and the loose dirt was shoveled in. The men rested on their picks and cursed the sun and the dust, and once more swung into the hard sunbaked wall before them.

"Bring the goddamn water barrel down," Billy Jo said.

"Where the hell is the trusty? Hey Evans, send down the water barrel," another said.

"I can't drink no water," Jeffry said.

"The rest of us can," Billy Jo said. "Evans! Tell the goddamn trusty to bring us some water."

Evans stood over them on the crest of the ditch. He frowned at Billy Jo.

"What's your beef?" he said.

"Some goddamn water."

"Go back to work."

"It's hotter than a bitch down here."

"I'll send the trusty. Keep swinging that pick."

Evans walked up the line and sent the trusty back. The aluminum water barrel was beaded with drops of moisture. A tin dipper hung from the lip of the barrel. Billy Jo pulled off the lid and filled the dipper. He swallowed twice and spit the rest in the dirt.

"This tastes like Evans washed his socks in it," he said.

"Drink it or go dry," the trusty said.

"Fuck you, ass kisser."

"Maybe you don't get no water the rest of the day," the trusty said.

"And maybe you'll get your fucking throat slit while you're asleep," Billy Jo said.

The trusty put the lid back on the barrel. "That's all your drinking water for today."

"Let me have a drink. I'm like cotton inside," Daddy Claxton said. The trusty pulled the lid back off and let him fill the dipper. The water rolled down Claxton's chin and over his chest. He lowered the dipper into the barrel and drank again. Jeffry watched him drink, and rubbed the back of his hand over his lips.

"You'll have the runs for a week," Billy Jo said.

"His tongue won't be blistering by one o'clock," the trusty said.

"Screw you, punk."

The dipper was passed around the gang. The trusty replaced it and the lid when they had finished.

"There's a freshwater spring over in them trees," he said. "I'm going over directly and have a drink."

"You mean there's clean water over yonder?" Jeffry said.

"It's coming right out of some rocks."

"Go fill up the water barrel. We'll pay you for it," he said.

"What with?"

"I got three bucks hid in the barracks."

"That ain't enough."

"The sonofabitch is riding you," Billy Jo said. "Don't pay him no mind."

"It's coming out of some rocks with moss on them."

"I believe him," Jeffry said. "This is hill country. There's always springs where there's hills."

"You're in barracks two, ain't you?" Billy Jo said to the trusty. "Well, I got buddies in there, so you better forget about sleeping for the next few nights unless you want to get operated on. It takes one swipe with a knife and your whoring days are over. Now get the fuck out of here, punk."

"It's a long day without no water," the trusty said, and lifted the barrel and moved down the ditch.

"You shouldn't ought to get him mad," Daddy Claxton said. "Maybe he won't bring the water back."

"He's got to," Billy Jo said. "Evans will make him. We can't do no work without water."

"I reckon you're right," Daddy Claxton said.

"I don't give a fuck for punks like that, anyway."

"I wouldn't mind making trusty," the old man said.

"That's for punks and ass kissers."

"You think there's a spring around here somewhere?" Jeffry said.

"There ain't no water in ten miles of here that don't have scum or mosquito eggs in it."

"I thought we might get some clean water."

"They might bring us some oranges with lunch. You can drink the juice."

"You think they will?"

"Today's Friday. Carp and fruit for lunch," Brother Samuel said.

"I seen some carp and garfish eating off a drowned cow once," Daddy Claxton said.

Evans walked over to the embankment of dirt and squatted on his haunches, looking down at the men. Small clods rolled from around his boots into the ditch.

"The captain wants a new latrine dug," he said.

"We dug the last one. It's gang six's turn," Billy Jo said.

"The captain likes the way we dig latrines. We do a good job. He might even let us keep digging them from now on. Boudreaux and what's your name, get up here."

Toussaint and Avery climbed out of the ditch.

"You see that line of scrub over there? Dig a trench fifteen feet long and three deep."

"We ain't got a shovel."

"Claxton, hand up your shovel."

"It's checked out to me. I got to hand it back in."

"Let's have it."

Evans took the shovel by its handle and gave it to Avery.

"Give Claxton your pick."

Avery slid it down the embankment to the old man.

They walked over to the line of brush. Avery marked out the edge of the trench with his shovel. Evans stood off in the shade of the trees to watch them.

"I'll break the ground and you dig after me," Toussaint said.

They went to work. Toussaint drove the pick into the cracked earth and snapped the brush roots loose. Avery dug from one end of the trench and worked in a pattern towards the other side.

"What makes Billy Jo and Jeffry think they can make it?" he said.

"Billy Jo has got a brother on the outside. He's supposed to help them."

"You think you could make it with somebody on the outside?"

"Not when everybody in camp knows about it," Toussaint said. "Billy Jo says his brother is going to meet them in a car. I'm surprised he ain't give out the license number."

"You might have a chance with help on the outside."

"You thinking about leaving us?"

"It passed through my mind."

"You can get out in a year. Serve your time. A year ain't nothing. If you break out and get caught they add five more on your sentence."

"Do you ever think about breaking out?"

"I wouldn't talk about it if I did," Toussaint said. "You're young. Wait it out."

The trench deepened. It was almost time for lunch.

"Why were you in detention?" Avery said.

"Talking during roll call."

"They gave you a day for that?"

"No, two days. They let me out to put somebody else in."

"Who put you in?"

"Evans."

"He must have it against you."

"He don't like nobody."

"He looks like he enjoys his work."

"It takes a certain type man to be a hack," Toussaint said.

"Does he ride you like that all the time?"

"You said you were from Martinique parish."

"Yes."

"Talk about Martinique parish, then."

They worked for a half hour in silence.

"What do you figure on doing when your time is up?" Toussaint said.

"I just got here. I haven't thought about it."

"You'll start thinking about it soon. You won't think about nothing else after a while."

"I might go to New Orleans."

"What for?"

"I've never been there."

"Ain't you got a home?"

"There's nothing left of it now. My daddy was a cane planter. We used to own twenty acres. The last I heard some man bought it at the sheriff's tax sale to build a subdivision."

"I lived in New Orleans. I worked on the docks."

"What's the chance of getting a job?"

"Fair. What kind of work you done?"

"Oil exploration."

"I know a man down there might help you."

"They say New Orleans is a good town."

"You planning on staying out of the whiskey business?" Toussaint said.

"I'll probably stay on the drinking end of it."

"You can't boil out the misery with corn."

"You can make a good dent in it, though."

"You're too young to have a taste for whiskey."

"I'm not too young to be digging a latrine with you, so let's get off my age."

"Whiskey can eat you up."

"I've seen a lot more eaten up, and whiskey didn't do it."

Evans blew his whistle for the lunch break. The men climbed out of the ditch and formed a line behind a pickup truck parked in the shade. Toussaint and Avery dropped their tools in the unfinished trench and got in line with the others. The tin plates and spoons were handed out. The trusties served the food from the big aluminum containers placed on the bed of the truck. The men sat in the shade and ate.

"You told me we was having oranges," Jeffry said.

"I ain't the warden. I can't know what they're going to do," Billy Jo said.

"You said we was getting oranges."

"Drink the tea. It helps your stomach," Brother Samuel said.

"It's just like the drinking water."

"Stop bitching," Billy Jo said.

"I seen some carp eating off a dead cow once," Daddy Claxton said.

"Maybe you're swallowing the same carp," someone said.

"It wouldn't bother me none. I eat worse. When I was a boy my pap used to bring home garfish that was caught up on land in the flood basin."

"This tea ain't no different from the water," Jeffry said.

"It's boiled. That makes it different. Drink it and shut up," Billy Jo said.

"I'll puke up my dinner."

"Let Brother Samuel work on you," a man from gang two said.

"He didn't do me no good."

"You wasn't cooperating," the man said.

"I ain't got my powers no more," Brother Samuel said.

"You know that ain't true, Brother. What's that thing around your neck?"

Brother Samuel touched the wooden disk that hung on a leather cord.

"The Black Man give it to me. These letters is written in a language that ain't even used no more. It means I got the power to control spirits."

"I thought you didn't have no powers."

"I still got my magic powers. I ain't got my spiritual ones."

"What's the difference?"

"My magic ones is from the Black Man, and the others is from the Lord. I ain't had no truck with the Black Man since he made me sin agin Jesus."

"Look at it this way," the inmate from gang two said. "If you use the Black Man's powers to do the work of Jesus, then you can get back at him for making you sin."

"I ain't thought of it that way."

"Ain't it the work of the Lord to heal people? Well, that's just what you're doing."

"That's the way I figure it, too," Daddy Claxton said.

"Use some of them things you carry around with you," the inmate from two said. His name was Benoit. He was dark complexioned and unshaved, with close set pig-eyes, and he smelled of sweat and earth.

"I ain't sure it's right. I gone back to following the Word."

"Lay down, Jeffry, and let him heal you."

"I don't want to be healed. I tried it once. It don't work."

"Sure it works," Benoit said.

"I'm about to puke from this fish already. I don't want nobody fooling with me."

"Tell him to get hisself healed, Billy Jo."

"Get yourself healed," Billy Jo said, his mouth filled with bread and carp.

"Let me be."

"Go ahead, Brother."

"I ain't sure."

"It ain't Jesus' will to let a man suffer when you can cure him."

"You want me to try, Jeffry?"

"No."

"Don't listen to him. He's sick in the head with fever," Benoit said.

"His head's all right. He ain't got faith," Brother Samuel said.

"You got no faith, Jeffry," Benoit said.

"You guys let me alone."

Most of the men had finished lunch and came over to watch.

"How about it, Brother?"

"I'll try."

The men held Jeffry's arms and legs to the ground and pulled up his shirt to expose his stomach.

"Goddamn you bastards! Leave go! Do you hear me! I'm sick! Turn loose!"

He struggled for a moment and then became still. He twisted his head up to watch his stomach and to see what Brother Samuel was going to do.

"What's them things you got?" Daddy Claxton said.

"Them's what I control the spirits with."

He knelt beside Jeffry, his face the color of mud under the straw hat that came down to his ears. His large ill-fitting clothes were damp with sweat.

"I'm going to use my moccasin fang and turtle foot first. It ain't going to hurt none, you'll just feel something pulling on you when the spirit leaves your body."

"You guys got no right to let him do this," Jeffry said.

"It's time you got religion," Benoit said.

"This ain't religion. It's conjuring. Don't let him touch me with that stuff."

"Lie still," Brother Samuel said. "I'm going to make a cross on your belly."

He drew a white impression of a horizontal line across Jeffry's stomach with the turtle foot, then drew a vertical line through it with the snake fang. He placed the fang and the foot on the ground beside a piece of string and the ball of hair taken from a cow's stomach. He folded his hands together and rocked slowly back and forth.

"Goddamn each of you bastards," Jeffry said. He struggled again. The men held him firmly. The figure of the cross was pink and white on his stomach.

"Great Belial," Brother Samuel began, "cast out of the spirits of

Zion that want this man to bow before the bloody hill where you wrecked the faith of mighty Jerusalem, and let him take the snake to his cheek." Samuel picked up the snake fang in his fingers and held the curved ivory point over Jeffry's stomach. "With the sign of your kingdom I plunge the poison of the shade into your enemy's heart." He brought the snake fang down and struck the center of the cross.

"I'm bleeding," Jeffry said. "Look at what you done. You stuck me full of poison. I heard you say so."

There was a small drop of blood at the joint of the cross.

"I never seen nothing like that," Daddy Claxton said.

"Jeffry don't look good."

"What the hell do you think I look like when somebody is sticking snake poison in me?"

"I didn't put no poison in you," Brother Samuel said.

"I heard you say it."

"That's just part of what I got to say to cast out the spirit."

"You feel any different?" Daddy Claxton said.

"Yeah. I got a hole in my belly that I didn't have five minutes ago."

"I reckon it takes some extra conjuring to get you healed," Benoit said.

"I had my fill. I don't want no more."

"It's a powerful spirit got hold of you," Brother Samuel said.

"It ain't no spirit. It's the runs. Everybody gets the runs," Jeffry said.

"Try another cure, Brother Samuel."

"Not on me. I ain't having no more." The men still held him to the ground.

"I ain't got but one left."

"Go ahead and use it. Jeffry is willing to do anything to get rid of the runs."

"You sonsofbitches."

"Don't use cuss words when we're talking about things of the spirit," Benoit said, his pig-eyes smiling at Jeffry.

"I wouldn't do this to none of you when you was sick," Jeffry said.

"That's because you got no charity. You got no faith, neither. Ain't that right? Jeffry's got no faith."

"You rotten bas . . ."

A man clamped his hand over Jeffry's mouth.

"Get on with the conjuring. We got to use force to get him healed."

Jeffry's eyes rolled wildly.

"What are you going to do with that ball of hair?" Benoit said.

"It's for casting out the spirit."

"How's it work?" Daddy Claxton said.

"I send the spirit out of Jeffry into the ball of hair, and then I set fire to it and let the spirit free again."

"What happens if he don't get free?"

"Belial will send another spirit into my body to make me turn him loose."

"Who's this Belial guy?" Billy Jo said.

"He was one of the angels the Lord run out of Heaven," Brother Samuel said.

"I never heard of no Belial," Billy Jo said.

"That's because you and Jeffry got no religion," Benoit said.

"I don't need none."

"Mmpppppppht," Jeffry said, beneath the clamped hand.

Brother Samuel held the ball of hair to Jeffry's stomach and closed his eyes and began to speak in a language that none of the men could understand. He rolled the ball in a circle and his voice became a chant. Jeffry's stomach started quivering under Brother Samuel's hands. The pink and white impression of the cross had disappeared, and only the small smear of blood remained. Brother Samuel chanted louder and rocked on his knees, with his body bent over Jeffry.

"Is that all there is to it?" Billy Jo said.

"I got to set the spirit free."

"You mean he's inside that ball of hair?"

"Take it and hold it in your hand."

"I don't want it," Billy Jo said.

Samuel offered it to Daddy Claxton.

"I ain't touching it," the old man said.

"I'll hold it," Benoit said.

Brother Samuel put it in his hand.

"It jumped! My God, there's something in it!" He jerked his hand away and let it drop to the ground. The men were grinning at him. "I tell you it jumped. I ain't lying. I felt it bump in my hand like it was alive."

"The sun must have fried your brains."

"One of you guys pick it up." No one did. "Go ahead, pick it up. See if I'm lying. It tried to jump out of my hand."

"You been drinking the kerosene from the line shack again?" Billy Jo said.

"All right, bastard. You pick it up."

"You can play witch doctor if you want. I ain't making an ass out of myself."

"Turn Jeffry loose," Brother Samuel said.

Jeffry wiped his mouth with his hand and tucked in his shirt. There was spittle and pink finger marks around his mouth.

"You see this piece of string?" Brother Samuel said. "I'm tying three knots in it. I'm going to give it to you, and I want you to put it in your pocket and not look at it till tonight. When the knots is gone your stomach won't bother you no more."

"You mean them knots is going away by theirself?" Daddy Claxton said.

"As long as he don't look at the string till dark."

"I ain't going to look at it no time. I don't want the goddamn thing. Hey, what are you doing?"

"I'm putting it in your pocket for you."

"I had my fill of this stuff."

"Shut up and do like he says," Billy Jo said.

Brother Samuel picked up the ball of hair. He took a kitchen match from his denims and scratched it across the sole of his work boot. He held the flame to the ball and waited for it to catch. A wisp of yellow-black smoke came up, and the sweet-rotten odor of burnt hair made the men draw back. He stood up and hurled the ball of flame into the air, where it burst apart in a myriad of fire. Pieces of burnt hair floated slowly to the ground.

"It's over. I set him free," Brother Samuel said.

Jeffry got up and walked across the clearing, his legs held close together.

"Where are you going?" Billy Jo said.

"To the goddamn latrine."

The whistle blew for the lunch break to end. The men filed past the back of the pickup and dropped their plates and spoons into a cardboard box. Toussaint and Avery went back to work on the trench.

"Does that go on all the time?" Avery said.

"That's the first time I seen him do any conjuring. He's usually talking about the Word and soul-saving."

"He stuck the snake's fang right in the center of the cross."

"I seen that done down home before. I knowed a man that did the same thing to get rid of a sickness. He said when he died he could pass on his powers, but it had to be to a woman. A man can only give them to a woman, and a woman only to a man."

"He puts on a fine show."

"He's a good man. He don't do nothing unless he thinks he can help somebody," Toussaint said.

"He didn't do much good for Jeffry. He's still on latrine duty."

Evans came over to watch the work. The width and length of the trench were dug out, and Avery had spaded the depth down to a foot. Evans chewed on a matchstick. He rolled it from one side of his mouth to the other with his tongue.

"We want it finished this afternoon," he said. "Put in a little less talk and more work."

"We was talking about this fellow Belial."

"What?"

"This is the place where you can get the spirit run out of you, the camp latrine."

"What the hell are you saying, Boudreaux?"

"You're the only hack in camp with a conjuror on your gang."

Avery threw a load of dirt to the side of the trench and didn't look up.

"You got no sense. You could be smart and do easy time," Evans said.

"That would put you out of a job. You wouldn't have nobody to lock up in the box."

"You got a lot more years to pull. You ain't going to make it."

"Don't put no money on it."

"You'll break down," Evans said. "I seen bigger guys than you crack. Some of them went to the bughouse at Pineville. You ever see anybody go nuts from stir? A stir nut is something to see."

"How deep do you want the trench?" Avery said.

"I told you before, three feet."

"It looks deep enough now."

"You better learn something now. You do like you're told in the camp."

"I thought I might give a suggestion."

"Don't."

"All right."

"This man you're with is trouble. Buddy with him and he'll get you time in detention," Evans said.

"I didn't ask to dig latrines with him."

Evans stared at Avery as though he were evaluating him. He flipped the chewed matchstick into the trench. The butt of his revolver and the cartridges in his belt shone in the sun.

"Do your stretch easy. It's the best way. Don't give me no trouble."

He left them and went to the trees.

"You didn't need to do that," Toussaint said.

"I didn't do anything."

"Don't think you ever got to take pressure off me."

"I got tired of listening to him talk."

"I don't want you putting your neck out for me."

"Why did you start that stuff with him?"

"I thought it might pick up the conversation."

"He's right. You'll never make your time," Avery said.

"You believe what he said about cracking a man down?"

"I don't know. A few years of this. Jesus."

"You think he can crack you?"

"I don't ask for trouble."

"It don't matter if you ask for it or not. You got one to three years of it when you walked through that front gate," Toussaint said.

"Free will."

Toussaint looked at him.

"It's a joke the brothers used to teach us," Avery said.

The sun went behind a cloud and the clearing fell into shadow. The breeze from the river felt suddenly cool; the sky was dark. A dust devil swirled by the trench and spun into the air. Its funnel widened, whipped by the wind, and disappeared.

The afternoon wore on, and at five o'clock the men climbed into the trucks and were taken to the barracks. The trucks rolled down the gravel roads over the railroad tracks and through the fields of green and yellow grass with the sun's dying rays slanting over the pines. The men showered and changed into fresh denims and lined up outside the dining hall for supper. They sat at the wooden tables and benches and ate the tasteless food that still seemed to smell of the carbolic and antiseptic that was used to clean the kitchen. They went back to the barracks and lay exhausted on their bunks, listening to the sounds of the frogs and night birds in the woods. Then it was nine o'clock and the lights went out and someone struck a match to the candle and the poker game began for those who were not too tired to play.

Toussaint's bunk was two down from Avery's. The army blanket on it was stretched and tucked so tightly across the mattress that you could bounce a quarter off it. The pillow was laid neatly at the head, and his foot locker was squared evenly with the base. He had a cardboard box fixed to the wall above his pillow, where he kept his razor, soap, toothbrush, tobacco, matches, and cigarette papers. He sat on the side of his bunk and reached up to get his package of Virginia Extra. He rolled a cigarette and popped a match on his thumbnail. He dropped the burnt match into a small tin can that he kept under his bed.

The poker game was being organized on the floor between the two rows of bunks. Jeffry's foot locker had been pushed out into the aisle to be used as a table, and an army blanket was spread over the top. The men played with pocket change, although it was against camp regulations for any inmate to have money. A visitor would slip a prisoner a few crumpled, hand-soiled bills, and they would eventually circulate through the entire camp by way of poker and dice games and bribes to the trusties and guards for favors. Billy Jo ran the poker game in Toussaint's barracks on a house system, by which he took a nickel out of every pot for the use of his candles and cards. He would cover any bet up to five dollars, and allow credit if the player could put up security.

"We need two more guys," Billy Jo said.

"We got four already," Benoit said.

"We need a couple more. You want in, Claxton?"

"Will you give me something on next tobacco ration?"

"You already owe it to me. What else you got?"

"Nothing."

"Brother Samuel."

"I ain't a gambling man."

"Who wants to play. We need two more guys."

"Get Jeffry."

"He's in the latrine."

"You ain't doing nothing, Toussaint."

"I only got a quarter."

"That's enough. Move over and let him sit down, Benoit."

Toussaint sat down on the floor in front of the trunk and changed his quarter for five nickels.

"Start dealing," Benoit said.

"We need another guy. You want to play?"

"I'm broke," Avery said.

"I'll give you two-bits on your first tobacco ration."

They made room for Avery. Billy Jo dropped two dimes and a nickel on the blanket.

"They pass out the tobacco on Monday. Bring me yours as soon as you get it," he said.

"Let's start playing," Benoit said.

"Five-card draw, no ante, jacks to open." Billy Jo dealt the cards around. The men looked at their cards in the light of the two candles melted to each end of the trunk.

"I can't open," the man on Billy Jo's left said.

"Me neither."

"Open for a nickel," Toussaint said.

"I'm out."

"Out."

Two more coins thumped on the blanket.

"Give me three," Toussaint said.

"One," Benoit said. His pig-eyes studied his hand thoughtfully.

"Two for the dealer," Billy Jo said.

"Your bet."

"Ten cents," Toussaint said.

"Bump you a dime more," Benoit said.

"Call," Billy Jo said.

Toussaint had opened on a pair of queens and had drawn another one.

"Call," he said.

"What you got?" Benoit said.

"Three queens."

"Fuck. I had two pair, ace high."

They threw in their cards and Billy Jo took a nickel out of the pot. Toussaint scraped in his winnings. They played four more hands; Toussaint won two of them. One man had dropped out and gone to bed, leaving five in the game. The deal went around again. Toussaint won the next hand on a straight. He had a dollar and a half in coins before him. Benoit dealt the cars.

"Open for a nickel," Avery said.

Everyone stayed.

"How many you want?"

"I'm pat," Avery said.

"You ain't taking no cards?"

"No."

"Three," Toussaint said.

The discards were scattered across the blanket. The man across from Toussaint drew one card.

"I'll take the same," Billy Jo said.

Benoit snapped two cards off the deck for himself. He mixed them in his hand and fanned them out slowly.

"Your bet, opener," he said.

"My last nickel," Avery said.

Toussaint had drawn to a pair of kings and missed. He threw in his cards.

"I'm out," the man across from him said.

"I'll see you," Billy Jo said.

"Call and raise it a quarter," Benoit said.

"That was my last nickel. I got to go in the side pot," Avery said.

"No side pot and no drawing light," Benoit said. "It's a house rule."

"I can't cover it, then."

"I'll back him," Toussaint said. He dropped three quarters in front of Avery.

Avery picked them up and threw them in the pot.

"Call and raise you fifty cents," he said.

"You splitting with him, Toussaint?" Benoit said.

"I got no part in this."

"How come you giving your money away?"

"I don't like to see nobody play freeze out."

"Call his raise or fold," Billy Jo said.

"Give me time."

Benoit ruffled the cards in his hands.

"Do one thing or another," Billy Jo said.

"He's playing on somebody else's money."

"You don't care whose it is when you put it in your pocket."

He waited, his pig-eyes studying the backs of Avery's cards. "All right, I fold," he said.

Avery tossed a nickel out of the pot to Billy Jo and took the rest in.

"Here's openers," he said. He showed a pair of aces.

"What else you got?" Benoit said.

"You didn't pay to see."

"I got a right to know."

"No, you don't," Toussaint said.

Benoit flipped over Avery's other cards, a pair of eights and a seven of clubs.

"You didn't have nothing but two pair. I was holding three tens."

"You should have paid to see those cards."

"Listen, kid," Benoit began.

"I don't like that crap, neither," Billy Jo said. "I run a straight game, and we play like the rules says. You got to put up before you see a guy's hand."

Benoit glared at the discards and was quiet.

"Hey, you guys, look here." It was Jeffry. He was coming from the latrine, barefooted, his belt unhitched and hanging loose, and his trousers half buttoned. He had the piece of string in his hand.

"You'll wake up the guys sleeping," Billy Jo said.

"Look at the string. Them knots is gone. It's like Brother Samuel said. There ain't one of them left!"

"Shut up," a voice said from one of the bunks.

"I went into the latrine and I was waiting to get rid of my supper, like I do every night, and I waited and nothing happened. My belly was all right. I didn't have to crap at all. I was hitching up my trousers and I took out this piece of string and them knots was gone. I don't feel sick no more. I swear to God I don't. Wake up, Brother Samuel! You healed my belly. It's like you said. No more runs."

Brother Samuel stirred in his bunk. He sat up and looked at Jeffry. His face was heavy with sleep.

"You done it," Jeffry said.

"I ain't sure you want to be obliged."

"This is the first time I held my food down since I come to camp."

"I healed you through the Black Man. Sometimes the spirits come back and make it bad for you in another way."

"I ain't worrying about no more spirits. They can do anything they got a mind to as long as they don't give me no more dysentery."

"You guys shut up," a voice said from the darkness.

"I told you there was something in that ball of hair," Benoit said.

"You guys been in stir too long. It's got to you," Billy Jo said.

"Look at the string. There ain't a knot in it."

"Who untied them? That Belial guy?"

"I don't know. I'd like to shake his hand, whoever he is," Jeffry said.

"Them spirits can come back," Brother Samuel said.

"They ain't coming around me no more," Jeffry said. "I swear to God I never thought nothing like this could happen."

"Button up your pants. You're hanging out," Billy Jo said.

"I knowed that ball of hair jumped in my hand," Benoit said. "I felt it, just like a frog leg jumps."

"Spread this around camp and you'll all go to the nut house," Billy Jo said.

"The spirits can put a grigri on you," Brother Samuel said.

"What the hell is a grigri?"

"It's a spell. It makes you have bad luck."

"I ain't worrying about no grigri. It couldn't be no worse than the runs."

"I ain't got the power to take it off. It takes a man that's sold his soul to get rid of a grigri."

"I ain't worrying."

Somewhere in the distance a train whistle blew. They could hear the rush of the engine and the rumble of the wheels. They never saw the train except the day they rode it to prison and the day they left. There was an old story that if an inmate saw the train's headlamp shining at him out of the darkness he would be released from the camp soon. The whistle blew again and the men sat in silence. Even Jeffry did not speak. The train was closer now and the whistle shrieked once more in the quiet of the night.

"The midnight special going to glory," Brother Samuel said. "Shine your light on me."

Three weeks passed and the sky became like scorched brass. The air was hot and dry, and the wind blew across the land like heat from an oven. Dark thunderclouds were spread over the horizon, but the rains didn't come. At night the heat lightning flashed in the sky, and black strips of rain clouds floated across the moon. The earth was cracked from lack of water. The grass in the fields was burnt yellow and whispered dryly in the hot wind. The men waited for the rains to drench the parched ground, and the thunder clapped and rattled over the horizon like someone beating a sheet of corrugated tin against the sky.

Gang five was still working on the irrigation canal the day LeBlanc was brought to camp. A pickup truck ground along the right-of-way in second gear and stopped close to the ditch. LeBlanc sat in the front seat between two guards. He got out on the driver's side, and the other guard slid out behind him. LeBlanc's face was marked with scars and the bridge of his nose was crooked. He hadn't had a haircut since he had been arrested, and the hair along his neck stuck down over his shirt collar. The two guards walked him to the area where gang five was working.

"Here's a new one, Evans. He just got in from Angola. The warden told me to bring him on down and get him started," the driver said.

"What's his name?" Evans said.

"LeBlanc."

"I been expecting him. You all can go on. I'll get him a pick and put him to work."

"Watch him. He spit on the cop that brought him on the train."

"He won't do that here."

The guards got into the pickup, turned it around, and drove back along the right-of-way towards the gravel road.

"Come with me," Evans said.

They went to the line shack and LeBlanc was issued a pick. They went back to the ditch.

"I ain't eat breakfast yet," LeBlanc said.

"You should have told them when they checked you through the office."

"I did. Them guards was supposed to take me to the mess hall."

"They was probably in a hurry. Get down in the ditch and go to work. You can eat at lunch time."

"I ain't used to working on an empty stomach."

"You'll get used to a lot of things around here. You come into camp with a bad record or they wouldn't have put you on my gang. Step out of line and you'll wish you was back in the hospital. Now start sweating some grease into that pick handle."

"I ain't got much use for people that wear uniforms."

"Get down in the ditch."

He climbed over the mound of clay and slid down the embankment.

"Hi, LeBlanc," Avery said. "When did they bring you in?"

"I come on the train this morning."

"How was it at the hospital?"

"They sewed up my face and put my ribs back together. I still got to wear some tape around my sides."

"I wasn't sure you were going to make it. You looked pretty bad when they carried you out of the jail," Avery said.

"I'm going to even up things back there sometime."

"You better forget about it for a while."

"I aim to get things straight. I owe some people for messing up my face."

"What was Evans talking to you about?"

"Who's Evans?" LeBlanc said.

"The hack."

"I give a cop some trouble."

"What did you do?"

"I spit on him at the front gate."

"Who's the new guy?" Billy Jo said.

"This is LeBlanc," Avery said. "He came in from Angola."

"What happened to your face?" Jeffry said.

"I fell on the sidewalk playing hopscotch."

"I was in Angola," Billy Jo said. "So was Daddy Claxton."

"I was there when they was going to set fire to the hacks," Daddy Claxton said.

"Who done that to your face?" Jeffry said. "Them stitches ain't been out very long."

"He was in a fight," Avery said.

"The other guy must have been using a ball bat."

"My face ain't your business," LeBlanc said.

"I didn't say it was."

"Stare at something else, then," LeBlanc said.

"This is the best gang in camp," Billy Jo said. "Everybody here is doing life or they showed the hacks they don't take crap."

"You got a cigarette on you?" Daddy Claxton said.

"They took them away from me at the office."

"What are you pulling?" Billy Jo said.

"Three and seven."

"Daddy and Brother Samuel is pulling life," Jeffry said.

The dust rose from the earth as the men worked. LeBlanc rested his pick and took off his shirt. There was a wide band of tape around his ribs and stomach. He swung the pick into the ground.

"You got something busted?" Billy Jo said.

"It's healed up now."

"Brother Samuel can heal it for you if it ain't right," Jeffry said.

"There ain't anything wrong with me," LeBlanc said.

"Who done it to you?" Jeffry said.

"Let the man be," Brother Samuel said.

"I was only asking."

"Listen to the thunder. Maybe we'll get some rain tonight," Daddy Claxton said.

"It ain't going to rain. We'll be breathing this goddamn dust the rest of the year," Billy Jo said.

"Not us. We only got a week to pull," Jeffry said.

"Shut up," Billy Jo said.

"Why is everybody on my ass today?"

"Because you ask for it," Billy Jo said.

"I ain't done a thing and everybody is getting on my ass about it."

"Then shut your mouth and we'll leave you alone."

"I can smell the rain in the air," Daddy Claxton said. "Like a paper mill. They say it means somebody is going to die when it stays dry a long time and then it rains."

"This weather ain't natural," Brother Samuel said. "I only seen it like this once before. The sky was yellow and the sun was like a red ball. When the rains come the fever come too, and people was dropping dead in the marsh like sick rabbits. They was still finding bodies two months later."

"It's a drought. Ain't you guys ever seen a drought before?" Billy Jo said.

"This one ain't natural," Brother Samuel said. "It means something."

"Where do you get a drink of water around here?" LeBlanc said.

"Call for the trusty."

"Where is he?"

"Down the ditch someplace."

"Don't drink too much water if you can help it," Avery said.

"What's wrong with it?"

"It makes you sick."

"Trusty! Bring the water barrel," Billy Jo said.

"Why ain't there any decent water?" LeBlanc said.

"The state don't want to pay for digging a new well," Jeffry said.

The trusty brought the water can. LeBlanc drank from the dipper.

"I wouldn't water stock with this," he said. He threw the dipper inside the can. The water splashed over the rim.

"What the hell!" the trusty said. "You got my shirt wet."

"Go put some clean water in the can," LeBlanc said.

"That's all there is. You drink the same as everybody else."

"What's going on down there?" Evans said from the top of the ditch.

"This guy don't want to drink the water."

"Let him go thirsty," Evans said.

"This water come out of a swamp," LeBlanc said.

The other men had stopped work to watch. LeBlanc's eyes shone hotly at Evans. The scars and the holes where his cuts had been stitched were pink against his face.

"You're starting off your stretch the wrong way," Evans said.

"Was you ever in the army? You look like the kind they got in the stockade," LeBlanc said.

"Cool down," Avery said.

"You always got a uniform and a gun, and sometimes they let you carry a stick to bust somebody's ribs with. I seen them like you in the stockade."

"You want to spend your first day in detention?"

The trusty started to move off with the water barrel.

"Come back here," LeBlanc said. He grabbed the water barrel and pulled the lid off. "Look at it. It's swamp water."

"That water come out of a tap," Evans said.

"You try it."

"You're talking yourself right into detention."

"Drink it," LeBlanc said. He held the barrel up at Evans. "Drink it, you fat swine. Drink it till your fat belly is full of worms."

"God damn you. Get up here. I'm going to make you sweat your ass off for that."

"You filthy swine." LeBlanc hurled the barrel at Evans' head. The water whirled out in a shower over the men.

Evans had his pistol in his hand and was blowing his whistle. Two guards came running from further down the ditch. The inmates had scattered along the canal when Evans drew his weapon. Picks and shovels were strewn over the ground. The wheelbarrow lay overturned on a mound of dirt.

"Bring him up here," Evans said.

The guards slid down the side of the ditch and came towards LeBlanc. He stepped back and raised his pick over his shoulder. They stopped and one of them, a lean rough-skinned man named Rainack, drew his revolver and cocked the hammer and aimed it at LeBlanc's head.

"I won't miss," he said.

"For God's sake, put it down, LeBlanc," Avery said.

"It's three to one, and you ain't got but one swing with that pick," Evans said.

"Come closer and I'll pin you to the ground," LeBlanc said.

"Quit while you got a chance," the other guard said.

"I seen your kind in the stockade. They know how to use a billy club real good. They know how to jab you where it hurts and it don't show."

"Let go of the pick."

"They've got you. Put it down," Avery said. "You can't beat them like this. LeBlanc, listen to me. For God's sake. He means what he says. He'll kill you."

"I ain't waiting much longer," the guard named Rainack said. "A few more seconds and you're a dead man."

Avery broke towards LeBlanc in an attempt to grab the pick. Toussaint dove into his body and dragged him against the wall of the ditch and held him there. Avery fought to get loose, saying, "He's sick, he was in the war and his mind's not right, don't you understand, he should be in a hospital, you can't shoot him down, Evans, he doesn't know what he's doing, he thinks you're somebody in a stockade—"

"Be still," Toussaint said.

"Make your play one way or another," Rainack said.

LeBlanc remained motionless, the pick held in the air above his shoulder, while his eyes moved slowly over the two guards in the ditch and then looked up at Evans. He lowered the pick and dropped it by his foot.

"I ain't going to let you kill me," he said. "You wouldn't have to worry about me no more. You'd like to shoot me. You want me to make it easy for you so there won't be no kickbacks from the warden or an investigation. Well, I'm going to stay alive, because when I get out of wherever you lock me up I'm going to kill that man standing on the ditch."

"You ain't going to do nothing," Rainack said, "except lay in the box and pray Jesus you was dead."

"I'm going to kill you," he said to Evans. "Do you hear me? I'm going to get you, or I hope I die and go to hell."

The guard jabbed his revolver in LeBlanc's side and shoved him towards the embankment.

"You'll think you're in hell when you've been in the box a few hours," Rainack said. "Get up there."

LeBlanc picked up his straw hat and his shirt and climbed up the embankment with the two guards behind him. He draped his shirt over his shoulder and put on his hat. Evans still held his pistol in his hand.

"Did you hear what I said? I'm going to kill you, you fat-bellied swine."

Evans whipped his pistol barrel across LeBlanc's taped ribs. He grabbed at his sides with both hands and doubled over. His teeth were clenched and his eyes glazed in pain. His black hair hung down over his face, and his knees were buckling as though he were going to fall.

"You goddamn, I'll get, oh you goddamn, oh goddamn. . . ."

"Get him out of here," Evans said.

A guard took him by each arm and led him, doubled over, to one of the trucks. The sweat on his back glistened in the sun. The tape around his ribs was moist and pulling loose from his skin. His hat fell from his head and rolled on the ground. Rainack stooped to pick it up, and threw it inside the cab of the truck and pushed LeBlanc in after it.

"Pick up the tools and go to work," Evans said to the men.

He put his revolver in his holster and snapped the leather strap over the hammer to hold it secure. Daddy Claxton turned the wheelbarrow right side up and began to refill it with his shovel, and the rest of the men picked up their tools and went to work. Evans watched them a minute and then walked farther down the line.

"Did you see Evans' face when he called him a fat swine?" Billy Jo said. "He would have shot him if the rest of us hadn't been here."

"He's mean enough to do it," Daddy Claxton said.

"I never seen him so pissed off. Not even at Toussaint," Jeffry said.

"He don't like to be called fat," Brother Samuel said. "He always wears his pistol belt over his stomach to hide it."

"I seen it in his face. He would have shot that guy dead if we wasn't here," Billy Jo said.

"That guy was talking like he was ready for the nut house," Jeffry said. "What was all that about the stockade and the army?"

"He was in a military prison somewhere," Avery said.

"You liked to got in the middle of it yourself," Brother Samuel said.

"It wouldn't make no difference to Evans who he shot. He don't care. He likes to hurt anybody," Jeffry said.

"The water can didn't miss Evans' head but about two inches," Billy Jo said. "God, I'd like to seen him catch it full in the face."

"You think he means it about killing Evans?" Jeffry said.

"He means it," Avery said.

"I served with some tough cons, but that boy can stand up with any of them," Daddy Claxton said.

"Somebody done him a lot of wrong," Brother Samuel said. "When he gets out of the box he ain't going to rest till he does Evans some bad."

"I want to be there to see it," Billy Jo said.

"It's going to be plenty hot in the box unless we get some rain," Daddy Claxton said.

"What's it like in there?" Jeffry said.

"It ain't nice," Toussaint said.

"I heard a man suffocated in there," Daddy Claxton said.

"I couldn't pull no time in the box. I'd go flip closed up in a place that small," Jeffry said.

"You'd pull it if you had to."

"Not in this weather. The sun will be like a blowtorch on them sides."

"Maybe the warden will ship him out to maximum security at Angola," Claxton said.

"Evans will make sure he does his time in the box. He won't turn in a report if he thinks the warden would ship him out," Toussaint said.

"I want to see him get Evans. Benoit's got a knife hid in his bunk. I'd get it from him and give it to this guy if he'd use it," Billy Jo said.

"Benoit ain't got a knife," Jeffry said.

"Yeah, he does. I seen him go in the latrine late at night and work on it with a whetstone."

"Leave LeBlanc alone," Avery said. "If you want Evans cut up, do it yourself."

"He can do it for me."

"You give him a knife and he'll end up being executed."

"That's his worry."

"Don't give him the knife."

"I do what I take a notion to. He says he wants to kill Evans. I ain't making him do it."

"You talk about getting Evans, but you got to have somebody else do it for you," Avery said.

"Get off my back, Broussard. I don't take orders from nobody on this gang."

"I'm telling you, let LeBlanc alone. He's got a ten-year sentence, and he's going to have enough trouble without you getting him into any more."

"You better mind your business."

"If you ain't enough man to do your own cutting, don't put a crazy man up to it," Toussaint said.

"You guys break my heart," Billy Jo said. "That nut ain't going to last a year in here. Why don't we let him get Evans while he can?"

"Get him yourself. You been talking about it ever since I come here," Toussaint said.

"I been waiting for the right time."

"You say you're breaking out next week. Get Benoit's knife and take a piece of Evans with you," Toussaint said.

"I ain't taking a chance on fucking up my break."

"Then don't put a knife in a crazy man's hand if you ain't willing to stick out your own neck."

"What's your part in this?" Billy Jo said. "Are you Jesus Christ or something?"

"I don't like to see you send somebody to the electric chair for what you can't do yourself," Toussaint said.

AVERY BROUSSARD

It was Sunday afternoon, and LeBlanc had been left in detention overnight, even though it was against normal disciplinary procedure. The day was bright and the sun reflected off the tin roofs of the barracks in a white glare, and the air was very still and heavy with the smell of the pines and dust and heat. Gang three had been assigned to police the area outside the barracks. They moved about slowly with their cloth sacks, picking up bits of paper and cigarette butts out of the dirt. Their wash-faded denim shirts were bleached almost white, and the stenciled letters LA. PENAL SYSTEM were black across their backs.

Inside Avery's barracks blankets were stretched across the windows to keep out the sun. The noise of running water came from the showers where the men were washing their clothes. Benoit and Jeffry were sweeping the grained floor with brooms, and three other men were scrubbing it behind them with soap and water. The bunks and footlockers were pushed back against the wall in order that the entire barracks floor could be well cleaned before five o'clock inspection. Avery and Toussaint stood at the window with the blanket pulled aside and looked out into the heat.

"It must be over a hundred degrees in the box," Avery said.

"It's hotter than that," Toussaint said. "They'll have to let him out this afternoon. A man can't take more than two days of detention."

"You guys move out of the way," Benoit said, sweeping the dust in their direction.

They stepped back and let him sweep past.

"Why are you all standing around? We got inspection in a couple more hours," he said.

"We were on cleanup this morning," Avery said.

"I been on cleanup all day. I ain't had time to do my laundry yet."

"That ain't our fault. You're doing Billy Jo's share because you couldn't pay off your card game last night," Toussaint said.

"Who says so?"

"Daddy Claxton."

"Claxton's ass. He don't know nothing."

"Wait a minute. I want to talk to you," Avery said.

"I got work to do."

"Do you have a knife?"

"I ain't got no knife. Who told you that?"

"What will you take for it? I got two dollars."

"I ain't got no knife, and it ain't for sale, anyway."

"I'll give you the two dollars. You can pay Billy Jo what you owe him and sleep the rest of the afternoon," Avery said.

"If I had a knife I wouldn't sell it for no two bucks."

"All right, keep it. And if Billy Jo asks you for it don't give it to him."

"What's he want it for?"

"He's going to give it to LeBlanc to kill Evans."

"Evans needs killing," Benoit said.

"If LeBlanc gets Evans with your knife I'm going to let the warden know where it came from."

"That ain't good talk."

"They'll think you were in on it. That could mean ten to twenty years," Avery said.

"You shoot off your mouth and you won't finish the week."

"Maybe you're right, but you'll spend the rest of your life in the work camp."

"I only got two more years."

"Don't give Billy Jo your knife," Avery said.

"I ain't saying I will or I won't, but it's going to hit the fan when you mouth off to the warden."

"Twenty years. There's a good chance they'll bury you here "

"I ain't going to say nothing about what you told me, because somebody might slip up on you one night and wrap a belt around your neck. But don't threaten me no more, or I'll give you that knife myself, personal."

"It works both ways, Benoit. You give away the knife and you'll rot in here."

Benoit's small eyes glared at Avery.

"You might get to ride the midnight special out of here in a wood box," he said.

He moved off with the broom, sweeping ahead of him.

"I don't think you got any sense," Toussaint said.

"It scared him. He won't give Billy Jo the knife," Avery said.

"Like he says, he might give it to you instead."

They looked out into the heavy stillness of the afternoon. Tufts of grass grew around the edges of the barracks, and the bare dirt grounds, trodden to dust, looked hot and dry. The men from gang three sweated in the sun. Avery watched one man pick up several cigarette butts and turn his back to the other men and conceal them in his pocket.

"Here he comes. They're bringing him in," Jeffry shouted from the other end of the barracks.

The men put down their brooms and mops and crowded to the windows. They pulled aside the blankets and pressed their faces against the wire mesh to see both ends of the grounds.

"Where is he? I don't see him," Daddy Claxton said.

"Around the other way. I seen them from the latrine. He looks like a baked apple."

The key turned in the lock and the door opened. Evans and Rainack brought LeBlanc inside by each arm. His legs wouldn't hold him and broke at the knees when he tried to set his weight down. His denims were smeared with black and red rust. His skin was raw, and his hands and forehead were spotted with dark red places. His heavy beard was covered with flakes of dirt and rust. They dragged him to his bunk and threw him across it. LeBlanc stared blindly at the two guards. His breath came in pants.

"Evans," he said. "I can't see nothing yet, but it's you. I been thinking about it since you put me in there. I know how I'm going to do it. God damn me to hell I'll cut your fucking stomach out."

"You want another two days in the box?" Evans said.

"Let's get out of here. He's stinking up the place," Rainack said.

"He smells like somebody pissed on a radiator, don't he?"

"Let's go. My relief comes on in a few minutes."

Evans took off his sun helmet and wiped his forehead with his sleeve. There was a damp smear across the khaki. He looked down at LeBlanc and put on his helmet.

"Just like piss on a radiator," he said.

"Come on, I want to wash this guy off my hands," Rainack said.

They walked out of the barracks, and locked the barred door behind them.

"Look at his hands. They're burned," Jeffry said. "He must have tried to push the lid open."

"His head's burnt, too," Billy Jo said.

"Who's got some grease?" Toussaint said.

"There's some around the pipes in the latrine."

"Go get it."

"I ain't going to get all dirty," Jeffry said.

"Get some grease, Billy Jo."

"I just got cleaned up."

"I'll get it," Brother Samuel said.

"He must have tried to bust the box open with his head," Daddy Claxton said.

LeBlanc had his hand over his eyes. He took it away and blinked at the ceiling. The pupils were small black dots.

"He can't see nothing," Jeffry said.

"He ain't seen light for two days," Toussaint said.

"I know how I'm going to do it," LeBlanc said. "I figured it out. I kept seeing his face like it was painted inside the lid. I thought of all the ways I could do it to him, and then I decided."

"How you going to do it?" Jeffry said.

"I got it figured."

"Get him undressed," Toussaint said.

Avery took off his shirt and trousers, and threw them on the floor. LeBlanc's underclothes were yellow and foul.

"He'll stink up everything in here," Benoit said.

"Shut up," Avery said.

"Here's the grease. There ain't much," Brother Samuel said.

"Put it on his hands and face."

Brother Samuel spread it thinly over the blistered swellings.

"What are you doing?" LeBlanc said.

"It will take the heat out of them burns," Samuel said.

"How you going to get Evans?" Jeffry said.

"You'll find out when the time comes."

"Let's strip him down and cover him up," Toussaint said.

They finished undressing him and covered him with the sheet. His hands lay on top of the sheet, taut like claws and black from the grease.

"We'll bring you some supper from the dining hall tonight," Brother Samuel said. "When you got some rest and something to eat we'll get you a shower. You can go on sick call tomorrow."

"I ain't going on sick call."

"They'll give you some medicine for them burns," Daddy Claxton said. "They might even keep you in the infirmary a couple of days. You ain't got to go out on the line."

"I don't want no sick call."

"You ain't in no shape to work tomorrow," Toussaint said.

"I'll be out for morning roll call."

The men went back to their jobs and let LeBlanc sleep. The floor was swept and wetted down and mopped. The bunks and footlockers were put back in place and squared away. The blankets were taken down from the windows and folded over the bunks. Someone in the shower was drying his laundry by slapping it against the wall. The brooms and buckets were put away, and the men sat on their bunks and smoked, waiting for five o'clock inspection. Avery cleaned out his footlocker and set things in order while Toussaint stood at the window.

"That man ain't going to finish his time," Toussaint said.

"Probably not," Avery said.

"How'd you get mixed up with him?"

"He used to run whiskey down the river. We were caught together after he shot at the state police."

Toussaint leaned on his elbows and looked out the window at the trees.

"This weather's got to break. It's too hot," he said.

"Brother Samuel says it's a sign."

"He's right about it ain't being natural. I never seen it stay hot so long without rain."

Avery closed his footlocker and tucked in the corners of his blanket around the bunk.

"I heard thunder last night," he said.

"I been hearing it for weeks. It's got to rain soon."

Monday morning the sky was black with clouds when the men lined up for roll call. The air was chill and moist, and lightning split the sky. The dark pines swayed in the wind, and a few drops of water made wet dimples in the dust. A great thunderhead was moving in from the Gulf. The wind blew clouds of dust across the grounds, and a straw hat was whipped from someone's head and swept end over end until it hit the wire fence and could go no farther. The captain and the guards had their slickers on. Some of the men asked to go back to the barracks and get their coats. A clap of thunder sounded directly overhead.

At ten o'clock the sky became storm-black and the rains came down. The men were working in the ditch, and the water drummed on the roofs of the trucks and ran off onto the ground and flowed into the dry and cracked earth. The men couldn't see farther away than the trees because of the steel-gray sheet of water. The ground turned to mud, and large pools formed and drained off into the irrigation ditch. The clay embankment washed away and the men worked in water up to their knees. They tripped over one another and lost their tools, groped for them, and tried to climb out of the ditch, sliding back down into the water again. They threw shovel loads of soggy clay up on the sides to rebuild the embankment, but the water washed it back in the ditch. Three pumps were brought in and set on the bottom, and the rubber hoses drained the water over the top of the embankment, but the waterline continued to rise. Only one handle of the wheelbarrow could be seen. The rain drove coldly into the men's skin like needles. The water was red and rising higher. The pumps clogged with clay and ceased to work. Half the men had lost their tools and were trying to pull themselves out of the ditch by the roots protruding from the sides. The guards couldn't tell which men belonged to which gang in the confusion. Evans stood on the embankment with the rain streaming off his helmet and slicker, shouting down at gang five. Farther down the ditch a wall of dirt caved in from one of the sides and the water poured through the opening.

The work captain walked up and down the line blowing his whistle for the guards to reassemble their gangs and to get them into the trucks. The men who still had their tools threw them up out of the ditch and started pushing one another up after them.

"Let's go, let's go. Everybody in the trucks," Evans said.

"I can't get up," Benoit said through the rain.

"You ain't in my gang. Get out of the way," Evans said.

"Where's gang three?"

"How do I know? Get out of the way and let my men up."

"Quit pushing," someone said.

"You dumb bastard. You knocked my hat in the water," another said.

"Gang five up here," Evans shouted.

"Help Claxton up."

"Grab hold of a root, Daddy."

Avery, Toussaint, and Brother Samuel pushed him up by his legs. His hands reached the top of the ditch, and then he fell backwards into the water and went under. He sat up with just his head and shoulders showing. His gray hair was matted with clay.

"Try it again."

"Gang five over here," Evans shouted. "Get the hell out of here, Benoit."

"I can't find my gang."

"Where's Rainack?" another inmate said.

"Down at the other end," Evans said.

"Stop shoving, for Christ's sake."

"Let me get on your shoulders."

"Cut it out."

They pushed Daddy Claxton up the side until he could get his stomach over and make the rest of it with his elbows and knees.

"Who's next?" Toussaint said.

"I'll go," Benoit said.

"Where's Jeffry and Billy Jo?"

"They went fishing," LeBlanc said.

"Benoit, I told you to find your own gang," Evans said, the rain beating against his cork sun helmet.

"I don't know where it is."

"Let Brother Samuel go," Toussaint said.

Toussaint made a foot-step with his hands and they boosted Samuel up the embankment. He crawled over the top.

"How about me?" Benoit said.

"Wait your turn," LeBlanc said.

"I can't find nobody. I'll go to detention if I ain't back with my gang."

"That'll break my heart."

"Come on, Avery."

LeBlanc and Toussaint shoved him to the top. LeBlanc followed, and Avery and Brother Samuel lay on their stomachs over the side to help Toussaint up. He dug one foot in the clay and leaped upward, grabbing some roots. He hung there and kicked his feet into the embankment. They caught him by the wrists and pulled him up. Benoit was left in the ditch.

"How about me?" he said.

"Go take a bath," Evans said.

"Be a good guy. I'll get time in detention."

Evans looked around him. His eyes snapped. He forgot about Benoit.

"Where's Billy Jo and Jeffry?" he said.

"They gone fishing," LeBlanc said.

"Shut your mouth. Who's seen Billy Jo and Jeffry?"

No one answered.

"God damn you, where are they?"

"I ain't seen them since it started raining," Daddy Claxton said.

"They was down in the ditch. You ain't blind. What happened to them?" Evans said.

"They could have got mixed up in another gang," Daddy Claxton said.

"Somebody here saw them. I want to know where they are."

"Go talk to a wall," LeBlanc said.

"I'm going to send you back to the box for that."

"You fat swine."

Evans struck him across the mouth with the heel of his hand.

"I'll use my pistol barrel the next time you say it," he said.

"It don't matter what you do. You ain't got long."

There was a smear of red across LeBlanc's lips. He wiped his mouth on his sleeve and spit.

"You got dirty hands," he said.

Evans hit him again, this time across the nose.

"Get in the truck, you sonofabitch. Get moving, every one of you."

"I know how I'm going to do it. It's going to hurt," LeBlanc said.

"Move! I'll get straight with you later."

They walked across the clearing through the mud and the rain and climbed in the back of the truck. LeBlanc got in and looked at Evans.

"You seen a hog cut before?" he said.

"You'll pay through the ass for this," Evans said, and slammed the doors shut and snapped the padlock.

There was no light inside the truck. The men sat on the benches in their wet clothes and listened to the rain beat on the roof. They could hear Evans speaking to the captain outside.

"I'm missing two," Evans said.

"Where are they?"

"I don't know. Maybe they got in with another gang."

"How long have they been gone?"

"I didn't miss them till I ordered the others out of the ditch."

"Can't you keep watch over seven men without losing somebody?"

"There was a dozen guys down there that didn't belong to my gang. I couldn't tell which ones was mine."

"We'll check the other gangs. You'd better hope we find them," the captain said.

"Yes, sir."

"Tell Rainack to phone in to the warden."

"We ain't sure they broke out yet."

"The warden wants a report when anybody's missing."

"Yes, sir."

"Check this end of the line and I'll start on the other."

Daddy Claxton had his ear pressed to the back door of the truck. His mouth was open in a half grin. The water dripped off his clothes onto the floor.

"By God, they done it. They broke out," he said.

"Did anybody see them?" Avery said.

"They was working next to me," Brother Samuel said. "When the sides started caving in they dropped their tools and took off down the ditch."

"Did you hear the captain chewing out Evans?" Daddy Claxton said. "He'll get busted if they don't catch them."

"We ain't sure they got away yet," LeBlanc said.

"They wasn't running down the ditch for no exercise," Toussaint said.

"They could have climbed up the other side when all that dirt fell in," Daddy Claxton said. "The hacks was worrying about the ditch flooding and them pumps going out."

"The dogs won't be able to follow them in the rain. They have a good chance," Avery said.

"Billy Jo said they had a car hid out somewhere," Daddy Claxton said.

"They'll be lucky if the police ain't sitting in it waiting for them," Toussaint said.

"They talked it around plenty," Brother Samuel said.

"Them boys is long gone. I wish I was with them," Daddy Claxton said.

"Why didn't you go?" LeBlanc said.

"I asked them. They told me I was too old."

"They couldn't have stopped you from going."

"I reckon they're right. I been in prison too many years to have any business on the outside."

"I ain't sure I want to be with them," Brother Samuel said.

"How come?" Claxton said.

"Jeffry's carrying a spirit. I seen the sign this morning. There was a big wart on his finger."

"You get warts from picking up frogs," Claxton said.

"Not this kind," Brother Samuel said.

"Them boys is gone. There ain't no wart going to hold them back."

"I told him the spirit might come back after I healed him."

"They'll be out of the state by tomorrow morning," Daddy Claxton said.

"It was a devil wart. It takes a special kind of conjuring to get rid of it."

"How long they going to keep us here?" LeBlanc said.

"We ain't got to work as long as the hacks is out on search," Claxton said.

Evans unlocked the back doors and threw them open. The wind blew the rain inside the truck. He and the captain climbed inside and left the doors open. Their boots and the bottoms of their trousers were covered with mud. A thin stream of water ran off the brim of the captain's campaign hat. Their slickers were shiny from the rain.

"Somebody in here saw them get away," the captain said. "I want you to tell me where they went."

The rain blew in the truck and formed small pools on the floor.

"Speak up. You ain't deaf and dumb," Evans said.

"What about you?" the captain said to Daddy Claxton.

"I was working all the time. I didn't see nothing."

The captain asked each one of them.

"I didn't know they were gone until we came out of the ditch," Avery said.

"There was too many people around," Toussaint said.

"I heard they went fishing," LeBlanc said.

"I didn't see nothing," Brother Samuel said.

"Everybody outside," Evans said.

"Where we going?" Daddy Claxton said.

"You're going to stand in the rain till we find them or somebody tells us where they are."

"The rest of the trucks is going to the barracks," Claxton said.

"This one ain't," Evans said.

They climbed out and stood looking at Evans and the captain. The rain ran off their straw hats down inside their clothing. The other trucks drove past them through the mud. Several guards were moving into the trees on the other side of the clearing. They carried rifles and shotguns. One of them was examining the area where the ditch wall caved in, an eroded pile of clay that sloped down to the bottom of the canal. He bent over and looked at the ground, the rain breaking across the back of his slicker.

"Here's where they come out," he yelled.

The other guards came back and looked at the deep boot marks in the clay.

"This is it, captain. They headed into the woods."

"Call the warden and tell him to get the state police moving in from the other side," he answered.

"What about us?" Claxton said.

"You'll stay here till we catch them," Evans said.

"It's getting cold. Let us get in the truck," Daddy Claxton said.

"I'm going to send Rainack over here to watch you. Don't move till we get back."

"We didn't help them. How come we can't go to the barracks with the rest," the old man said.

"Because you all think you're so goddamn smart playing closemouth," Evans said.

"Go get Rainack," the captain said.

Evans walked down the line and came back.

"He's coming. I told him to get a couple of rifles out of the pickup," he said.

"I'm an old man. I can't stay out in the wet like this," Daddy Claxton said.

Rainack came through the rain with two rifles that were slung upside down over his shoulder to keep the barrels dry. They were '03 Springfields that had been bought from the government. He swung them off his shoulder by the slings and handed them to the captain. He reached under his slicker and took a handful of shells out of his pocket.

"This is all there is," he said, giving the cartridges to the captain. "The rest is corroded."

The captain handed one rifle to Evans, and they opened the bolts and loaded. The heavily grained military stocks were rubbed with linseed oil. There was a thin spray of rust on the butt plate of Evans' rifle.

They went around the farther end of the ditch to the far side of the clearing and moved into the trees with the other guards. The captain spread his men out through the woods. Rainack got in the back of the truck and sat on one of the benches. He took out his tobacco and rolled a cigarette. He struck a match on the wall of the truck, covered the flame with his hands, and exhaled the smoke into the damp air.

"They're gone now," Claxton said. "Let us get out of the rain."

Rainack smoked in silence.

"Come on, nobody will know the difference. We ain't going to say nothing. I'm soaked plumb through."

"You heard the orders. You got to stay there till they get back."

"They ain't going to know," Claxton said.

"I got my orders. If it was just me I wouldn't mind," Rainack said.

Claxton stepped towards the truck.

"Stay where you are."

"I had pneumonia once. I ain't strong enough to pull through it again."

"I can't do nothing for you."

"Don't expect a bastard to act like a decent man," LeBlanc said.

"What did you say?"

"I said you're a bastard."

"The box didn't seem to teach you nothing," Rainack said.

"Let the old man out of the rain," LeBlanc said.

"I'm going to tell Evans about this when you get back."

"Come out here and do something yourself."

"You should be in a crazy house," Rainack said.

"Why didn't you go with the others? You're going to miss the shooting."

"I don't want to hear no more from you."

"You can hit a man through the eye at two hundred yards with a Springfield," LeBlanc said.

"Shut up."

Daddy Claxton began to cough.

"Let him get in the truck," Toussaint said.

"I got my orders."

"Don't ask him nothing. He'd let the old man spit blood before he'd do anything," LeBlanc said.

"Take my hat," Avery said.

"I'm obliged to you," Claxton said.

He put it low on his head. The wet locks of gray hair stuck to his forehead. He began coughing again. The rain poured out of the sky in steady swirling sheets. The irrigation ditch was almost filled. The embankment was washed smooth with the level of the ground. Roots and pieces of broken tree branches floated on the water. A moccasin slithered across the surface. The red water rippled back in a V behind his black head. He tried to work himself up on the bank and the current sucked him out again. He reared his head up as though climbing into the air and struck at the bank and tried to coil his body on the clay. He slipped out and was caught by a floating branch and pulled under.

The rain stung Avery's eyes. His fingers were pinched and white from the water. He felt the cold beginning to numb his feet. Brother Samuel looked straight ahead at the trees. His oversized clothes hung wetly from his body. Toussaint, Claxton, and LeBlanc stood with their heads slightly bowed, the rain sluicing off their hats. They looked blankly at the rivulets running through the mud. Brother Samuel stared at the place in the woods where the guards had entered.

"They ain't coming back," he said.

"They'll be in Mississippi come morning," Claxton said.

"He was carrying a spirit. I seen the sign. I shouldn't have used my powers to heal him."

"Don't worry about them boys. They're young. They can take care of theirself," Daddy Claxton said. "It's us old ones got to stand out in the rain and die from pneumonia."

"I thought I was doing right and I done wrong," Brother Samuel said.

"You didn't do nothing wrong," Toussaint said. "If they get shot it's their bad luck. You didn't have nothing to do with it."

"I went back on my promise to the Lord and had dealings with the Black Man. I should have knowed better. Billy Jo and Jeffry is going to pay for what I done."

He took the wood disk and its leather cord from around his neck and held it in his hand. The letters on it were cut deeply in the wood. He wound the cord tightly around the disk.

"What are you doing?" LeBlanc said.

"I'm giving up my powers." He threw the disk across the clearing into the canal. It splashed into the water and floated along in the current. He took the snake fang and turtle foot from his pocket. He jabbed the fang into the shriveled foot and threw it against the opposite bank. It hit and rolled into the ditch.

"You mean you ain't got no more powers now?" Daddy Claxton said.

"I done renounced," Brother Samuel said.

"Just throwing them things away and you can't heal no more?"

"I done it too late. Jeffry and Billy Jo is going to stand before judgment today."

"They can take care of theirself. They ain't old and wore down," Claxton said.

"They'll go before the Lord with the evil spirit clinging to their souls, and the Lord will look down at them and turn His face away. He'll point His finger at them and lightning will strike from His hand and the spirit will drag them down to the shade."

An hour passed. The rain lessened and then began again in a fresh downpour. The trees shook in the wind. Bits of dead leaves lay in the pools. The clearing was rutted with deep tire tracks where the trucks had passed. The warden, the parish sheriff and two deputies had driven out to the line and had become stuck. The car sunk down to its hubs and the tires spun and whined deeper. The smell of burnt rubber filled the air. The deputies got out and pushed and the mud splattered their uniforms, but the car didn't move. Gang five was ordered to push them out. Toussaint got the jack from the trunk and jacked up the rear end. They put leaves and brush under the wheels and let the jack down. They lifted up the rear bumper, and while the warden accelerated they bounced the car out of the ruts. Then Rainack took them back over to the truck, and he got inside and they remained in the rain.

It was two o'clock and Avery's legs felt weak under him. He had his eyes closed and his face tingled from the steady beating of the rain. He shifted his weight from one foot to the other. He thought of when he used to work on the exploration crew on the Gulf. It seemed long ago. He remembered the hot, clear days on the drill barge and the easy roll of the swell, the few whitecaps in the distance, the long flat blue-green of the water and the way the trout jumped in the morning, their sides silver and speckled with red in the sun, and at night when they laid the trotline out. The next day it would be heavy with catfish, and there was the good feel of rope in his hands when he moored the jug boat to the rusty bulkhead of the barge, and the pitch of the deck when the weather got rough and they had to put on life jackets because someone was always getting washed overboard when they went out to pick up the recording cable, and the cans of explosives that were screwed end to end and were run down through the drill pipe below the floor of the Gulf, and the battery and detonator that the shooter used to set off the charge and the way the iron barge would slam and jar when the explosion went off, and the acrid yellow smoke that floated back off the water and would give you a headache if you breathed it, and going back inland on the launch after the hitch was over with everybody getting drunk and talking about going to whorehouses and staying there until the next hitch began, and the island off the coast with the pavilion among the cypress where they served chilled wine and the beer came in beaded mugs.

He remembered his last year in high school when his father was alive and he had gone out with a girl named Suzanne, and they were always together and they talked about getting married. Her skin was very white and her hair hung to her shoulders like black silk, and at eighteen she looked like a mature woman. There was that Saturday they went fishing together in his boat and he rowed down the bayou with the oaks and cypress and willows on each side, and she sat forward in the bow and her eyes were dark and happy and she lifted the hair from her neck to let the breeze blow on her, and he put into the bank and got out and dragged the boat through the shallows, and he didn't have to ask or even say anything because she already understood. And for the rest of the spring it was the same. On Saturday morning he would meet her at the levee and they would row to the same place on the green bank among the azaleas and jasmine, and later they would drink wine and fish and he would row her back in the afternoon.

They graduated from high school and he began to drink more, and there was the weekend they drove to Biloxi in the sports car her father had given her for graduation, and Avery left her in the hotel room to get a package of cigarettes and came back three hours later blind drunk, and she lay in bed with her eyes wet and her hair spread out on the pillow and she turned away from him when he tried to touch her; he left the room and bought a bottle at the bar and went down on the beach and passed out. He woke in the morning with a bad hangover and his clothes and hair were full of sand, and the sun was hot and the white façade of the hotel gleamed in the light. He went to the room, but there was nothing to say or do because when he told her he was sorry it sounded meaningless. She was very hurt and she tried not to show it, and that made him all the more angry and ashamed. So they drove back home not talking, and things were never the same after that. The summer became fall, and she went to school at the state university and he took a job on a shooting crew. She wrote him a few letters during the time she was at L.S.U., and then she went to Spain to study painting and he never heard from her again. It had ended undramatic and unpoetic and unanything, and he wondered why he should think of her now. He had been in prison only for a short time, but everything that had existed before seemed to belong to another world and she with it. The Saturdays that they had together and the things they did were no longer real, nothing was real except the wet clothes and the rain and the mud and the cold in his feet and Daddy Claxton's coughing and Rainack sitting in the back of the truck in his uniform and slicker with the holster strapped around his waist and the .45 revolver that meant he could crack the barrel across your head if you tried to get out of the rain, and two men somewhere off in the woods running for freedom with an armed search party behind them.

"I got to take a leak," Claxton said.

"Go ahead," Rainack said.

"Can't I go off in the brush?"

"I got to keep watch on all of you."

Claxton looked embarrassed.

"I ain't going to run off nowheres," he said.

"Act your age. We ain't going to look at you," Rainack said.

"It'll just take a minute. I'll be right back."

Finally he turned to the side and urinated on the ground. He buttoned his trousers and stared at the irrigation ditch, not wanting to look at anyone.

"How's it feel to be a bastard?" LeBlanc said.

"You ain't getting a rise out of me," Rainack said. "Your time is coming when Evans gets back."

"If Evans owes you any money you better get it from him while you can," LeBlanc said.

"You're talk, LeBlanc. Guys like you shoot off their mouth. They never do nothing."

"Wait around a while."

"Evans will be alive to piss on your grave," Rainack said.

"Maybe you ought to pay up your debts too."

"I should have killed you out in the ditch and saved everybody a lot of trouble."

The sound of rifle shots came from the woods. They were distant and faintly audible through the rain. There was a single report followed by two more, and then someone was firing in rapid succession. A minute passed and it was quiet except for the even patter of the rain. Rainack got out of the truck with his hand on his revolver and looked at the trees. The front of his khaki clothes, where his slicker was open, was drenched through. Gang five waited and listened. There was a final *whaaap* of a rifle and almost immediately after a burst from a shotgun and then silence again. A few minutes went by and the woods remained quiet.

"That's the end of your pals," Rainack said. He got back in the truck and shut one door to keep out the rain. He wiped the water off his face with his handkerchief.

"Them shots was too close," Daddy Claxton said.

"They've been gone three or four hours," Avery said. "They should have been in the next parish."

"Maybe Evans was having rifle practice on a friend," LeBlanc said.

"I know it ain't them. They're young. They could make ten or twelve miles in the time they been gone," Claxton said. "Billy Jo said they had a car waiting for them. They might be over the state line by now."

"They're standing before the Lord," Brother Samuel said. "They crossed the big river, and the Lord's sitting in judgment. Tonight their souls will be flying through the dark with the evil spirit dragging them by a chain."

"I ain't going to believe it. They're young. An old man couldn't make it, but the young ones got a chance."

"I seen the sign this morning. I knowed it wouldn't do no good to warn them."

Daddy Claxton coughed violently. His breath rasped in his throat. He gagged on his shirt sleeve.

"There ain't no reason to keep us out here now. Let the old guy get inside," LeBlanc said.

"Talk to Evans," Rainack said.

"You got no call to keep us in the rain," LeBlanc said.

"It's going to be a hell of a lot worse for you when Evans gets back."

"Billy Jo and Jeffry is dead," Brother Samuel said.

"I got my orders."

"Try using your mind. You're going to kill the old man," Avery said.

"You keep quiet."

"Why don't you throw him in the irrigation ditch? You'll be sure he catches pneumonia that way," Avery said.

"Evans is going to hear about this."

"There's some deep places in there. He probably can't swim," he said.

"Keep it up. You'll have your name on detention list with LeBlanc," Rainack said.

"Or you could take him into the swamp and find some quicksand," Avery said. "It's not much different than dying from pneumonia. His lungs would fill up with sand instead of water."

"You're pushing it. I ain't taking much more."

"You ain't going to do nothing," LeBlanc said.

"Keep running off at the mouth and see."

"I knowed people like you in the army. You won't drop your britches to take a crap till you get an order. We're five to one against you. Lean on one of us and you'll have to use that pistol. Then there will be an inquiry and the warden will bust you out of a job to save hisself."

"It's your ass when Evans gets back."

The warden's car came back down the line and went past the men. It was splattered with mud. The tires spun in the mire, and the warden steered around the place where he had stuck before. The sheriff sat in the front seat and the two deputies were in back. The end of a rifle barrel showed behind the glass in the back seat. An enclosed truck followed them, the back covered with canvas like an army truck. The guards sat inside, crowded towards the front because the sheet of canvas that closed the rear had been torn loose from its fastenings by the wind and flapped over the top. The captain's pickup came through the ruts in second gear and hit the soft place where the warden had become stuck. His wheels whined in the mud and he shifted into reverse and fed it gas and shifted into second again, rocking it, until he got traction and spun out of the soft spot to harder ground. Evans sat next to him. They stopped the truck and got out and went around to the back. Their rifles were propped against the seat by the gear-shift stick.

"Bring them over here," Evans said.

Rainack snuffed out his cigarette and buttoned his slicker. He got down in the rain.

"You heard him. Start moving," he said.

Avery and the others walked unsteadily across the clearing to the pickup. His legs felt loose and uncoordinated from having stood in one position too long. His feet hurt from the cold when he walked. Daddy Claxton wavered from side to side. He coughed and spit up phlegm. There was a tarpaulin laid across the bed of the pickup. Pools of water collected in it and ran down through the folds and creases. There was a dark smear on top of it. Evans had his hand on one end of the canvas to raise it up.

"I want you to know what happens to guys that think they can bust out of here," he said. "Look at them and tell everybody back at camp what you saw."

He lifted the tarpaulin and exposed the two bodies. They lay on their backs and their faces looked up blank and empty and the rain fell in their eyes. Billy Jo had been shot twice through the chest and a third bullet had cut through the left eye and come out at the temple. Pieces of cloth were embedded in the chest wounds. The blood had congealed and his shirt stuck stiffly to him. He was barefooted and his pants were torn at the knees and stained with mud and grass. His remaining eye was rolled back in his head. The wound where the bullet had emerged from the temple was very large and fragments of bone protruded from the matted skin and hair. Jeffry wore only one shoe. The ankle of his bare foot was broken. It swelled out in a big, discolored lump like a fist and the foot was twisted sideways. His shirt was torn in strips like rags. He had been hit with a shotgun at a close distance and the pellets covered his trunk and part of one thigh. An artery had been severed in his neck and there was a large area of red around the top of his chest like a child's bib.

"Where were they?" Rainack said.

"They fell in a clay pit. They was just climbing out when we saw them. Billy Jo started running for the trees, and me and Jess let go. We missed Jeffry but Abshire got him with the shotgun. It blew him right through a thicket."

"Who got Billy Jo in the head?" Rainack said.

"It's hard to tell. We was shooting at the same time. Part of him is still sticking to a tree out there."

"Cover them up and let's go back," the captain said.

Evans replaced the tarpaulin. The water ran down from the creases in the canvas onto his boots.

"You goddamn swine," LeBlanc said. His skin was white and the burn on his forehead turned dark as blood.

"Shut that man up," the captain said.

"I been having trouble with him ever since you left," Rainack said. "I started to bust him a couple of times."

"Can't you keep control of your men, Evans?" the captain said.

"I'd like to take him off in the woods and not come back with him," Evans said.

"Sonsofbitches."

"Do you want to keep shut, or you want something across the mouth? Evans said.

Spittle drooled over LeBlanc's chin. He sprang on Evans and grabbed him by the throat. The guard fell backwards in the mud with LeBlanc on top of him. Evans' mouth opened in a dry gasp and his eyes protruded from his head. LeBlanc's hands tightened into the soft pink skin. Evans fumbled weakly at his holster for his pistol.

Rainack and the captain hit at LeBlanc's head with their revolvers, and amid the hard bone-splitting knocks he shouted into Evans' face, the saliva running from his mouth: "You wouldn't let me wait I had it planned and you wouldn't give me time goddamn you to hell if you'd only waited I could have done it right—" and then Rainack whipped his pistol barrel across LeBlanc's temple, and he fell sideways into a pool of water.

J.P. WINFIELD

The show had returned to town two months after it began its tour of the southern portion of the state. It was night, and a large flatbed truck, painted firecracker-red, followed a black sedan over a railroad crossing down a dirt road into the Negro section of town. At first there were board shacks with dirt yards and outbuildings on each side of the road, then farther on, the road became a blacktop lined with taverns, pool halls, shoeshine parlors, and open-air markets which stank of refuse and dead fish and rotted vegetables. The doors to the taverns and pool halls were opened, and the night was filled with the noise of loud jukeboxes and drunken laughter. Negroes loitered along the sidewalk under the neon bar signs and called back and forth to each other across the street. A hillbilly band stood on the open bed of the truck with their instruments. A boxlike piano was bolted to the bed with its back against the cab. Several wood casks were stacked along the side of the piano. The firecracker-red truck was painted with political slogans in big white letters:

LET A HUNGRY MAN KILL A RABBIT
BRING HONEST GOVERNMENT BACK TO LOUISIANA
LET THE GOOD CHURCH PEOPLE HAVE THEIR BINGO GAMES
VOTE FOR JIM LATHROP, A SLAVE TO NO MAN AND A SERVANT TO ALL
THE COMMON MAN IS KING

The sedan and the truck stopped by the taverns. The Negroes on the sidewalk looked at them cautiously. More Negroes appeared in the doorways, and small children ran down the road from the shacks to follow the truck.

"What you want down here?" a Negro said from the sidewalk.

Jim Lathrop got out of the sedan. He was dressed in a light tan suit with a blue sports shirt buttoned at the throat without a tie. He looked at the Negro.

"This is campaign night. Don't you know this is election time?" he said.

"You ain't going to get no votes down here," a woman said.

"How do you know that, sister?" Lathrop said. "How you know you don't want to vote for me if you haven't heard what I got to say? How do you know I'm not the only man running for office that can do something for you? Tell me that, sister, and I'll go on home. Of course you can't tell me, because you haven't listened to what I got to say. And that's why I'm here tonight. You folks don't have one friend in Baton Rouge and you don't have many friends in Washington, and I'm down here to tell you how you can get one; I'm here to tell you that there's one man in this state who is a slave to nobody and a servant to all, and I mean all, no matter if he's colored or white."

"You ain't going to do nothing for us," a Negro man said.

"You're wrong, brother. If I get in office you'll get an even shake. I promise you that. Anyone who ever knew Jim Lathrop will tell you that he takes care of his friends. We got a band tonight and we got plenty to drink. I want you folks to enjoy yourselves while you listen to what I tell you. There's J.P. Winfield on the truck, star of the Louisiana Jubilee and the Nashville Barn Dance. He's going to sing you some songs. There's enough to drink for everybody, so line up at the back of the truck and we'll get things started."

No one moved off the sidewalk. Lathrop watched them a minute and went to the truck and took a carton of paper cups from behind the piano and pulled one from the box.

"Bring a cask over here, J.P.," he said.

J.P. rolled a cask on its bottom to the edge of the truck bed. Lathrop turned on the wood spigot and filled the cup with wine. He drank it empty and crushed the cup in his hand and threw it on the concrete. He filled another and walked to the sidewalk with it.

"I never knew good colored folks to turn down a cup of wine," he said. "I wouldn't have bought all them kegs if I'd thought I was going to have to drink it by myself. What about you, brother? You drinking tonight?"

"I drinks any time, morning, noon, or night," the Negro said.

"See what you can do with this." Lathrop handed him the cup.

The Negro drank it off, the wine running down his chin and throat into his shirt. He wiped his mouth and laughed loudly.

"I'm one up on you," he said.

"How's that?"

"I never registered. I can't vote."

Everyone laughed.

"He's got you there, boss," someone said.

"Ain't none of us registered. Can't pass the reading test."

"Better go on the other side of town and drink your wine. I told you there ain't no votes down here."

They were all laughing now.

"I didn't come down here to make you vote for me," Lathrop said. "I just want you to listen to me for a little while. If you want to vote and you ain't registered, by God I'll take you down to the polls and register you myself. Now go on and line up for some wine. It don't matter if you vote for me or not; I came here to have some drinking and some singing, and by God we're going to have it. Sing us a song, J.P., while these people get something to drink."

The band started playing and J.P. sang the song he had written for Lathrop's campaign. The Negroes gathered around the back of the truck, and Lathrop left the spigot of the cask open while they passed their cups under it. The cask was soon empty and another was brought up. J.P. sang three more songs, and April and Seth sang one each. The crowd around the truck became larger. Several Negroes were dancing in the street. Their faces were shiny and purple under the neon. The air was heavy with the smell of sweat and cheap wine. The empty casks were thrown into the gutter, and small children tried to stand on their sides and roll them down the street. The people at the back of the truck began to push each other to get their cups under the spigot. Lathrop smashed in the top of the keg and set it in the street. The Negroes dipped their cups through the top into the wine. The keg was drained in a few minutes. A man tried to pick it up and drink the residue from the bottom. He lifted it with both hands and put his mouth to the rim and tilted it upward. The wine poured out over his face and clothes. He laughed and threw the empty keg into the air. It crashed and splintered apart in the middle of the street.

"Police going to be down here."

"Hush up, woman. Police don't bother me."

"You're going to spend the night in the jailhouse, nigger."

"Hush yo' mouth."

"How's everybody feeling?" Lathrop said.

"Bring out some more of them barrels."

"Right here," Seth said.

He put the keg on the edge of the truck and broke the spigot off with his foot. The wine ran in a stream into the street. The Negroes crowded around with their cups. The wine splashed over their clothes and bodies.

"God, what a smell," April said. "How long do we have to stay here?"

"Till Lathrop makes his speech and gets tired of playing Abraham Lincoln," J.P. said.

"The smell is enough to make you sick," she said.

"Drink some wine with your brothers," Seth said.

"You're cute," she said.

"April don't like the smell. Tell them to go home and take a bath," Seth said.

"You're very cute tonight," she said.

Lathrop called up to the truck from the street, where he was handing out election leaflets that instructed the reader how to use the voting machine and what lever to push for Lathrop as senator.

"Let's have some music up there," he said.

J.P. sang an old Jimmie Rodgers song.

> *I'm going where the water drinks like cherry wine*
> *Lord Lord*
> *I'm going where the water drinks like cherry wine*
> *Because this Louisiana water tastes like turpentine.*

Seth rolled another keg to the edge of the truck bed. Someone grabbed it by the top and pulled it over into the street. A stave broke loose and the wine poured into the gutter. A fight broke out between the man who had tipped over the cask and another man who had been waiting to fill his cup.

Lathrop got up on the truck and motioned for the band to stop playing.

"Here it comes," April whispered. "God, I hope he makes it quick. I'm getting sick."

"Now that I met most of you folks I'd like to tell you what I got planned when I get in office," he began. His tan suit was spotted with wine stains. "You see that dirt road we came up on? When I'm elected we're not going to have roads like that. No sir, we're going to have the best streets and highways anywhere. You're not going to have to sit on your front porch and eat all that dust everytime a car comes down your street. We're going to get electric lights in the houses and plumbing and running water, and there's going to be good schools you can send your children to."

"Lawd-God," Seth whispered.

"They ought to bring a fire hose out here and wash them down," April said. "None of them must have bathed since the Civil War."

"Don't you like nigger politics?" Seth said.

"And we're going to have unemployment insurance and social security and charity hospitals for the poor," Lathrop said. "We're going to run that bunch of politicians out of the capitol and put the common man back in his rightful place. We're going to get rid of the fat boys that are draining the state dry and giving nothing to the people; we're going to raise the wages and the living standard, and the only way to do it is to get this big city trash out of office and let a man of the people serve and represent the people."

"This is the last time I'm going around kissing niggers for Lathrop," April said.

"You thinking about quitting?" Seth said. "Doc Elgin ought to give you a job. They say there's good money in pushing happy powder in the grade schools."

April turned to him and formed two words with her lips.

"And there's a lot more benefits coming to the state," Lathrop said. "For years you been paying taxes to the rich, and the only thing you got for it is hard work and poverty. I've seen colored people working in the fields twelve hours a day and not getting enough money to buy bread and greens with; I've seen them sweating on highway gangs and railroad and construction jobs and getting nothing but sunstroke for their pay. Well, that's going to change. Every man in this state is going to have an even chance, and there's not going to be any rich men walking over the poor—"

His speech went on for another half hour. A police car came down the blacktop and cruised slowly by the crowd. An officer in the front seat waved to Lathrop. Lathrop nodded in return, and the car disappeared down the road. The last cask of wine was emptied, the band put away their instruments, and Lathrop said good night to the crowd. He went among the Negroes and shook a few hands before he got in his sedan and drove back to the other side of town, where he was to make a late speech at a segregationist rally held in a vacant lot under a big tent. The truck followed the sedan past the board shacks and across the railroad crossing.

At the hotel J.P. stopped off in the bar and had a whiskey and water. He had another. He got some change from the bartender and went to use the telephone in the booth. He phoned Doc Elgin at his home.

"You didn't come around today," J.P. said.

"I've been busy. I asked you not to phone me except at my office," Elgin said.

"I need some candy."

"Everybody needs candy."

"I'm almost out. I'll need some by tomorrow."

"I have a lot of people to see," Elgin said.

"Listen, I need it in the morning."

"Where will you be?"

"At the hotel."

"You owe me for the last two deliveries."

"I'll make it good tomorrow."

"I advise you to," Elgin said, and hung up.

J.P. had a glass of beer and a ham sandwich at the bar and went up to April's room. Through the door he could hear the shower water running. He went in without knocking and sat in a chair by the window and waited for her. He lifted the shade and looked down into the street. The lamp on the corner burned in the dark. A Negro fruit vender pushed a wood cart along the worn brick paving in the street. The night was quiet except for the creak of the wooden wheels over the brick and the slow shuffle of the Negro.

April came out of the bath in her robe. She was drying the back of her neck with a towel. Her hair was damp from the shower. She looked at him without speaking and took a cigarette from a nickel-plated case on the table and lighted it.

"What did you want to tell me?" he said. She had told him earlier on the truck to come to her room after they came back from the Negro section of town.

She threw the towel on the bed and sat in the stuffed chair across from him. She smoked the cigarette and looked at him.

"It can wait. Did you call Elgin?" she said.

"He said he'd come around tomorrow. He wants some money."

"Give it to him."

"The bastard is worse than cancer."

"He's better than some," she said.

"Why ain't they taken his license away?"

"They did a long time ago. How many bags do you have till tomorrow?"

He took a small folded square of paper from his coat and held it between two fingers.

"This is it, and I'm fixing to take it right now," he said. He unfolded one end and lifted it to his mouth and let the white powder slide off under his tongue. He walked to the desk and put the paper in the ashtray. He lighted a match to one corner and watched it burn.

April went to the dresser and took a shoe box out of the bottom drawer. She went into the bathroom and remained there a few minutes, and then came back out with the shoe box and replaced it in the drawer. The sleeve of her robe was rolled up over her elbow. She pulled it down to her wrist.

She turned off the light at the wall switch. She took off her robe and lay on the bed. J.P. got up from the chair and walked to the window. He had swallowed some of the cocaine before it dissolved in his mouth, and there was a feeling of nausea in his stomach. She turned her head on the pillow and looked at him. The pupils of her eyes had contracted to small points. The light from the street lamp cast J.P.'s shadow on the ceiling. April laughed.

"You're upside down," she said. "You are. Look at yourself. The white candy horse is galloping and you ride him upside down."

He sat on the bed. He was high, but he felt that he might get sick and then the shaking would start and he would sweat and have chills at the same time.

"When are you going to mainline?" she said. "Little boys can't eat candy all their life." She laughed steadily now. "Little boys get sick when they eat too much candy. Does J.P. feel sick? Poor J.P. always feels sick. Poor poor poor poor J.P. Nice little boy with too much sweet in his mouth."

She reached around him and touched him.

"Let April be your nurse. We'll have some nice medicine."

He got up to undress. He stood in his shorts, and then the room shifted under him and something went yellow in his head and crimson and then black, and he felt his mind slip out of time and something rush away inside him to darkness. He fell on the edge of the bed and rolled off on the floor *in the woman smell of her robe satin soft against my face the reek of yesterday's love and she laughing get up J.P. too much sugar in little boy's mouth come let April make it right she leans over the side of the bed and looks at me smiling her hair wet and sticks to her neck her hand comes down and touches me not even the whores behind the railroad depot come on J.P. not on the floor we can't have fun on the floor she laughing louder if I could move and slip again in time and her hand touching me warm like the woman smell in her robe like the sweat and sour milk and soap smell of her breasts that time in Lafayette when she put them in my and I no I was high I wouldn't have done it if I wasn't high can't stop now her hand like warm water and I rushing to meet her in the final burst of white corn cast upon the ground.*

He woke in the morning with a pain in the back of his head. He was stiff from sleeping on the floor. He walked across the room in his shorts and became dizzy and had to sit down. April was still asleep. Her head was turned towards him on the pillow. Her mouth was open, and the wrinkles around her face and neck showed clearly in the morning light. J.P. didn't remember what had happened the night before, and then it came back to him. He looked down at himself and felt disgusted. He picked up his clothes from the chair and went into the bath to shower. He wrapped the soiled underwear in a towel and put it in the clothes bag hanging on the door. He dressed and went into the room. April was awake.

"Give me my robe," she said.

He picked it up off the floor and threw it to her.

'That's a nice way to hand it to me," she said.

"You look like hell."

"What's that for?"

"Goddamn it, what do you think?"

"You mean that! Oh God, you were funny. You should have seen yourself. I laughed until somebody next door started hitting on the wall. You lying on the rug with that expression on your face. I'd give anything for a picture of it."

"Stop laughing."

"I can't help it. You were so funny. Your face looked like a child's when he's sucking on his first piece of candy."

"You ain't got no more decency than a whore."

"You shouldn't say things about the girl you're going to marry," she said.

"You're still hopped."

"I'm pregnant."

"What?"

"I waited to make sure before I told you."

"Why didn't you take care of yourself?"

"I did. It happened anyway."

"Can't you do something to get rid of it?"

"You want me to drink gasoline or have my stomach cut open?"

"Why the hell did you let it happen?"

"It's here and you're stuck with it, so think about getting a marriage license," she said.

"How do I know it's mine?"

"It would take you to say something like that."

"Seth says you and Doc Elgin got something going on."

"You and me are going to stand up before a justice of the peace. You don't have any way out of it."

'There ain't no shotgun laws in this state. You can't force me into it. All I got to do is support the child."

"But wait till your Baptist-Methodist audience finds out about it."

"Are you going to put signboards on the highway?"

"I'll have a blood test made and take it into court. Then all the hicks can read about it in the paper. Lathrop and Hunnicut will give you bus fare back to your tenant farm."

"I got half a mind to take that bus ride."

"How are you going to pay for your habit?"

"I can still kick it. It ain't too late," he said.

"You're a fool."

"I ain't stuck it in my arm."

"You will."

"Everyone don't have to end in the junkie ward."

"I don't feel like hearing about your cures this morning."

"You and that bastard Elgin got me on it," he said.

"Go cry to somebody else about it."

"Don't it bother you none fixing up Elgin with customers?"

"A girl looks out for herself."

"You let yourself get knocked up on purpose."

"I don't want a child. I never liked children," she said.

"Why in the hell weren't you careful?"

"The courthouse closes at five o'clock. We'll apply for the license this afternoon and three days from now we'll be married. Isn't that nice?"

"I got to think it over."

"I'll meet you in the lobby at one."

"I can't do it today. Elgin is coming by with a delivery."

"There's some in the drawer. Get it and take it with you."

"I got to pay Elgin anyway."

"He'll be back tomorrow."

"Look, we can put it off a while. It don't hurt to wait."

"Stop being an ass."

"We wouldn't be no good married together."

"I'm not getting caught with your brat and no husband."

Two hours later he was downstairs in the lobby waiting for her. He had coffee in the café and went outside to the cigar stand for a shoeshine. The stand was under the brick colonade of the hotel. A large oak tree grew through an opening in the sidewalk. The day was not hot yet, and there was a slight breeze that carried the watermelon smell of summer from the country and the odor of old brick. J.P. gave the porter a half dollar and went inside to the bar for a drink. He left word at the desk for April.

He sat on one of the tall bar stools and drank a draught beer. April came in and sat next to him. She wore a dark blue skirt and a white blouse and black high heels.

"You want a beer?" he said.

"No. Let's go to the courthouse."

"Bring me another draught," he said to the bartender.

"We have to go," she said.

"I feel like drinking some beer."

"You can drink later."

The bartender drew the beer from the tap and put the filled mug on the bar. J.P. paid him and drank half of it without putting the mug down. He wiped the foam off the corners of his mouth.

"You ought to have a drink," he said.

"I don't feel like it."

"Are you still shaky from last night?"

"Finish your beer and let's go," she said.

"I ain't in no hurry."

He swallowed down the rest of the beer and motioned to the bartender for another.

"Can't you do anything without getting high first?" she said.

"I feel like getting blind."

"After we come back you can pass out in the lobby if you want to."

"You'll be a sweet wife."

The beer came. He watched her over the top of the mug as he drank.

"Pay for it and let's go," she said.

"Did you ever have a boilermaker? This seems like a good day to have one." He called the bartender over and had him put a double shot of whiskey in the glass. He drank it down in two long swallows and put a dollar on the bar.

They took a taxi to the courthouse. They went into the clerk of court's office to fill out the applications. He paid the license fee to the clerk and left April in the office. He walked down the marble corridor towards the front entrance. He heard her high heels clacking on the floor behind him.

"Where are you going?" she said.

"There ain't nothing else, is there?"

"Why did you walk off and leave me alone in there?"

"I'm going somewhere, and I don't reckon you want to come along," he said.

He walked out the front door and down the wide concrete walk to the street. The sun was very hot now, and the glare from the cement hurt his eyes. He heard the high heels clacking behind him again. He didn't look back. He signaled a taxi and got in and slammed the door before she reached the street. He saw her face go by the window as the taxi pulled away from the curb.

"What are you laughing at, mister?" the driver said, looking at him in the rear-view mirror.

"It's so goddamn funny you wouldn't believe it."

"Are you all right?"

"I'd tell you about it, but you wouldn't believe it."

"Where did you say you wanted to go?"

"Jerry's Bar, back of the depot."

The driver looked at him once more in the mirror and drove down a side street through the old part of town and across the railroad tracks. They slowed down behind the station and stopped in front of a bar across from the freight yards. The bar was a two-story board building with dirty front windows and a shorted-out neon sign that buzzed loudly and lighted up only half of its letters.

J.P. went inside. It smelled of flat beer and the sawdust that was spread on the floor. The mirror behind the bar was yellowed, and the rough-grained floor was stained with tobacco spittle. Some of the chairs were turned over on the tables, and two railroad workers were drinking at the other end of the bar. A middle-aged man in a dirty apron was drying glasses behind the bar. His hair was combed over the bald spot in the middle of his head.

"Good afternoon, Mr. Winfield," he said.

"Give me a whiskey and water, Jerry," J.P. said.

"Yes, sir."

He mopped the area in front of J.P. with a rag and set down the drink.

"We ain't seen you in a while. You must be busy in politics."

"When are you going to stop cutting your whiskey?" J.P. said.

"We don't do that here, Mr. Winfield. I can give you another shot if it's too weak." He filled the jigger and poured it in J.P.'s glass.

"I want a room upstairs for the afternoon."

"It's a little early. I don't know if any of the girls are in."

J.P. took out his billfold and put five ten-dollar bills on the bar.

"Let me ask my wife," the bartender said. "Emma, come over here a minute."

The woman who had been sweeping propped her broom against a table and came behind the bar. She was stout and had big arms like a man. There was a large wart on her chin. She didn't look at J.P.

"Mr. Winfield wants to go upstairs. I told him it was a little early for the girls," the bartender said.

She took the money off the bar and rang the cash register and put it in the drawer.

"Come with me," she said.

J.P. followed her off into a narrow hallway at the back. She opened the door to a stairway and climbed the steps with J.P. behind her. The upstairs was divided by a hallway with a series of doors on each side. The floor was covered with a tattered maroon carpet. The hall ended in a single large room that served as the kitchen. There was a curtain pulled across the doorway. The woman left J.P. standing at the top of the staircase and went down the hall opening doors and looking into rooms. She came back and went past him to the kitchen, not looking at him.

"They keep their rooms worse than niggers," she said.

He watched her pull aside the curtain and look into the kitchen. Four women were sitting around the table eating. She held the curtain and stepped back for him to look in.

"You want one in particular?" she said.

"Is Margaret still here?"

"She got sick."

"It don't matter, then."

"There's a customer, Honey," the woman said.

"Yes, ma'am," a girl at the table said, and wiped her mouth with a napkin and got up from her chair. She came out into the hall. Her hair was long and honey-colored. She wore a pink flowered house robe. She was a little overweight and the pink polish on her fingernails was chipped away.

"Honey is one of our best girls. We never had complaints about her," the woman said.

The girl smiled at J.P. He put a bill in the woman's hand.

"Tell Jerry to send up a bottle and some glasses," he said.

"This has always been a good place. We never had trouble with townspeople or police," the woman said.

"I ain't going to tear up your place. Tell Jerry to bring the bottle."

The woman put the bill in her dress pocket and went back down the stairs. J.P. followed Honey into her room.

"Say, aren't you that singer? The one on the Louisiana Jubilee?" she said.

"No."

"You look like him. What's his name?"

"I don't know. I'm a vitamin tonic salesman. You want to buy some vitamin tonic to keep strong in your work?"

"You even sound like him. You sure you're not him?"

"I sell vitamin tonic to working girls that keep late hours," he said.

"Salesmen don't have money for an all-afternoon date."

"You're a smart girl."

"We get all kinds of people here. I can tell what a fellow is when he walks in. I know you're the one on the Jubilee," she said.

Three days later J.P. and April picked up their marriage license at the courthouse. He had a fresh supply of powder from Doc Elgin, and he stayed high all evening. That night they drove to a justice of the peace's house on the edge of town. The official considered his marriage office a very important one. He smiled and spoke of the many young people he had married. There was a scent of whiskey on his breath. The house had the smell of old wallpaper, dead flowers, and old ladies. His wife served as a witness. J.P. was very high and he kept wanting to laugh during the ceremony. He looked at the homely slogans on the wall in the gilt and scrolled frames. He thought he heard himself laughing. The marriage was over and they were sitting in the back seat of the taxi on the way to the hotel and he could still smell the old wallpaper and the withered flowers.

AVERY BROUSSARD

After he had served a year Avery was up for parole. The board met once every two months, and he had to wait five weeks after his minimum sentence was completed before his case was reviewed. He had never spent time in detention, and no bad reports concerning him had ever been filed with the warden's office, chiefly because Evans never took time to file reports on anybody in his gang. The board met at the warden's house at the edge of the camp on a hot Friday afternoon. Avery was taken off work at noon and driven back from the line to the barracks by a guard. He showered and changed into clean denims while the guard sat on a bunk by the doorway and waited. He was then taken over to the warden's house to be interviewed by the board.

He walked up the veranda with the guard beside him. In the dining room six men sat around the table in their shirtsleeves. The ceiling fan ruffled the papers on the table. The guard brought Avery into the room and motioned for him to sit down in a chair against the wall. The chairman of the board looked at Avery across the table. His face wore no expression save the confidence of his position in dealing with prisoners. He was the kind of man who could speak of correction, punishment, and rehabilitation without ever seeing the gangs working in the ditch or smelling the stench of sweat and urine when someone was brought back from detention.

"We've considered your case," he said, "and although we've decided in your favor, I have to tell you that a parole is not a guarantee of complete personal freedom. Your crime was a first offense, and because you were relatively young when you committed it, you're being given another chance on the street after doing only a third of your sentence. However, there are restrictions attached to parole that you are going to have to follow the next two years. You can't associate with criminal or antisocial company, and you can't leave the state without permission of your local board. You can't overindulge in alcoholic beverages, nor own a firearm, and you must check in with your board every month. Would you like to say anything before you're taken back?"

"When can I get out?" Avery said.

"Our recommendation has to be sent to Baton Rouge for approval. Then a letter will be sent to the warden ordering your release."

The other men at the table were hot and bored.

"Is there anything else you'd like to know? One aim of the board is to help you make the adjustment back to normal life."

The chairman waited for Avery to speak. He expected some expression of gratitude from men to whom he granted parole.

"If you have nothing to say, the guard will take you back."

Avery went outside with the guard. They walked to the truck parked at the barracks. He asked if he could change into his soiled clothes before going back on the line. The guard said there wasn't time. Avery sat beside him in the truck as they drove through camp out the wire gates and down the dirt road towards the line.

"It looks like you're going to be the only one from gang five to make it out," the guard said. "Billy Jo and Jeffry is dead and LeBlanc is locked up in the nut house, and the rest is serving life except Boudreaux."

"How long does it take for them to get that letter here?" Avery said.

"Four or five days. It's good for you Evans didn't turn in no report. You wouldn't be making parole."

"Is that a fact?"

"Yeah. He don't like you."

"I thought we were close friends."

"He ain't got no use for anybody that would buddy with LeBlanc. He had them blue marks on his neck for a week. I heard LeBlanc was slobbering like a sick dog. Is that true about them beating him over the head a half dozen times before he let go of Evans?"

"Ask Rainack."

"Didn't you see it?"

"No. I was in the truck," he said.

Avery's letter of release came later that week. A guard told him in the dining hall to have his things ready before breakfast the next morning. He got up at six o'clock with the rest of the men and cleaned out his footlocker and folded his army blanket and bed linen. He rolled his mattress up on the foot of his bunk and laid out his clothes issue on top of his locker. From the window, he could see the sun through the pines. Toussaint sat on the next bunk and rolled a cigarette.

"How's it feel?" he said.

"Good."

"You'll be walking down Bourbon Street tonight."

"Not with less than ten dollars in my pocket."

"Try the docks. You can make good money handling freight."

"Nobody is hiring ex-cons," Avery said.

"You ain't got to tell them where you come from."

The breakfast whistle blew. They lined up outside the dining hall.

"Stay out of trouble. Don't let them send you back to this place," Toussaint said at the table.

"They never will."

"Them parole boards can send you back for the rest of your stretch."

"They won't get me in here again," Avery said.

"Don't give them no excuse."

They finished eating and lined up outside for roll call. The captain told Avery to return to the barracks after his name was called and wait for the guard to come get him.

"So long, whiskey runner," Toussaint said.

They shook hands.

"Take care," Avery said.

"Worry about yourself. They can't do no more to me."

"I'll write you a letter."

"You ain't got to do that."

"Maybe I'll see you in New Orleans," Avery said, and then felt stupid for saying it.

"That'll be a long while."

They shook hands again.

"So long," Avery said.

"So long."

Avery went to the barracks and waited for the guard. Rainack came in with a brown paper bundle under his arm. He dropped it on the bunk.

"Here's the stuff you come in with. See if it's all there," he said.

Avery broke the string and unwrapped the paper. The package contained the clothes he had worn when he was arrested. They had been washed, pressed, and wrapped in a bundle nearly a year ago. He looked at the scuffed brown shoes, the print sports shirt faded almost white, and the gray work trousers. There was a brown envelope on top with his name and prison number printed across the front. He opened it and shook out a pocketknife, three quarters, a billfold, and a leather-band wristwatch with the crystal broken.

"What happened to my watch?"

"Talk to the trusties at the office. Is everything else there?"

"Yes."

"Change into your own clothes. You got to go by the warden's office before you leave."

Avery got dressed. He sat on the bunk and put on his shoes.

"You can take your boots with you. We never issue out boots twice," Rainack said.

"You can keep them."

They went over to the warden's office. The trusty who served as a secretary sat behind a small desk inside the hall.

"Take him in to see the warden. I got to go back to the line," Rainack said to the trusty. He went out and let the screen slam behind him.

The trusty knocked on the warden's door.

"Broussard's here, sir," he said.

"I'm busy. Wait a minute."

Avery waited a quarter of an hour, then he was told to go in. He sat down in the straight-backed chair before the warden's desk.

"You see this ten-dollar bill?" the warden said. "It will buy a bus ticket to any part of the state you want to go to. We don't care where you go, we just don't want you back here. It cost the state a lot of money to keep you in camp, and we figure that after you've spent some time here you don't want to cost us no more money. You'll be outside in a few minutes and the choice will be up to you. You can obey the law and keep clear of us, or you can come back. But I'm going to warn you that we don't like to see nobody here twice."

"Is that all?" Avery said.

"That's all."

Avery took the bill off the desk and put it in his billfold.

"Do you know how to get out to the highway?" the warden said.

"I'll find it."

He got up and went back out through the hall.

"Hold on," the trusty said. "I got to take you to the gate."

They walked across the dirt yard of the camp. He looked at the white barracks in the sun and the corrugated tin roofs and the wire fence with the three barbed strands at the top. The guard at the gate sat in the shade of a tarpaulin that was stretched out from the fence and attached to two wood poles stuck in the ground. He had a double-barrel shotgun across his knees.

"Broussard's coming out," the trusty said.

The guard propped the shotgun against the fence and unlocked the gate.

"Come calling again," he said.

Avery walked out and heard the gate lock behind him. The camp road led through some pines and divided into a fork ahead. There were tire marks in the dirt where the trucks turned right at the fork to take the men out to the line. The gravel lane to the left became a farm road that led to the highway. He walked in the shade of the trees. The trunks looked dark and cool, and off in the distance he could see the cotton fields and the red clay land and the Negroes chopping in the long green rows. He followed the farm road for a mile with the sun hot on his shoulders and the back of his neck. The dew on the grass was dry and the grasshoppers flicked across the road in the sun. He thought how long it had been since he used to catch the big black and yellow grasshoppers on the bank of the bayou and nigger-fish with a cane pole. A mile further on the farm road ran into the highway. He stood on the shoulder of the highway and tried to hitch a ride. He waited two hours and no one stopped. It was mid-morning and the day was beginning to get hot. He unbuttoned his shirt and let the wind blow inside. The cars came down the highway with the sun reflecting on their windshields and their tires whining on the pavement; they sped past him and disappeared down the road. An old coupé with a smoking radiator slowed down and pulled off onto the shoulder. Avery got in the front seat and shut the door.

The driver was a farmer. He wore overalls and a checkered shirt and an old Stetson hat that was wilted with sweat. His face was lean and burned by the sun. He shifted the floor stick and pulled back on the highway.

"Bad place to be hitchhiking," he said.

"Why's that?"

"Didn't you see them signs they got along the road?"

"No," Avery said.

"They say hitchhikers might be escaped convicts. There's a prison camp over yonder."

"How far are you going?"

"About twenty miles up the road. Ain't you traveling light?"

"My suitcase was stolen."

"Where you coming from?" the farmer asked.

"North of here."

"You sure picked a bad place to catch a ride. Most people is afraid they'll get one of them convicts in their car."

"Aren't you afraid?"

"I pick up boys along here all the time. Sometimes they're just getting out of prison. I ain't afraid of them."

They drove down the highway for fifteen miles. The heat waves looked like pools of water on the road. The grass was tall and green in the fields. The clouds moved across the sun and made places of shadow over the countryside. The river was off to the left, curving through the slow-rolling hills of cotton and corn.

"You look like you been working outdoors a lot," the farmer said.

"I have."

"What doing?"

"I worked for the state. You can put me down at the crossroads."

"Look, it don't matter to me where you come from."

"It doesn't? You seem to want to know pretty bad."

"I was talking to pass the time. I don't grudge a man his past," the farmer said.

"This is where I get off, anyway."

The coupé stopped where the road intersected with the federal highway. Avery got out and watched the car pull away. There was a country store on the corner under two big shade trees. Some old men sat on a bench under a Hadacol sign chewing tobacco and spitting in the dust. They watched him walk up the sandy drive past the broken gasoline pump into the store. It was cool inside. A clerk came from the back and stood behind the counter. Avery bought some lunch meat, a loaf of bread, and a can of sardines. He looked up at the package shelf behind the clerk.

"How much for a pint?" he said.

"Two dollars."

"You don't have any that comes in glass jars, do you?"

"We only sell bonded whiskey here," the clerk said.

"Give me the pint."

The clerk put the bottle in a paper bag. Avery stuck it in his back pocket and picked up his groceries and went out to the highway.

He sat under a pine tree and ate lunch. There were brown pine needles spread over the grass. He opened the sardines and picked them out with his pocketknife and ate them with bread. He was still hungry and he wanted to eat the lunch meat, but he would have to save that for supper. The sun was very hot now. He threw the empty can to the side of the road and wiped his knife clean on the grass. He took the pint bottle out of his pocket and cut the seal off. He unscrewed the cap and drank; he felt the whiskey hot in his stomach. It tasted good after so long. He took another swallow and put the cap back on and replaced the bottle in his pocket. He wrapped the rest of his groceries in the paper sack and got up and stood by the shoulder of the highway to hitch another ride. Three cars passed him by, and then he caught a lift with a salesman who was going all the way to New Orleans.

He got into the city late that night. The salesman gave him directions to an inexpensive rooming house and dropped him off on the lower end of Magazine. Avery walked through the dark streets of a Negro area until he found St. Charles. He caught the streetcar and rode downtown to Canal. He stood on the corner and looked at the white sweep of the boulevard with its grass esplanade and palm trees and streetcar tracks, and the glitter like hard candy of the lighted storefronts. The sidewalks were still crowded, and he could hear the tinny music from the bars and strip places. He walked down to Liberty Street and found the rooming house the salesman had told him of. It was an old wood building that had a big front porch with a swing. It was one block off Canal and three blocks from Bourbon, and the Frenchwoman who owned it kept it very clean and she served coffee and rolls to her tenants every morning.

He took a room for the night, and in the morning the woman brought in his coffee on a tray. She poured the coffee and hot milk into his cup from two copper pots with long tapered spouts. She wore a housecoat, and her hair was loose and uncombed.

"Will you keep the room for another night?" she said.

"I'm looking for a job. I'll stay if I find one," Avery said.

"Your name is French. *Tu parles français?*"

"I understand it."

"D'où tu viens?"

"Martinique parish."

"What kind of work do you do?"

"Anything. I'm going down to the docks today," he said.

"My husband is a welder on the pipeline. He can get you work."

"I've never worked on a pipeline."

"You can learn. He will teach you."

"Where is he?" Avery said.

"He is eating breakfast. Finish the coffee and you can talk with him."

Avery met her husband and drove to work with him. He got a job as a welder's helper on a twelve-inch natural gas line that had just kicked off and was to run from an oil refinery to the other end of the parish. He worked with the tack crew, cleaning wells, driving the truck, and regulating the welding machine. He liked the job. Each morning they went out on the right-of-way that was cut through the woods and marsh, and the joints of pipe would be laid along the wooden skids by the ditch; he followed behind the truck with the electric ground that he clamped on the pipe to give the welder a circuit and with the wire brushes and the icepick in his back pocket that he used to clean the joints; the welder would bend over the pipe with his dark goggles on and his bill-hat turned around backwards and his khaki shirt buttoned at the collar and sleeves, and the electric arc would move in an orange flame around the pipe, and there was the acrid smell of tar and hot metal and the exhaust from the heavy machinery.

He stayed on at the rooming house, and sometimes in the evening he went down into the Quarter and ate dinner in an Italian place off Bourbon Street, then he would walk through the narrow cobble lanes and look at the old red and pink stucco buildings and the iron grillwork along the balconies and those fine flagstone courtyards with the willow trees and palms that hung over the walls. At night he could see the back of Saint Louis Cathedral with the ivy growing up its walls under the moon, and there was the park in the square across from the French Market where the bums and the drunks slept under the statue of Andrew Jackson.

One night he found a small bar on Rampart where the band was good and there were no tourists. He had been drinking since he had gotten off work. He sat at the bar and drank whiskey sours and listened to the band knock out the end of "Yellow Dog Blues." The drummer twirled the sticks in his hands and played on the nickel-plated rim of his snare. The man on the next stool to Avery was having an argument with the bartender. He was dressed in sports clothes, and was quite handsome and quite drunk. He had thin red hair and blue eyes and a pale classic face like Lord Byron's. He didn't have enough money to pay for his drink. He turned to Avery.

"I say, have you a dime?" he said.

Avery pushed a coin towards him.

He gave the dime to the bartender with some other change.

"The fellow was going to take my drink away," he said.

"You're spilling it," Avery said.

"Spilling?"

"On your coat. You're spilling your drink."

"Don't want to do that." He wiped his sleeve with his hand. "My name is Wally."

"I'm Avery Broussard."

"You look like a good chap. Do you want to go to a party?"

"Where?"

"On Royal. A friend of mine is giving a debauch."

"I wouldn't know anyone."

"Of no importance. The literary and artistic group. We'll tell them you're an agrarian romanticist. Do you have a bottle?"

"No."

"We'll have to get one. The artistic group asks that you bring your own booze."

They left the bar and went to a package store down the street.

"Do you mind making it Scotch?" Wally said.

Avery went in and bought a half pint.

"Good man," Wally said.

"Are you English?" Avery took a drink and passed the bottle.

"Who would want to be English when they can belong to the American middle class?"

"You sound English."

"Went to school in England. Drank my way through four years of Tulane, then tried graduate work at Cambridge and was sent down. Acquired nothing but a taste for Scotch and a bad accent. Now make my home in the Quarter writing."

"Pass the bottle," Avery said.

"What do you do?"

"Pipeline."

"I say, we're emptying the bottle rather fast."

"Have to buy more."

"I'm stony broke. Hate to use your money like this."

Avery took a long drink.

"Mind if I have a bit?" Wally said.

Avery gave him the bottle. He leaned against the side of a building and drank.

"I think I'm tight," he said.

"Where is the party?"

"Royal Street."

"We're going the wrong way," Avery said.

They turned the corner towards Royal. The half pint was almost finished.

"You have the last drink," Wally said.

"Go ahead."

"Your bottle."

Avery drank it off and dropped the bottle in an alley.

"Puts us in an embarrassing way. Can't go to party without liquor," Wally said.

"Dago red."

"Never drink it."

"It's cheap."

"Unconventional to go to party with dago red," Wally said.

"There's an Italian place with good wine."

"A little restaurant off Bourbon?"

"Yes."

"Have to wait outside. Can't go in," Wally said.

"Why not?"

"Broke some glasses they say. Don't remember it. Was inebriated at the time."

"They have good wine," Avery said.

"I'll wait for you. It's always awkward to have scenes with Italian restaurant owners."

Avery walked down two blocks and bought a large two-liter bottle of red wine in a straw basket. He met Wally at the corner.

"I forgot to get a corkscrew," he said.

He cut out the top part of the cork with his pocketknife and pushed the rest through the neck into the wine.

"Good man," Wally said.

They each had a drink. They could taste the cork when it floated up inside the neck. They walked along, Avery holding the bottle by the straw loops of the basket. They came to an apartment building with a Spanish type courtyard that had an iron gate and an arched brick entrance. The courtyard was strung with paper lanterns, and there was a stone well with a banana tree beside it in the center. The walls were grown with ivy, and there were potted ferns in earthenware jars on the flagging. People moved up and down the staircase, and laughing girls called down from the balcony to young men in the court.

"Hello!" Wally said.

"It's Wally," someone said.

"I say, is there a party here?"

"Come in. You look shaky on your feet," another said.

"Does anyone know if there's a party here?" he said.

"Someone help Wally in," a girl said.

"We're agrarian romanticists. This is Freneau Crèvecoeur Broussard."

"Avery."

"That's not agrarian enough. You'll have to change your name," Wally said.

Everyone turned and looked at Wally.

"Do you remember my party last Saturday?" a girl said.

"I was helping out at the mission last Saturday. We're starting a campaign to make New Orleans dry."

"He said he was somebody out of *War and Peace*," she told the others. "He stood backwards on the edge of my balcony and tried to drink a fifth of Scotch without falling."

"Couldn't have been me. I've never read Chekhov."

"You would have broken your neck if you hadn't fallen in the flower bed," she said.

"Don't like those Russian chaps, anyway. A bunch of bloody moralists," Wally said.

"Sit down, fellow. You're listing," someone said.

"Won't be able to get up."

"Tell Freneau Crèvecoeur to sit down. He doesn't look well," the girl said.

"Avery."

"Beg your pardon?" she said.

"My name is Avery."

"Excuse me, Mr. Avery."

"We're agrarian romanticists," Wally said.

"Avery is my first name."

"Who wants to read a bunch of bloody Russians when they can have the agrarian romanticists?"

"What does your friend have in his bottle?" the girl said.

"The best Italian import that a pair of unwashed feet could mash down in a bathtub. I say, let's have a drink."

He took the bottle from Avery and turned it up.

"Your turn, old pal."

Avery sat down on the well and drank.

"Damn good man. Wonderful capacity," Wally said. "Everyone take a swallow. Pass it around. I insist. Each of you must take a swallow. I never drink alone. It's a sign of alcoholism."

"You're impossible, Wally," the girl said.

"I cannot stand people who do not drink."

A man took the bottle and held it for his girl to drink. She laughed and a few drops went down her chin. The bottle was passed from one couple to another.

"I refuse to go to parties where everyone is not smashed," Wally said.

"Do you live in the Quarter, Mr. Crèvecoeur?" another girl said.

"No writer would live in the Quarter," Wally said.

"Are you a writer?"

"Work on the pipeline," Avery said.

"What did he say?"

"He's a disillusioned agrarian," Wally said.

"Have you really written anything?"

"We've made an agreement with a publisher to write dialogue for comic books," Wally said.

"Be serious."

"He did his thesis on Wordsworth's sonnets to the dark lady."

"I'm interested in writing myself," she said to Avery.

"She's a copy reader for the *Picayune*."

"Where is the wine?" Avery said.

"All gone."

"Have to get more."

"I've written a few poems and sent them off," the girl said.

"We had a full bottle when we came in," Avery said.

"It's a lovely trick. You let everyone have a sip of yours, and then you drink out of theirs for the rest of the night."

"Do you publish often?" she said.

"I'm a welder's helper."

"You said you were a writer."

"He is."

"I almost failed high school English," Avery said.

"Why did you say you were a writer?"

"I tell you he is," Wally said.

"We need another bottle."

"Let's go upstairs."

"I wouldn't have told you about my poems," the girl said.

"Crèvecoeur will be happy to read your poetry and give you a criticism."

"You take things too far," the girl said.

"Oh I say."

"It's true."

"Apologize to her, Crèvecoeur."

"I'm going down to the package store."

"These other chaps owe us a round. Let's toggle upstairs."

They went up the staircase and entered the living room of an apartment. It was crowded and they had to push their way through to the kitchen where the liquor was kept. Wally took a bottle of Scotch off the sideboard and two glasses from the cabinet. There was a sack of crushed ice in the sink. He fixed the drinks and handed one to Avery. They went back into the living room. There was a combo playing in one corner. The guitar player was a Negro. It was very loud in the room. Someone dropped a glass on the coffee table. Someone was saying that a girl had passed out in the bathroom. Avery tripped across a man and a girl sitting on the floor. The glass doors to the outside balcony were open to let in the night air. He started to go out on the balcony but he heard a girl whisper and laugh in the darkness. The piano player in the combo was singing an obscene song in Spanish. Avery couldn't find Wally in the crowd. Two men who looked like homosexuals were talking in the corner by the bookcase. One of them waved girlishly at someone across the room. The girl who had passed out in the bath was brought out to the balcony for some air.

Avery moved through the groups of people. He finished his drink and put his glass on a table. He could feel the blood in his face. The noise in the room seemed louder. He wanted to get outside. He remembered that he had to be out on the job at seven in the morning. He looked up and saw a girl watching him from the other side of the room. She smiled at him and excused herself from the people she was with. It was Suzanne. She wore a wine-colored dress, and there was a gold cross and chain around her throat. She looked even better than when he had seen her last.

"I couldn't tell if it was you or not," she said.

"Hello, Suzanne."

"You kept walking through the crowd. I wanted to call out, but I was afraid it wasn't you."

"I thought you were in Spain or someplace."

"I was. What are you doing here?"

"I'm not sure. I was leaving when I saw you," he said.

"Don't leave."

"I'm not."

"Let's go outside. It's too loud in here."

"I've tried. Couldn't make the door."

"We can go out through the kitchen," she said.

They went out through a back door that opened onto the balcony over the courtyard. The air was cool, and the moonlight fell on the tile roofing of the buildings.

"I didn't believe it was you. You look changed," she said.

"You look good," he said. She really did. She had never looked so good.

"It's been awfully long since we've seen each other."

"Did you like Spain?"

"I loved it."

"Are you living here now?"

"Over on Dauphine. Another girl and I rented a studio. You have to see it. It's like something out of nineteenth-century Paris."

They sat on the stone steps leading down to the court.

"I'm one of those sidewalk artists you see in Pirates Alley," she said. "Daddy was furious when he found out. He said he would stop my allowance."

"He won't."

"I know. He always threatens to do it, and then he sends another check to apologize."

He looked at her profile in the darkness. She kept her face turned slightly away from him when she talked. The light from the paper lanterns caught in her hair. He wished he had not drunk as much as he had. He was trying very hard to act sober.

"I came with some fellow named Wally. He put a drink in my hand and I never saw him again."

"How in the world did you meet Wally?"

"He was broke. I lent him a dime."

"One night he went down Bourbon asking donations for the Salvation Army."

"What happened?"

"He used the money to buy two winos a drink in The Famous Door."

A couple brushed past them down the steps. Others followed

them. Part of the party was moving outside. Wally came out on the balcony and called down.

"Who in the hell would read a bunch of Russian moralists?"

"Let's go to the Café du Monde," Suzanne said. "They have wonderful pastry and coffee, and we can sit outside at the tables."

"What about the people you're with?"

"I've been trying to get away from them all evening. They come down from L.S.U. to see the bohemians."

They left the party and walked towards the French Market through the brick and cobbled streets. They passed the rows of stucco buildings that had once been the homes of the French and Spanish aristocracy, and which were now gutted and remodeled into bars, whorehouses, tattoo parlors, burlesque theaters, upper-class restaurants, and nightclubs that catered to homosexuals. They could hear the loud music from Bourbon and the noise of the people on the sidewalk and the spielers in front of the bars calling in the tourists, who did not know or care who had built the Quarter.

"I didn't find out what happened to you until I came back from Spain," she said. "I'm very sorry."

"It's over now."

"I couldn't believe it when Daddy told me. It seems so unfair."

"I did a year. They might have kept me for three."

"Was it very bad?" she said.

"Yes."

"I wish I had known. I was enjoying myself, and you were in one of those camps."

"I'm finished with it now."

"It makes me feel awful to think of you in there."

"You're a good girl."

"It must have been terrible."

"It was worse for some of the others," he said.

"I couldn't bear thinking about you in a prison."

They walked across Jackson Square through the park and crossed the street to the Café du Monde. They sat outside at one of the tables. There was a breeze from the river. The waiter in a white jacket brought them coffee and a dish of pastry.

"We never wrote to each other after my first year in college," she said. "I wanted to write but anything I could say seemed inadequate."

"I wasn't sure you wanted to hear from me."

"You know I did. It all went to nothing over such small things."

"I passed out on the beach in Biloxi."

"I wasn't angry. It just hurt me to see you do it to yourself."

"I felt like hell when I saw the way you looked the next morning," he said.

"I didn't sleep all night. I was so worried over you."

"You were always a good girl."

"Stop it."

"You were always damn good-looking too."

"Oh for heaven's sake, Avery."

"Did you see those men turn and look at you in the park?"

"You're being unfair."

"Why are you so damn good-looking?" he said.

"I want to show you my apartment. Can you come over tomorrow evening for supper?"

"You're changing the subject."

"Can you come?"

"All right."

"I cook beautifully. My roommate refuses to eat with me."

"Good. Tell her to leave."

"What were you drinking tonight?" she said.

"I thought I fooled you."

"Your face was white. I was afraid to light a cigarette near you."

"Tell your roommate to leave, anyway."

"You're still tight."

"Dago red leaves me like this for a couple of days."

"It's good to be with you again, Avery."

"Let's walk home," he said.

BOOK THREE

WHEN THE SUN BEGINS TO SHINE

TOUSSAINT BOUDREAUX

They were clearing a field of stumps the day he escaped. Toussaint waited with the team of mules while Brother Samuel cut the stump from its roots with a chain saw. The field looked flat and bare with the trees cut down. Pieces of splintered wood were strewn over the ground. The air was loud with the knock of the axes and the whine of the saws. There was a big pile of brush burning on the edge of the field. Samuel put down the saw and chopped the remaining roots loose with an axe. His mud-colored face was slick with heat. He rested on one knee and swung the axe down over his shoulder. Toussaint backed up the mules and fastened the chains around the stump. Easing the mules forward, he let them tighten against their harness, then slapped the reins down on their backs; they strained for a moment and then pulled the stump free. He and Samuel took up their axes and split it in pieces to put in the wheelbarrow.

"You ain't talking today," Brother Samuel said.

"Got something on my mind," Toussaint said.

Most of the gangs were working at the other end of the field. Evans was the only guard close by. He stood off to the side of the burning brush, from where he could see all his men. The fire was very hot. Toussaint rolled the wheelbarrow past Evans and began throwing pieces of the stump into the flames. He looked back across the field. It was almost time for lunch and the other guards were taking their gangs back to the road to wait for the food truck.

The fringe of the woods was just behind the brush pile. Toussaint left a thick piece of tree limb in the bottom of the wheelbarrow. Evans stood about thirty yards away in his khaki uniform and cork sun helmet. He took off his helmet and wiped the inside of it with his handkerchief. Toussaint knew that once he was past Evans he could get across the short span of ground into the safety of the trees before the other guards realized anyone had escaped. He looked back across the field again. None of the other guards was looking this way. He pushed the wheelbarrow along the rutted ground until he was opposite Evans. He let the wheelbarrow drop on its side, and knelt with his back to the guard and wrenched the rubber tire from the wheel.

"What's the matter?" Evans said.

"The wheel busted."

"Fix it."

"The tire split. I got to go back to the line shack for another one."

"You ain't going nowhere. Let me see it."

Toussaint gripped the tree limb tightly. He waited for Evans to get close. He raised up quickly and struck him squarely across the forehead. The limb was rotten and it broke in his hand. Evans fell back heavily and lay still, his cork sun helmet beside him. Then Toussaint was racing across the bare strip of ground beside the brush pile, expecting to hear a guard call out to the others, into the protection of the woods, the branches whipping against his face and tearing his clothes. He tripped across the vines that covered the ground, and the thornbushes broke his skin. He ran through the undergrowth and briar, and then the woods began to thin and he could see the green grass on the riverbank through the trees.

He ran down the slope and dove into the water. Swimming out to the middle, he let the current catch him and carry him downstream. He looked at the high clay banks and the trees hanging over the water. There was a houseboat tied to the shore. He didn't see anyone on it. He went underwater and stayed down until he believed he was past it. Some sunken tree branches brushed under his legs. He came up for air and swam towards the opposite bank.

The river made a curve ahead, and beyond it a logging company was working in the woods. He walked up through the shallows onto the mud flat. The police would be delayed while the dogs had to hunt along the bank for his scent after crossing the river. He entered a pecan orchard and stopped to get his breath and pull off his boots. The leather was wet and would blister his feet, and running was faster barefooted. The orchard opened onto a meadow; to the right there was a narrow bayou that cut back through a thicket. He carried his boots in one hand and followed the bayou, walking in the shallows as much as possible so the dogs wouldn't be able to track him. He took off his shirt and turned it inside out to hide the stenciled prison letters and put it back on again.

By late afternoon he had reached a crossroads off the main highway. There was a grocery-and-hardware store on the corner and some farmhouses in the distance. A bridled mule was hitched to the porch railing of the store. A Negro came out with a cloth sack of groceries, got on the mule, and rode down the gravel lane. Toussaint knew the police would have the main roads blocked, and the town constables would be watching for him in the small settlements. He needed food, a change of clothes, a gun, and ammunition. He wanted to keep going south until he hit the swamp country around Bayou Lafourche; once there, he could get a pirogue and slip through the canals into Barataria where he could hide indefinitely. He had relatives in Barataria, and people in that part of the country cared little for the law. Later, when the police had stopped looking for him, he could get out of the state.

He hid in a cornfield and waited for nightfall. A police car came down the road and stopped in front of the store. An officer got out and spoke to the men sitting on the porch. He went back to his car and stood with one foot on the running board and talked into the microphone of his radio. Toussaint could see the sunlight glint on the butt of his revolver. He wished he had a gun. He felt helpless without one. There was a chance they could take him back to the work camp if he had no weapon.

The officer got in his car and drove off. Toussaint smelled the clean odor of the earth. He rubbed some dirt between his hands. This was good land. The corn was high and green, and there was a field of strawberries across the road. Around his home most of the men were fishermen, but he liked the land and things growing. It had been a long time since he had been on a farm. There had been his time in prison, and before that the city where he saw nothing except concrete buildings and the faces of people he didn't understand, nor who understood him. He could have lain in the field without ever getting up. The soil was cool and a thin breeze ruffled through the cornstalks. A cottontail jumped into his row and stopped, its ears pressed down against its back, the nose twitching. We got to keep moving, don't we, rabbit? Toussaint thought. If we don't there won't be no more cornfields or strawberries or going home. There won't be nothing.

That night he waited until the store closed. He could see two men playing dominoes through the window. The light went off in back and the two men and the owner came out on the porch. They got into a car and drove down the road. Toussaint moved forward to the edge of the field and remained watching to make sure they were not coming back for anything. He could see the lighted farmhouses in the distance. The moon was down, and the road was dark. He could hear the crickets and the frogs in the woods. He crossed the road and went around to the back of the store. He pushed in the screen on the door with his hand until it broke from its fastening. The inside door had a glass pane in it. He tried to force the door by slowly pushing his weight against it. It was bolted. He got a piece of brick and wrapped it in newspaper. He broke out the glass near the corner of the frame and reached in and slid the bolt loose.

He was thirsty. He hadn't had a drink of water since he swam the river. He took a bottle of pop out of the cooler and drank it. He opened another and drank it while he went along the shelves and took the cans of food he would need. He found a gunnysack behind the counter and put in the cans. There was a rack with used clothing and work clothes by the front door. He took a shirt and a pair of trousers and put them in the sack with the cans and tied a knot in the top. He set the sack on the counter and looked around the store. The guns rested on wooden pegs against the wall. They were all secondhand. He took a Winchester off its pegs and worked the action. He could find only two boxes of shells for it. He loaded the magazine and put the rest of the shells in his pocket. He would need a knife also. He slid back the cover of a glass case and chose a good Queen knife with a yellow bone handle and two long blades. He picked up the gunnysack from the counter and looked out the front window at the road. He went out the back door and circled around the store, crossed the road, and ran through the cornfield into the woods.

He went deep into the trees before he stopped. He took the shirt and trousers from the sack and changed clothes. He rolled his prison denims into a ball and dug a hole in the leaves and soil with his hands and buried them. He traveled south through the meadows and wooded areas, avoiding the roads and farm settlements. He made good time, and by dawn he had found a deserted cabin in a pinewood where he could hide until the next night. One side of the cabin was stored with grain, and there was a damp cool mealy smell inside. There were tracks in the grain where the squirrels had come to feed. The roof of the cabin had a big hole in it, and Toussaint could see the blue light in the east spreading across the sky. He was tired, and after he had eaten he lay back in the grain and slept.

It was noon when he awoke and heard the dogs barking. They had picked up his trail at the crossroads. He grabbed his rifle and ran out of the cabin into the hot light. He hadn't thought they would catch up with him so soon. He cut through the woods and hoped that he could find a bayou where he could throw the dogs off his scent. The trees were thickly spaced and slowed his running; there was no bayou. The barking of the dogs seemed farther behind him now, but that was because the police had stopped to search the grounds around the cabin; it would not take them long to discover that he had just fled and was less than a mile away. He had left the sack of food behind.

He headed for the marsh. It was the only thing left. If they caught him in the open he would either be killed without a fight, or worse, handcuffed and returned to camp. The marsh was a long way, and he had to travel at a steady pace without halting to rest. The main highway was off to his left and the state troopers were skirting the woods to the right, trying to cut him off. His path was laid out for him like a geometric rectangle; on one extreme was the dead end where he would make his stand, and on both sides were the police, who tightened the rectangle like a vise with each passing hour.

Once they almost got him. He was crossing a dried-out river bottom when the deputies opened fire. The river bottom was flat and reddish brown and baked by the sun, and the clay broke up and sank under his boots. He splashed through the few remaining rivulets of water that flowed through the low places in the bottom. He ran up the opposite bank and crouched behind a log and shot at them until they retreated from the bluff out of sight. The log was a cypress trunk that had washed over the bank in a flood and had been left when the water receded. The trunk was eaten by worms. A bullet splintered against it and filled his face with slivers of wood. A trooper had climbed down into a wash and was shooting at him from his flank. Toussaint fired back and saw a puff of dust jump up behind the trooper. He shot again as the man crawled rapidly back to the bluff and took cover. He sighted his rifle across the log and waited. They weren't going to try again. They were going farther down the bluff to slip across the river bottom and flank him. He ran up the levee and down the other side into the woods. His face stung and bled slightly from the cypress splinters. He had been lucky. If they had been more careful they would have taken him.

He continued due west, pausing at intervals to fire at the police. He came out of the woods at evening and crossed a railroad embankment. He could see the swamp ahead of him. He saw the oaks with the moss in their limbs, and the cypress with their trunks swollen out at the waterline, and the alligator grass and bamboo and willow trees, and the white cranes that flew above the gray of the treetops.

The troopers had finally closed the rectangle. He broke through the underbrush, holding the Winchester at port arms, and started up the slope in a full run towards the marsh. It was almost dusk, and if he could reach the top of the rise without being hit the troopers would have to wait until morning before they tried to take him again. There was a rifle report behind him and a bullet slammed into the dirt by his feet. He hunched his shoulders and zigzagged from side to side as two more shots rang out. They were getting closer. He knew they were missing their mark by only a couple of inches whenever he heard that hollow *throp* near his head. He stumbled and fell, landing on his elbows so he wouldn't drop the rifle. He dug his boots in the ground and lurched to his feet. There were more shots behind him, but they were shooting too fast now to be accurate. He thought his lungs would burst before he reached the top of the slope. He dove headlong over the crest and lay panting in the weeds.

They had stopped shooting. Toussaint raised his head just enough to see a dozen men spread out in an even line behind the undergrowth. The swamp was to his back, and there were two deep clay gullies that flanked each side of the crest. He had been in this part of the country before. The state had used convict labor to sandbag the levee when the river overflowed a year ago. He had deliberately chosen this particular place to make his stand. He could knock them down one at a time if they tried to move up through the gullies. He didn't think they would come up behind him. The marsh was twelve miles across, and it would take more than a day to get a flatboat through, because there was only one channel and it was shallow and choked with logs and sandbars. They could enter the marsh farther down on this side and try to circle him, but there were many quicksand bogs and deep holes and he doubted if they would risk losing any men in the water.

They would come in the morning. They didn't have machine guns now, but they would have them in the morning and the sun would be at their backs. They had it all in their favor, but he would make their job hard. He took his handkerchief from his back pocket and spread it neatly on the ground. He counted out his cartridges on the handkerchief. Fifteen, plus nine in the magazine. He wouldn't waste a round. He would wait until they came into full view (and they would have to) before he shot. He put the shells back in his pocket. The bluing of the rifle was worn off. There were specks of rust along the barrel. He rubbed the thin rust off with the palm of his hand. He opened the breech and wiped it and the action clean of grit with his handkerchief.

The afterglow of the sun faded to darkness. He heard a truck grinding in low gear through a field opposite him. They were bringing in more men and guns. He thought about water. He could go without food, but he would have to have something to drink in order to last through the next day. The July sun would beat straight down into his eyes until afternoon. Toussaint crept down the backside of the slope to the edge of the marsh. He would take a deep drink now, and just before daylight he would take off his shirt and soak it in the water so he could suck the moisture from the cloth throughout the morning. The water was thick with lily pads and reeds. He cleared the scum off with his hand. It wasn't good to drink from the swamp, but he had no choice. He could bear the mosquitoes, the hunger, and the long hours without sleep, and if he didn't become sick he could make his fight a good one. The water tasted sour in his mouth. He climbed back up to the crest and lay down, cradling the Winchester in the crook of his arm. A fire was burning down the slope. They were making coffee. He could see a man shadowed against the light throwing sticks in the fire. The range was too far for an accurate shot, and Toussaint would not have fired, anyway. He would wait and give them their chance in the morning.

He waited on his stomach in the dark for dawn to come. He weakened during the night and there was a hard cramp in the lower portion of his body. The swamp water had been bad and he was beginning to feel its effect. He felt light-headed, and the campfire in the distance was blurred and out of focus. He pressed his fist in the pit of his stomach to ease the pain. God, don't let me pass out, he thought. Let me be ready for them in the morning. I got to be at my best tomorrow. This is the end of the line and it's got to be right. I'd rather turn this gun on myself than have them come up here and find me passed out.

He wiped the sweat out of his eyes and shook his head. His mind cleared for a moment, then something twisted inside him like a piece of hot metal. He clenched his teeth to keep from crying out. He had had dysentery in the camp, but not this bad. He gripped his stomach so tightly that his fingernails tore through his shirt. The pain was getting worse. That was the way swamp fever was. It came in spasms. One minute his forehead was hot as an iron, and then he would be shivering with cold.

If only he had a blanket. Or a big, warm quilt like the one he and his brothers slept on behind the French Market in New Orleans. He was thirteen then and the twins were a year older. They came to town on the weekends and stayed behind the Market where the trucks were unloaded. It always smelled of dead fish and rotting vegetables. At night they went down to Bourbon Street and danced on the sidewalk for the tourists. One of his brothers beat on a cardboard box while he and the other brother clapped their hands and sang.

> *Oh Lord I want to be in that number*
> *When the sun begins to shine.*

The tourists threw their nickels and dimes on the pavement, and he hated them for it. He even hated himself when he stooped to pick them up and say Thank you, suh. Yes, yes, thank you, suh. My daddy don't have money to put clothes on our back and we got to crawl around on our hands and knees to scrape up your pocket change, but thank you anyway.

> *Lord I want to be in that number*
> *When the new world is begun.*

After the Quarter had closed for the night they went back to the French Market and counted their money in the dim light of the streetlamp. He felt ashamed when he saw his brothers laugh and shake the change in their hands. They would turn up their palms for the white man's tip the rest of their lives. When they went to sleep he hid his face in the quilt and cried.

Toussaint rolled over in the grass and unhitched the top button of his trousers to ease the knotted ball in his abdomen. The campfire burned lower as the night passed. He bit his lips and his face strained as he tried to straighten his legs. The pain was spreading into his loins. The crickets and the nightbirds were quiet, and he could faintly hear the troopers talking. He thought of Billy Jo and Jeffry, and he wondered if the police would return him to camp in the back of a pickup truck with a tarpaulin over him. Evans would uncover him, and everyone in gang five would stand motionless and sullen and look down at him while the captain made his speech, and Daddy Claxton would cough up phlegm and spit, and Brother Samuel would stand with his straw hat over his ears and pray something about devil warts and the Black Man, and maybe somebody would turn aside and get sick, and Evans would pull the tarpaulin back over him and the truck would drive off and he would roll back and forth with the motion of the truck until it stopped and they put him in a box which would be picked up by the state health board and either buried in the parish cemetery without a headstone or turned over to the medical school.

It was nearly dawn. The eastern sky was rose-tinted with the morning's first light. He pumped a shell into the chamber of his rifle and shifted himself so he could watch the troopers. The slope was covered by a mist from the marsh. His clothes were wet from the dew. His body ached terribly, and he felt like water inside, but the worst part of the fever was over. His head was clear and he would be ready for them when they came.

The sun was red and just above the horizon. The mist over the slope began to thin as the morning became less cool. The troopers were gathered in a circle while the parish sheriff spoke to them. Off to one side a man held the dogs by their leashes. Toussaint squinted down the slope; he couldn't mistake the cork sun helmet and the sunburnt face. It was Evans. The sheriff left the other men and walked to the foot of the rise. He was within range of Toussaint's rifle. He put his hands on his hips and glared up at the crest.

"Come down, Boudreaux."

Toussaint chewed a weed between his teeth. You got courage, he thought. I could bring you down like a coon in a tree.

"I gave you your chance," the sheriff said, and went back to the troopers. They moved up to the base of the slope. Toussaint sighted at a man's throat to allow for the drop of the bullet and fired. He ducked his head just as a burst from a machine gun raked the crest. He ejected the spent cartridge and rolled sideways. They would be waiting for his head to appear at the same place. Two troopers tried to get farther up the rise. They wore campaign hats and Sam Browne belts. He shot at the first one and watched him grab his knee and tumble back down the slope. The other trooper kept coming. He was a heavy man and his face was sweating from the effort. Toussaint worked the lever action and hit him in the chest. He spun around and dropped on his back. He tried to sit up and pull his revolver from his holster. His rifle lay behind him. He fell flat again with his mouth and eyes open, staring at the sky.

Toussaint wished he had a bolt action rifle. It was hard to shoot from a prone position with the Winchester. A deputy fired from behind a log with a machine gun while another trooper ran for the gully. The deputy fired until his clip was empty, the bullets cutting pockmarks in the dirt, ripping up divots of grass around Toussaint's head. Toussaint waited until the hammering of the machine gun had stopped. He put the V of his sights on the campaign hat that showed just above the log. He shot and the hat flew in the air, and he turned his rifle on the trooper in the gully. He missed and the trooper slid back down the clay embankment to safety, then the firing stopped altogether.

Evans came out from behind the truck with the dogs. They were going to turn them loose. Evans released the two German shepherds and kept the bloodhound on its leash. The dogs charged up the hill towards Toussaint. They were fine animals and he didn't want to hurt them. Only a man like Evans would turn his dogs loose to get killed, he thought. He pulled back from the crest, standing erect, and held the rifle by its barrel. He swung and hit the first dog across the muzzle with the stock. The dog flipped sideways and lay quivering on the ground. There was a split along its jowl that ran back to the thick gray-black fur around the neck. The second dog bounded over the crest and tore into Toussaint's legs. He kicked and pounded its neck with the rifle butt. The dog's jaws were locked around his ankle, cutting to the bone. He inverted the rifle and shot it through the back. The bullet broke the dog's spine, and he had to shoot it again to put it out of pain.

He limped back to the crest and took his position. The troopers had moved up the gullies while he fought the dogs. The firing was heavy and it came at him from both flanks. The acrid smell of burnt powder filled the air. He took the last cartridges from his pocket and pushed them down into the magazine. He crawled to the edge of one gully and tried to hold them back. There was a shot behind him, a whine like a bullet ricochetting off rock, and suddenly his stomach was aflame. His eyes throbbed and he couldn't breathe; he was spitting blood. He held his forearm across his belt line, his rifle in one hand, and stumbled away from the crest to the water's edge. He fell in a sitting position with one leg bent under him.

This is it, he thought. I ain't got to go no more. *The wound in my side turns the grass to red.* He saw the troopers come over the rise, silhouetted against the sun. He could see Evans among them, as though he were looking at him through a long tunnel. He could have raised his rifle and shot him, but he knew it would do no good. There would always be another Evans and another after him. Toussaint was very tired. *I wish I could lie in the corn and look up through the stalks.* His head sagged on his chest, and he fell backwards in the leaves with his arms stretched out by his side.

J.P. WINFIELD

He had a morning appointment with the doctor. He took a cab to the doctor's office and gave his name to the nurse and read the newspapers in the waiting room while she told the doctor he was there. Later the nurse took him into a small white room that had the depressing antiseptic smell of a hospital to it. The doctor came in a few minutes later. He was slight and dark featured and he had a gray mustache and his hair was beginning to thin along his forehead.

"What's the trouble?" he said.

"I want a checkup."

"Is it anything in particular?"

"I blacked out a couple of times," J.P. said.

"Under what circumstances?"

"I just blacked out."

"Take off your shirt."

The doctor listened to his heart and breathing with the stethoscope.

"Do a couple of knee bends," he said.

J.P. did them. The doctor listened some more with the stethoscope.

"Let's check your blood pressure."

He wrapped the rubber tourniquet around J.P.'s arm and pumped it up with the rubber ball in his hand.

"It's high," he said.

"How much?"

"Considerably more than it should be. Did you know that you had a heart murmur?"

"No."

"I want to make a cardiograph test."

"What's that?"

"It will tell us more about the condition of your heart."

"How bad is a murmur?"

"It depends. It might mean you have to take things a little easier." J.P. put his shirt back on.

"Do you drink excessively?" the doctor said.

"No."

"Are you taking any kind of drugs?"

"Barbiturates."

"Nothing else?"

"No."

"Who prescribed them for you?"

"Another doctor."

"Why do you need them?"

"I'm a singer. I keep late hours."

"You'll have to stop taking them. Your blood pressure is too high."

"What will happen if I don't stop?"

"They can put a severe strain on your heart."

"Can you give me that test now?"

"Tell the nurse to make an appointment for you tomorrow. I can't give it to you this morning," he said. "Don't take any barbiturates today, regardless of whether you have a prescription or not."

"It's a habit with me. I can't get rid of it just like that."

"You'll have to unless you want to seriously damage your health."

It was raining when J.P. returned the next afternoon. The sky was yellow from the rain, and the trees along the street were wet and very green. He went into the office and put his hat and raincoat on the rack. He went into the small white room and lay on the table while the doctor put the recorders on his chest. When the test was over the nurse came in and removed them. She and the doctor left the room. J.P. dressed and sat on the table. He looked out the window and saw the rain falling on the street out of the yellow sky. There was a magnolia tree in the yard by the side of the building, and the white petals of its flowers were scattered on the grass. The doctor came back in and closed the door behind him.

"I can't tell you much more than I told you yesterday," he said. "The murmur isn't a bad one, but you will have to be careful."

"About them barbiturates. I been taking them a long while. It ain't easy to stop right off."

"You might try a withdrawal period."

"Ain't there a treatment to let you down easy?"

"Is it only barbiturates you're worried about?"

"I done told you."

"You should commit yourself to a hospital if you're addicted to anything stronger."

"I ain't taking nothing else."

"I could get you into a private hospital."

"Listen. You're supposed to help my heart."

"There's nothing to do for a murmur. I can only tell you not to put a strain on yourself. Will you let me contact a friend of mine who treats narcotic cases?"

"No," J.P. said.

"Then good day, sir."

J.P. left the office and walked out on the street in the rain. He caught a taxi and rode back to the hotel. He listened to the tires roll along the wet concrete. He thought about what April had told him of her hospital cure. Six months to a year in a small room without any furniture except a bed that was bolted to the floor, and the shock treatments when they turn the high-pressure hoses on you or strap you to a table and run an electric current through your body, and when they gradually reduce your dosage of narcotics and then one day shut you off completely and you start the nightmares and your nose runs and you get sick if someone talks of food and everything inside you goes crack like a broken plate. Then someday you would get out and think you were clean, and like April you would be on it again in a couple of weeks. He couldn't do it, he thought. It was too much. The taxi arrived at the hotel. He stepped out on the curb and stood under the colonnade out of the rain and paid the driver through the window. A year of treatment and it would start all over. He couldn't beat it, and that was the end of that.

A week later was election day. Lathrop's ticket won the Democratic primary by the largest majority in the state's history, and the opposition was considered fortunate to have taken four parishes in the southern part of the state since it took none in the north. J.P. was at the hotel that evening, and April, Seth, and Hunnicut were listening to the returns over the radio in the next room. Seth opened the door that joined the two rooms. He had a glass of bourbon in his hand, and his face was red. He came over to the bed where J.P. was resting and put his hand on J.P.'s arm.

"Abraham Lincoln took the state," he said.

"I ain't interested," J.P. said, opening his eyes.

"A bonus and free nigger pussy for us all."

"Pour me a drink There's a glass on the table."

Seth went to the other room and brought his bottle back. He clinked the lip of it on the glass and poured.

"I'm going to get me a big redheaded nigger woman," he said.

J.P. sat up in bed and took the drink. He put on his shoes, leaving the strings untied, and went over to the ice pitcher on the dresser and poured some water in the glass.

"Mr. Lincoln has promised free nigger pussy to all white male voters," Seth said.

"Did the sonofabitch really take the whole state?"

"He missed it by four parishes."

"Is J.P. up?" April said from the next room.

"He ran off with a nigger woman," Seth said.

"You're very cute," she said, still in the other room.

"He was with one of them big redheaded ones."

"Why don't you go somewhere else?" she said, now standing in the doorway.

"Your wife don't want me, J.P."

"Let it alone," he said.

"Have a drink with us," Seth said.

"Please leave," she said.

"Sit down and drink some of Lathrop's bourbon."

"Tell him to leave," she said to J.P.

"I offered her a drink."

"You're a drunk pig," she said.

"My, my."

"Tell him to get out, J.P."

"Tell him yourself."

"Both of you make me sick," she said.

"You better go, Seth."

Seth went to the door and toasted them with his glass.

"Peace be with you, my children."

April shut the door after him and put on the latch chain.

"I can't stand that ass," she said.

"Do you have any whiskey?"

"No."

He called down to the bar for a bottle. A few minutes later a Negro porter knocked on the door. J.P. took the bottle and tipped him.

"Are you going to sit around and drink all night?" she said.

"For a while."

"I'm sick of this place. Take me to a movie."

"I'm leaving town in an hour," he said.

"What?"

"I'm going back home for a few days."

"What in the world for?"

"I ain't been there since I went to work for Hunnicut."

"I'm not going to stay here by myself."

"Do what you like."

"I'll go with you," she said.

"You wouldn't enjoy it."

"I'm sick of this hotel."

"Hunnicut will take you to a movie."

"It's not fair to go off and leave me alone. You didn't even tell me."

"I'm going to pack my bag," he said.

He opened his suitcase on the bed and took some clean shirts out of the dresser drawer.

"Damn you," she said.

"Let's don't have no arguments tonight."

"You have to be back for the show Saturday."

"I'll be here."

"I'm going with you. Anything is better than staying here."

"It's a little hick town south of the Arkansas line, and you'd be ready to leave five minutes after you was there."

He wrapped the bottle of bourbon in a soft shirt and put it in the suitcase. He phoned the desk clerk and told him to send up the porter. The Negro came in and took the suitcase out.

"I got to go now," J.P. said.

"Don't you want to stay and do something nice?"

"Goodbye."

He carried his guitar with him in its gray felt cover and caught the nine o'clock train at the depot. It was an old train that pulled mostly freight to a few towns along the state line; it carried only two passenger cars hitched to the rear before the caboose. He sat in the front car in one of the leather seats, and felt the train jolt under him and the couplings bang as it moved out of the station past the lighted platform and baggage wagons and into the yards through the maze of tracks and the green and red signal lamps on the switches, and on past where other trains were pulled off on the sidings and the water tower and the board shacks with their roofs blackened by the passing locomotives. He looked out the window into the dark and saw the lighted glow of the city against the sky far behind him.

There were just a few people in his car. He took his suitcase off the rack and went into the men's room. A gandy-walker was sleeping on the seat by the window. He wore overalls and heavy work shoes and a trainman's cap. There was a lunch pail by his foot. He had a faded bandanna tucked into the bib of his overalls. He slept with his mouth partly open, and his face was unshaved and sunburned. J.P. opened his suitcase and took out the bottle. He mixed a drink with water in a paper cup. The gandy-walker woke up and went to the basin to wash his face. He sat back down and took a sandwich from his lunchpail and began eating. J.P. asked him if he wanted a drink.

"Yeah buddy," he said.

He unscrewed the top from his coffee thermos and held it out for J.P. to pour.

"Have a sandwich," he said.

"No, thanks."

"Go ahead. My old lady makes up more than I can eat."

J.P. took the sandwich. It was a piece of cold steak between bread.

The trainman was eating and drinking and talking at the same time.

"You're the fellow that got on with the guitar. I seen you on the platform," he said. "Go get it and let's play a tune."

"It'll wake up the people in the car."

"We can go out in the vestibule. It ain't going to bother nobody."

"You want another drink?"

He held out the red thermos top while J.P. poured.

"Go get the guitar. I play a little bit myself."

"All right." J.P. pushed aside the curtain that hung over the door of the men's room and went back into the car. The lights were down, and the few people in the car were sleeping. He took the guitar off the rack and unzipped its cloth cover. He put the cover on the seat and went back to the men's room.

"You don't mind, do you?" the trainman said. "I'd like to hear some music before I get off at the next town."

J.P. got his bottle, and he and the trainman went out to the vestibule. The area between the two cars swayed back and forth with the motion of the train. They could hear the wheels clicking loudly on the tracks. The door windows had no glass in them, and the wind was cool and smelled of the farmland. They could see the fields of corn and cotton in the night under the moon, and a pinewoods that stretched over the hills into the dark green of the meadows.

"Play if you want to," J.P. said, handing him the guitar.

"You sure you don't mind? Some fellows don't like other people picking their guitar."

"Help yourself."

"You know 'Brakeman's Blues'?"

"Play it."

The gandy-walker held the fingers of his left hand tight on the strings and frets and strummed with the thumb and index finger of his other hand. He propped his leg on the metal stool that the conductor used to help passengers off, and rested the guitar across his thigh.

I'll eat my breakfast heah,
Get my dinner in New Or-leans
(Right on down through Birmingham)
I'm going to get me a mama
Lord I ain't never seen.

I went to the depot
And looked up on the board,
It said there're good times heah
But it's better on down the road.

He played quite well. J.P. listened and drank out of the bottle. Through the window he could see the black-green of the pines spread over the hills and the moon low in the sky and there was a river winding out of the woods across a field and he saw the moonlight reflecting on the water.

Where was you, mama,
When the train left the shed?
Standing in my front door
Wishing to God I was dead.

"You do all right," J.P. said.
"I reckon you can pick, yourself."
"Play another one."
"No, I'm getting down pretty soon."
"Take a drink."
"Much obliged," he said. He drank out of the bottle. "Play one yourself. I'd like to hear."

J.P. took the guitar from him. He leaned back against the wall of the vestibule, slightly bent over the guitar, and moved the callused tips of his fingers over the frets. The trainman drank from the whiskey and listened.

I'm going to town, honey,
What you want me to bring you back?
Bring a pint of booze
And a John B. Stetson hat.

"That's good. You got a nice style," the gandy-walker said. "I ain't heard good twelve-string guitar like that in a long time."

J.P. set the guitar down and took a drink.

"You must be one of them professionals," the gandy-walker said.

"I used to be a farmer."

"You from around here?"

"A little further north. Up by Arkansas."

"I worked in Arkansas. I railroaded all over the country. I was all the way to California once. I heard a lot of good picking, but you're good as any. Where did you learn?"

"From a bum in a Salvation Army camp."

"Is that a fact?"

"He didn't own nothing but a five-dollar pawnshop guitar, but Jesus he could play. He come up to the house one day and asked for a drink of water and directions to the camp. I give him some meat and biscuit, and about a week later I was walking past the camp to the store and I seen him sitting under a tree with his guitar. He called me over and said he was going to teach me to play. I didn't pay him no mind, and then he started playing and it was like nothing I ever heard. I went down to see him every evening for almost a month, and he'd let me keep the guitar overnight to practice with. Then one day he grabbed a freight and I never seen him again. He was the best, though. I never heard nobody except Leadbelly that could play as good."

J.P. and the trainman both took a drink off the bottle. It was good whiskey. They were nearing a town. The train whistle blew at the crossing, and the red signal light was swinging mechanically from a wood post by the side of the road and a bell was clanging to warn the automobiles. Another train sped past them in the opposite direction, and the noise was loud in the vestibule. The gandy-walker tried to say something and had to stop. He picked up his lunch pail and pointed out the door. The other train finally went past.

"I get down here," he said when it was quiet again. "Thanks for the drink."

"You bet."

"Close the door after me. The conductor don't like it open."

"Sure thing."

"So long, buddy."

"So long," J.P. said.

The gandy-walker swung the vestibule door inward and put his feet on the single steel step. The train was in the yard now and it was not moving very fast, but it was still dangerous to step down unless you did it right. He stood backwards on the step and held to the handrails with the handle of his lunch pail hooked over his thumb. The gravel bedding next to the track rushed by the open door. He eased one foot back and let it barely touch the ground, the rocks skipping up under his shoe, and put his weight down agilely and released his hold, and then he was gone into the dark somewhere behind the last lights of the train.

J.P. stood alone in the vestibule and thought of the tramp that had taught him guitar, and he thought of the songs he had wanted to write which would probably never be written. He thought of Woody Guthrie, an Okie who bummed his way across the Dust Bowl to California during the depression with thousands of others to live in the Hoovervilles and tarpaper shacks and to ride the rods with never enough to eat and to get thrown in jails by town constables who feared a man with a hole in the bottom of his shoe. Guthrie wrote ballads about the Okies and America, and he drifted across the nation from the West to the East Coast and all the time he was writing and singing songs about the things he saw, and other people were singing them in the Hoovervilles and tarpaper shacks, and he never copyrighted what he wrote and his music about the diamond deserts and the redwood forests and the New York island got him almost nothing. And there was Joe Hill, who had belonged to the I.W.W. and sung the songs of the working class that fought outside the factories with axe handles and lengths of pipe when striking was considered Red and the beginning of revolution, and Joe Hill was an I.W.W. spreading revolution and anarchy and his songs were sung by the Marxists, so he was stood against a wall in the Utah penitentiary and shot to death. J.P. thought about Jimmie Rodgers, a railroader from Meridian, Mississippi, who was the finest country guitarist of his time, and who had to quit railroading and make a living by singing when he contracted tuberculosis. But his songs were about the great trains that rolled from California to Texas and he was never able to get away from his life as a railroader. His last days were spent in a

New York recording studio where he made records and became sick with fatigue and slept on a cot until he died.

J.P. looked out the window into the dark. The train was past the station now, and he was out in the country again with the cool night air blowing in his face, the moon rising through the clouds above the green hills. He wondered at what point in his life everything had slipped loose and why he had never written the song about the train that came out of the woods in the late evening with the red sun just above the trees, and why hadn't he written about the heat lightning flashing in the east and the rain falling slowly on the young cotton with the white and red flowers showing along the tops of the rows, and the nigger funeral marches down by the river where the dead were buried on a mud flat that was washed away once a year by the flood? He had never written anything except a campaign song for Jim Lathrop, and now with a heart condition and a cocaine habit there wasn't much time left for writing.

It was still dark when he arrived in town and stepped down on the platform from the train. He carried his suitcase and guitar through the waiting room and out the other door down the front walk towards the town square. The morning was cool and dark and there was just a thin ridge of blue light on the horizon. He crossed the street and walked a block to the square, and he saw the old brick courthouse set up high on the lawn and the luminous face of the clock on the steeple, and there were big shade trees in front and wood benches where the farmers came to sit on Saturdays, and around the four sides of the square there were hardware and drygoods stores and barber shops and feed suppliers, and everything was quiet now and the trees looked black on the lawn and he could hear a cat-squirrel chattering.

He went to the hotel on the corner and took a room over the street. He lay on the bed and watched it grow light until he fell asleep. When he woke at ten o'clock, the sunlight was bright through the window and he had slept with his clothes on. The ceiling fan was turning slowly over his head, but the room was becoming hot as the sun got higher, and he changed his shirt and went out to a café to eat breakfast.

J.P. had no family to speak of. His father had been a tenant farmer who brought his family down from Arkansas during the depression, and after he had located them on a seven-acre company farm he put his single change of clothes in a cardboard suitcase and caught a bus out of town and no one saw him again. The mother worked the fields with the children and sold eggs and butter at back doors in town, and she died two years later from cancer, for which she never had treatment. J.P. and his sister were raised by the older brother, and they continued to live on the seven acres of burnt-out land that would not yield enough cotton to come out with a profit at the end of the year, and when J.P. was almost grown the brother became involved with a Negro woman and was found dead on a country road one night with razor cuts all over his body, and although several Negroes were arrested and one was executed no one was ever sure who had done it. The sister stayed on another year, and one time J.P. caught her laying in the woods with a man, and he beat the man senseless with a stick and dragged her home and locked her in the bedroom, and she got out during the night and he called the sheriff to bring her back and this time he kept her locked in for three days and she got out again and the last he heard of her she was working in a brothel in Little Rock.

So he had no one in town to go see and he didn't really know why he had come, except that he was sick of his wife and vitamin tonic and nigger politics.

He ate an order of eggs and bacon and drank a second cup of coffee. He paid the check and walked down the street to the barbershop. He looked at the courthouse and the trees and the green lawn in the sunlight. The barbershop had a candystriped pole in front of it and an awning that stretched out over the sidewalk. Two men sat in the shade on wicker chairs. The cement by their feet was stained with tobacco juice. J.P. went into the shop and sat in one of the chairs along the wall and picked up a newspaper. There was only one barber, and he was shaving a large fat man in the chair. There were some other men sitting in the chairs farther down the wall.

Look, it's J.P., someone said. It sure is. I didn't recognize you. Hey boys, it's J.P. How are you all doing? We didn't figure to see you back here no more. I'm just visiting a couple of days. Hey, fellows, come on in and see J.P. You don't look like the same fellow. He's been running with them rich women. We been hearing about you. You gone right up to the top. Me and the old lady listen to you every Saturday night. There was a piece about you in the town paper a while back. I was saying to my old lady we used to shoot pool together down at the billiard hall. You fellows look like you're working hard. Farming ain't no good no more, J.P. A man does just as good setting in the barbershop. You sure done all right for yourself. Tell us about some of them rich women. I'm married now. Did you hear that? Old J.P. has got hisself a woman. I bet that don't keep him out of trouble. Let's go down to the billiard hall and I'll buy the beers. Come with us, Sam. I got to keep the shop open for these loafers to set in. Ain't one of them got six bits in his pocket for a haircut. Sam ain't changed none, has he, J.P.? Let's get a beer. He's a buying.

The six of them went to the billiard hall two doors down from the barbershop. There were four pool tables inside and one billiard table, and a long bar with a foot rail ran the length of the room, and there were places to play checkers and dominoes. The room was dimly lighted except for the electric bulbs in the tin shades over the tables, and the fans attached to the walls oscillated back and forth and cleared the smoke from the air. They stood at the bar and J.P. ordered the beers and paid for them. The bottles were sweating and cold, and the beer tasted good. They had another round and J.P. paid. The men he was with were farmers who seldom farmed; they spent their time in the billiard hall or in the barbershop or sitting in front of the courthouse and sometimes in jail. He didn't remember all of their names and there was a couple of them who had recently come over from a pool table and were now drinking that he didn't know at all.

"You remember when we used to go see Ella across the river?" a man named Clois asked. There was a stubble of beard on his face and he wore overalls; he had never worked since he had learned how to switch a pair of dice in a game and not get caught. "We was inside with her and her old man come home and we had to crawl out the back window and hide in the cotton field because he was looking for us with a horse quirt."

"I reckon J.P. is getting his share now," another man said.

"Didn't you hear him say he was married?"

"That don't keep a good man from tomcatting."

"Is you going to be in the movies, J.P.?"

"I ain't figuring on it," he said.

"He's got plenty of what he needs right here."

"You fellows have another beer. I got to run along." He put two dollars for the next round on the bar and finished his beer.

"He's a going to see old Ella, I bet," a man said.

"She's still out there. A dollar a throw," Clois said.

"Come on back later. We're going to have a game in back."

"You all are too sharp for me," J.P. said.

"Listen to that. He used to roll sevens like there wasn't no other numbers."

"See you later," J.P. said.

"Tell Ella we're coming out to see her," Clois said.

J.P. left the billiard hall and walked down the street towards the hardware store. The sun was above the courthouse now, and the day was getting hot. The shade trees across the street shadowed the lawn, and some old men sat on the benches out of the heat whittling shavings on the grass and spitting tobacco juice and watching the people move along the sidewalk. He went into the hardware store and bought some light fishing tackle—a detachable cane pole that came in three sections, twenty feet of six-pound test line, a wood float, some number four hooks, a piece of gut leader, and several small weights. The clerk wrapped the cane pole up and put the rest of the tackle in a paper bag.

J.P. hired one of the town's two taxis and rode down to the river where it made a bend by a deserted sawmill and the logs were jammed up along the shore under the overhanging trees. He walked down the green slope of the bank and looked out over the water, red from the clay and swirling in eddies around the logs; across the river there were more trees and some Negro shacks and a pirogue was tied by its painter to a willow tree and pulling in the current. He laid his tackle down in the grass and found a piece of board to dig worms with. He squatted on the ground and dug in the soft dirt around the roots of a tree, sifting the dirt through his hands and picking out the worms one by one and putting them in a tin can. The worms were small, not like the big night crawlers he used to look for with a flashlight behind the barn at home. He scooped some dirt and leaves into the can and sat down under a tree on the bank and inserted the joints of the detachable pole

into each other. Letting out the twenty feet of line, he tied a knot
one foot from the end of the pole and another right at the tip to
even out the pull of a fish along the whole cane. He slipped his
float up the line and plugged the wood stick in the hole to keep
it secure, and put on two small weights and mashed them tight on
the line with his teeth, and tied the gut leader and the hook with
a slip knot at the end. He threaded a worm carefully over the
hook, not exposing the barb, and dropped the line into the water
between the logs where the catfish nested.

The wind was cool coming through the trees, and he sat in the
shade and looked at the sun reflect on the water. The river had
overrun the bank around the sawmill and the outer door to the
logging chute was partly under water and wood chips stacked in
a pile by the wall were lapped over and pulled out in the current.
He could see the gars turning in the water, their backs and tails
just fanning the surface, and he picked up his line and moved it
to another place between the logs and then the cane jerked hard
in his hand and the float went under. The line was taut and pulling
from side to side in the water as the catfish tried to tangle it in
the logs. J.P. stood up and pulled the catfish out of the river,
swinging him in the air clear of the logs onto the bank beside him.
The fish flipped in the grass with the hook protruding from the
corner of his mouth and tangled himself in the line. J.P. lifted him
up carefully, putting his fingers behind the stingers, and removed
the hook. It was a mud cat, pale yellow from living on the bottom
of the river, with whiskers and a wide-slitted mouth. J.P. cut a
forked twig from a bush and shaved it clean of bark and sharpened
one end to a point. He ran the pointed end through the fish's third
gill and out the mouth and dropped him in the water and stuck
the other end of the twig firmly in the side of the bank. The fish
ginned the water with his tail and tried to get off the twig.

J.P. put another worm on the hook and threw his line out among
the logs. He caught three sun perch, another catfish, and two
cottonfish which he threw back. He wanted to catch some bass
but it was too early in the year. The time to catch bass was in the
early fall when the weather was cool and he could go upriver in
a boat beyond the sawmill to those deep ponds cut back in the
bank and surrounded by trees and the water was dark and still.
About evening he would fish the reeds with a flyrod and the fly

would rest motionless on the surface and he would snap it back over his head and whip it dry in the air and cast again; there would be a flick of silver in the water when the bass hit and the rod would throb in his palm, and he would take up the slack in the line with one hand and use the automatic reel with the other. The bass would fight hard and finally J.P. would dip him out of the water with his net and put him in the straw creel in the bottom of the boat.

He caught two bullheads, and it was late afternoon and the sun was red in the west over the green of the trees. He took the forked twig out of the water and slid the fish off and laid them on the bank. He cleaned the perch first, scaling them and leaving the heads, and then he cleaned the catfish. He slit their stomachs open from the gills back to the tail and scooped out the entrails and threw them in the river, then he snapped the heads off cleanly by breaking the vertebras backwards; then he cut two long slices along the dorsal fin from front to back and peeled the skin off in strips. He washed each of the fish in the water and wrapped them in the paper sack his tackle had come in.

He walked the two miles back to town along a dirt road with trees and fields and farmhouses on each side. The sun was now setting and the day had become cool and the wind dried the sweat on his neck. There were a few rain clouds beginning to build and the sky looked green, the way it does before it rains at evening during the summer. The fish felt moist in his hand through the paper sack. He wanted to come back tomorrow and fish farther upstream for the bass, even though he knew it was too early. He looked at the sky and hoped that the rain would only be a shower so the fishing would still be good the next day. He walked into town and stopped at a café and had the cook prepare the fish for him. They were fried in cornmeal, and he ate them with his hands, the grease hot on his fingers, and drank two bottles of beer. He gave the cook a dollar and paid for the beer and picked up his pole, which he had left outside, and went to the hotel.

It started to rain after he reached the hotel, and he looked out his window and watched the water streak down the glass and the evening twilight diminish from green to lavender and the neon sign come on over the billiard hall. The street and the high sidewalks and the courthouse lawn and the one-story brick buildings were empty of people. The afterglow of the sun faded in the wet sky, and the small crack of red in the clouds low on the horizon sank out of sight, then it was dark.

He went down to the billiard hall, since everything else in town was closed after seven o'clock except the gas station, the café, and a couple of taverns. He went inside and drank a beer at the bar. Some of the men he had been with earlier were still there. He listened to the crack of the billiard balls and the squeak of the cues being chalked and the cursing when someone missed a shot. Clois, the man who could switch a pair of dice in a game or make them walk up a backboard and come back sevens so often that he was required to throw with a cup, come over to J.P. and asked him to join the others in back.

"What are you playing?"

"Craps. We never play nothing else," Clois said. "Like the nigger says, them galloping dominoes ain't done me wrong yet."

They walked the length of the bar past the pool tables and went through a door in the back. There was a room bare of any furniture with no windows and a single light bulb with a green shade like those over the pool tables. A dirty blanket was spread on the floor, and six or seven men were kneeling around in a circle and one was bouncing the dice off the wall back onto the blanket.

"Mind if me and J.P. gets in?" Clois said.

The men looked at them and then back at the game. The man who was shooting smacked the dice off the wall.

"Ain't you fellows ready to let some more money in the game?" Clois said.

"Shut up. Can't you see I'm shooting?" the man with the dice said.

He hit them off the wall again and crapped out.

"All right. You done made me lose my point. You can get in now," he said.

"Whose dice?" Clois said.

"You got money?" a man said.

"What the hell do you think I come in here for?"

"Put it on the board."

Clois dropped two crumpled one-dollar bills on the blanket and took the dice.

"None of your stuff, neither. This is a straight game," the man said.

"I ain't pulling nothing on you boys," Clois said, and rolled his sleeves up over his elbows.

The bets went down on the blanket. Clois knelt on one knee and rubbed the dice between his hands. J.P. watched and didn't bet. Clois rolled.

"Six is my point. Right back the hard way," he said, and put two more dollars on the blanket. He cracked the dice between his palms. "Come on, cover it. I ain't got all night."

He shot four times. His shirt collar was damp with sweat. There were small beads of perspiration over his face and in the stubble of his beard. He retrieved the dice and on the fifth throw he made his point.

"Thirty-three, the hard way," he said. He picked up the bills and put them in front of him. "Shooting it all."

The others covered him. He rolled a seven.

"Let it ride," he said.

He made three more passes and he had a good pile of bills and change in front of him.

"I'll shoot five this time," he said.

"What's the matter?" a man said.

"The dice ain't good forever." He picked up all the money except a five-dollar bill and put it in his pocket. He bounced the dice off the wall.

"Boxcars. You get some of your green back," he said.

"You always drag at the right time," a man said.

"It's part of knowing how to play."

"Give me the goddamn dice," the man said.

"You fellows don't know how to lose."

"You talk too much."

"Roll the dice."

"You want in, J.P.?" a man said.

"All right."

He knelt in the circle with the others and put three dollars in the center of the blanket. He rolled a four.

"Little Joe at the cathouse do'," Clois said. "I'm betting he makes it."

"Put your money down, smart man."

"Ten bucks. Give me three to one," Clois said.

"You're on," the man said.

J.P. made it on the second pass. He let his money ride and crapped out. The bartender brought in a tray of sandwiches and beer. One of the men put a bill on the tray. The dice came around to J.P. again and he shot five dollars and threw a three.

"I ain't hot tonight," he said.

"You ain't made your point yet. You still got another shot," Clois said.

"Shooting ten," J.P. said.

"Fade," a man said, covering his bet.

He rolled an eleven and doubled his money. He shot the twenty and doubled again.

"I'll drag half of it," he said.

"Let it ride," Clois said. "You can break the game."

"I ain't hot."

"You done made two passes."

"Dragging half of it," J.P. said to the others.

"You ain't making no money like that," Clois said.

"I ain't feeling it tonight."

"One more pass and it's eighty bucks."

"Shut up and let him play," a man said.

"Coming out," J.P. said.

He crapped out on a deuce. The other men split up the twenty dollars he had left remaining on the blanket. J.P. put the rest of the money in his wallet.

"You quitting?" Clois said.

"I reckon."

"Wait a minute. I'll go with you."

Clois picked up the bills in front of him and folded them neatly and put them in his shirt pocket and buttoned it. The others didn't want him to leave. He was ahead a good bit.

"That's too goddamn bad," he said, looking at them with his dull gray eyes. He and J.P. left the room.

They drank a beer at the bar and watched the pool games. It was still raining outside. The light from the neon sign was red and green on the front window.

"Let's go out on the highway," Clois said.

"Are they still doing business out there?"

"The sheriff raided it a while back but it's open again now. They caught one of the church deacons trying to zip up his britches and hide in a closet. I reckon they figure they better not raid it no more unless they want to find the preacher and the mayor next time."

They finished the beer and went outside in the rain to Clois's car, a 1941 Ford with a smashed fender, one headlight, and a broken back window. They drove down the main street out of town with the windshield wipers switching against the glass and the rain falling in the light of the single headlamp. Clois opened the glove compartment and took out a half-empty pint of bourbon and unscrewed the cap and drank. He passed it to J.P. They went on for several miles and turned off the highway onto a dirt road, the mud and the gravel banging under the fenders. There was no moon, and the fields on each side of them were wet and dark. Ahead, there was a large two-story white house that was set back from the road with nothing around it. It looked like one of those big frame farmhouses built during the early part of the century. The shades were drawn, and there were two cars parked in the yard. Clois stopped by the side of the house, and they got out and walked through the rain to the front porch and knocked. The door opened a small space and a dark-haired woman of about forty-five looked out at them. She had a gold tooth and her face was thin-featured and pale. She opened the door wider and let them in.

"Good evening, Miss Sarah," Clois said.

"Wipe your feet before you track up my rug," she said.

"You remember J.P., don't you?"

"I don't keep count of who comes in here. You still got mud on your feet."

"Yes, ma'am. Sorry."

They went through the hallway into a big living room that was lighted by a single lamp in the corner. The only furniture was a sofa, a scarred coffee table, and a few uncomfortable chairs. Three women sat on the sofa, and there was a drunk oil-field worker in one of the chairs trying to make another woman sit on his lap.

"Business ain't too good tonight," Clois said.

"Do you want something to drink?" Miss Sarah said.

"I don't reckon."

She looked at him hard.

"A couple of beers will be all right," he said.

She went into the back of the house and returned with two bottles.

"That's one dollar," she said.

He gave it to her. J.P. looked at the women on the sofa. Two of them looked old and a little used. The third, a big blond woman, sat at one end. She wore white shorts and a silk blouse, and she had good thighs and her breasts were heavy and loose, and he could see that she wore no underwear. He put his beer down on the table and went in back with her.

Her room was near the back porch, and he could hear the rain falling against the side of the house. She turned on a table lamp and tilted the shade so that most of the light would fall in the corner away from the bed. She undressed without looking at him or speaking. Her breasts were very large. She lay down on the bed and put a pillow under her.

It had stopped raining the next morning, and the sun was bright outside the hotel window when he awoke. He thought about the prostitute from the night before, and for a moment he wanted her again. There was a bad taste of whiskey in his mouth. He went into the bath and brushed his teeth. He had gone back to the billiard hall with Clois after they left the brothel, and both of them had gotten drunk on a bottle of cheap bourbon, and now he was thirsty and dry inside. He drank too much water from the tap and it made him dizzy again. He went back to bed and lay on the cool sheets under the ceiling fan and put the prostitute out of his mind and didn't think of anything except the coolness around him. He slept for a while and awoke and the fan was turning over him, its long flat wood blades making a flicking circle of shadow and light on the ceiling. The breeze felt very good and he went to sleep again. By noon he was feeling much better, and he showered with cold water and went out to eat.

Later, he returned to the hotel and picked up his fishing tackle. He felt pleasant after eating, the day was fairly cool from last night's rain, and the whiskey taste was gone from his mouth. He walked the two miles along the farm road to the river, with the fields of cotton and corn and watermelon and the red dirt land on each side and the Negro shacks and the big cotton gin made from tin and the pine and oak trees that grew back from the river bank in the distance. He walked through the trees to the river, and the ground felt soft under his feet. He saw an armadillo move through the grass looking for insects; its hard armored shell was hunched on its back, and it had a spike tail and a small head with little ears and shrunken black eyes. He remembered when he used to hunt them with a .22 after the rains.

He came out of the trees by the sawmill. The river was higher than it had been yesterday, and it swirled around the door of the logging chute that hung open in the water. He looked along the bank for grasshoppers, but the grass was too wet for them to be jumping. A Negro boy of about fourteen came down the bank on the other side of the river and got into the pirogue tied to a willow tree. He wore a ragged wash-faded shirt and short pants that hung to his knees. He sat in the stern of the pirogue and pushed it out in the current from the bank with the paddle. J.P. called to him.

The boy stroked across the river and held the boat steady in the back current along the bank by sticking the paddle in the soft clay at the water's edge.

"You want to make fifty cents?" J.P. said.

"What I got to do?"

"Let me use your boat for a while."

"My daddy don't let nobody else use it."

"Then I'll give you the fifty cents to row me down to the ponds." The boy looked at him, unsure.

"You want the fifty cents, don't you?" J.P. said.

"Yes, sir. I wants it, but I don't want no whipping when I get home."

"Come up here and help me dig some worms."

"Yes, sir."

The boy got out of the boat into the shallows and dragged the bow onto the bank. He took the bailing can from under the seat and squatted on his haunches by J.P. and helped him dig in the ground. They filled the can with worms, and the boy got into the pirogue's stern and took up the paddle while J.P. slid them off the mud back into the water and jumped in. The boy swung them into the current and headed downstream towards the ponds. There were oaks and cypress on each side of the river leaning out over the water. It was cool in the shade of the trees, and when they went around a bend close to the bank the overhanging moss swept across the bow of the boat. J.P. put his pole together and fixed his line as they neared the place where the river widened and cut back into the ponds. The water was dark from the rain. He could see the gars breaking the surface with their backs. He hoped there were none around the ponds. The fishing was never any good when the gars were near, since they preyed on smaller fish. The boy paddled them into a cove that was fairly large and shaded by the trees. The water was covered with lily pads along the bank, and they rose and swelled in the waves from the boat. The boy grabbed a willow limb and pulled them close to the bank and tied the painter to the trunk of the tree. J.P. threw his line near the lily pads. Bass always stayed in the shady places in hot weather. The boy touched him on the back and pointed to the bailing can with the worms. He had a throw line in his hand with three hooks and a lead washer for a weight. J.P. handed him the can. The boy baited only one of his hooks and let the line hang over the side down in the mud. He waited a few minutes and pulled his hook out of the water and spit on the bait and put it back in again. It was a Negro superstition. They believed that fish would bite if you spit on the hook, even a bare one.

They fished for an hour and a half. J.P. caught one sun perch and one smallmouth black bass. It had rained too much for the fishing to be any good. The boy caught a gar. The line was wrapped around his wrist, and it cut his skin when the gar hit and started to run. The boy pulled with both hands, the veins standing up hard in his wrist, as the gar thrashed the water with his tail and tangled himself in the line. The boy got him against the side of the boat and held him partly out of the water and got his pocket-knife open with one hand and worked the point into the weak spot in the back of the gar's neck where the armored skin joined the head. He pushed the knife to its hilt and pulled it free and then plunged it in again. The gar snapped his long pointed jaws at the line, and then his body went weak when the vertebra was cut and his tail stopped ginning the water. The boy pulled the gar into the boat by the gill and laid him in the bottom. He smiled at J.P. His face and neck were beaded with sweat, and a thin rivulet of blood ran down from his wrist over the back of his hand. He took the knife off the board seat and cut down the back of the gar and pulled the hard skin away, then he slit open the belly and scooped out the entrails and threw them onto the bank. He let the head remain. The gar was a big one even after he had been dressed. The eyes looked like glass now and the jaws were open, exposing the long rows of teeth. The boy would take him home and his family would barbecue the meat over an open fire on a spit. J.P. had never tasted gar; only Negroes would eat it (along with mullet and cottonfish and coon and possum), but they said it was good. The boy was quite happy. He rowed them back down the river and talked about the fish. He asked J.P. if he had ever seen one that large. J.P. said he hadn't. The boy was very pleased and he wanted to give J.P. part of the meat.

He paid the boy and gave him his tackle since the fishing would not be any good until a few days from now when the water went down, and he would have to return to the show before then. He went back to the hotel and read the newspapers in the lobby for a while. He ate dinner at the café and walked down the street as the glow of the late afternoon sun lessened to twilight and the faint evening wind blew through the trees on the courthouse lawn. He had nothing to do except shoot pool with Clois and the others or get drunk or go whoring, and he didn't feel like doing any of it.

He caught the night train to the city. As he rode through the dark fields, he realized that his hometown held nothing for him anymore. Time had removed him and it would not allow him to go back. The fishing had taken him back for a short while to the way things had been two years ago, but he knew now that he existed only in the present moment of the wheels clicking over the tracks, and time would carry him farther away from the world of small towns and Saturday night whorehouses and the red clay cotton fields and the nigger funeral marches and fishing for bass in the ponds during the early fall.

He was hopped when he arrived back in the city. He had opened one of the white packets from his suitcase on the train, and he stayed high on cocaine and whiskey for the next two days. He slept little, and he lost any sense of night and day. Later, he could not remember how much he had taken or drank. He walked the streets all one night, and was asked to leave a bar after he became involved in an argument with another man. He picked up a prostitute, although he didn't recall it afterwards, and she rolled him for his watch and wallet. On Saturday he was with April in their room, and he hadn't changed clothes or shaved since he had gotten off the train. His shirt was soiled and there was a thick feeling in his head.

"You've got the show tonight," she said. "Don't you understand what I'm saying? Listen to me."

He wanted to get out of the room. He didn't know how he had gotten there, anyway.

"Don't give a goddamn," he said.

"You let those hicks know what you are and you're finished."

"Kick the habit with Live-Again."

"Oh, you stupid—"

"Sonabitch said something in a bar."

"Will you please listen to me? You have to go to the auditorium at eight o'clock."

"I ain't going."

Virdo Hunnicut didn't see him that night, or he would not have let him go onstage. J.P. had shaved and put on fresh clothes, but there were razor knicks on his face and his blank eyes showed that he was still high and his fingers couldn't find the right chords on the guitar. April talked to the director, and they decided to let him sing without his guitar and to use the band for accompaniment.

"What the hell is this? Give me my goddamn guitar."

"Your wife thought it might be better if you just sang tonight," the director said.

"I ain't singing with no band."

He went on the stage and the lights were hot in his face and made his eyes water. He heard the people applauding for him, and then the auditorium became quiet and he was standing behind the microphone with the guitar in his hand. The director was saying something to him in a hoarse whisper from the wings. *Go on, man. They're waiting for you.* Still he didn't begin. He looked out at the audience for almost a half minute. There was the scraping of chairs and a few coughs in the silence. Some of the people thought it was a joke and part of the show. *For God's sake, do something*, the hoarse whisper said. Those who thought it was a joke laughed, and then the laughter stopped and it was silent again. The building was hot and poorly ventilated. He started to sing. His voice sounded strange and far off. He hit the wrong notes on the guitar and he couldn't remember the lines to the song. He stopped playing and looked out at the audience. His face was sweating from the heat of the lights. *Get him off there*, a voice from the wings said. He started to play again and it was worse than before. He suddenly became aware of where he was, and he tried harder to get the song right. He was singing the words faster than the tempo of the guitar. His throat went dry and his voice cracked. Then he heard someone in the audience; it was a single sound from one person, not loud, but it carried through the auditorium: "Boooooooooooh."

AVERY BROUSSARD

Early the next afternoon he had dinner with Suzanne at her apartment. It was on the second floor of an old white brick building on Dauphine. The red of the bricking showed through where the paint had flaked away, and there was a balcony around the courtyard and a big willow tree by the iron gate; the flower beds in the court were planted with Spanish daggers and jasmine and oleander, and the interior was furnished from antique shops in the Quarter with dark handcarved wood chairs, an old Swiss clock, French curtains, and a folding Oriental screen decorated with dragons and embossed birds separated the living and dining rooms. The back room where she worked had a skylight that was stained green by moss and rainwater and there were big glass doors that opened onto the narrow brick-paved street below. There were reproductions of Cézanne and Velázquez and Goya along the walls and a charcoal sketch of a street scene near St. Louis Cathedral was attached to her easel, and five or six pastels of other scenes in the Quarter which she sold to the tourists in Pirates Alley were spread out on her table.

She wore a white dress and her hair was dark like her eyes, and her figure was fine to look at. She served the food from the kitchen, and there were drops of perspiration around her temples. As she reached across Avery to set his plate he could see her dress tighten across her breasts and he thought of the first time he had taken her fishing in the rowboat and they had put into the bank, and he had to look away from her. She put a slender green bottle of Barolo wine in front of him and two glasses. There was an empty wine bottle with a wicker basket around it in the center of the table and she had burned red candles down over it until the sides were thickly beaded with melted tallow. She put a fresh candle in the top and lighted it and sat down across from him and served the spaghetti and the light of the flame reflected in her eyes and made them look darker.

"Don't you like it? I think it's one of the best in the Quarter," she said.

"What?"

"The apartment."

"Yes." He was still thinking about the way her dress tightened.

"I knew you would like it. I furnished it myself. It was a mess when we first took it. I think it must have been a brothel. Strange men knock on the door sometimes and we have to convince them that we're not running a business."

He poured the wine for her. She sipped it and looked at him over the top of the glass. He tried not to think about the times they went down the bayou in the rowboat. He knew she would know what he was thinking, and their conversation would become strained and he would blurt out something and both of them would be embarrassed. He felt her dress brush him under the table. He pulled his foot back under the chair self-consciously. They finished eating and went into the living room. They took the wine bottle and the glasses with them. He sat down on the sofa while she opened the doors to the balcony to let the breeze in.

"What did you do in Spain?" he said.

"I studied in Madrid most of the time. It's so lovely there, even though it's not Spain. You have to go out in the country to see Spain. I went to some of the small villages to paint. The people are terribly poor, but they're friendly and simple and they like Americans. I got some wonderful sketches in Granada and Sevilla. The old Moorish buildings are like lacework, and the cafés and parks are splendid."

She sat down on the sofa beside him. The wind was cool through the open door. She ran her fingers over the stem of the wineglass.

"Would you like to go out?" he said.

"Let's stay here."

"Won't your roommate be home?"

"She has a date with some graduate student from Tulane."

He could feel it growing inside him. He wanted to hold it back but he knew he wouldn't be able. He looked at her fingers on the wineglass. She set the glass on the table and put her hands in her lap. She crossed her legs and the edge of her slip showed at the knee. He watched her hand curve around the wine bottle as she picked it up to pour in his glass. He leaned over and kissed her. She put her palm lightly on the back of his neck. He could smell the slight scent of perfume in her hair. She turned her face up and he kissed her again. He couldn't stop it now. He tried to pull her down on the sofa. She pressed one hand against his chest.

"You knew it would be like this when I came over," he said. He still held her.

"You can't drop something for three years and then pick it up again just like that."

"You want it as much as I do."

"Yes. But we can't. Please, Avery."

"It's all right."

"No. Please."

He kissed her and held himself close to her and ran his hand along her thighs. He heard her breathing increase.

"You'll hurt both of us," she said. "You must know that. We'll both feel bad about it when it's over." Her eyes were wet. She relaxed and didn't try to push him away anymore. He put his hand inside her blouse and felt her breasts. He unbuttoned the blouse and tried to pull it back off her shoulders. "Let me up. We can't do it here," she said.

He had to wait a moment in order not to embarrass himself before he could stand up and follow her into the bedroom. His shirt stuck to his back with perspiration. She drew the curtains on the window and undressed and lay on the bed with her hair spread out on the pillow. Her skin was white and her waist was slender and she wore the gold cross and chain around her throat, and when he looked at her he felt something drop inside him. He lay beside her and kissed her. She reminded him of how she had looked the night they had the argument in Biloxi.

"I'm sorry to hurt you," he said.

She put her arms around his neck and held her cheek to his.

"I always loved you. I was never as happy as when I was with you," she said.

"You're a swell girl."

"Do it to me. I want you so badly."

"You won't cry anymore?"

"No. I promise. It was just because I didn't want everything to turn out bad again. Oh, Avery."

"Does it hurt you?"

"It's lovely. I'd forgotten how good it is. Do you still like me?"

"You're wonderful. Was there anyone between?" he said.

"No."

"You're my lady."

"I was always your lady."

"My darling lady."

She kissed him hard on the mouth and he felt her body tense as her arms tightened around his back.

"Hold me. Do it harder. Oh Avery darling hurt me please hurt me. It's so good. My lovely sweet darling hold me. I love you terribly."

They lay in bed and drank wine and smoked cigarettes. He pulled her to him and kissed her on the cheek and bit the lobe of her ear. The back of her neck was damp. She held herself close to him and put her forehead under his chin.

"I'm sorry for the way I acted," she said.

"You don't feel bad about it?"

"Of course not. Do it to me once more."

"Aren't you tired?"

"I could never be tired of this."

"Your roommate might come home."

"We have time. Let me do it to you. We've never done it like this. I want to do it every way we can."

She changed her position. He looked up at the gold cross swinging from her throat and her hair on her shoulders.

"Am I good like this?" she said.

"It's fine."

"I want to always make it good for you."

"You're nice inside," he said.

"You're being bad."

"I'm sorry."

"I want you to be bad. I want you to say bad things."

"I like your thighs," he said.

"Do you love me?"

"Yes."

"Very much?" she said.

"I love your thighs."

"Now you are treating me bad."

"I do love you."

He pulled her down on him and felt the softness of her breasts against him and rubbed his hands over her back and down the insides of her legs. She propped herself on her arms again and smiled down at him, and he looked at the whiteness of her breasts and the curve of her neck and her dark Creole eyes and then he held her very tightly and he felt his loins grow warm and then hot and everything went out and away from him. She leaned down and kissed him and then lay beside him and put her arm across his chest. He felt empty and cool inside, breathing her perfume and the smell of her hair, and he didn't want to move or get up or even talk.

"We'll have to get dressed, darling," she said later. "I'm sorry."

"Let's go to a hotel."

"It's too late. You have to work tomorrow."

"Lock your roommate out," he said.

"You're unkind."

"Your roommate is unkind."

"We'll go to a hotel tomorrow evening and stay together all night."

"Do you promise?" he said.

"We can get some good wine and you can drink and I'll take care of you."

"You're my wonderful lady."

"I'll always be your lady."

They dressed and she made up the bed and combed her hair. She took the two glasses and the wine bottle into the dining room and put them on the table.

"Good night," he said.

"Good night. I love you."

"You're very pretty."

"Come over as soon as you get off from work," she said.

"Will you keep your promise?"

"Yes. Kiss me good night."

"Pretty lady."

"Good night," she said.

"Good night."

He met her at the apartment the next evening, and they had dinner at a small French restaurant on Burgundy Street that had red-checkered cloths on the tables, and they sat at the bar and ate oysters on the half shell and drank beer, and the Negro waiter opened the oysters with a knife and squeezed a lemon on the muscle and if it didn't twitch he threw it away and opened another. They bought a bottle of Liebfraumilch from a package store and they stayed in a hotel outside the Vieux Carré and she was there beside him whenever he wanted her. They finally went to sleep after midnight, and he awoke later and felt it grow in him again. Her body was cool from the breeze through the window and her legs were long and white. They lay undressed on top of the sheets with the green wine bottle in an ice bucket by the side of the bed, and when the sky turned dark blue just before morning he didn't want to see the sun come up and the night to end.

The following afternoon he had to check in with the parole board, and afterwards they went to the beach and rented a cabana under some palm trees. They watched the waves roll up on the sand and the crimson sun going down beyond the water's edge and a single sailboat with a red sail tacking in the wind. They brought their bathing suits and dressed inside the canvas cabana, and after dark they went swimming in the surf. The moon reflected off the water and the palm trees hissed in the breeze. In the distance they could see the glow of the city. She ran through the breakers and swam out quite far from shore and then swam back and knelt in the shallows, sitting on her heels, laughing and panting for breath, with the small waves breaking around her waist. They went back to the cabana and lay down in the sand. He kissed her on the mouth and smelled the salt in her hair. The moonlight came through the open flap of the cabana and shone on her ankles, and he wanted to do it right there but there were other people further down the beach.

"As soon as we get home," she said.

"What will we do with your roommate?"

"We'll send her out."

"You're getting cruel also," he said.

"She won't mind. She's quite nice."

"I don't like her."

"You don't know her."

"I don't like her, anyway. She stays home too much. Tell her to have an affair with someone," he said.

"Wasn't it nice in the hotel? Let's go there again."

"I don't get paid until Saturday."

"I have money."

"You always have money," he said.

"Daddy spoiled me. I want you to spoil me too."

"I'll spoil you in a particular way. Will you really ask your roommate to go?"

"Yes, darling."

"I'll spoil you the rest of the night."

"I wish we could always be in bed and do good things to each other," she said.

"We could close the flap now."

"Those people might come by."

He slipped the strap of her black bathing suit off her shoulder and put his hand on her breast.

"You're taking advantage," she said.

"I'll do other things when we're in bed again."

"We'll do them together. But not now."

"You have nice breasts."

"Oh, Avery."

"They are."

"You're terrible."

"Do you like me terrible?" he said.

"Yes. I love it."

He unrolled the canvas flap over the door opening, and as they dressed he looked at the smooth curve of her waist and the indentation of her stomach when she bent over to get her sandals, and he felt that same feeling of something dropping inside him. They rolled their bathing suits in a towel and walked up the beach along the white sand by the edge of the surf towards the lighted walkway and the amusement park where her car was. A few hundred yards behind the beach they could hear the music from the carousel and see the brightly lit Ferris wheel revolving against the sky. They stopped at one of the open-air stands in the park and drank a beer with the sea breeze blowing in from the Gulf. Her car was in the darkened gravel parking lot, and he drove them back to town. It was the same low-slung, wide-based, Italian sports convertible that she had gotten for her graduation from high school. It had four forward gears, and when he stepped on the accelerator he could feel the guttural roar of the exhaust through the steering wheel and the power of the take-off pressed him back comfortably in the thick leather of the seat. She sat close to him with both her hands on his arm and her cheek on his shoulder and her wet hair whipping behind her in the wind. They drove along those wide curving cement drives outside New Orleans that wind through groves of oak and cypress trees with the moss hanging in the branches, and the night air smelled of lilacs and jasmine and freshly cut grass.

They were alone at the apartment and they made love in her bed. She got up to make sandwiches in the kitchen and she brought them back on a silver tray with two iced drinks of cognac and orange juice. They ate the cold chicken sandwiches and drank the brandy and then did it again.

"Am I making you too tired?" he said.

"Don't be silly. It gets better every time."

"The cognac makes it better."

"Darling?"

"What is it?" he said.

"Can those parole board people do anything to you?"

"Why do you ask that now?"

"I was worried about it. I know you don't like to talk about it, but I worry."

"I just have to go see them once a month."

"You looked angry when you came out today," she said.

"I get sick at my stomach every time I go in there."

"Don't do anything that would make them send you back. I couldn't stand it."

"I won't."

"I'm sorry for talking about it. I know you hate it," she said.

"It's all right."

"Does it bother you much?"

"No," he said, thinking of the nightmares he had been having in which he was back in the work camp, expecting to wake to the morning whistle for breakfast and roll call and then the ride in the trucks out to the line.

"I know it bothers you. I can tell," she said.

"You're a good lady."

"I wish I could take it all away. Do you think about it when you're with me?"

"I think about your thighs."

"Always think about my thighs."

"I like to stay between them."

"Tell me something else."

"You have good hands," he said.

"Do you really forget the work camp when you're with me?"

"Yes."

"I'm so glad. I want you to be happy. We can stay in a good position and you don't have to think about anything except me."

"Can you do it again?"

"I'll do it any time you want me."

"I want you all the time," he said.

"Tell me bad things. I want you to. I think I'm becoming degenerate."

"Is it good?" he said.

"It's wonderful. Do it hard. Make me hurt."

"You're worse than I am."

"Is there any other way to do it?"

"Not that I've thought about."

"We'll find new ways," she said.

"I don't think so."

"Let's drink some more cognac and make it nicer. Good Lord, I know I'm becoming degenerate."

"Do you want some cognac?" he said.

"Yes. You can feel the fire go down inside you. Will you mind if I leave you a minute? I'll be right back."

She returned with the square, dark-colored bottle and filled each of their glasses half full. She sat beside him and drank hers down fast. It was strong brandy and it made her eyes water.

"Can you feel it get hot inside you?" she said. "Isn't it nice? I'm going to have some more."

"You'll be tight."

"Will you like me better?" she said.

"I like you any way."

She drank more of the brandy and set the empty glass on the floor by the bottle.

"God, that's strong," she said.

He kissed her mouth and neck.

"I'm sorry. You've been waiting," she said.

"I love you very much."

"I'm so happy with you, Avery."

He kissed her again and he felt the coolness of her arms around his neck and then it began to swell inside him and he held her very tight with his face in her hair and he felt it go through his body and his entire existence was concentrated in that one moment and he could feel the muscles in the back of his legs quiver and then he was quiet and relaxed inside, and they went to sleep.

They saw each other every evening, and sometimes they stayed in the apartment or checked into a hotel outside the Quarter or went dancing or went to the parties that one of her friends gave, and one time when the pipeline shut down for a couple of days because of rain and Avery was free they spent the night in a small guest house down by the beach and he rented some flounder gaffs and flashlights and they hunted along the edge of the surf for the flat-sided fish lying in the sand, he barefoot and in dungarees and stripped to the waist and she in toreador pants with a white blouse held closed by a knot tied at the stomach; and he cleaned the fish on the beach and built a fire from pieces of driftwood while she opened two bottles of beer from the cooler they had brought with them. He fixed the fish on sticks, and they baked them over the fire and peeled them off in strips to eat. They sat in the sand, still warm from the day's sun, and drank another beer. There was no one else on the beach, and they put out the fire and undressed and went swimming. Later, they walked along the edge of the water and hunted for seashells with the surf rolling over their bare feet and the moon low on the horizon and the sky clouded from a thunderstorm that was building in the Gulf.

They went to a party one Saturday night and left early. It was like the other parties they had gone to. The rooms were crowded with people, and there was a progressive combo trying to play above the noise; the bass player passed out in the hallway, and Wally, the redheaded, blue-eyed Cambridge boy with a taste for Scotch, gave an imitation of a Baptist preacher. Someone opened the door of a bedroom at the wrong time and there was a scene and a girl began crying and left by herself since her date had been one of those in the bedroom. The people in the upstairs apartment knocked on the walls and floor, and Wally went out and came back with a bum he had found in Jackson Park and the bum got sick in the flower bed of the courtyard and Wally was told to leave by the hostess. The knocking on the walls and floor continued, and finally Avery and Suzanne left by the side door without saying good night to anyone and walked down the quiet cobblestone street in the dark and breathed the cool night air. They stopped in a bakery and bought some pastry and went to her apartment to make coffee.

She fixed café au lait in the kitchen and brought the coffeepot and the hot milk out on a tray and they drank it in the living room and ate the pastry.

"Did you mind leaving the party?" he said.

"Not if you wanted to go."

"I like it better here."

"I like it too," she said.

"Who is Thomas Hardy?"

"He was an English writer."

"Somebody asked me if I'd read him."

"What did you say?"

"I told him I didn't keep up with professional baseball anymore," Avery said.

She put her napkin to her mouth as she laughed.

"I know who asked you," she said. "It was the little buglike fellow with the baggy trousers. He's Wally's roommate. He pays the rent for both of them. He thinks Wally is a talented writer."

"Is he?"

"He never writes anything," she said.

"What does the bug fellow do?"

"Reads Thomas Hardy, I suppose."

She poured more milk and coffee into his cup.

"Could you ask Denise to go out for a while?" he said.

Denise was Suzanne's roommate. She was a pleasant, intellectual girl, and she would have been attractive if she didn't wear a wash-faded pair of slacks and an unpressed blouse stained with paint all the time.

"She's painting in the back room now," Suzanne said. "Some woman is paying her twenty-five dollars to paint a portrait from a photograph."

"Would she mind leaving for an hour?"

"I couldn't ask her to. She's been very good about everything, and it wouldn't be fair to ask her to stop work because of us. She needs the money badly."

"Do you want to go to the horse races tomorrow? The park is open for the season now," he said.

"Let's go to Tony Bacino's. I've always wanted to see what it was like inside."

"What is it?"

"One of those nightclubs where men dress up like women," she said.

"I'd rather see the horses."

"Don't you want to go?"

"No."

"Denise went one time. She said she saw two men dancing together. God, what a sight. Can you imagine it?"

"Do you want to go out to the park?" he said.

"I'll go anywhere you ask me to. Are you angry?"

"Why would you want to see men dressed like women?"

"I don't know. I was teasing. Don't be mad."

"I'm not," he said.

"We'll watch the horses and have a lovely time."

"Could you pick me up at my room? They run the races in the afternoon and we'll be late getting out."

"We'll do something first, won't we?" she said.

"Yes. That's always first."

She leaned over and kissed him on the cheek. They walked together out to the balcony and looked down over the iron railing at the flagstone courtyard with the moonlight on the flower beds. The white paint over the bricking of the walls looked pale in the light, and away in the distance they could hear the jazz bands playing on Bourbon. It was getting late and he kissed her good night and walked down Dauphine towards his rooming house.

On Sunday afternoon she was parked in front of the rooming house in her sports car when he got back from work. She smiled when she saw him. His denims were stiff with dirt, the skin of his face was stained from the black smoke that comes off a fresh pipe weld, his crushed straw hat was frayed at the edges and the brim was turned down to protect him from the sun. There were two thin white circles around his eyes where he had worn the machinist's goggles while cleaning the slag out of the welds, and his shirt was split down the back from being washed thin. He talked with her for a moment at the car and went up the front walk and across the veranda into the house. He showered and shaved and changed clothes and came back to the car. She slid over on the seat and he got behind the steering wheel.

They drove to the apartment and parked the car in the brick-paved alley behind the building, and later they went to the park. The best racing in New Orleans was at the Fair Grounds, but it was open only in the winter season, and the races at the park were generally good. They sat close down in the stands near the track. The sun was in the west above the trees on the other side of the park, and the track was a quarter-mile smooth brown dirt straightaway. At one end was the automatic starting gate, and the three-year-olds were being lined up for the second race. The silk blouses of the jockeys flashed in the sun and the horses were nervous in the gate just before the start. Then the bell rang and they burst out on the track and charged over the dirt, still damp from the rain, and the mud flew up at their hoofs; they stayed close together at first and then began to spread out, the jockeys bent low over their necks whipping their rumps with the quirts, and as they neared the finish a roan had the lead by a length and Avery could see the bit working in its mouth and saliva frothing into the short hair around its muzzle while the jockey whipped its rump furiously, his knees held high and the numbered sheet of paper pinned to his blouse partly torn loose and flapping in the wind. They thundered over the finish line under the judges' stand, the clods of dirt flicking in the air, with the roan out ahead by a length and a half, and the jockeys stood up in the stirrups and tightened the reins.

"Isn't it exciting?" Suzanne said. "I've never been before. It takes your breath away."

"Do you like it?" he said.

"Very much..Why didn't we come before? Can we bet?"

"If you want to."

"How much do you bet?"

"Anything."

"Bet two dollars for me in the next one," she said.

"On which horse?"

"Any one. You decide."

Her eyes were happy, and she wore a white dress with a transparent lavender material around her shoulders, and she had on one of those big white summer hats with the wide brim that Southern ladies used to wear to church on Sunday.

"Let's bet on that one," she said. "The black one. Look how his coat shines. Isn't he handsome?"

Avery left the stands and bet her money and two dollars of his own at the window.

"I bet it across the board," he said.

"What does that mean?"

"You collect if he wins, places, or shows, but your odds go down."

"I know he's going to win. Look at him. He's beautiful. Watch how the muscles move in his flanks when he walks."

They were taking the horses down to the starting gate.

"I wish I could paint him," she said. "Have you ever seen anything so handsome? Does a horse like that cost much?"

"Yes."

"I wonder if Daddy would buy one for my birthday."

"What would you do with him?"

"I don't know. But God he's gorgeous. I'd love to own him."

The horses were in the gate now. The black one tried to rear in the stall and the jockey had trouble keeping him calm until the start.

"What's the matter with that man? Doesn't he know how to handle horses?" Suzanne said. "Why are you laughing?"

"It's nothing."

"There they go. Oh, they're pushing him into the rail."

"It just looks that way from here."

"It's unfair. He's getting behind," she said.

"He's no good on a wet track. Watch how his legs work."

"What's wrong with his legs?"

"He doesn't have his stride."

"That's silly," she said. "What does a wet track have to do with anything?"

"Some horses can't run in the mud."

"He's dropped back to fourth."

The horses crossed the finish line in front of them. Suzanne looked disappointed.

"He'd do all right on a good track," Avery said.

"I'd still love to own him. How much would he cost?"

"Around a thousand dollars. Maybe more."

"Will he run in another race?"

"Not today."

"Let's come out next Sunday and see him again. Will he be here?"

"Probably," he said.

"Oh, good. The track will be dry and he'll win next time." She looked happy again.

"Are you glad you came?" he said.

"Of course, darling. I always like the places you take me."

"In the winter we can go to the Fair Grounds. They have some of the best horses from over the country there."

"What happened to the mare you used to own?"

"She died in foal," he said.

After the races they drove to the beach and went swimming. The sun had set and the afterglow reflected off the water in bands of scarlet, and then it was dark with no moon and the white caps came in with the tide and roared over the sand. The water was too cold for them to stay in long, and they lay on the beach and looked out towards the black horizon and the black sky.

Later, the moon came out and the sand looked silver against the black of the water. The wind was getting cool and everyone else had left the beach. She was shivering a little from the cold. Avery put his shirt over her shoulders.

"Do you want to go?" he said.

"Only if you want to."

"You're cold."

"I feel fine," she said.

"Let's go back to town."

"Hasn't it been fun today?"

"Yes."

"Maybe Denise will be gone when we get back," she said.

He had to check in with his parole board the next afternoon. The board was located in an old office building built of weathered gray brick, and the plaster in the hallways was cracked and the air smelled close and dusty. He sat on a bench in the outer office with three other men and waited his turn to see the parole officer. The man next to him had a fat coarse face with large red bumps on his nose. He wore a windbreaker that had a ring of sweat around the collar, and his slacks were worn thin at the knees and his brogans had been scuffed colorless. He held his hat in his hand between his legs. There was a dark area around the crown where the band had once been. He cleared his throat and looked around for a place to spit. He emptied his mouth into his handkerchief.

"They ain't even got a fucking spittoon," he said.

The secretary looked at him across the room.

"Where was you?" he said to Avery.

"In a camp."

"I was at Angola." He looked at Avery as though expecting an answer. "I was there twice."

"Fine place, Angola."

"Better than one of them fucking camps." He blew his nose on the handkerchief and put it in his pocket. "What was you up for?"

"Transporting whiskey."

"Ain't they a trash can over there?"

"No."

"Ain't even got a place to spit. The bastards," he said.

Avery went in to see the parole officer, a sallow middle-aged state appointee in an outmoded business suit with big lapels and an off-colored bow tie. His coat hung damply from his shoulders. His eyes were yellow-green and his face was slick with perspiration. He had Avery's file open on the desk before him. He unclipped a sheet of paper from the rest and read over it.

"You'll have to get your employer to send us another letter," he said.

"I already had him send one."

"Yes. I have it right here, but it's not notarized. It has to be notarized by a state notary."

"It says I'm working steady. That's what you wanted to know, wasn't it?"

"It's not a legal document without an official seal. Anyone could have written this letter."

"Where can I get it notarized?" Avery asked.

"He has to sign it in front of a notary."

"He might not want to write another letter."

"We can't accept this one."

"Could you phone out to the main office? They'll tell you that I'm working."

"We have to have an employer's letter for the file."

"All right. I'll ask him again."

The official crumpled the sheet of paper and threw it in the wastebasket. He thumbed through the rest of the file and his yellow-green eyes went over each page.

"Are you still living in the same place?" he said.

"Yes."

"Have you been going to any bars or keeping late hours?"

"No."

"Are you associating with anyone who has a criminal record?"

"I told you these things the last time I was here."

The official repeated his question without looking up from the file.

"I don't know anyone with a criminal record," Avery said.

"That's all. Get your employer to write a notarized statement this week or you'll be listed as unemployed."

"What will that mean?"

"Your case will go before the board for review. You can't stay out on parole without an honest means of support."

Avery left the building and walked down the street to the drugstore on the corner. He could feel his temples pounding with anger. He looked up the number of his crew foreman in the telephone book. He didn't know the foreman well and he didn't want to ask a second favor of him. Also, the foreman had been hesitant in writing the first letter, because he hadn't known that Avery was an ex-convict when he hired him on the job. Avery phoned him at his home. The foreman sounded irritated and he didn't understand why another letter had to be written. At first he said he didn't have time to see a notary, but he finally agreed and said that he would post the letter that week.

After he left the drugstore, he caught a streetcar to the Vieux Carré and walked along the streets in the summer evening to Suzanne's apartment. Denise told him that she was out shopping in the stores and she wouldn't be back for another hour. He went down to the sports parlor on the corner and bought a newspaper and read the ball scores. He sat in one of the chairs along the wall by the pool tables. Three men were playing a game of Kelly pool. He bought a beer at the bar and watched the game. There was a table free and he played a game of rotation by himself. He shot a second game with a merchant sailor from Portugal. The sailor spoke bad English and he used much obscenity when he talked, but he was good with a cue and he paid for the game even though he had won. Avery folded his newspaper and drank another beer at the bar and went back to the apartment. The cool dank smell of the sports parlor with its odor of draught beer and cue chalk had taken away the parole office, and he felt good walking down Rampart with the sun low over the buildings and the Negro children roller-skating on the sidewalk and the old women on the balconies calling to one another in French.

He saw Suzanne going up the steps to her apartment as he entered the courtyard. She had several boxes in her arms. She wore high heels and a dark suit and a small white hat with a white veil.

"Hello," she cried. "Come up and see what I bought."

He followed her up the steps and into the living room. She left the doors open to the balcony. She looked out of breath. She threw the boxes on the couch and tore them open and pulled out the new dresses amid the rustling of the tissue paper.

"Do you like them?" she said. "God, what bedlam. I'll never go shopping at five again. I'm sorry I'm late. Where have you been?"

"The parole board and the pool hall."

"Oh? Did anything happen?"

"No."

"Did you have to talk with that same little man you told me about?"

"He's been assigned to me as my counselor on readjustment."

"Poor darling. You must be tired. Do you want a drink?"

"Do you have a beer?"

She went into the kitchen and got one out of the icebox and opened it. The foam came over the lip of the bottle.

"Did you meet any literary people at the pool hall?" she said.

"A Portuguese sailor."

"Has he written anything?"

"Only on bathroom walls."

"I've always wanted to go to a pool hall. What's it like?" she said.

"Most of the upper-class people from the Quarter are there."

"They're lovely company."

"Is Denise in?" he said.

"I don't know. Denise!"

She looked in the bedroom.

"She must have gone out with that Tulane boy."

"Let's go to bed."

"That's a subtle way of putting it," she said.

"I've been thinking about you all day."

"I've wanted you all day, too. It must be true that once you get in the habit of it you can't do without it."

"Do you feel that way?" he said.

"I don't think I could go a week without you."

"We won't ever have to go without each other."

"We'll always be together and nothing else will matter," she said.

He drank down the foam in the bottom of the bottle.

"Do you want another one?" she asked.

"Let's go to bed. We'll go out and drink beer afterwards."

"I know a German place we can go to. They have beer in those big mugs with the copper lids."

They went into her bedroom and she slid the bolt on the door. She drew the French curtains on the big window overlooking the courtyard. He watched her undress.

"We have such good times, don't we?" she said.

"We always will."

"We won't get tired of each other like married people do, will we?"

"No."

"We'll have each day like this. Always and always and always," she said.

"Are you very happy?"

"You make me happy in a nice way."

"You're getting to be a bad girl."

They lay on the bed. She put herself close and tongue-kissed him.

"How do you like me best?" she said.

"We'll take turns. Am I too heavy for you?"

"Ummmm. This is fine."

"Could we get an apartment together?"

"I've thought about it, but it would get back to Daddy and I don't want to hurt him."

"It's hard with Denise around."

"She said she might find another place. Poor thing, I guess we've almost driven her out. But wouldn't it be nice? I'd have the apartment to myself, and you could come over and we could do it anytime we wanted. Again and again and again with no one to bother us."

"When is she leaving?"

"She isn't sure yet."

"Could we let her find us in bed?" she said. "That should hurry things up."

"Stop being mean."

"She's nice, but it will be better when she's gone."

"You can come here after work, and we'll undress and lie in bed and you won't have to go home. Won't it be wonderful?"

"Yes, it will."

The last rays of the summer evening fell through the crack in the French curtains and the room became dark.

J.P. WINFIELD

Virdo Hunnicut was furious. His tie was pulled loose from his shirt collar, and he paced up and down the room talking loudly and jabbing his finger at J.P. to emphasize a point.

J.P. sat in the chair with only his trousers and undershirt on. His bare feet looked yellow on the rug. The razor nicks on his face were thinly flecked with blood, and his eyes were sunken. His hair was uncombed and it hung down over his forehead and ears. There was a throbbing pain in the back of his head; when he moved he felt something shoot through his neck and shoulders hot like ice. He heard Hunnicut speaking from afar. He tried to remember what had happened last night. He remembered going on the stage, and then somebody had booed and the curtain had been drawn and Seth was trying to pull him into the stage wing by his coat sleeve. Or was it April? It was like that bitch to do something like that. What was Hunnicut saying now? He didn't give a goddamn, really. He wished Hunnicut would take a bath before he came into the room. He'd have to leave the window open all morning to get the stink out.

"—you'll be finished, out on your ass in the street. I fired that goddamn stage manager for even letting you go on—"

Why didn't he shut up, the fat unwashed bastard?

"Do you hear me? Open your eyes and look at me. We're going to make an announcement over the air that you were sick last night. You had pneumonia but you wanted to go on anyway because you love the hicks so much. I'm going to wait a month and put you on the show again, but if you make another hophead performance like that you're canned for good. Are you listening?"

Go fuck yourself.

"I don't know how I picked you up to begin with," Virdo Hunnicut said.

"Stop your goddamn shouting. I had my fill of it this morning," J.P. said.

"I put you on top and you blow it."

"I made a bundle for you."

"You wasn't nothing but a poor white trash farmer when you went on my show."

"Listen, I ain't—get the hell out of here. You're stinking up the room."

"What? What did you say?"

"You're stinking up the room."

Hunnicut's face reddened. The sweat rolled off his neck onto his shirt. Everything about him was sweaty. His slacks stuck to his legs, and even his tie was damp. His face was strained with anger.

"You're finished," he said. "You take yourself and your cocaine and your slut wife with her douche bag and get out of town because I'm through with you. I've had enough. You ain't worth the spit on a sidewalk. I don't know how I put up with you this long. Go up to Little Rock and Nashville and see if they'll give you a job when they find out you're a junkie. I'm glad to get shut of you."

Hunnicut walked out of the room, leaving an odor of sweat in the air behind him.

J.P. sat in the chair and felt the throbbing pain in his head increase. He couldn't see clearly to the opposite side of the room. He wanted to get up from the chair and walk to the bed to lie down, but when he moved the pain dropped down in his neck and shoulders and he remained still. He wondered if he had said too much to Hunnicut. Pack your cocaine and your douche bag wife and get out of town. The stinking bastard. Don't want junkies in Nashville and Little Rock to sell glow-in-the-dark tablecloths painted with the Last Supper. What about big-print Bibles miracle water actual photographs of Jesus books on faith healing flower seed egg formula vitamin tonic cut-out pictures of your favorite country singers? Snowbirds ain't wanted. The pain in my head swells and lessens and swells again. My fingers twitch and the cigarette in my hand burns down to my knuckles. Got high Wednesday or Thursday night. Can't remember after. My watch. Where the hell is my watch? Bitch of a wife probably sold it for a shot. If she ain't spreading her legs for Doc Elgin. Back home we'd go after him with a gelding knife. Hopping a man's wife for drugs. Couldn't get in a whorehouse with a fist full of green. Eyes aching, feel full of sand like I looked at a welder's torch too long. I need a drink or powder to get flat again and lie in bed with a soft belly woman on top of me. That blond-headed whore up home with the rain falling outside. Tried to get her hot. You can't get a whore hot. You hear stories about a fellow getting one hot and she keeps asking for more and then he gets it free whenever he wants. They ain't got no interest in it. Even though they give you better loving than them tight-leg bitches that think they're giving you something if they let you have a couple of inches. Take some snow now and a little whiskey and then go over to Jerry's and get fixed up for the afternoon. Wonder if Hunnicut meant it. Who gives a goddamn? The unwashed bastard.

April comes into the room and stops behind my chair. We look at each other's reflection in the dresser mirror. She is beginning to swell with child. Her dress is too tight. She don't want to wear one of them maternity things. Don't want to believe the baby is there. She told me she'd like to have a miscarriage. When she gets high she pretends she ain't knocked up. I see the lines around her eyes and neck. Said she was twenty-seven. Must be older by ten years. Older than me. Hard to tell. She's been jazzing since she was fifteen. First time in a woodshed with her uncle. She ain't going to look good pregnant. Probably get fat and swole up like a sow. Wonder if she's laying anybody besides Elgin. She always smells like she's rutting when she takes off her pants. She ain't going to get no more laying with a swole belly. A man don't like to climb over a baby to get to it. She's got a look in her eyes. She's on it. She walks past my chair and out of the mirror and sits on the side of the bed and takes off her shoes. Her eyes stare at me flat. Sunday morning. She was over at Elgin's. Prayer meeting with a needle in the tangle of sheets.

Need to dress and catch air before she starts talking. One paper of snow wrapped up in a sock in the drawer. I got to walk across the room and get it and cut out. She pulls her skirt over her knees and lays down in bed. She ain't got any pants on. Rutting. I walk to the dresser jesus my head throbbing like the marrow of my skull brittle and cracked dust breathed into my brain and the pain drops down my back and circles my chest. Untwist the sock and tear the paper open. Put the powder under the tongue and wait. I feel it sucked into the skin taste it in the throat. Bitch was wrong. Never had to mainline. Ain't going to neither. It don't hurt you under the tongue. Niggers do it all the time. Don't bother them none. You're okay if you don't jab it in the arm. Troy was hypo. Snow ain't no different than getting drunk. Remember when I got tight on moon once. I could smell it in my sweat the next day. It ain't no worse than moon. It don't drive you blind or insane. Feel it spreading through my head and chest. Put on my shoes and shirt and get a drink at the bar and go down to the depot. Honey-colored hair. A little overweight but it makes it better.

"What did Virdo say?" April said. Her voice was slow and far away.

"He says I'm through."

Her eyes turned from the ceiling and looked at him and blinked.

"I'm through," he repeated.

"What?"

"He called me white trash."

"He's not going to fire you. He told me so."

"Ask him again."

"He's just going to leave you off the show for a while."

"I ain't taking no more insults from him."

"Don't be foolish. I talked with him. He's not going to fire you, and that's all there is to it."

She's really hyped, he thought. She sat up on the bed with her skirt over her knees. Her eyes blinked at him again.

"We talked it over. He said he would give you another chance. Why did you tell me you were through?"

He buttoned his shirt and laced his shoes and didn't answer her. The pain in his head and body had lessened. The fingers of his right hand twitched as he tied his shoe string.

"Why did you tell me those things?" April said.

He left the room without putting on his coat or tie. He rang for the elevator and waited. It didn't come. He heard April open the door of the room.

"Where are you going?" she said. "Come back and explain to me why you said Virdo fired you."

He walked down the stairs to the lobby. He had to pause at the second flight and rest. The twitching in his fingers spread to the muscles of his arm. He walked two more flights and stopped again. He leaned against the wall and breathed hard. He felt his heart twist from the strain. Didn't have no sleep, he thought. I'll sleep this afternoon and let the whore fix me up. Makes a man right. Cleans the fatigue out of him. I need another piece like that blond slut back home. Should have gone to see her again before I left. He went down the last flight to the lobby and entered the bar.

The bartender was chipping up a block of ice in the cooler. The pick splintered a few pieces of ice on the floor. The bottles behind the bar were covered with a white sheet. There was no one else in the room save a Negro who was wiping off the tables with a rag. J.P. asked the bartender for a straight whiskey.

"I'm sorry, sir. It's Sunday. We can't serve drinks until after one o'clock."

"Give me a bottle to go."

"We can't do that either, sir."

He left the hotel and walked down the sidewalk in the sunshine to the cabstand. He rode out to Jerry's Bar behind the depot with the hot summer wind blowing in his face through the car window. He ran his fingers along his jaw and felt the dried blood of the razor nicks flake off as he touched them. He looked down at his shirt. It was the same one he had taken off last night. There was a small drop of blood on the soiled collar. The cab drove through the train yard over the railroad tracks and stopped in front of the bar. The electric sign over the door with the shorted-out letters buzzed loudly. He paid the driver and went inside. Jerry was behind the bar.

"Good morning, Mr. Winfield," he said. The bald spot in the center of his head shone dully in the light. He had an ingratiating mercantile manner that made J.P. want to spit. "What will you have?"

"A straight."

"Yes, sir."

Jerry put the jigger on the bar and filled it from a bottle that had a chrome spout fixed to the top. J.P. drank the bourbon neat and had the jigger filled again. The whiskey burned the inside of his stomach. He didn't remember when he had last eaten.

"I want a girl for the afternoon," he said.

"Talk to my wife. She takes care of all that."

"Where is she?"

"Upstairs."

J.P. started towards the back.

"Mr. Winfield, you didn't pay for your drinks."

He reached in his pocket for his wallet and found that he didn't have it.

"Give me a blank check and a pen," he said.

"We don't cash checks as a rule, Mr. Winfield."

"Don't you think it's good?"

"It ain't that. I know it's good coming from you, but Emma don't like me taking checks from nobody."

"You ain't running the only can house in town. You want me to go somewhere else?"

Jerry took the empty jigger off the bar and looked up the stairs at the back of the room.

"All right. I'll cash it for you. But don't let Emma know about it," he said.

J.P. wrote out a check for a hundred dollars. Jerry took out for the two drinks and placed the rest of the bills and a couple of coins on the bar. J.P. folded the money and put it in his pocket. The room smelled of sawdust and flat beer.

Emma, the bartender's wife, met him at the top of the stairs. She was big for a woman, and she had masculine features and thick muscular arms. She looked at him with her opaque colorless eyes.

"You pay here before you go any further," she said.

J.P. took some money out of his pocket, counted it, and gave it to her.

"Where is Honey?" he said.

"She's got a customer. You want to wait?"

"No."

"Go into that room on the right. I'll send a girl in."

He went into one of the bedrooms. The single window was

boarded on the outside. The only furniture was a wood chair, a large double bed that was covered with a spread tucked in tightly on all sides, and a night table ringed with glass stains with a tin washbasin on top. There were cigarette burns on the floor, and a half-empty glass of beer on the windowsill. There was a lipstick print on the rim of the glass. He turned on the overhead light and looked at the cracked wallpaper and the stains on the bedspread and he turned it off again. He sat in the wood chair and took his package of cigarettes out of his pocket. It was empty. He crushed it and threw it on the floor.

The door opened and the girl came in. She was thin and tall with long straight black hair, and she looked as though she had been up all night. She had on light blue shorts and a knitted sweater without sleeves. Her mouth was thin like a spinster's, and she used her lipstick to make her lips look larger. She undressed by the bed and put her clothes on the chair. She looked at the crushed cigarette package on the floor.

"Say, this room ain't a garbage can," she said.

"Get in bed."

"Listen. We have to keep our rooms clean. Miss Emma don't like them dirty."

"You ought to set fire to the whole goddamn place, then."

"Wait a minute, mister. I've had a hard night. I don't have to put up with any stuff from you."

"I ain't come in here to talk about your dirty floor. Get on the bed," he said.

"I have to look at you first."

A half hour later he sent down for a bottle. The girl asked for beer. She said whiskey made her sick. She got drunk very easily, and she talked obscenely while they made love. She hadn't taken off her lipstick and she smeared it on the side of his face. He felt the whiskey go through his body, and he had that same thick feeling in his head of the night before, and the strain of the alcohol and sexual labor made him short of breath. He wished he had taken another girl. She had had only three bottles of beer, but she was very drunk. He drank down the whiskey and felt it hit hot in his stomach. The girl opened another beer and smoked a cigarette. She got up once to use the bathroom. They could hear the music from the jukebox down in the bar and she popped her fingers in time to the tempo. After a while she became half asleep, her mouth open, and lay relaxed on the bed and didn't move her body with his.

"Go tell that woman to send in another girl," he said.

"What's the matter?"

"Just tell her to bring someone else in, and you can take the day off."

"What's wrong with me? You want a special kind of jazzing or something?"

"I didn't pay you to fall asleep."

"You must think you're some kind of wonderful lay. I've had better lays from a sixteen-year-old boy than you. You don't even know how to get it in."

"Get the hell out."

"I hope somebody else gives you a good case of clap, you bastard," she said.

She put on her light blue shorts and knitted sweater and house slippers and left the room. A minute later somebody knocked on the door.

"Put something on. It's me," Emma said.

J.P. got up from the bed and slipped his trousers on. He felt dizzy when he stood up. Emma came in and shut the door behind her.

"What's the trouble?" she said.

"Bring Honey in."

"What's wrong with the girl I gave you?"

"I don't like her," he said.

"I ain't had any complaints about her before."

"Send me another girl. I done paid for the afternoon."

"It will cost you twenty-five dollars more," she said.

"I already give you fifty."

"You paid for Rita."

"What difference does that make?"

"If you want somebody else you got to pay again."

"The bitch went to sleep on me," he said.

"She's one of my best girls. I never had no complaints."

"She sleeps with her mouth open."

"A man told me last night she was the nicest lay in the house. Her customers don't complain," she said.

"I didn't hire a wore-out whore that can't stay awake."

"If you're one of these flip guys with different tastes you can go down the street. They'll take care of you. I run a respectable place. There's others waiting for this room that will pay extra to have Rita."

She folded her heavy arms across her breasts and looked at him.

"All right. Here. Tell Honey to come in," he said, giving her the money.

"She's in another room now. You'll have to wait a few minutes."

After the woman had left he poured a glass of bourbon and sat in the chair and drank slowly and looked at his bare yellow feet on the floor. His fingers shook slightly on the glass. He thought about Honey and her soft belly and pink breasts. He had made love to the first girl twice, and he should have felt spent, but he could feel it go through him again, weak in the loins and the pit of his stomach, and he put the tip of his tongue between his teeth when he thought about it. He drank down the whiskey and filled the glass again. The bottle was two-thirds empty. He tried to remember what had taken place the last three days. Everything was confused in time, and he couldn't concentrate on any one thing long without its becoming confused with something else. He knew that something had happened in a bar somewhere and there had been a fight. Maybe someone had taken him outside and rolled him. His watch. Yes, and his billfold. That had been it. There was a fight and he had been rolled. Saturday night he had been on the Jubilee. That was last night. He didn't have his guitar with him or he could have played right. They had given him one of them goddamn electric things that sounded like somebody was twanging on a strand of bailing wire. The only person who could use an electric guitar was Charley Christian, and he was dead. A man gave a guitar its tone. It didn't need nothing else but the man playing it. J.P. could hear and feel the rosinous squeak of his fingers working over the frets and the chords vibrating through the dark wood.

The girl he had wanted came into the room. She had on a pink robe and sandals. Her hair had dark and light amber streaks in it. He expected her to smile or to make some show of recognition when she saw him. She didn't speak, and her pale blue eyes looked at him for a moment and then turned away blankly as she took off her robe and dropped it over the brass bedstead.

"Miss Emma said you give Rita some trouble. This is just a straight date without no trouble, hear."

"I didn't bruise nothing of yours the last time I was here," he said.

"Miss Emma says you give Rita a bad time."

"I didn't pay for no drunk whore to yawn in my face."

"Well, I don't want no trouble. Rita says you were acting flip. I give a straight lay and that's all. You go see one of the other girls if you want something else."

"Do you remember me?" he said.

"Lots of fellows come in. They're one and the same to me, honey."

She lay down on the bed in a receptive position. She rubbed the insides of her thighs with her palms. He poured a drink in his glass from the fifth and drank it down.

"Let's go, honey. There's others waiting," she said.

"Get on top."

"That means you got a complex about your mother."

"Watch it."

"Some fellows want to lay their mother and they don't know it. I read it in a magazine once."

"Get on top and do what you're supposed to," he said.

"I know my job. You don't have to worry about that."

She got on top of him and smiled stupidly. She raised up on her knees and then sat back. She touched him and adjusted herself again, supporting herself with one arm, and sat once more on his legs.

"You're going to have to do better than that," she said.

"It's the whiskey."

"You give Rita all you had. You ain't got another lay in you," she said.

"Wait a minute. I'll be all right. I was all right before you come in here."

"Are you saying you can't get nothing on for me?"

"No. It's just the whiskey. I'll be all right in a minute."

"Come back tomorrow," she said.

"I hired you for the afternoon."

"You ain't got it to put in, honey."

"I paid seventy-five dollars for you and that other bitch, and you ain't taking off."

"You see me tomorrow night and I'll give you one free."

"You bitch," he said.

"Take it easy."

"You ain't cutting out on me."

"I'm not going to stay here and play hand games for you, mister. When you can get something on come back and I'll take care of you."

She took her robe off the bedstead and started to put it on. He sat up and pulled it off her. The sleeve caught on her arm and ripped at the shoulder. She grabbed the robe in both hands and jerked it away from him and got off the bed.

"All right, flip man," she said. She pushed a buzzer on the wall by the light switch and put on her robe. Her shoulder showed at the rip in the seam. He got off the bed and came towards her. She pushed the buzzer again.

"I'd like to watch him beat the piss out of you," she said, and went out the door.

"You goddamn whore."

He put on his shirt and trousers. He felt shamed and enraged at the same time. His head spun when he reached over to pick up his shoes. He forgot to put on his socks. He wanted retribution against the two prostitutes and the madam. They had gotten him for seventy-five dollars. He was going out in the hall and either make the girl return to the room or get his money from the madam. Back home they'd burn a whorehouse down with coal oil if a man got treated like a nigger. They'd put the whores in jail and let any bum with a dollar in his overalls lay them. Said she'd gotten better jazzing from a sixteen-year-old. I could split her in two. I ain't going to take no insults from a bunch of whores.

The door opened and a big man whom he hadn't seen before walked in. The man had a flat, scarred face and tattoos showed through the black hair on his arms. The hair on his chest curled out over the top of his shirt. He had a short wood club in his hand, the handle wrapped with black tape and a hole drilled in the end filled with lead. Emma stood behind him in the doorway. Her hard eyes looked over the man's shoulder at J.P.

J.P. backed away and got his knife out of his pocket. He opened the single blade and held it before him. He had seen a knife fight in a poolroom once and he remembered to keep the knife at an upward angle to parry a thrust or blow. He tripped backwards over the chair. The big man flicked the club across J.P.'s hand and knocked the knife to the floor. J.P. felt the bones in the back of his hand break, and a pain shot up his arm into his shoulder. He held his wrist with his other hand, and the man hit him across his good arm. He fell back against the boarded window and dropped to the floor. His trousers came loose and uncovered his buttocks. The pain was more than he could bear. His mouth opened and the muscles in his stomach tightened and convulsed. He felt that his arms were jerking without control when he tried to move them. The room was pink like blood diffused in water.

"The sonofabitch," Emma said.

"Do you want to put him in back?" the big man said.

"I knowed he was going to cause trouble when he first come in here."

"He don't look like much now," the big man said.

"I give him the two best pieces in the house, and he gets one of them drunk and he tells Honey he can't get nothing on for her."

The man picked up the knife off the floor and folded the blade and put it in his pocket.

"Give me the stick," she said.

She leaned over J.P. and hit him across the jaw with the club. His face snapped sideways against the floor. His eyes were still closed and his mouth was open and a mixture of saliva and blood drained out on the hard-grained wood. His expression didn't change. His broken hand had begun to swell.

"Put him behind the tracks," she said. "Maybe one of the bums will give him the kind of swish action he wants."

The big man picked J.P. up over his shoulder and carried him through the hallway and down the stairs. Honey stood in the doorway of the kitchen, smoking a cigarette, and watched them. She picked her teeth with her fingernail. The man took J.P. out the back door towards the railroad tracks. The brambled area behind the building was littered with broken glass and refuse that had overflowed the garbage cans. The man carried him over the tracks and the gravel bedding to the jungle. The trees and grass

were powdered with dust from the passing trains. The man put
J.P. down and went back to the building. J.P. lay on his stomach
with the side of his face in the dirt and his arm twisted under him.
A train roared by and the ground thundered under him, although
he was only vaguely aware of it. He slipped in and out of conscious-
ness; he was at the bottom of a dark place without pain, and then
the yellow light of afternoon came into his mind and he felt he
could open his eyes but the bone-throbbing pain in his hand began
and he choked on the blood in his throat and fell away into nothing
again.

Two men walked through the dust-covered trees and brush. One
of them was thin and suntanned with a sharp, lean face. He had
only one eye; the iris of his blind eye was broken and its color
had run out into the cornea. His hair was stiff and uncut, and he
wore a pair of pin-striped trousers that were shiny from wear. The
other man was smaller and thinner than the first, and his trousers
sagged on his buttocks. He had a hand-rolled cigarette in his mouth
that had gone out, and his teeth were brown with rot. There was
a needle hole in his arm which he had gotten when he sold blood
at the blood bank. He followed the man with one eye through
the trees. He took a sip off a bottle of port and screwed the cap
back on and put it in his pocket. He didn't want the first man to
see him drinking. They were supposed to share the bottle. They
stopped when they saw J.P. on the ground. The man with one eye
touched J.P. with his foot.

"Let's get going. I don't want to get found with no dead man,"
the one with the rotted teeth said.

"He ain't dead. A dead man don't bleed. Don't you know that?"

"He must have fell off the train."

"Look at them shoes. He ain't no bum." He had to turn his good
eye around to look at the other man. He took off J.P.'s shoes and
sat on the ground and put them on his own feet. "Go through his
pockets."

"Let's go. There might be some dicks around."

"You want another bottle, don't you? Get his money."

"They lock you up for keeps in this fucking town."

"There ain't no dicks around."

The smaller man went through J.P.'s trouser pockets. He felt
the loose bills but he didn't pull them out.

"He ain't got nothing," he said.

"See if he's got a watch."

"He ain't carrying nothing, I tell you." He waited until the other man turned his good eye down to tie his shoes, and then he tried to get the bills out of J.P.'s pocket without being seen.

"You lying bastard. Give me that. I ought to beat the crap out of you."

"I was going to give it to you."

"Shut up."

"You spent all the last money we got at the blood bank on a whore."

"So what?" the man with one eye said.

"It was half mine."

"You'd be in jail in Baton Rouge if I hadn't talked the dicks out of it and told them we'd clear town."

"Let me have half of it."

"I'll give it to you later."

"You'll get juiced with a woman and I won't see none of it."

"I let you carry the port, didn't I?"

"Yeah, but—"

"I don't let nobody give you no shit, do I?"

"What if the dicks grab you and I get away? I don't get no dough."

"You tried to steal it from me. That don't give you no rights."

"Come on, Jess."

"Piss on it. Let's get out of here."

They walked off arguing through the trees.

J.P. became completely conscious late that afternoon. His eyes opened and he looked at the ants crawling on the ground and the tin cans and bits of moldy newspaper. He pulled his arm out from under him. The back of his hand was swollen and purple. He sat upright and let the hand lie limply in his lap. He felt something hard roll inside his mouth and spit the broken tooth on the ground. He looked at it dumbly and touched the side of his face with his good hand. The pain ripped along his jawbone and into his ear. When he swallowed some blood it made him retch, but he could only heave dryly, out of breath, the muscles in his chest and throat straining violently from the effort. He saw his bare feet and the old pair of shoes the tramp had left. He stood up, holding his bad hand at the wrist, and looked around. The blood raced in his head and everything went out and away from him and blurred and then came back again. He didn't know where he was. He walked through the dust-powdered trees and knocked against the trunks with his body, and the branches swung back against his face. He had to get someone to help him before he passed out again. He could die out there and no one would find him until the smell got so bad that the parish health man would be sent out to investigate it. He stepped on a sharp rock and bruised his foot. He looked through the trees and saw the railroad tracks, and on the other side, the brothel. He was in the jungle behind the tracks. They had worked him over and dumped him in the jungle. That big sonofabitch with the flat scarred face. J.P. thought of what he would do in retribution to the man and the madam and the two prostitutes. He became confused and thought he was back home. He saw Clois and the other men from the billiard hall and himself packed in a coupé at night with the cans of coal oil on the floorboards, riding out in the country to the brothel; they would park the car on the road and move quietly up to the building and saturate the porch and the walls from the cans and set a torch to it. He could see the building burn against the dark sky and the whores climbing out the windows and the big man with the club rolling on the lawn trying to put his clothes out.

He walked in an uneven line to the railroad and crossed the tracks. The rocks cut his feet. The sun was low in the sky, and it shone just above the freight cars in the yard. He heard a whistle blow in the distance. He went through the vacant field by the side of the brothel to the street. He stepped on some thorns and he could hardly bear to put his weight down on his feet. His breath rasped in his throat and there was a close feeling in his chest. He held his hand by the wrist, and when he walked the movement made his whole arm throb. He came out of the field onto the dirty side street that ran past the train yard in front of the brothel. There was nobody on the street. He saw a brakeman locking the door on a freight car in the yard. An automobile came down the street, and as it passed J.P. waved his arm to stop the driver. The man looked at him strangely and drove on.

Goddamn lousy bastard.

A few minutes later J.P. lay on the sidewalk unconscious. He didn't know that he had had a heart attack. He hadn't had time to think about it. He felt his heart twist inside him, and there was one great pain that exploded in his chest, and then the cement rushed up to hit him and that was all. A taxi that had just let down a man at the brothel stopped and the driver got out and came over. He knelt on one knee beside J.P. and felt his wrist for the pulse. He went back to his cab and called the dispatcher at his company on the radio and told him to send an ambulance. The sun went down, and one of the locomotives in the yard was pushing a string of freight cars off on a siding. A Negro boy walked down the street, throwing a baseball up in the air and catching it in a fielder's glove. He stopped on the other side of the street and looked at the cabdriver and J.P. The long cream-colored ambulance glided down the street with the siren low and parked by the curb. The two attendants took the stretcher out of the back and put J.P. on it and strapped down his legs and chest with the cloth belts. They put him into the ambulance, and one rode in back with him and the other drove.

They took him to the emergency receiving room at the charity hospital, which was an old building in the poor section of town built by Huey Long during the depression. There was a big green lawn in front and trees along the walkway and the walls were orange like rust. The emergency room was overcrowded, and the nurse told the ambulance driver that all the doctors were busy at the moment and they would have to put J.P. in an oxygen tent and wait until the intern on the floor was free. There were two Negroes in the waiting room who had been cut in a razor fight, an emaciated three-year-old girl, and a man with a compress on his head who had been hurt in an auto accident.

The ambulance men pushed the stretcher down the hall on its rubber wheels to one of the rooms with an oxygen tent. The ambulance men were tired and they wanted to put J.P. in the tent and go to coffee before they were called out again. Having been exposed to death often, they had learned that the end of man's life is as significant and tragic as water breaking out the bottom of a paper bag. The doctors worked on J.P. for several hours. Two of the heart chambers had ruptured and filled and couldn't expel the blood back into the arteries. One of the doctors suggested opening the cavity and massaging the heart, but there wasn't a surgeon available at the time who could perform the operation. J.P. died alone in the room shortly after midnight, and when the nurse found he was dead she called the intern and the body was removed, because the space was needed for others.

AVERY BROUSSARD

It was Friday evening and they were having a barbecue and beer party at the apartment. The afternoon sun had already died in the west as he walked down Dauphine, and the old stucco buildings and the iron-railed balconies stood out against the acetylene-blue glow of the sky after dusk. He had gotten a haircut and a shoeshine at the barbershop, and he felt good after the day's work on the pipeline. He walked under the green colonnade in front of a corner grocery store and went inside and bought twelve bottles of beer in a paper bag. An old man was selling the *Picayune*, and there was a hurdy-gurdy playing on the other side of the street. Avery carried the beer in the sack down to the apartment and went through the gate under the willow tree into the courtyard.

Suzanne was cooking chickens on a small portable barbecue pit she had set up on the flagging. She wore a blue and white summer dress, and there were drops of perspiration around her temples. She had borrowed some Japanese lanterns from a friend and had strung them over the court. There was a large tin tub of crushed ice and beer by the stone well. Several other people sat in deck chairs or on the steps, sipping highballs and drinking beer and talking. Wally was telling a couple that the *Paris Review* had accepted two of his poems and that the *Atlantic Monthly* was considering one of his short stories. He was drinking Scotch and soda, and his face was flushed and his English accent kept becoming more pronounced. Avery went over to Suzanne and smiled at her and put the bottles in the crushed ice. She had washed her hair the night before and it was loose and soft around her shoulders.

"I was waiting for you," she said.

"We worked overtime today."

"You look nice."

"I had a haircut."

"Taste the sauce."

He tasted it with the wooden spoon.

"*C'est pas trop chaud pour toi?*" she said.

"I thought you had forgotten French."

"*Dis moi de la sauce.*"

"It's good."

The light of the paper lanterns, which swung slowly in the breeze, flickered on her face. Her dark eyes were bright and cheerful. Her arm brushed against him and he wished they were alone and not at the party. He opened a beer and drank out of the bottle. She took a sip and turned the chickens on the grill. The grease dripped down into the fire and sputtered on the coals. Wally came over with a highball glass in his hand.

"Hi, fellow. What did you bring?" he said.

"Dago red. Would you like some?"

"There's a bottle of Vat 69 upstairs in the cabinet," Suzanne said.

"Were you speaking French?"

"I don't know any French," Avery said.

"Seriously. Can you speak French?"

"We were practicing our Church Latin. We're thinking of taking holy orders," Avery said.

"That's right. You *are* a Catholic, aren't you? Denise told me. I say, have you read any of Joyce?"

"Why don't you get another highball, Wally?" Suzanne said.

"What do the Jesuits think of Joyce?"

"I didn't go to school under the Jesuits," Avery said.

"You look like a Jesuit. Melancholy eyes and that sort of thing."

"For heaven's sake, Wally. Get a highball," Suzanne said.

"I've been doing some work on the Trinity theme in *Ulysses*. I think Joyce was actually orthodox in his Catholicism. Tell me, do Catholics really have to accept all of the Nicene Creed?"

"I'm not Catholic," Avery said.

"Suzanne's roommate told me you were."

"Wally, go upstairs and get the Scotch. I'd like a drink, too," Suzanne said.

"I'm sure there's a relation between the Trinity and the Bloom family."

"Who is the Bloom family?" Avery said.

"Isn't it true that you're Catholic?"

"No."

"You are, aren't you, Suzanne?" Wally said.

"Once in a while."

"Well, do you have to accept all the Nicene Creed?"

"I suppose. What does that have to do with anything?"

Wally forgot why he had asked. He began talking about Baudelaire.

"I've been reading him in French. You lose a lot in the translation," he said. "Have you read *The Flowers of Evil* in French?"

"I read Ring Lardner and Rudyard Kipling my last year in high school," Avery said.

"You don't consider Lardner a serious writer, do you?"

"I'd like a highball. Would you fix me one, Wally?" Suzanne said.

"Do you really compare Lardner with someone like Baudelaire?"

"I liked his short stories," Avery said.

"Tell me if you think Lardner could be compared with any French writer of worth."

"You're tight," Suzanne said.

"I just want to know if anybody can believe Ringgold Lardner was a good writer."

"If you won't get the Scotch, open a beer for me, please," she said.

"Lardner never wrote a decent page of prose in his life," Wally said.

"Wally, will you please be quiet."

"And Kipling, for God's sake. Can you tell me of anyone more undeserving who has received as much attention?"

Avery looked at his whiskey-red face and didn't say anything. A young man came over from the steps and put his arm on Wally's shoulder. He winked at Suzanne.

"Come talk to us, old sock," he said. "We want to hear about your poems."

"They're completely worthless."

"Also about your short story in the *Atlantic*," the young man said.

"It's worthless, too. The *Atlantic* has a policy of not publishing anything of merit."

"Come sit down and have a Scotch with us," the young man said. He was a portrait painter who had done well with the Saint Charles Avenue upper class. His hair was black and he had a good suntan and his teeth were white when he smiled.

"Stop this goddamn patronizing attitude," Wally said. "If there is anything I can't stand, it's to be patronized when I'm drunk."

The others in the courtyard stopped talking and looked at Wally. The young portrait painter felt that attention was being focused on him, also. He smiled and put his hand on Wally's shoulder again. His teeth shone, and he gave an appearance of composure and easiness of manner.

"I'm not patronizing you," he said in a low voice, smiling.

"Do you know one thing about the amount of work that goes into a good piece of fiction?"

"Come over and tell us about it."

"Do you think that painting some aristocratic pig on Saint Charles is art?"

"Now look, Wally."

"Tell me."

"I'll discuss it with you when you're not cross-eyed."

"You don't know anything about art, whether I'm sober or not."

"Let's have a drink. This is rather pointless, isn't it?"

"Hell it's pointless. I want to know right now if you think painting these pigs is art."

Suzanne turned to Avery and spoke quietly. "Take him outside for a while. I'll serve dinner."

"I'm going out for cigarettes. Do you want to come?" Avery said to Wally.

"How am I in any way involved with your smoking habits?"

"I thought you might like to take a walk."

"All right. I know I'm obnoxious. I'll leave," he said. "I apologize, painter. You're an artist. Your pigs will be hung in the Louvre someday."

They went out of the courtyard into the street. They walked along the sidewalk in the dark under the balconies and colonnades in front of the apartments with the trees hanging over the walk, the tattoo parlors, antique shops, the small lighted restaurants with the steamed windows, the ten dollar a week rooming houses that catered to the Tony Bacino clientele, the pool halls and bars and Salvation Army missions, past the girls who stood in the darkened doorways and smiled woodenly, and across the street to the grocery store on the corner with the big screen doors and the green shutters and coarse-grained floors and the rusted Hadacol sign and the glass cases of chewing tobacco and cigars.

Avery bought a package of Virginia Extra and poured the tobacco into the wheat-straw paper. He and Wally walked back towards the apartment. Avery struck a match and lighted the cigarette and watched the paper curl away from the flame.

"How do you feel?" he said.

"Nonrepentant," Wally said.

"You made it a little hard on Suzanne."

"I didn't mean to, old pal. My bile is directed only towards pretentious painters. I can't tolerate that fellow. He's such a goddamn boor."

"Do you think you can go back in now?"

"I'm in excellent shape. By the bye, can we forget that Lardner business?"

"Sure."

"I know I'm bloody insulting when I get on the grog."

"Forget about it."

"It's merely that I don't like Kipling or Lardner. Neither of them could write. I can't understand how these people are given attention."

"Do you want a smoke?" Avery said.

"Lardner wrote *Saturday Evening Post* fiction."

Avery walked on listening and not answering. They passed a package store just before they got to the apartment.

"I say, could you let me have a couple of dollars?" Wally said. "I'm out of booze and I don't like drinking off the others all evening."

Avery gave him the money. Wally bought a pint bottle and put it in his coat pocket, and they went back into the courtyard. The guests were eating the barbecued chickens from paper plates with their fingers, and Suzanne was serving several other people who had just arrived. Avery looked at her damp temples and the way her body moved against her dress. He took a beer out of the tub of crushed ice and opened it. The foam came out over the top of the bottle and slid down the side onto his hand.

"How is he?" she said.

"Still plastered."

"Get a plate. You haven't eaten anything."

"Can we be together later?" Avery said.

"We'll have to go somewhere else. Denise is going to be home."

"Let's go to the beach."

"All right. Maybe everyone will leave early."

"We can rent the beach cabin," he said.

"Ssssh." She smiled.

"They can't hear us. Wally is talking too loud."

"We'll have to get him to leave early, too. He's always the last one to go. He spent the night on our sofa one time."

"Maybe we can send him home with the painter. They seem to get along well."

"Excuse me a minute, darling. I have to go upstairs and get some more chickens."

"I'll help you."

"I can do it by myself."

"I'll help you, anyway," he said. She smiled back at him.

They went up the stone steps to the apartment. When they were inside he closed the door behind them. He kissed her on the cheek and mouth in the darkened living room.

"Ummmmm," she said. "You're nice."

She put her arms around his neck and held him close.

"Do you think they would miss us for a few minutes?" he said.

"Oh, darling, wait until tonight."

"It would only take a few minutes."

"We can't. Someone might come in."

"Let's stay at the beach house all night, then."

"Won't you be too tired to work tomorrow?"

"We probably won't get to work a full day. It's supposed to rain."

"We haven't gotten a whole night together in a long time. Won't it be lovely?" she said.

"Do you think the others will go home early?"

"I'll ask Denise to suggest that everyone go to that cellar place on Burgundy."

"Will they do it?"

"I think so. It's one of those sandal and beard places. It's artistic to be seen there."

He kissed her on the neck and held her and put his face in her hair. He felt the smoothness of her body against him.

"I want you so much," she said.

"You're a precious lady."

"I love you terribly."

"Can't we go in the other room?"

"It will only be a couple of more hours."

"We haven't had each other in four days."

"I know, darling. But it will be so good tonight. Let's wait."

He kissed her cheek again and bit the lobe of her ear.

"We have to go back," she said.

"Stay a little longer."

"I have to cook."

"Let's don't go to any more parties for a while."

"All right, darling."

"We're around other people too much."

"We won't go to any more parties unless you want to, and we'll only see each other."

"Do you mind not seeing anyone but me?" he said.

"Of course I don't. We have good times together."

"Don't go back yet."

"We have to. Be good and help me carry the food down."

They went down the stone steps to the courtyard. The light from the Japanese lanterns fell on the oleander and jasmine and Spanish daggers in the flower beds. There was the whisper of silk and petticoats, and the quiet talk of couples in the shadows, and the clink of ice in cool glasses of gin and quinine water. Avery reached his hand down into the tin tub and took out one of the last bottles of beer and opened it. The cap clicked on the flagging of the court. Suzanne stood under the willow by the iron gate to greet some people who had just come in. She came over to Avery.

"We'll have to get more beer," she said. "Can you go down to the grocery store?"

"It's closed now."

"That place on Esplanade is still open. Go in the car."

"Where are the keys?"

"Upstairs, I suppose. You don't mind going, do you? I'd ask Wally, but he'd never come back."

"When are they going to leave?"

"It won't be long. I'll talk with Denise. Be a good darling."

Avery went upstairs and got the keys and came back down and started out the courtyard.

"Where are you going, old pal?" Wally said.

"To get beer."

"Is it all right if I go along? That painter has started talking again. I swear to Jesus I can't tolerate listening to that fellow."

"I'm only going to be gone a few minutes."

"Maybe he will have left when we get back. If he's still here I think I'm going to hit him."

"You'd better come with me."

"Rather. I'm not keen on getting into a bash with such a disgusting fellow."

They went around the side of the building to the cobbled alley where the car was parked. Avery started the engine and drove out onto the street with the convertible top down and pressed on the accelerator. The exhaust roared against the pavement and echoed off the quiet buildings. The car, low-slung and flat with a wide wheelbase, could turn a corner with a slight twist of the steering wheel. You couldn't use all the gears except on the highway; and when he pushed down on the gas he felt the power pull him back in the leather seat. They went to the grocery store on Esplanade and bought a half case of beer. They put it on the front seat between them. Wally opened one of the warm beers on the bumper of the car by putting the cap against the metal edge and knocking it down with the palm of his hand until it popped loose. The beer foamed up over the front of his coat. He upended the bottle and drank fast, his throat working, to avoid spilling any more. Avery put the car into gear and pulled away from the curb and made a right turn into the Quarter.

"One-way street," Wally said.

Avery stepped on the brake and put the car in reverse. He backed into a driveway to turn around. The exhaust throbbed against the stucco wall of the building. An automobile was coming down the street towards them. Avery waited for it to pass before he pulled out. It stopped in front of them and blocked the driveway. The headlights went out, and Avery saw the city police emblem on the door. He could hear the police calls coming over the mobile radio inside. The officer got out and walked towards them. He had a flashlight in his hand.

"Put the beer under the seat," Avery said.

"There's no room."

"Cover it with your coat."

"Too late, old pal."

The officer shone the large three-battery flashlight at them and into the car. The bottles were amber in the light. The officer was young and looked as though he hadn't been on the police force long. He wore a tight, well-fitting light blue shirt and dark blue trousers with a black stripe down the side. He had a pistol and holster on his hip and a thick leather belt with the .45 cartridges protruding through the loops and handcuffs in a black leather case and a short billy with a spring and a lead weight in it. He was tall with dark hair and athletic features. There was a pair of sunglasses in his shirt pocket.

"Do you know this is a one-way street?" he said.

"I didn't see the sign," Avery said.

The officer shined the light on the bottles.

"Have you been drinking?"

"Not in the car."

"Let me see your driver's license, please."

Avery took out his billfold and opened the celluloid viewers.

"Take it out of the wallet, please."

Avery gave it to him. The officer looked at it under the flashlight.

"This expired last year, Broussard."

"I didn't look at the date on it."

"I say, I'm the only one drinking, officer. This fellow is quite all right," Wally said.

"You'll have to come down to the station with me."

"I'm not drunk," Avery said.

"You have liquor in your possession and you've been drinking."

"Look, couldn't you give me the ticket and let it go?"

"Both of you get in my car, please."

"I say," Wally said.

The officer opened the door for Avery to get out.

"Let's go," he said.

"You can't get me on a D.W.I. I'm not drunk."

"He's disgustingly sober," Wally said.

"Don't make it hard on yourself, Broussard."

"I haven't had more than four beers this evening."

"Get out of the car."

"I'm not going to jail for a D.W.I."

"You just have to go to night court and pay your fine."

"We're absolutely broke. That means the can, doesn't it?" Wally said.

"Come on, Broussard."

"All right, but I want a test. Do you understand? I'm not going to jail on a drunk charge."

"Have you been in jail before?"

"No."

"Put away your beer and come along, too," he said to Wally.

"Righto. Just a moment. I never leave an unfinished drink about." Wally drank down the last of the beer in the bottle.

"I want the test right away. As soon as I get in the station," Avery said.

"You'll get it."

"No jail, either. You understand."

"Both of you get out."

"Let go of my shoulder," Avery said.

"I told you to get out."

"Take your hand off me."

"You're making trouble for both of us. Now climb out of there."

Avery knocked his hand away.

"All right, stand up," the officer said. "You heard me. Put your hands against the car."

"Isn't this a bit absurd?" Wally said.

"Put your hands on the car and lean on them, Broussard."

Avery stood with his feet wide apart and his weight on his arms. The officer shook him down carefully. He kept one leg inside Avery's as he patted with his hands along his trousers so he could kick his feet out from under him if he attempted anything.

"You're next. Lean against the car," he said to Wally.

"You haven't any abnormal complexes, have you?"

"Do what I tell you."

Wally turned around and placed his hands on the car fender. The officer searched his pockets.

"Get in the back seat of my car," he said.

The inside of the police car was fitted with a thick wire screen which was attached to the roof and bolted to an iron bar that ran along behind the driver's seat so that the driver was protected from anyone behind him. Wally and Avery got in, and the officer pulled the car up to unblock the driveway and went back to move Suzanne's sports car out into the street and park it by the curb.

As they rode down to the police station Avery began to feel afraid. It was an empty sick feeling in his stomach, the same sick feeling he had when he was taken to the work camp on the train in handcuffs and a prison guard met him and the deputy sheriff at the depot and they drove down the dirt road in the pickup truck and he had looked out the window and had seen the white barracks through the pines and the denim uniforms of the men and the high fence with the strands of barbed wire at the top. He felt in his pocket for his cigarettes and found that he had only the package of Virginia Extra he had bought earlier in the evening. He tried to roll a cigarette and the tobacco shook out of the paper. He took a cigarette from Wally, but the smoke tasted bad in his mouth. He tried to remain reasonable and to think of the best thing to do, and then he knew that there was nothing to do; they had him and maybe they would fine him and let him go, or someone might check and discover that he was an ex-convict, and that would mean the jail without bond and a trial for parole violation and then the ride on the train back to the work camp and two more years on the gang.

They walked up the steps of the police station, a brown brick building with yellow shades on the windows. There was a big marble corridor inside and spittoons were placed along the walls, and at the end there were two varnished swinging doors with panes of frosted glass in them. Wally and Avery and the officer went through the doors into a large room where there were several desks, filing cabinets, spittoons, and telephones. There were only two men at the desks. One of them was in uniform. The officer told Avery and Wally to sit down on the bench by the wall and wait. Avery rolled another cigarette and the tobacco fell out the ends, and when he lighted it the paper flared up and made the smoke hot in his throat, and finally the cigarette broke apart in his hand. The officer made out his report and started to leave.

"Am I being charged with a D.W.I.?" Avery said.

The policeman didn't answer him and walked back out through the wood doors.

The officer in uniform at the desk came over to them with some papers and a fountain pen in his hand. He had a square, blunt, red face and brown hair that had begun to thin and recede at the forehead. He sat down beside them on the bench and crossed his leg and held the papers on his thigh to write.

"What is your name?" he said to Wally.

"Wally Laughlin."

"Age."

"Twenty-five."

"Why did you give the officer some trouble?"

"I assure you I didn't. The fellow seemed intent on making a fool of himself."

"That's enough of that."

"What am I being charged with?"

"You're not charged with anything. You can go if you like. Just try to cooperate with the police next time."

"Why was I brought down here?"

"You'd better go, son."

"Do you want me to do anything?" he said to Avery.

"What time is night court?"

"Eleven o'clock," the officer said.

"Go tell Suzanne what happened. Ask her if she can raise the fine," Avery said.

"Are you sure you don't want me to stay around?" Wally said.

"Just see Suzanne."

"We'll get the car and come back before eleven."

"Thanks."

"Take care."

"So long."

Wally went out through the doors, which swung back behind him.

"How do you want to enter your plea?" the officer said, his red, square face looking at Avery.

"What are the charges?"

"No license, going the wrong way on a one-way street, and driving while intoxicated."

"I'm not drunk. I wasn't drunk in the car."

"Do you want to plead not guilty?"

"The officer said I would get a test."

"A test won't tell us anything now. You might be sober at the station, but that don't mean you weren't tight earlier."

"That man knew I wasn't tight."

"You had liquor in your possession."

"Where did the other officer go?"

"Out on call."

"If I plead not guilty and he's not in court, that means I get off, doesn't it?"

"It will be better for you to plead guilty. You'll only get a fine that way."

"I'm not getting caught for a D.W.I."

"All right, son. Not guilty. Were you ever arrested before?"

"No."

The officer wrote on the papers held against his thigh.

"Whose car were you driving?"

"My girl's."

"What is her name?"

"Is that important?"

"Yes, it is."

"Suzanne Robicheaux."

"We'll have to check you through for a previous violation."

Avery felt that sick empty feeling in his stomach again. The officer gave the papers to the detective at the desk and asked him to check Avery's name through their records. The detective was dressed in a pair of unpressed slacks and an open-neck sports shirt, and his undershirt showed at the top of his chest. He had a cold and he blew his nose often on a soiled handkerchief. There were deep pockmarks in the back of his neck, and his skin was coarse with large pores. His eyes squinted as he read the papers on his desk and he held the handkerchief to his nose with both hands and blew. He turned around in his chair and looked at Avery, wiping his upper lip with the handkerchief.

"Are you Broussard?" he said.

"Yes."

"Where is that list of resident parolees the parole board sent us?" he said to the officer in uniform.

Avery felt everything go weak and sick inside him.

"It's in my desk. What do you want it for?"

"I thought I saw this guy's name on it," the man with the handkerchief said.

The officer in uniform took the list out of his desk drawer and looked through the names.

"Broussard, Avery. On parole for two years," he read. His blunt red face looked at Avery. "Let's go upstairs, son."

"Is that where the jail is? Am I going into the drunk tank?"

"You shouldn't have broke parole."

"It's the drunk tank and then back to the pen. Is that it?"

The man with the handkerchief blew his nose loudly.

"You want me to take him up?" he said.

"No. I'll take him."

"A girl is going to be here in a little while. Can I see her when she comes?" Avery said.

"You'll have to wait until tomorrow. Visitors are only allowed in the afternoon."

They went out the side door of the room into another hallway and rode upstairs in the elevator. The officer slid back the elevator door and they entered the third floor of the building which served as the jail. The corridor ran in a rectangle around the building, and there were four rows of cells facing the outside walls. There were dim ceiling lights along the corridor that were protected by wire screens. Avery could hear the men in the cells snoring or talking in low voices. There was a sound like a man retching, and someone coughed and cleared his throat of phlegm and spat through the bars on the floor. The officer unlocked one of the cells, and Avery walked into the darkened room, with the three iron bunks fixed to the wall and the obscene words burned on the ceiling with matches and the tobacco spittle and cigarette butts on the floor. A man with some torn newspaper in his hand was relieving himself on the toilet. Another man slept in one of the bunks with his back turned towards them and a striped pillow without a case over his head. The officer clanged the door shut behind Avery and went back down in the elevator.

The man who had been on the toilet stood up and buttoned his trousers. He was rawboned and tall, and his hair was gray and his face pallid. One of the straps of his undershirt was frayed almost in two. He walked barefoot across the concrete floor of the cell and sat on his bunk.

"You got any cigarettes?" he said.

Avery looked out the bars across the corridor through the window. He could see the night glow of the city and hear the sound of the automobiles below.

"Hey, you got any cigarettes?" the man said.

Avery threw him the package of Virginia Extra. The man took out one of the very thin yellow-brown wheat-straw papers and poured the tobacco neatly and rolled it into a cylinder between his thumb and fingers.

"You in on a stew-bum?" he said.

"Parole violation."

"What have you got left?"

"Two years."

"Hell, I got ten to fifteen facing me. I'm really fucked."

I'll probably go back on the same gang, Avery thought. We'll cut cane and clear fields of stumps and dig irrigation canals, and Evans will be there with his sunburnt face and sunglasses and khaki uniform and pistol, and we'll line up for mess and roll call and somebody will get time in detention for talking in line, and on Sunday we'll clean the barracks and Evans will make inspection, and on Monday we'll start all over again. He thought of the homosexuals who always made advances to the new men in camp, and the sound of the man in the next bunk masturbating in his sleep, and the phlegmy hacking cough of Daddy Claxton, and the inevitable talk about women and sadism and escape, and the story everyone told about the convict who had tried to climb over the barbed wire on top of the fence and how he had been caught in the lights and the guards had cut him to pieces with the shotguns and everyone was made to come out and see it after it was over.

"Bang on the door for the hack," the man said. "I got the cruds. There ain't no more newspaper."

"Shut up, will you," the man who had been sleeping in the bunk said.

"I got to shit. I ain't got no more paper."

"You kept me awake all night."

"I told you I got the cruds. It ain't my fault."

"Do it through the bars. They'll bring you some paper."

Avery closed his eyes and tried to think of Suzanne and the past months. He tried to think of her dressed in the big white Sunday hat and the white dress with the transparent lavender material on her shoulders, and of the times they had been in bed together; but he couldn't keep the thought of her in his mind, and nothing seemed real to him except the jail and returning to the work camp. He listened to the men arguing in the dark.